TIDAL FATES

BOOK I
CALLING

———

THOMAS USLE

To William, James, Oliver, and Evelyn

CONTENTS

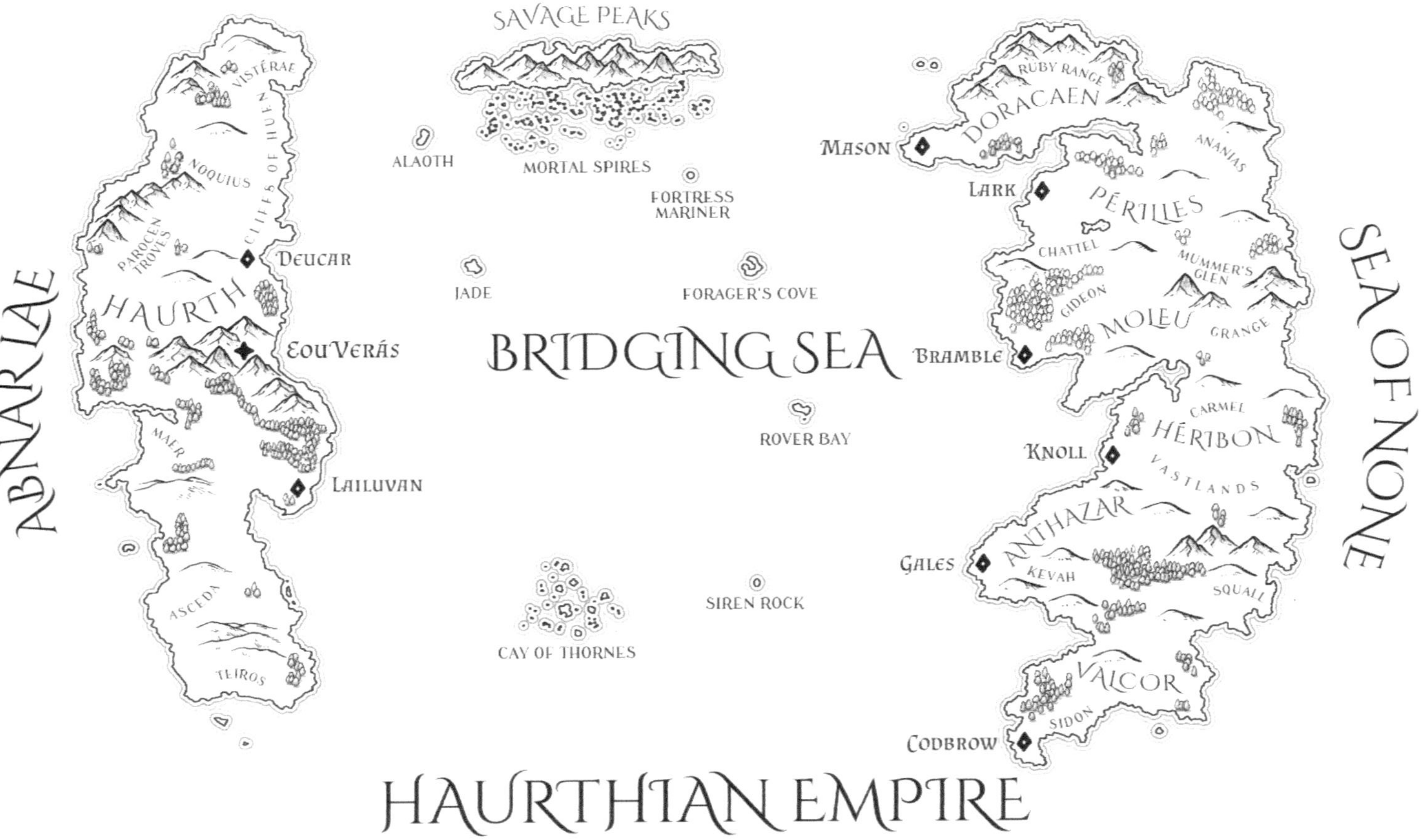

SAVAGE PEAKS
MORTAL SPIRES
ALAOTH
FORTRESS MARINER
JADE
FORAGER'S COVE
ROVER BAY
SIREN ROCK
CAY OF THORNES
BRIDGING SEA
ABNARIAE
SEA OF NONE
HAURTHIAN EMPIRE
VISTERAE
NOQUIUS
CLIFFS OF HUEN
PAROCEN TROVES
HAURTH
DEUCAR
EOUVERAS
MAER
LAILUVAN
ASCEDA
TEIROS
RUBY RANGE
DORACAEN
ANANIAS
MASON
LARK
PERILLES
CHATTEL
MUMMER'S GLEN
GIDEON
MOLEU
GRANGE
BRAMBLE
CARMEL
HERIBON
KNOLL
VASTLANDS
ANTHAZAR
KEVAH
GALES
SQUALL
VALCOR
SIDON
CODBROW

CHAPTER I

THE HUNT

The forest held its breath as wafts of dense fog roved aimlessly between limb and trunk. Trees loomed barren in the young spring, with no leaves to clothe the towering thicket. Trickles of daylight pierced through shallows in the drifting haze. Cascading shimmers danced like a rippling stream overhead. Were it not for the direction given by the shrouded sunrise, all sense of direction would be lost to a stranger in these woods.

Noiselessly, a tall figure crept amongst the timbers and across the moistened ground. A pair of sandals stepped in awkward patterns, careful to avoid trodding upon those twigs undisturbed since the autumn. At each thick trunk, the creeping figure halted to turn an ear towards the neighboring brook. Amidst the gurgling of the coursing waters, a soft, rhythmic slurping could be discerned. A dark eye peered around the tree and fixed upon a creature taking in a drink. The doe's pale brown coat stood out amongst the gray bark of the surrounding oaks. The man drew a short dagger from his side, which would surely have given him away in the pure sunlight.

Beyond the doe and the stream, a dark shadow emerged in the distant fog, its outline sharpening as it neared the stream. It strode unlike any creature of prey that roamed these woods. The lank oaks were hardly wide enough to conceal the entirety of the stocky figure as it made its stealthy approach. The thin silhouette of a bow was raised up as the man across the way crouched in silent anticipation, the dagger held close to his chest.

The shriek of an arrow wailed through the dank, foggy air and vanished with a sharp splinter of bark. The doe sprang to life and broke into an almighty sprint away from the brook and the archer, who had abandoned his cover. The pattering of hooves grew louder as the man, still concealed behind the oak trunk, watched the doe flee unknowingly to its end. When the creature was nearly upon him, he lunged from his cover and into its path. Casting his free arm around its neck, man and beast hurtled to the ground with a violent thud. Before the doe could wrestle free, the dagger rose and ran across the creature's throat. The thin legs thrashed, and its head jerked, but the man's hold did not slacken. The animal's futile attempts to cling to life grew faint and desperate until only a twitch remained in one of its hooves. There was a final kick, and the doe went limp. As the man freed one of his arms from beneath the fallen beast, the archer came to his side just in time to help his companion to his feet with a toothy grin.

The archer was as short and stout as he had appeared in the shadows. This was made all the more prominent as he stood beside his companion, who was at least two heads taller and far leaner. For one descended from dwarf kin, however, no one could claim that the archer was not a respectable height and as healthy as anyone his age could endeavor to be. The dwarf had a thick, rounded nose, beady eyes, long, matted hair, and a beard that shrouded most of his pale face. The gray in his mane had overtaken all but a few remaining patches of auburn, the last remnants of a distant youth.

The man brandishing the dagger took his weapon to the stream for a wash. As he walked, he brushed away the dead leaves and dirt from his wavy hair. His tunic had also picked up some earth from his tumble with the animal, though its tawny color did not reveal too much. He had rich olive skin and a beard shorter than the dwarf's, though no less full. Not a fleck of gray tarnished the midnight hair, which fell to his shoulders. Both hunters wore laced sandals upon their feet and a rigid, patterned scarlet cloth about the waistline of their tunics. The vivid colors of their sashes made concealment during a hunt considerably more challenging, but it bothered neither man nor dwarf.

When the short blade was spotless again, the man sheathed it to brush the last of the forest residue from his arms and legs. The archer fetched the arrow lodged in the bark and returned it to the quiver upon his back. As the aged dwarf made to hoist the felled creature, a firm clasp on his shoulder halted him. A slight look of indignation momentarily grew on the dwarf's face. But as he met the dark eyes, he silently conceded the laborious task to the young man, who threw the carcass over his shoulders with ease. They took a moment to gather their bearings before the pair set off on the path that had brought them so deep into the forest.

As he carried the doe through the stream and over fallen trees, Ira recollected his first venture into these parts. Many of the local children wiled away their days in these woods, forgoing their chores in the homes and shops. Érnog had been one of these children in his youth, and so he was most intimately acquainted with every tree and twig. That forest, which Ira had known best in his youth, was quite unlike this one. Those trees were never void of color, even in the dead of winter. Critters of all kinds meandered across grassy mounds and hills. Birds danced on high and sang in the day and night to the amusement of any wanderer. If he closed his eyes, Ira could almost recall that garden so distant from where he and Érnog now strode.

The two came upon a clearing as the mist dissipated with the dawn. Rolling mounds dressed in stalks of barley stretched wild and far. Jagged boulders scattered about erupted from the golden sea. Upon a bare patch between barrow and bramble, a wagon was settled beside the fading embers of a quaint fire. Seated upon a rock by the fire was another dwarf, a lady, as could be discerned by her bare upper lip. Her beard was also aged, though her figure was not as wide as her husband's. As the dwarf lady pulled the blanket around her closer, a young woman could be seen brushing a dapple-gray horse tethered to one of the oaks. Her raven hair and smooth olive skin matched her brother's, though her eyes were not as dark as his. Both ladies wore the same patterned cloth as the hunters, theirs draped over their heads as veils. Concealed beneath the young woman's veil was a long scar stretching across her left cheek to her ear.

Érnog called to the women from the clearing as Ira made for the wagon, heaving the doe from his shoulder to the back of it. He shifted some packs and cargo around to leave enough room for the women to sit comfortably. As he did, Érnog bid the ladies a good morning as he sat on the rock with his wife.

"Did you get enough sleep, Torzara?" asked Érnog.

"Yes, I am quite ready to resume our travels," said the lady dwarf. "Esther was so kind to prepare breakfast before I awoke. But"—she touched a thinning hand to her husband's cheek—"I worry you are not rested enough, my love."

"Not to worry," Érnog assured her. "Ira and I are quite accustomed to this journey by now."

"Nevertheless," said Esther, "a hearty meal will serve you well before we set off."

She brought forward two plates of roast chicken and eggs, which the hunters graciously accepted. As they ate, Esther fetched another blanket from the wagon and wrapped it tenderly around Torzara. The weary dwarf held the blanket close as she peered into Esther's eyes endearingly. Esther smiled weakly as she turned to gaze upon the wild pastures opposite the wood. The hills swayed to the bidding of the cool breeze like windswept waves. Those enormous chunks of stone across the hills remained the only inert landmarks. But as sunlight broke through the morning gloom, the lands awoke, and the mighty boulders rose to meet the new day.

The stony giants across the rolling hills stretched their arms as a few made to rise to their stubby feet. Their hardened bodies were coated in thick patches of moss. It could be rather difficult to distinguish a giant from those lifeless boulders that protruded across nearly every hill within sight. Their habits of slumbering soundly through the day or night were well known across the lands. Walking, even standing, was enough to tire a giant into settling for a long nap. Few in the Eastlands could attest to having seen one of these stony beasts show any sort of emotion. While it was considered unwise to irk any creature of such enormity, local villagers often chortled that it would take all the miners of the Ruby Range and their sharpest picks to spark any reaction out of a giant.

The hunters finished their breakfast as the stony creature nearest their camp lay on his front and dragged his hands through the golden stalks, an impassive expression chiseled on his face. Érnog and Esther began loading what little they had unpacked into the wagon as Ira took the plates and pot around the wood's edge to the stream for a wash. He also took those waterskins nearly dry from the journey thus far. Ira returned as Esther was helping Torzara into the wagon's rear while Érnog hitched the horse, Selah. When all was ready for their departure, the hunters climbed into the wagon's front, checked once more on the ladies seated together, and the party set off.

"Only a two-day ride to Gales from here," Érnog informed the ladies. Torzara sighed as she rested her head on Esther's shoulder and closed her eyes.

The echo of a path was trampled into the ground where countless horses and wagons had trod before. Though the dwarf had a far superior knowledge of the forest, Ira was content to admit to knowing this road quite as well as Érnog. The two passed along this route every few weeks, and Ira even more on his own. Though their crafts were widely sought in the neighboring ports of Gales and Codbrow, the profits to be had in the former far surpassed those of the latter. Érnog was a tanner from the outskirts of the village of Squall, and Ira served as his apprentice. The dwarf had learned all he knew of leathers and skins from his kin, and those of the southern provinces who knew of his goods would gladly exclaim that no other could compare in make or quality.

Few beyond the House of Érnog knew the reason why his wares had earned such a grand reputation. It was Érnog's ancestor, Deerdun, who first discovered the secret properties of mashed gnome mushrooms and implemented them into the sealing coat of his hides. As a result, the leathers exhibited fierce durability through rain or sun. This fantastic discovery had arisen from the curiosity concerning what gave those wandering imps of the forest such tough skin to allow them to burrow and dig for days without so much as a scrape. And it was this unusual quality that made a craft of Érnog's last considerably longer than any other skin before it would begin to wilt or crack. The dwarf tanner had secured a contract with the local magistrates in Gales and Codbrow for deliveries of fresh leather armor no less than once a month. The enlisted men of the Provincial Guard, posted out of every port in the Eastlands, were constantly growing in numbers and were always in need of new or replacement armor. Pricey as the skins came, importing iron makes from the Westlands for the captains of the Guard alone would mean a tax lofty enough to send every house into destitution.

The wagon rolled gently along the lonely path as the early haze faded away. Plumes of barley swayed and parted in narrow trails as critters and creatures sallied along. The wild and unkept life engulfed the trail until it was near impossible to distinguish through the brush. Ira did not bother to search for the path but continued west along, between, and over the countless mounds stretching to the horizon. Érnog sat by Ira's side, his arms crossed and his head bobbing as he fought a losing battle against his drooping lids. Torzara was fast asleep in the back of the wagon; her head still rested upon Esther's shoulder. Esther did not mind. After all, it was a long way for the dwarf to travel in her state. It had been some years since she had ridden as far as Gales. Despite Érnog's initial protests, Torzara had been determined to join the company for this particular journey.

As their wagon approached the peak of yet another golden hill, a rolling noise called from across the way. Ira called Selah to a halt to listen more closely. Dormant atop the stalk-veiled plateau, the ground beneath their wheels rumbled and shook the wagon. Érnog woke with a start, Torzara lifted her head wearily, and Esther peered eagerly in search of the tremor's cause.

"That will be the herd," said Érnog, straightening himself up as he observed the hilltops.

As the thundering of hooves upon earth boomed ever louder, a pack of horned beasts scurried over one of the southern mounds. The bison's fur was a rich chestnut brown and as long as the golden blades they trampled. In seamless unison, the herd shifted its direction as hundreds of beasts poured over the mounds, along the vales, and around an idle giant napping peacefully in the heart of the stampede. Amidst the swarm, three magnificent steeds carrying riders clad in beige followed along the outskirts of the herd. The riders raised their bows and let loose their arrows into the great drove. With each arrow that met its mark, a heavy bison would topple to the ground as the herd around it would instantly veer to avoid a collision.

As the stampede continued towards the east, one of the riders parted from the commotion and headed towards the wagon. The man's features were kind. His hair was not as long as Ira's. His skin had long been kissed by the sun, and like all other men, he, too, had a short but thick beard. It was considered improper for any man to appear bare-faced without a title or some noble position, much as it would be for a woman to remove her veil in the presence of any but her kin. The exception to the former custom was awarded to the naturally bare-faced race of elves. This was still uncommon to see, however, as the provinces were inhabited mainly by the race of men and several dwarves. The rider trotted up the mound to the wagon's side, and Ira's face broke into a grin as he greeted his dear friend.

"I thought it was you," said the rider cheerily. "We thought you would not reach Kevah until sundown. Had we known to expect you sooner, I would have brought you a steed."

"Have you been out for long?" asked Érnog.

"Not long. It was our luck that the herd roamed so close to the village. My brothers and I were about to return with our last kills of the day." The man took notice of the ladies in the back of the wagon and offered them a courteous smile. "And this must be the family I have heard so much about. My name is Nathanael. It is my pleasure to welcome you to our village at last."

"Your hospitality is most appreciated," Esther replied kindly. "I am Ira's sister, Esther, and this is Torzara." She gestured to the dwarf by her side, and Torzara offered the man a weak nod. "My brother has told me the riders of Kevah are skilled bowmen; now I see for myself that it is true."

"That is high praise from one as skilled as he," said Nathanael. As he spoke, his eyes lingered on the long scar upon Esther's cheek. Catching his momentary imprudence, Nathanael quickly averted his gaze. In the corner of his eye, Ira saw Esther casually attempt to draw her scarlet veil closer to better conceal the mark she bore. "You must be weary from your travels," Nathanael said to the company. "Everyone in the village is eager to meet the ladies of the House of Érnog. My wife, Ruth, has talked of nothing else for days. Allow one of my brothers to escort you, and Ira, you can help us haul the bison if you are willing."

Ira glanced at Érnog the way a child might wish to ask for permission, but Torzara responded first with a feeble smile and a nod. With a wide grin, Ira hopped down from the wagon as Nathanael whistled a tune of three notes towards the two riders in the distance. Before long, Nathanael's younger brother, Simeon, had joined them atop the mound on a midnight stallion with white hooves. Simeon greeted Ira heartily before clambering into the wagon and taking the reins from Érnog. Ira mounted the steed he knew to be named Edna and set off with his companion.

"Race you there?" Nathanael proposed eagerly.

Without another word, the two set off at the pace of a racing chariot in the Circus of Lark. The howling wind and pattering of hooves sent both men into a state of immaculate elation. They sped down and over slopes, watching the golden stalks part violently in their wake. Their laughter could hardly be heard over the trampling of the brush and earth. As they neared the third rider,

Nathanael eased upon the reins. But Ira and Edna's pace quickened as they rode to join the herd of bison running wild and free beyond the next barrow. When they had caught up, hunting the scurrying beasts was the last thought on Ira's mind. In this glorious moment, he was reserved to allow Edna to carry him to her heart's content. His eyes bathed in the lavish fields that stretched for what appeared to be an eternity. When he had engrained every detail of the sight in his mind, he turned around and rode away from the herd at a light trot.

The thundering of the herd receded into the east as Ira dismounted and joined Nathanael and his elder brother, Meshach, in preparing the felled beasts for transport to the village. Together, they wrapped three massive bison in thick sheets and latched each to a saddle. Once Ira had fastened his tarp to Edna, they set off with the animals dragging behind them over the soft plumes. As they rode, the three exchanged their latest tales and exalted the spoils of the hunt. The familiarity of the scene brought warmth to Ira's heart, followed by a tinge of bitter sorrow.

For years, whenever skins began to run short in Érnog's shop, Ira was sent by his master to hunt for bison hides in the knolls of the Province of Anthazar. The beasts roamed the hills year-round, though the vast expanse sometimes made for difficult tracking. Ira first crossed paths with Nathanael and his brothers on one of these lonely hunts for the same prize. The hunters of Kevah soon found Ira to be a welcome addition to their party, what with his keen marksmanship and swiftness on a saddle. On their first collective excursion, they felled a dozen bison after less than a day's search for the herd. Having little use for the beasts beyond the skins his trade required, Ira struck a deal with the brothers. He would offer up the flesh of his bison for the hides of the brothers'. The exchange was more than worthwhile for the hunters of Kevah, and it became a standing practice as Nathanael invited Ira to join their hunts whenever the dwarf tanner required fresh skins. Not long after the newcomer fostered a strong bond with the brothers, the village began to welcome Ira and any of the House of Érnog whenever they passed their way.

As Meshach went on about the state of the village and its inhabitants, Ira could not help but note a peculiar expression across Nathanael's face. It was a hollow look he had not often seen, and not even Meshach's lavish imitations of one of Simeon's missed shots from the hunt were enough to spring Nathanael from his private daze.

"Do you intend to share this daydream of yours with us, Nathanael?" asked Ira. The man started at the sound of his own name. "I wish I were as taken with Meshach's storytelling as you appear to be with your own thoughts."

"Has he not told you?" said Meshach, staring at Nathanael in astonishment. "Honestly, brother, I thought the news would have burst out of you by now."

"News? News of what?" implored Ira.

Nathanael took a moment to collect himself before he said in a meager voice, "Ruth is with child."

At once, Ira exploded with congratulations and well wishes for his beloved and their house. Nathanael smiled and laughed as his friend patted him on the back. But even in the merriment, Ira could not suppress the feeling that his friend was concealing some heavy burden despite his happy news. Indeed, when the cordial thanks had left Nathanael's lips, his expression of emptiness instantly returned to his face.

"Come now, Nathanael," said Ira cheerily. "What possible reason can you have to look so dismayed with your first child on the way?"

"Do not mistake me," began Nathanael. "I am overjoyed, as is Ruth. If it were not for—"

"Oh, not this again," sighed Meshach. He turned to Ira and said, "My brother believes he ought to neglect his upcoming voyage and stay with Ruth until the child comes."

With this, Nathanael's unusual behavior became all too clear to Ira. His friend was due to set sail aboard a merchant ship from the Port of Gales tomorrow. His position as a relief sailor meant that he was randomly called upon to serve if one of the regular crewmates fell ill or was otherwise indisposed. Voyages such as these kept him abroad for weeks, even months, at a time. Ira could see in Nathanael's eyes that the prospect of being so far removed from his bride and his child was weighing heavily upon his mind.

"It is not as though we are hailing to Lark and back in a fortnight," contested Nathanael. "A voyage to Haurth? I should be lucky to return in two months."

"And the child will not be along until summer's end," retorted Meshach. "I have two little ones of my own, and my Naomi would tell you the same as Ruth has told you. Forfeit this voyage, and Halruc will never take you on again. There is no shortage of able-bodied men in Gales who would clamor for half of your commission. And Ruth will not thank you for being by her side when the Guard makes their way to Kevah as soon as another tax is levied."

Nathanael opened his mouth to speak but found no words. Turning to his friend, he raised his eyebrows, begging Ira to come to his aid.

"Ruth will not be on her own while you are abroad," reasoned Ira. "All of your kin reside in the village. And Meshach is right; you will be back with plenty of time to welcome the child."

With an air of reluctance about him, Nathanael conceded and vowed not to raise the subject again. As they crossed the hill, a lone acacia could be seen growing wide in a low valley. Settled beneath its winding limbs was a score of weathered cottages of timber and stone. The fields surrounding the village of Kevah were evidence enough of the resident civilization. The barley was trimmed unnaturally low, standing out amongst the wild growth surrounding the homes. Ira searched for the wagon and his company, but they had yet to arrive.

As Meshach, Nathanael, and Ira approached the square, they were met by calls and cheers from the people scattered about the village. As the three dismounted and untethered their tarps, men and women garbed in plain tunics, dresses, and veils came forward to greet them before making quick work with their sharp tools. They took to skinning and butchering the carcasses as a swarm of children rushed from their play to spectate. Meshach hoisted his two daughters into a great hug as the young begged Nathanael and Ira for tales of their conquest. Nathanael only managed to tame their pleas with the promise of regaling them with the whole story that night after supper.

The children accompanied the returned riders and their horses to the aged stone well on the outskirts of the village. Ira dropped the bucket into the fount many times to fill the barren trough before the riders took a drink for themselves. As the horses slurped to their content, a wagon came into view over the wild turf to the north. The fleeting attention of the children sent them off to meet the newcomers. As the wagon came to a halt in the square, Simeon sprang from Érnog's side to help the ladies down from the back. Ira, Nathanael, and Meshach tied up the horses before making their way to the huddle, where introductions were being made.

Érnog and Torzara, being the only dwarves in the crowd, could hardly be seen amidst the men and women of Kevah.

"We are delighted to have you with us," said a kindly woman Ira knew to be the mother of his rider friends.

"We are once again indebted to you and your kin, Dinah," said Torzara appreciatively. "How many times now have you hosted Ira and Érnog on their trips to the port?"

"Indeed, I seem to have lost count," laughed Dinah's husband, Reuben. "But we would have it no other way. You are most welcome here, all of you." These last words lost some of their cheeriness as Reuben caught a glimpse of Esther's marked cheek beneath her veil. Like Nathanael, he quickly collected himself and reassumed his happy demeanor. "You will be hungry after your long travels, no doubt? Supper will soon be prepared."

"As usual, you are too kind, Reuben," said Érnog. "And for your kindness, we bring a token of our thanks." From the back of the wagon, Érnog retrieved the limp doe slain and offered it to the gracious villagers. "It was Ira's prize in the woods," the dwarf proclaimed proudly.

"I have never been so skilled at the hunt in surroundings so dense and quiet," said Nathanael. "Perhaps it is best that I remain with the bison in the open hills."

"I do not think the bison would object to your absence," chuckled Ira.

They laughed together as a young woman with her hair tied back emerged from one of the cottages. She strode towards Nathanael, her hand resting upon her midriff. Any trace of doubt or worry he had held for his imminent voyage faded from Nathanael's face as Ruth came to his side. She welcomed Ira as he wished her every happiness for her news. Torzara and Esther came forward to introduce themselves, while Meshach made another impression of Simeon, this time of his younger brother falling dramatically off his horse.

As the sun sank closer to the stalk-strewn hills surrounding Kevah, some of the men started a fire in the town square to roast the doe they had been gifted. Ruth had taken Esther by the arm and presented her to the other wives and daughters of the village. Most were courteous and friendly to the visitor, while others nodded shortly and resumed their former chores or discourse. Nevertheless, Esther was glad as she strolled about the square with her new friend. A few boys had resumed play with a ball in the trimmed brush of the village outskirts. They called out to Nathanael to join them for a game and, with some additional coaxing, managed to summon Ira and a few of the younger men to join in as well. They scrummed for a long while through the dry fields that had now lost all trace of the morning dew. It was nearly sunset when the panting men left the boys to continue their sport without them.

Worn and famished, Ira and Nathanael headed to the blazing pit, where a slab of flesh was crackling on a spit. The doe's rich aroma was enough to make the children's mouths water. Along the edge of the cottages, Ira spotted his sister strolling about with a new companion. A girl of no more than eight or nine was by her side, gripping Esther's hand and chattering about something he could not make out. Whatever it was, Esther was engrossed in every word, beaming down at her with a delicate smile. In the corner of his eye, Ira caught a glimpse of a woman striding anxiously towards the meandering pair.

"Merab, go inside and finish your chores," the woman said sternly.

"But I have finished them, Mother," stated the little girl.

"Do as you are told!" snapped her mother. "Inside, now!"

The girl pleaded with Esther longingly before her mother snatched her by the hand and, after shooting the marked woman a dirty look, led her daughter back to the cottages. Esther watched them stride away before turning to face the sunset. Ira parted from Nathanael without a word and made his way towards the outskirts of the village. Habitually, Esther pulled her veil close to her cheek as she heard the approaching footsteps.

"It is only me," Ira said reassuringly.

"I know," she replied with a hollow voice.

"Soon, all of this will be behind us."

"I hope so."

Behind him, Ira could see the townsfolk huddled in deep conversation about the square. Érnog was marching towards the mass, a disapproving glare under his thick brow.

"We could make camp somewhere along the road," suggested Ira. "It would mean a shorter journey for us tomorrow. And I know Torzara—"

"These people have shown great kindness by welcoming us to stay with them," said Esther quietly. "To leave now would be a poor repayment for their generosity."

Esther did not meet her brother's gaze as she spoke, while argumentative voices sounded from the village. Understanding her desire to be alone, Ira dismissed himself and headed towards the commune. He arrived at the gathering just in time to hear Érnog hiss sternly, "I will have no more of it, do you hear?"

A robust man with a nasty frown stepped forward and glared at the dwarf.

"You bring one bearing that mark to our village, and you expect us to abide?" the man said gratingly. "You have some nerve, Érnog, to take advantage of our hospitality so."

"We meant no disrespect, Achan," retorted Érnog with a forced sense of calm, "but if it is a problem—"

"It most certainly is!" bellowed the man, looking to his neighbors for support. "It is indecent to keep something like that a secret!"

"It was no secret."

Nathanael stepped forward and faced the robust man with a steely glare.

"You knew of this? And when were you planning on telling us, boy?"

"I told all in the village that the family of Ira and Érnog would be passing our way," Nathanael preached to the gathering, "and that our house would offer them food and shelter for the night. There were no qualms then, and I fail to see what has changed now."

"What has changed? You failed to mention that one of their kin was a criminal! Had we known—"

"And what do you know of this girl, Achan?" asked Dinah as she entered the huddle. "What I know is that this village has welcomed Ira as one of its own every time he has passed our way. To think so little of those he trusts, let alone his own blood, is an insult to any trust you would claim to hold in him."

Achan reproachfully held his tongue as the crowd looked on in silence. Dinah gave Ira a gentle smile that he returned before speaking himself.

"We did not mean to cause a row by our presence," he said to the huddle, "and we will take no offense if you ask us to—"

"You will do no such thing!" Reuben barked over Ira. He came to his wife's side as he scowled at Achan. "It was agreed that all of you would stay with us for the night, and so you shall.

And Achan, I should ask you to show more civility to guests of my house in the future."

With a sour huff, the robust man stormed from the crowd to one of the cottages and slammed the door behind him. The men and women gathered around and stood idle and awkward before parting from the scene. Dinah also strode away from the square towards the edge of the sheared field. When she returned, it was with Esther by her side, and the two took their seats with Ruth and Torzara around the fiery pit. As darkness hovered and others congregated around the roasting doe, Achan and his wife peered out from their cottage before closing their shutters. Ira found himself a spot under the acacia and seated himself, a fair but not disrespectful distance from the villagers. He was not in the mood for food or company. But when Simeon approached him with two plates, Ira did not refuse him. With a nod of thanks, he took the plate as the young brother joined him under the broad tree.

"Achan cannot resist making trouble every chance he gets," remarked Simeon. "If boorishness were bravery, he would make a soldier to rival the finest of the legions."

Ira gave a hollow chuckle. Simeon seemed to grasp that he did not care to speak of what had just transpired and so changed the subject.

"Nathanael's ship sets off tomorrow. He tells me he is riding with you to the port."

"He is. Érnog and I were already scheduled for delivery to the garrison when Nathanael informed me of his own plans. It is the least we could do to take him with us, and we will be glad of the company."

Simeon nodded and, after checking that no others were close enough to overhear them, leaned in close to speak in a low voice.

"And is it true then," he whispered, "what Nathanael tells me?"

"What have you heard?" asked Ira quietly.

"That you and your sister are leaving the provinces, that you are bound for the Westlands, and . . . and you will not be returning."

Ira took a deep breath before uttering his next words. "It is true what your brother has said. Esther and I have long discussed taking this journey, and a few weeks ago, we finally arranged passage to the Realm of Haurth."

"Why did you not tell us?" implored Simeon. "We can still make this feast a proper send-off for the both of you."

"A touching gesture, and one I am grateful for," Ira said with a grin, "but I prefer a common night like this to be my last in Kevah. Farewells are so bitter a thing. I would much rather part like this—in secret. The leaving does not feel so heavy this way."

They stared into the fire for a time, allowing the whole meaning of this remark to sink in.

"Well, sad as I will be to see you go," said Simeon, "I trust your reason for voyaging so far to be a strong one. But, if I may ask, why are you not heading north to Périlles? Your kin hail from there, do they not? I seem to recall you mentioning it some time ago."

Something stirred uncomfortably inside Ira at these words. As he searched for an answer, he noticed Nathanael standing within earshot of their dialogue. From his grim expression reflected in the firelight, Ira could tell he had overheard his brother's query. And of all the villagers of Kevah, only Nathanael knew why Ira could not answer truthfully.

"Is it not clear to you, brother?" Nathanael said as he took a seat beside them. "The life Ira and his sister had in that place is long behind them. Their kin misses them, I am sure, but a new home free of memory or connection can be cleansing for the soul. Not all are content to live and die in one place without leaving their mark on the world around them."

As Simeon took in his brother's reasoning, Ira managed to sneak his friend an appreciative smile for coming to his aid.

"I do not mean to pry, of course," Simeon assured them. "It is only that I do not recall you ever mentioning a desire to leave the provinces before now, Ira."

"Please do not mistake my intentions for leaving. I have cherished my years with Érnog and Torzara, as has Esther, and I would not trade those days and nights we scouted in the hills for anything. But our time here has only been a passing thing. It has long been a dream of mine, and especially of Esther's, to sail across the Bridging Sea and settle in some secluded place. There, we might begin our lives anew in quiet contentment. If I never spoke of it before, it was because I never believed the dream was within our grasp. But I am ever grateful to be wrong, and I have your brother to thank for his part in realizing our dream."

"And how did Nathanael make all of this possible?" asked Simeon, a note of concern in his voice.

Ira held his tongue as he contemplated whether to divulge the truth to Simeon. No ship carrying passengers to the Westlands would harbor Esther or himself. But Nathanael, having connections in Gales, had secured their places aboard a merchant ship bound westward to the Port of Deucar. Taking on individuals with criminal histories was hardly uncommon for masters who wished to profit from discounted labor, so long as they were not suspected of associating with the Pirate Horde. However, illegal passage was a crime punishable by life on the Isle of Ruin, as was forging documents of identity. But thanks to Nathanael's efforts, it was arranged that Ira and Esther would be granted such passage. Once near enough to the coast of the Westlands, they would disembark in a rowboat and hail to some remote beach to avoid discovery. For risking so much on his and Esther's accounts, Ira was eternally grateful to his dear friend.

With a sly grin at Simeon, Ira replied, "Never you mind how your brother helped us. Nathanael is too smart to play the fool. And yet, he is too foolish to do anything considered wise."

"And that is what keeps everyone guessing," chuckled Nathanael. "What will I ever do without you to humble me, Ira?"

"I dare not imagine."

They ate in good cheer as the moon chased away the last glimmer of daylight. Those faces in the square could only be discerned by the light of the still-blazing pit. After pouring himself a mug of ale, Meshach rose and called for the village's attention. At the behest of the children, he delved into a theatrical retelling of the day's encounter with the herd. Ira knew from experience that these hunts were largely uneventful before the part of the story when the bison were finally discovered. Nevertheless, Meshach began at the hour of their departure that morning and shared every detail with the air of a seasoned bard. Ira's attention drifted from the man to the radiant pit, and Meshach's lofty voice grew distant and mumbled. The luminous arms of the fire stretched and grasped at the stars before vanishing into wisps of smoke. As he stared vacantly into the light, Ira's thoughts dwelled on all he had told Simeon and all he had refrained from saying.

It had been twelve years since Ira and Esther first came to the little town of Squall along the eastern shores of the Sea of None. As they could travel no further from the masses, the young brother and sister considered it an appropriate place to remain. Without so much as a bronze assarius to buy a loaf of bread and with Esther's cheek bearing the fresh mark of a hardened criminal, no man or woman in Squall would so much as speak to the wandering strays. One night, as they lay shivering in the desolate street, a dwarf passing by bid them to accompany her to her home on the outskirts of town. She and her husband offered them a warm meal and a spare room for the night. Ira could not remember a more comfortable night's rest than that he spent in the cottage, which had been in Érnog's family for generations. The following day, after some hard-fought negotiation, the siblings persuaded the dwarf couple to accept what repayment they could offer. What began as Esther's help in the cottage and Ira's hands in the tanner shop grew into a kinship to last for years to come.

This new family quickly turned the house on the banks into a home, though life did not grow any easier when they ventured to town. Those who had spotted the strangers quickly spread the word of their being taken in by the childless dwarves on the far end of Squall. For this, Érnog and Torzara were shunned by many who considered opening their home to unknown wanderers, especially a marked one, as nothing less than a disgrace. Ira received even more backward glances any time he passed through the town streets. But no one could stand the sight of Esther in public spaces, and for this, she isolated herself. Most of her days were spent inside with Torzara, most recently tending to the elderly dwarf's dwindling health. Those rare times Esther found herself away from the cottage, she walked the secluded banks, wiling away the days with a book or with nothing at all. Years passed, and the people of Squall eventually grew used to their neighbors, yet their demeanors towards them never altered.

The dying fire brought Ira back to his place beneath the acacia. He looked up and saw Érnog and Torzara seated on either side of Esther. Distracted from life's troubles, they laughed with the townsfolk at Meshach's animated portrayal of one of the bison from earlier that day.

27

townsfolk at Meshach's animated portrayal of one of the bison from earlier that day.

CHAPTER II

THE TEMPLE OF ÉROSAI

Across the Bridging Sea in the land of dawn, a flood of brilliant orange crept from the sea's edge and into the sky. The Realm of Haurth met the young day as the dazzling sunlight rippled across the briny waters. The ocean view was set between two jagged mountains encircling a vast jade meadow. The peaks began abruptly at the shore and rose like naturally carved walls surrounding the valley below. The northern and southern mounts stretched for leagues until, at last, they met in the west, becoming one crescent range behind a glorious city of stone.

The rigid masonry of the city was composed of magnanimous slabs of granite. Their color resembled a blue sky hardly visible behind a patch of gray clouds. Paved lanes rose slenderly with the gradual incline of the mountain's foundation. Along the streets were shops and abodes uniform in make and majesty, and a bell tower jutted high enough to be seen from the winding roads below. One edifice had a perfect view from the main streets of the Hallowed City to the watery horizon in the east. The Temple of Érosai glistened in splendid grandeur. Pillars of pale marble with cascading emerald veins rose high for all the city to see. A towering archway faced the plaza, set many steps below. No roof or cover was erected over the temple, and the last specks of starlight could be seen from within as the day gave them chase. In those spaces between each pillar stood grand statues of pure white marble. Taller than life, the stony figures faced the temple courtyard, each with a small fire at its base and a thurible burning incense. The courtyard was of the same stone as the statues but with golden patterns etched far across. At the center of the ornate floor was an elongated star with four points, and behind it was a pale, vacant throne facing to the east.

Up the steps from the plaza and through the archway, there came a man striding into the temple. He bid the blue-clad temple sentries a good morning as his sandals clapped against the cool stone and echoed throughout the empty place. Under his traveling cloak, he wore elegant white robes with a royal blue sash tied about his waist. His ashen hair was finely braided, and his olive face was shaved clean. In one of his thin hands was a letter heavily creased from the man's tightened grip. Another pair of footsteps, softer and quicker, sounded from the temple's rear. Emerging from behind the throne, a young man, barefoot and wearing a plain blue tunic, approached.

"A table and chairs, please," said the ashen-haired man as he removed his cloak and handed it to the servant, "and some wine."

The servant bowed and scuttled off to fetch the requests. The man stood in the quiet courtyard, tapping the letter anxiously upon his side. On one of the fingers clenching the letter, he wore a silver ring with the crest of a horned creature upon it. When the young man returned, he was accompanied by other servants carrying a fine mahogany table and chairs. The finely clad man seated himself with a heavy sigh as an ornamental jug filled with crimson wine was set upon the table along with seven silver goblets. Pouring into the nearest one, the man dismissed the servants absentmindedly as he sipped and stared up at the vanishing twilight sky. Faint voices of early risers going about their day could be heard from the streets. Despite the city's dense population, there was never as much rush in the streets as one might typically expect from the ports. In Eou Verás, any sort of hurry was ill-favored. Established more than a millennium ago, the Hallowed City carried an air of peace and tranquility that all citizens of the Haurthian Empire respected deeply.

The ashen-haired man was about to refill his goblet when another figure passed through the archway and into the courtyard. The dwarf had a long, straight beard and hair, and the color of his robes and cloak were akin to the man's. While the race of men shaved their faces as an outward sign of their authority, having one's hair cut in the Westlands was a great punishment and shame amongst the elves and dwarves. The finely clad dwarf nodded politely to the man before tossing his cloak to the young servant. After seeing the lone jug of wine, he called after the young man to bring some food and another jug of wine for the table.

"How was the theater, Doracaen?" asked the ashen-haired man between sips of his goblet.

"You were wise not to show," groaned the dwarf, seating himself across the table from the man. "*The Thieving Band of Hesed* was an utter bore. Indeed, I might have escaped sooner had they not seated us in the royal box. We could not escape unnoticed." When the servant brought a platter of grapes, figs, pomegranates, and pears, Doracaen began to pile an assortment onto a plate. "But tell me, Anthazar, why were you absent last night? The wife and I were expecting you."

"Forgive me," said Anthazar. "I did mean to show, but I was otherwise preoccupied." His eyes fixed on something in the distance, though he could not tell what it was.

"Not to worry, there will be another show this evening," mumbled Doracaen through a mouthful of fruit. "You can honor the citizens with your presence then, but do not say I never warned you." As the dwarf chuckled, he took notice of the letter grasped in Anthazar's palm. Doracaen opened his mouth, either to speak or to take another bite of pomegranate, but was distracted by the appearance of two more men in the courtyard. One had a stoic expression carved upon his sallow face, and the other was rather scrawny beneath his fine robes. The new arrivals joined the table, soon followed by a dwarf with pearly hair and an extremely portly man. Only one seat remained vacant at the head of the table. As the pearly-haired dwarf and the scrawny man began to chatter animatedly about their favorites for the Race of Itherios, Anthazar spotted Doracaen gazing at him between bites of pear. He looked down at his hand on the table, the creased letter tapping rhythmically against the mahogany. At once, he ceased his tapping and laid the letter to rest on his lap.

The discussion of charioteers and their steeds was hushed by several footsteps marching from the rear of the temple. Half a dozen temple sentries clad in royal blue tunics, shining iron armor, and glimmering helmets entered the courtyard armed with spears in hand and short gladiuses by their sides. The elves stationed themselves around the table as the governors rose. From the garden, behind the polished pillars, came a tall figure. He was dressed in regal sapphire robes and a white sash, diametric to the threads of his companions around the table. His appearance was most likened to the men's, though the elf was of a paler complexion with longer features in face and stature. His hair cascaded behind his pointed ears down to his waist, the locks glistening the same shade as the polished mahogany table set before him. As windless as the courtyard was, the elf's hair flowed gracefully and in unison with his elegant robes. His years were apparent, yet his skin remained unblemished. A belt around his waist held a sheathed gladius quite different from those of the sentries. The elf's long-fingered hand rested upon its hilt with gold etchings akin to the marble floor's. A midnight gem the size of a walnut was set into the sword's hilt. This dark jewel was the only part of the gladius that did not shimmer in the morning sun's rays. As the elf approached the table, each servant in the courtyard bowed low and did not stand upright until he had passed them by.

"Good morning, governors," bid the elf with a bow to the men and dwarves around the table. "Shall we resume where we left off yesterday?" The table murmured their agreement, and they took their seats once more. "Very well, then. Governor Héribon, have you any news from the Magistrate of Knoll?"

"Yes, premier," answered the scrawny governor. "I had a letter from the magistrate last night. The Provincial Guard of Héribon has found no less than sixty homes in the port with one or more residents showing symptoms of pestilence. The magistrate has also dispatched some enlisted men to those remote parts of the province, but they have yet to report their findings."

"It is enough to go on for the time being," said the premier. "So, accounting for the other provinces and their numbers, we are looking at several hundred dwellings in the Eastlands suffering from this new plague. Medicine will have to be delivered, and there is presently not enough to send to the ports. Fortunately, the fields beyond Deucar will be in full bloom once this primaveral season is behind us; no later than early May, I would venture. At that time, the flowers' remedial oils may be procured and dispatched at once to the Eastern ports. Are we all in agreement?"

Each of the governors nodded their assent.

"This will, of course," said the portly governor, "mean levying another tax to cover the cost of labor and shipment."

"Governor Moleu is correct," remarked the premier. "I dare say four denarii a head will sufficiently cover the cost."

"That will be rather steep for a home with many mouths to feed," suggested Doracaen concernedly.

"The cost of silver will hardly weigh greater than the lives of ailing children," uttered the sallow-faced governor.

"Shall we say three denarii then?" interjected Héribon. "And perhaps extra barrels can be sent and stored in the garrisons in the case of another wave of illness?"

The governors turned their heads down the table to the premier, who contemplated the terms.

"Agreed," said the elf, "and I also think it prudent to send a convoy to escort the shipment, lest the Pirate Horde take advantage of a lone galley trekking the Bridging Sea. Granted, the Horde had seldom raided the empire's warships since the days of the Snakeheart. Nevertheless, I consider it a warranted precaution." This suggestion was met with further approval. "Well then, shall we put it to a vote?"

The governors murmured their agreement once more, and with the raising of seven hands, the ordinance was passed. One of the servants standing by, an older man with a thin beard, approached the table with a wax-covered tablet. As the premier dictated, the scribe recorded his words in the wax with an iron stylus. When the ordinance was finished, the members of the court took it in their turn to imprint the seal of their rings at the bottom of the tablet. When six animal crests and one of an elongated star were set into the wax, the scribe gave a bow and parted from them.

"Governor Moleu, when can we expect the warships being constructed in Bramble to join the fleets?" inquired the premier.

"I have been assured that the galleys will be seaworthy before April's end," answered the portly man.

"Excellent. Well then, the High Court has already tended to the next order of business. I carry with me the newly appointed admiral's first set of orders regarding the empire census. Today, the galley *Requiarda* will depart from the Hallowed City for its maiden voyage. I dare say the admiral is well up to the challenge of his new post." There was some light laughter from the governors at these words. Anthazar gave a hollow chuckle before peering again at the letter held in his lap. "And so, that should conclude old business. I now invite any man to rise and bring new business before the court."

Anthazar anxiously rose, but not before the sallow-faced governor across from him had bolted to his feet. After a short look of shared apprehension, Anthazar conceded the floor and resumed his seat.

"Premier, if I may be so candid, I wish to address the High Court with my concerns regarding the census." As the elf made no verbal refute, the man permitted himself to continue. "The incidents that have arisen in the Province of Périlles have been neither scattered nor solitary. We have all received similar accounts from all our magistrates as of late. Despite their efforts to quell unrest in the ports and the provinces, these accounts of citizens questioning the authority of their governors and the Haurthian Empire have only grown more common. I can only surmise this is due to our not dealing with the situation strongly enough."

"May I remind you, Périlles," interrupted the pearly-haired dwarf with annoyance, "that all of this has been said already. Is this not the reason the court voted for a census to be held in the first place? So that the Guard might account for and investigate any civilians creating tensions in the Eastlands?"

"All you say is true, Governor Valcor," replied Périlles.

"Surely, your mind has not been altered on the matter," suggested Moleu.

"Not in the matter of the census, governor, only in the manner of its conduct. My concerns regarding the census stem from the prospect of leaving an ordinance so vital to be headed by the Provincial Guard. Forgive me, governors, but we are delegating much to the very recruits who have thus far failed to apprehend the brigands who brought about the need for a census in the first place. We must hold those who threaten the Haurthian Empire fully accountable for their transgressions if we are to move forward with strength and unity!"

Only when he had concluded did Périlles seem to note the fiery alteration in his formerly calm voice. He took a deep breath and collected himself as all eyes around the table drifted from the governor to the premier. The elf did not appear troubled by the governor's words but sat in contemplation of the man. He quietly stroked his chin with one hand while the other rested still upon the golden hilt of his gladius.

"You have voiced your concerns, governor, and your candor does you credit," said the premier genially. "Now, I wish to hear your proposal. With such solidarity in your stance, I presume you have a solution to offer the court."

"I do," responded Périlles. "I propose sending the Legions of Haurth to oversee and carry out the census in each of the six provinces."

Doracaen sputtered wine down his front as the mouths of the other governors gaped. Anthazar, for the first time, lifted his gaze from his lap to stare wide-eyed at Périlles.

"You cannot be serious!" laughed Valcor, though his laugh did not echo any humor at the proposition.

"Have you forgotten what happened when the mariners last governed over the Eastlands?" exclaimed Héribon.

"I have not forgotten," muttered Périlles, fighting to maintain his composure.

"These accounts you cite, we have all received them from our homelands," admitted Doracaen as he dabbed at the crimson spot on his pale robes. "I will not deny there are those displeased with some of the High Court's decisions, but they are too few to warrant a full-scale occupation of the provinces. It is not so grave as you make it out to be."

"It may be so grave."

The whole table turned to stare at Anthazar with a look that suggested they had entirely forgotten he was present. The governor's words lingered in the courtyard as he took the letter from his lap and offered it to the premier. The elf opened the crinkled parchment and read silently while the rest of the table observed with bated breath. A grim expression fell upon the premier's face as the little color in his cheeks faded away.

"When did you receive this?" inquired the premier, unable to tear his eyes from the parchment.

"It arrived yesterday evening," replied Anthazar. When the premier said nothing but began to reread the letter, the governor addressed the rest of the table. "The displeasure with the High Court has now risen to a degree we cannot ignore. It is now confirmed that there is talk of the people demanding the empire release the Province of Anthazar from its governance. The Magistrate of Gales reports a rogue band of citizens meaning to establish its own rule." Anthazar took a deep breath and uttered his next words in barely a whisper. "The people are calling for my expulsion as governor."

Morbid astonishment painted the faces of the horror-stricken men and dwarves around the table. Doracaen nearly toppled over as he leaned back in his seat. Périlles turned to the premier, who offered him the letter.

"But what else do we know?" demanded a bewildered Moleu. A sense of urgency had overcome the portly man as his knee began to shake like an anxious schoolboy's. "I mean, these agitators are everywhere in the Eastlands. Do they mean to come after the rest of us as well?"

"Your guess is as good as mine," Anthazar said quietly. "But underestimating the breadth of this movement brewing in the East would be a dreadful mistake."

"You see?" exclaimed Périlles, waving the letter on high. "We cannot wait for our enemies to act before we do. If we are too late to make examples of these rebels and blasphemers, we will face a much graver threat down the line."

"But that is exactly where you are wrong, Périlles," contested Anthazar, rising to his feet. "These people you call our enemies are the citizens we are charged to serve. We must uphold the will of the people, and if those of my homeland will risk imprisonment because we failed to uphold that duty, then I must humble myself and forfeit my position."

"We are not talking about every citizen of the provinces," scowled Périlles, "only a small but formidable band of apostates who would threaten the union and all we have built. They have no right to dictate the fate of the empire!"

"And we have no right to demand unearned loyalties," spat Anthazar briskly.

"Enough!"

Both governors recoiled at the premier's interjection. The sentries around the table looked on in uniform silence. As the young servant who had taken their cloaks replaced the empty jug of wine with a full one, the elf rose from his seat, his hand clutching the gladius at his side.

"It occurs to me that the Legions of Haurth may be necessary to ensure the census is carried out most effectively. Half measures will not benefit the people if the situation is as dire as this letter claims."

Anthazar took a moment to contemplate his address to the leader of the Westlands.

"Premier, I ask you to consider how sending the legions will appear to the people. Such brash action can only sever the thinning trust that holds our lands together. We seven established the rule of this allied empire, East and West, the provinces and Haurth, all to serve the will of our people. And for that time, I honestly believe that we have served them well. But if release from empire rule is this widely sought, we would be fools to try and temper the torrential waters with soldiers and galleys."

"You were once from that land, governor," Périlles said coldly. "Would you so eagerly offer them your blessing to break that alliance we have labored so hard to maintain?"

The songs of nightingales above filled the courtyard as the seven sat in grim consideration. Carts and chatter from the plaza could be heard as the people of Eou Verás went about their day. After a period of hush, Valcor stood and straightened his long, snowy beard.

"I cannot say that I entirely agree with Governor Anthazar as it pertains to those who wish to break from the empire," he began proudly, "but I do concur that the legions will do more harm than good in this instance."

The dwarf took his seat and regarded the other governors, waiting to see which would follow his statement.

"It is too early to put such drastic measures to a vote," said Héribon shortly.

"Agreed," chimed in Doracaen. "Let us wait until we have seen the fruits or thorns of the census."

Moleu only noticed that he was the last to offer his thoughts as the other governors eyed him inquiringly.

"Yes, quite right," he said awkwardly. "Best to leave it for another time."

The premier looked to Périlles; they were the only two who remained standing. The governor looked around the table and gave a heavy sigh as he regained his seat.

"Very well then," concluded the premier, "we shall resume this discussion some other day. Now, if you will excuse me, I must deliver the new admiral his orders."

As the court adjourned, many governors remained in their chairs to murmur amongst themselves. Périlles could not quite contain his tone of indignation as he turned to address Valcor. Anthazar rose to his feet, but before he could call the young servant to fetch his cloak, the premier invited the man to take a turn about the courtyard with him. Anthazar obliged, and the pair sauntered across the white and gold floor.

"Your burdens are heavy this morning," uttered the elf in a low voice, "but they have been growing heavier for some time now."

Anthazar peered towards the other governors before replying softly, "I have failed in my charge to the province I serve, and so the burden of my deeds should weigh great upon my soul. Moreover, I fear we may fan the flames of unrest rather than douse them if we are not careful."

"Nothing is yet decided on the role of the mariners."

"But you believe they would restore order?"

"I would have it so that interference from Western forces was not deemed necessary. But the sickness left to fester will corrupt its host and those around him. Left unchecked, plague and malady will lead others to ruin, even the innocent or well-intentioned. I have no desire to see our empire perish when we stand to rescue her."

"If you are so firm in your convictions, why do you allow us to deter you? You could order the legions to preside over the provinces if you wished; it is your birthright to command them."

At these words, the premier and the governor's gazes turned upon the empty throne before them. It was true that the power to command the Legions of Haurth to the provinces was within the elf's rights. But such a unilateral act had not been decreed since last an emperor sat upon the pale throne. By Haurthian law, for any ordinance of the High Court to be passed, a majority of at least three governors and the premier must vote in favor of said ordinance. However, even the unanimous votes of the governors could not pass any law without the support of the leader of the Westlands.

"I was not born of this land," said Anthazar, his eyes spanning the courtyard and the many statues erected between emerald-veined pillars. "At times, I still count myself a stranger to the people of Haurth. Now, I count myself a stranger to the people of my own land. My service to them from so far away feels weak and hollow."

"I would wish for a way to put your heart to rest," said the premier, "but we stand here amongst one another so we might serve the people of our lands in communion. Were it not for the great distance that separates the provinces from the Realm of Haurth, I would agree with your sentiments. But such a distance between leaders would only divide us further." When the premier spoke next, it was with the air of one tending to an ailing friend. "These are uncertain times, Malachi, and in times such as these, I choose to hold my trust in you and the governors. You have never given me cause to question your loyalty or your constitution."

This was a far more personal form of address, for Malachi was the man's true name. Only when he was appointed Governor of Anthazar did he assume his title and forfeit himself. As his decisions bore the weight of the province he served, such a title was only fitting. The premier placed a hand upon the man's shoulder and pressed it firmly.

"You have served your people well, governor," assured the elf. "My trust in you is steadfast and well-earned. Now, put aside these thoughts of dereliction. I must be off."

A sense of calm spread throughout Anthazar at these words. With a final bow, he dismissed himself to rejoin the table. The premier summoned the young servant, who brought him a thick white traveling cloak. Donning the garment, he strode to the noble archway and looked upon the plaza of the Hallowed City. Elves and dwarves of all ages strolled through the square at the foot of the temple steps. Even the poorest of citizens wore tunics, mantles, dresses, and veils of delicate fabrics. Children skipped and played in small gatherings as shopkeepers and tradesmen bartered with passersby. Carts teeming with imports and exports rolled in all directions through the many winding avenues. Despite the distance separating him from the crowd, the premier felt the scattered commotions swarming around him.

"*Sidrena cudaulis ém,*" the elf said in his native tongue to one of the sentries posted at the archway.

The sentry hurried down the steps, around the temple, and out of sight. Closing his eyes, the elf allowed the cool breath of the wind to wash upon his face, through his fingertips, and between his toes. He was unaware of how long he had been standing idle until the sentry returned with the premier's request. A freshly painted chariot pulled by two chestnut horses awaited him at the base of the steps. The dwarf driver stood with the reins in hand, and behind him was an elven lady in a royal blue gown and a cloak to match the premier's. Her pale eyes and golden hair reflected the brilliant sunlight beneath her sheen veil. The premier stepped into the chariot and kissed the lady's hand as the driver called the horses onward.

"I am sorry to have kept you waiting," he told her.

"The wait was no bother," she replied gently. "It is always so soon that we must say goodbye to him. And yet, this time has come even sooner."

"It is a great honor he has accepted, Filia. I have seen his leadership at the helm, and there is none more suited for the task."

They rode through the city streets paved with oceanic cobblestone between small shops and the morning crowds. From the dwellings above the shops, several people called down to the royal couple as they passed, waving and bidding them a good day. Children wandering about or strolling with their parents shouted and waved or whispered to their friends with pointed fingers. Slowly, the city streets grew sparse until they faded into a valley lush with buds not yet in bloom. The premier let his hands fall at his side as he closed his eyes. As noisy as the chariot wheels were, the elf labored to recall the last time his mind had been this quiet.

"Lysias?"

The voice of his love recalled him to his body. Lysias gazed upon her and fell into the eyes he knew so well. He took Filia's hand and held it in his own. She did not speak; she rarely had to. The journey to the harbor passed in an instant, and before either of them knew it, they were brought to a halt before a vessel of incomparable magnitude.

A heavy warship longer than any other in the harbor, the virgin cedar planks of the galley *Requiarda* glistened unweathered by trials of the sea. A tall mast rose from the deck, and a royal blue sail was laced to the yard. Three banks of oars spanning the length of the hull would offer the galley speed unmatched by any vessel constructed before. Fixed to the bow was a ram of shimmering bronze, ready to strike any warship daring enough to challenge the pride of the Haurthian Navy. Men of the Eastlands commissioned as rowers carried crates of rations and barrels of fresh water aboard the galley *Requiarda* while several mariners stood watch. The soldiers of Haurth wore iron helmets and chestplates over their sapphire tunics, as well as shimmering gauntlets and greaves upon their bare arms and legs. The officers were distinguished by their likened armor of bronze as well as the short blue capes upon their backs.

Lysias and Filia stepped down from the chariot and approached the admiral, who was conversing with the galleymaster of this mighty vessel. While both wore the same armor as the officers scattered about the harbor, the galleymaster's cape was silver with blue embroidery, and the admiral's as pearly white as Governor Valcor's beard. To further denote their ranks, the traditional tassels were fastened to the fine belts they wore. The admiral was of mature age, though notably younger than many of the officers under his command. Nevertheless, the tone of his voice did not waver in the wake of his youth. His face was long, and his mahogany hair, like every soldier and officer's, was woven into a single braid. As the premier and the lady strode to the harborside, the admiral bid his galleymaster, a bare-faced man with a sheen of long gray hair, to continue in his stead. He approached the pair and bowed cordially to them.

"Your new commission suits you well, Praelaum Ambrose," said Filia with a loving gaze.

"Indeed," said Lysias, "I see now that the High Court chose well in its new appointment."

"You grace me with your presence and your praises," replied Ambrose, "but I shall feel much more the part once we are underway."

"Nonsense," protested Lysias. "You mastered the command of the galley *Cuenoros* for years and warranted high regard from your predecessor, I might add. Undoubtedly, your renewed service to the fleet will garner as much praise in time. Which reminds me . . ." He stretched out an arm from within his cloak and offered the admiral his sealed orders. "If all goes well, we shall see you back here in a few short months."

"Let us hope," said Ambrose. "How go matters with the court?"

"I would trade all the days in that temple to be a humble gailaum again," Lysias said with a longing spirit.

"Well, I will not pretend to miss those days of separation," said Filia with a grin.

The gray-haired galleymaster approached the three, bowed to the premier and the lady, and addressed his admiral.

"All provisions and crew have been accounted for, praelaum."

"Very good, Gailaum Zaccai. Prepare the crew to make sail."

The galleymaster dismissed himself, and Ambrose offered one last bow to the premier and lady.

"Praelaum Fenthres assured me that none but you could take his place," said Lysias. "You are ready, and upon your return, we shall host a glorious feast in your name! Then, you may recount the many tales of your voyage to a courtyard of ardent ears."

"I shall await that day most eagerly, Father."

As the admiral strode away, the tethers to the harbor were loosened, and officers on deck called out orders to unfurl. The brilliant sapphire sail fell into the wind, displaying the Star of the Sea embroidered in silver. Ambrose stood at the helm as the sheets were fastened, and the galley floated gracefully towards those waters that stretched beyond the eye. The mariners atop the harbor towers bid the vessel farewell as Filia and Lysias stood by the chariot, watching the ship sail until it vanished on the horizon.

CHAPTER III

THE PORT OF GALES

The company hailing to the Port of Gales rose earlier than most of the villagers, not counting those men who had taken to gleaning the wild grain in the cool of the morn. The House of Reuben had risen with their guests to see them off and especially to bid farewell to Nathanael. Dinah offered Érnog a small package of bread and cheese for the road and insisted they return to Kevah to stay another night once their business in Gales was settled.

"You are most kind," said the dwarf, "but we will be lucky to return to these parts by nightfall if we are not held up. We shall set up camp along the road but should be honored to accept your hospitality another day."

Meshach lent Torzara a hand as she clambered into the back of the wagon once more. As Ira took the reins, he caught sight of Nathanael holding Ruth's hands underneath the lone acacia. They gazed at one another, heart and soul lost in mutual adoration. As he watched them exchange soft words of farewell, the memory of the couple in that very spot beneath a chuppah came to Ira. The branches had been lush with striking autumn leaves the day they took their vows. Music and dance had filled the night, and a feast of olives, dates, honey, and enormous jugs of milk and wine had been prepared. The taste of the memory was fresh on his lips as Ira recalled the glorious union. When the family of three had parted at last, Nathanael joined Esther and Torzara in the back of the wagon. His kin waved to them until they and the cottages had disappeared behind the golden barrows. Only the massive acacia remained in sight as the wagon rolled west until that landmark had gone as well.

As the sea of blade-strewn mounds flattened into broad, low plains, Nathanael entertained his companions with tales of his family spanning many generations. Ira suspected a desire in Nathanael's heart to distract himself from all he was leaving behind, and so he chuckled heartily with the others. The custom of sharing stories of one's kin rather than of oneself was a common pastime in the Eastlands. To tell others of an ancestor, offspring, sibling, or parent, especially in kindly jest, was considered a great honor to all parties concerned. Even Érnog conceded to share a few fables after much cajoling from Ira. The wagon roared with laughter as the dwarf recounted one particular time in his youth when he was bucked off a wild pony and into the mud. Érnog could hardly keep himself upright as he chortled over his late father's stern words regarding that foolish errand. As Ira clutched his stomach in laughter, he saw the smile under his sister's veil lose some of its life as her eyes reflected a sorrow held at bay. Ira was not the only one to notice as she fought to produce a convincing chuckle for the company. With a somber crease upon his brow, Érnog fell silent and elected to reserve himself to the reins as Selah pulled them along.

By midday, the beating sun had banished the chilly air they had departed in. Ripples of heat radiated from the barren trail they followed westward. Beads of sweat trickled down Ira's face as he passed around his waterskin, the supply of crisp spring water he had collected that morning reduced to a few warm gulps. Torzara drank some as Esther wiped away the sweat on her brow. She passed it to Érnog, who, at Nathanael's insistence, had swapped seats with him so the aged dwarf could rest in the back with the ladies. To pass away their time under the sweltering blaze, the two men in the front delved into lively discussions of those battles and conflicts most renowned in the annals of history. The distraction did them well, and Ira was halfway through recounting the Battle of the Blooming Vale when he received a hard nudge in the side from Nathanael, who pointed ahead.

It was difficult enough to see past the road before them in the glare of the beating sun. Blocking it with his hand, Ira squinted hard for the first landmark of their destination. Sure enough, between the blonde meadows and the clear sunbathed sky, a vivid sliver of deep sapphire was painted along the horizon. With the Bridging Sea finally upon them, the men began to scout the shore until, through their dry eyes, they spotted the blurred outline of a city not a league away. Nathanael woke the others to announce their arrival as the scent of salty sea air flushed their nostrils.

Gales was composed of several sandstone structures and dwellings of varying heights. The constructs were huddled so close together that, from a distance, the port appeared to be one massive construct. Other wagons and carts began to occupy the road heading eastward, while others followed along those trails bound south to Valcor or north to Héribon. Posted outside the entrance to the port were two men in dirtied white tunics with blue hems beneath their leather armor. The enlisted men of the Guard paid the company of the wagon no mind and casually admitted them into the flooded main street.

Swarms of civilians bustled in front of and around Selah and the wagon. Narrow alleys and streets weaved about, many of them too small to admit a single wagon. Sets of stairs ascended along the stacks of grainy stone, making up the tiered homes of those who dwelled in the port. Lines strung across the rooftops held tunics and dresses drying overhead. Men bartered in the streets, discreetly exchanging bronze assarii and silver denarii for items of sale or notes of debt. While homes and abodes were situated on higher levels, the base of every sandstone structure was brimming with shops and tradesmen busy at work. As a dwarf's beads of sweat sizzled on the hot iron he hammered, a whaler examined the price of one of the smith's long harpoons. Women carried baskets of fresh clay from the neighboring stream to ceramists, who shaped pots and jugs to be blazed in an enormous kiln. Carpenters chopped and shaved away at timber, carefully examining every angle of their crafts. Threads of rope were strung together to create casting nets for local fishermen. A scribe was seated behind his bench, scrawling upon sheets of parchment as men and women took his letters to the local mews to select an osprey for delivery. Not even the children of Gales were without their duties, though many became easily distracted as they admired the masters of trade at work.

Carefully avoiding those citizens rushing around Selah and the wagon, Ira brought the company to a split in the road that followed the shore's path. In either direction, even more shops and laborers were at work on the eastern side of the street. To the west was a stretch of beach spanning as far as the eye could see. A scattering of rowboats loaded with nets, barrels, or crates was strewn across the damp sand, and ships of many makes and commissions were anchored off the banks. One mass of ragged-looking men stood huddled on the sands near a couple of mariners and one Haurthian officer, all dressed in royal uniforms. The elf stood opposite the paupers as he drew slips of parchment from a wooden bowl. While he called numbers aloud, the mariners weaved through the mob and pulled from the ranks those who had lucked into a rower's position and pay for the length of the galley's next voyage. Even as the last recruit was brought forward, several of the illiterate men waved their slips at the Western soldiers, begging them to check their numbers again.

As the wagon rode down the seaside street, they passed the most open space between any two structures in the whole of Gales. The bazaar was brimming with all those crafts from the shops already passed, as well as many more goods for sale. Hung on the surrounding walls were lengths of plain cloth and simple tapestries. Snappers hung from hooks, crates of chickens were stacked upon one another, and carts of produce could be seen between the many outstretched hands turning over melons and apricots. Sacks of barley were heaved over the shoulders of shoppers, and skins of wine were filled from barrels and jugs. People shuffled about the market, examining and bartering loudly with the merchants. A gaunt man in a filthy tunic trudged from the street towards the bazaar, a thick scar reaching from his forehead to his chin. As the beggar reached for an apple in one of the carts, a passing soldier of the Guard jabbed him with the hilt of his sword and threw the marked man back into the street. None in the bazaar paid the vulgar display any mind, but Esther pressed her scarlet veil tightly against her own marked cheek.

The wagon continued in uncomfortable silence until it came upon a structure unlike any other in the port. Amongst the plethora of sandstone constructs stood a gray stone wall making up the garrison of the Provincial Guard. The ward within the colossal walls could be glimpsed through the grilles of the iron gate facing the street. A couple of enlisted men peered down from their posts along the wallwalk, and a gigantic blue banner with an elongated silver star was draped high for all the port to see. Ira peered uncomfortably at the banner as he brought the wagon to a halt in front of the iron gate.

Érnog hopped out of the wagon and helped the ladies down the paved street. "We shall not be long," he said to them.

Taking Torzara's arm, Esther walked with her towards one of the shops, where a woman could be seen weaving baskets out of reeds. As Ira and Nathanael waited in the wagon, Érnog marched to the gate and called into the ward. One of the recruits within the walls came forward and addressed the dwarf through the grilles.

"What do you want?" the man said gruffly.

"We have business with the clerk," replied Érnog.

Glancing towards the wagon, the soldier gave a lazy nod and called for the gate to be opened. The iron bars were raised and granted the wagon entry. Nathanael gazed up at the walls in awe, their inner appearance even more domineering than the outer appeared from the street. In one shady corner of the grounds, the enlisted men of the Provincial Guard were taking refuge from the blistering sun. Many were standing around a low table watching two men gamble with silver denarii in a game of twelve lines.

The soldier who had shown them in trotted up the steps leading to the clerk's office in the garrison's keep. Érnog, Ira, and Nathanael waited for some time under the sun as hoots and cheers exploded from the crowd spectating the game. When, at last, the soldier returned from the offices, he was accompanied not by the clerk who handled trades and payments but by the Magistrate of Gales himself. His ivory hair was the same hue as his robes, and a broad smile broke upon his shaved square jaw. Ira turned his glaring face away from the man as he suggested to Nathanael that they join the crowd around the game. The haunting look on his friend's face told Ira that he understood the meaning of the suggestion. They were about to take a step towards the gamblers' huddle when . . .

"Well now," called a lofty voice as the magistrate strode their way. Ira's heart stopped and did not beat again until the man said, "You must be Master Érnog. I am honored to make your acquaintance at last."

The man had eyes for Érnog alone. Taking their chance, Ira and Nathanael strolled casually towards the off-duty soldiers.

"The honor is all mine, magistrate," Érnog said cordially. "Forgive me, but I believe I am expected presently by Clerk Lemuel."

"So you were. Unfortunately, the poor clerk has come down with the illness that has been going around. He is in no condition to assume his duties."

"I am sorry to hear it, and I wish him a swift recovery."

"As do we all," the magistrate said in an airy, less-than-authentic voice. "But never you worry. I shall be handling the trade in his stead. Now, let us see these fine crafts you have brought."

A little taken aback, Érnog beckoned the magistrate to the back of his wagon and lifted the sheet to unveil his makes. He counted each of the tunics out loud and casually reminded the magistrate of the price he had secured in his latest contract with the Guard.

"If I am not mistaken," said Érnog with a tone of civility, "the total comes out to two gold pieces and four silver for the lot."

One of the soldiers from the offices brought forward a set of scales and placed them beside the leathers as the magistrate sifted through them. For a while, the man said nothing but continued to smile broadly. When he had looked at each tunic no less than three times, he let out a dramatic sigh.

"It pains me to tell you, Master Érnog, and especially after so many years of faithful service to the Guard," the magistrate added in a shallow attempt at sympathy, "that I have not the means to offer you the price in your contract for these exquisite crafts."

Ira glanced towards the wagon and saw Érnog's eyes shift between the magistrate's freshly polished belt and his sandals, which held not a trace of mud on them.

"And what price can you offer?" the dwarf inquired patiently.

"I am at liberty to offer you twenty denarii for the lot."

The tension on Ira's face was nothing compared to that in his fists as he forced himself to stare at the game before him. The price offered, less than half of what had been contracted, was nothing short of an insult to Érnog and his reputation.

"This is not the first time the Guard has altered a price after delivery has been made, magistrate," Érnog stated steadily. "I was quite clear with the clerk that should you wish to negotiate, I would be happy to consider it once my present contract has expired."

"Were it in my power—" The dismissive look from Érnog gave the magistrate pause. The theatrical tone of friendship lost what little charm it held as the magistrate went on with a conceited demeanor about him. "It would seem the ledgers have come up short this season, and not for the first time, I might add. If citizens would pay what is owed to the province, I should be happy to pay you in full. My soldiers do not take advantage of those homes incapable of paying their taxes," Nathanael scoffed, but only loud enough for Ira to hear. "But I can always enforce stricter punishments upon those who come up short when the Guard arrives to collect. Would you have me take such measures, Master Érnog?"

"I would not wish for anything of the sort on my account," Érnog assured him, "but I cannot accept a price so much less than was agreed upon."

"Times are hard, Érnog. Were there any way to—"

"Certainly, somewhere within these walls, there is bound to be enough gold to make up the difference."

The retort was regretted the moment it left Ira's lips. Nathanael had gone stiff at his side, and the soldiers around them looked on in muddled shock and anticipation.

"You two!" the magistrate barked at the pair of strangers. "Come forward!"

Dreading every step, they trudged towards the wagon, each of them fighting the impulse to quicken their breaths. When they stood by Érnog's side, Ira focused on one of the stone slabs behind the magistrate's head, determined not to meet the gaze of the man he had met only once before.

"Who are these men?" the magistrate demanded of Érnog.

"This is my apprentice," the dwarf began hesitantly, "and his companion is a friend who traveled with us to Gales."

Every muscle in the man's face was taut, and he looked Nathanael up and down thoroughly before continuing on to Ira. All Ira could find himself grateful for was that the magistrate was so severely fixed on him that he could not notice the worry beneath Érnog's bushy beard. When the magistrate had finished examining the two, he muttered, "Your apprentice could use a lesson in manners, Master Érnog. That tongue of his is liable to get him into trouble someday."

"I will thank you to keep quiet throughout my dealings," grumbled Érnog as the wagon filled with unsold leathers passed through the iron gate into the street.

"He had enough to pay you and then some," said Ira defensively.

"He certainly did. And it will be his regret for not abiding by our contract when he cannot trade with any other tanner in all of Anthazar."

"What makes you say that?" asked Nathanael.

"Word travels quickly, and the trust of tradesmen is a deeply held institution. We may tussle and vie for our commissions, but our first loyalty is to our craft. When the magistrate's welching on an agreed contract is made known, no one will wish to do business with the Guard. The soldiers may have muddied sandals and wilted armor for as long as the magistrate wills it. And my patience will be rewarded with a greater commission than that I was first refused."

"I doubt beaten leathers would bother him as much as if the garrison's supply of Western wine ran dry," observed Ira. "He may be content to play the long game with you and the other tradesmen."

"Perhaps," admitted Érnog, "but what is life without a bit of a gamble."

These words did not entirely reassure Ira, but a chuckle and pat on the back from Érnog lightened his spirits a bit. As they searched the crowded street from the wagon, they found Esther and Torzara listening to a man speaking to a small gathering from atop a cart. Behind him was a scarlet banner embroidered with what appeared to be a long golden star set between two crescents.

". . . ignore the needs of the people! Where are our governors now? They do not live according to the rules they enforce on us, the citizens they—"

"We ran into an old friend, my love," Torzara said happily. "Leah of Sidon. I cannot remember the last time I—what is this?"

Torzara was staring at the pile of covered leather still sitting in the wagon. Ira and Érnog glanced at one another.

"Never mind that now," said Érnog casually. "How is Leah?"

"Oh, she is well enough. Her youngest has lately been commissioned into the Guard of Valcor."

"I could not stand it if one of my kin enlisted," Nathanael muttered to Ira. "If Simeon ever arrives at my doorstep to collect, I should throw him to the herd to spare our house the shame."

Ira had to stifle a laugh as the wagon passed along the bustling street.

A few hours of daylight remained, and the ship carrying Ira and Esther to the Westlands was to depart at sunset. Though Nathanael had spotted the merchant ship he was to serve aboard, he insisted on first seeing the brother and sister to their own vessel before embarking on his own voyage. After searching the sands as they rolled along the seaside, Nathanael sighted the man he had bartered with for his friends' passage. Érnog pulled the wagon over to the busy street's edge, careful not to let the wheels sink into the sand beside the paved road.

"I will give you a moment," said Nathanael, and he left the company to bid their farewells in private as he made his way down the beach.

"Come here, Ira," whispered Érnog. They strolled to the back of the wagon, where the dwarf reached one of his hairy arms into his pack and removed the dagger Ira had hunted with many a time. Ira was lost for words as the blade was offered to him by his master and friend. The feel of the dazzling knife in his hand had grown natural, even commonplace, over the years. Yet he had never considered it to belong to anyone but Érnog. "Say nothing of it," the dwarf urged as Ira tried to return the simple gift. When Ira finally accepted the gift, a somber smile grew beneath Érnog's lengthy gray beard.

"This is . . ." But the thanks Ira wished to express for this and every preceding kindness could never be enough. Érnog gave a light chuckle, and the two embraced one another. Ira could see Torzara offering Esther a gift of her own, a book entitled *Fables of the West*. Esther held her gift close to her heart as the frail dwarf caressed her face. When the brother and sister traded places, Ira took Torzara's hands and held them in his own.

"Do not worry for our sakes, we shall be just fine," Torzara assured him as she looked over to see Esther and Érnog exchanging soft words of parting. "Watch over her."

"Now and always," he replied.

"I hope you find what you are looking for, the both of you."

Abandoning searching for grand words of affection, Ira whispered to her, "Thank you, Torzara."

He and Esther stood on the sands as the dwarves in the wagon said with their eyes what their lips could not. Érnog and Torzara hardly watched the road as Selah pulled them down the bustling seaside street. Ira and Esther did not look away until the wagon turned the corner onto the main road, leading them out of the port along their homeward trail.

"We shall never see them again," Esther said under her breath, more to herself than to Ira. Ira picked up their small pack and hoisted it over his shoulder in an effort more to distract himself than anything else.

"We ought not leave Nathanael waiting," he said quietly.

When Esther could finally tear herself from her place in the sand, they strolled towards the rowboat settled on the moistened beach. They trod past a horde of footprints left by the beggars, who had earlier been clambering to serve as rowers aboard the

Haurthian galley. As they approached the crashing waves, Nathanael could be heard speaking to the master of the merchant ship they were to embark upon.

"Here they are now. See, your schedule shall not be delayed."

The master, a man with a haughty demeanor, wasted no time in looking Ira up and down far more intimately than the magistrate had. Ira had expected to be called upon to labor with the rest of the master's crew. But it still came as a surprise when the man began to grab his arms and feel their firm muscles. This uncouth behavior, hardly fitting for the Circus of Lark, continued until the man finally nodded his approval. To Esther's great relief, she was not so much as glanced at by the master.

"Well?" the man grunted, his eyes glancing anxiously down the beach. "Do you have it or not?"

Nathanael looked to Ira, who reached into his pack and retrieved a leather coin purse. He handed it to the man, who poured the gold and silver into his hand and began to count at an irritatingly slow pace.

"It is all there," hissed Ira urgently, peering around for any soldiers who might happen upon the illegal exchange. The master also lifted his gaze from the coins to examine the beach but did not quicken his counting. When, at last, he was satisfied with the bribe, the man returned the coins to their purse.

"All right then, in you go," he said with a nod to the rowboat beside him.

"Well," Nathanael said to the brother and sister, "this is where I leave you then." In a low voice, he muttered, "Send word when you have reached the garden."

"And we shall expect a letter from you when the baby has come," said Esther.

Ira thanked his friend once more as Esther made to step into the crammed rowboat. But as she did, the master halted her with a grasp of her arm.

"Not you," he growled.

"What is this?" demanded Ira, lunging forward to yank her arm from the master's grip.

"You," the master said with a nod at Ira, "not her."

"Passage for two, that was the deal," snarled Nathanael. "You have your gold; now let her pass."

"Payment for one sailor's labor and passage," retorted the master nastily. "If I am expected to take on a freeloader, it will cost you extra."

"Do not test me, Isaac!" Nathanael scowled in a low voice so as not to be overheard.

"I can work! I can!" pleaded Esther, but the master ignored her pleas. Ira's face was so close to the master's that he could smell the fish on his breath.

"Either permit us aboard your ship or return our payment."

"What have we here?"

An enlisted man of the Guard was striding down from the street towards the rowboat. He shot a solitary look at the master before turning on Ira, Esther, and Nathanael, who had all gone stiff.

"These three were attempting to bribe me for passage to the Westlands," boasted the master gallantly. He offered the purse to the soldier, who took it with a callous smirk.

"That is a serious offense," said the soldier. "The magistrate will not be pleased when I report this." Ira's clenched knuckles grew pale as Esther tried to conceal her mark beneath her veil. The sounds of the street and the bazaar were drowned by those of the waves ebbing and flowing around them. The soldier's shrewd grin broke as he jingled the contents of Ira's purse. He weighed them in his hand before saying, "Of course, I would not wish to bother the magistrate with so petty a matter as this." Then, holding the purse aloft, he hissed at the three, "Consider this payment for my silence. But should I catch wind of another attempt like this, it will be straight to the garrison with you. Now clear off this beach before my mercy runs dry."

And with a final glance at the master, the soldier strutted off towards the street.

"You heard him; scram!" barked the master severely.

Neither Ira nor Nathanael broke their glares at the man until Esther pulled them by their rigid arms towards the market. They halted at the edge of the street, where they could disappear into the throng of people shuffling about their errands.

"This is all my fault," lamented Nathanael, having not the heart to face either Ira or Esther. "I will see the gold returned to you; I swear it."

"It matters not," said Esther with an effort. "This journey was never ours to make. It is time we accept that." Her voice cracked as she spoke, and Nathanael looked adamantly towards Ira.

"There is still my first proposal to consider," he said.

"And I have told you already," said Ira firmly, "he will not have it. Moreover, you will be sacked for the mere suggestion of it."

"What are you talking about?" asked Esther, glancing between them.

"My ship is bound for Eou Verás this very day," explained Nathanael. "And I know I can convince Halruc to grant you passage and deliver you to some remote place beyond the Hallowed City."

Esther beamed at her brother with wide eyes. "Why not? Surely, if Nathanael will vouch for us—"

"We have not an assarius to offer him," Ira pointed out.

"Let me worry about the payment," said Nathanael.

"Come now, Nathanael. You know as well as I that your master will not have us. It is risky enough harboring us across the sea, let alone delivering us to the Western shores. If caught, your master would face life imprisonment in Alaoth. He could have you jailed for proposing the idea."

"Halruc is many things, but he would never stoop to that level," affirmed Nathanael. "Let me do this for you!"

Aggravated at his friend's rash desire to amend their present situation, Ira turned to Esther for support in swaying Nathanael's mind from recklessness. She quietly considered both sides before addressing the matter in a most serious tone.

"If you firmly believe your master will not turn you into the Guard, then we shall speak to him. But if you hold even the slightest reservation about approaching him, we will drop the matter and repeat nothing of it."

Nathanael took a moment to consider the risk and said with finality, "We can trust him."

Esther strained to temper her hopes as Nathanael led them north along the side of the road at a brisk pace. They passed many a merchant ship anchored along the coast, along with some smaller fishing boats scattered between. Ira and Esther hurriedly followed as Nathanael suddenly veered from the street onto the hot, coarse sands, heading towards two rowboats settled along the shoreline. Loading the rowboats with jars and barrels was a tall, burly man clad in a scarlet worker's tunic.

"Tabor!" Nathanael shouted to the sailor.

The man turned to see who had called to him and gave a wave upon setting eyes on Nathanael. Like many sailors, his appearance was weathered more by service than age. He had a crooked nose and a mane of dark hair flecked with gray. It was neither a sinister appearance nor a kindly one. The man wore around his neck an ancestral pendant in the shape of a ship, the sign of a trade passed down for generations. As Nathanael braced arms with the man called Tabor, his knuckles displayed many cuts and scrapes mended over the years, the trophies of a faithful servant.

"You are cutting it rather close, Nathanael," said Tabor. "We were ready to set off without you."

"And you would have been the sorrier for it," replied Nathanael.

"So says you," the sailor said with a grin.

"Tabor, may I introduce two friends of mine, Ira and Esther of Squall."

"A pleasure," remarked Tabor with a cordial nod to the brother and sister. "I hope you left your family well, Nathanael."

"Well indeed, my Ruth and I are to welcome our first child later in the summer," acclaimed Nathanael with a note of true felicity in his voice.

"My congratulations to you both, and may there be many more to come! A large house makes for many working hands." He gestured towards an adolescent boy carrying two small crates across the street from the bazaar. He was lanky and not as tall as his father but garbed in the same scarlet tunic. Though his features were not as irregular and worn as Tabor's, the resemblance was plain. "My eldest," Tabor said to Ira and Esther. "He is stronger than he appears and a diligent worker. There are four more at home tending the land, as well as their mother. She was taken ill a few days before we departed for Gales."

Nathanael gave both Tabor and his son an apprehensive look. Illness, especially at sea, was no trivial thing. A harsh fever aboard an isolated ship could bring down an entire crew if allowed to fester. And if pestilence did not cost any lives, it could just as well wary the most veteran sailor into sloppy seamanship, enough to risk sending every soul to the depths and the vicious maritime creatures lurking below.

"Fret not," Tabor added hastily, understanding Nathanael's cautious gaze. "We traveled three days to Gales, and I have been in perfect health since. The lad, too."

"Well, is everything settled then?" asked Nathanael.

"We shall be ready to shove off before dusk."

"Is the master already on board?"

"He had some dealings in the market to tend to, but he shall be along shortly. Lend us a hand with the provisions, will you?"

"Of course, but first," said Nathanael as he glanced towards the edge of the bazaar in search of his master, "I have a matter to discuss with Halruc."

At these words, Tabor's eyes drifted between Nathanael and his pair of companions. After giving his fellow crewmate an inquiring look, which Nathanael did not return, Tabor appeared to grasp what sort of business he might have with the master. Leaning in a little closer, his next words came as a whisper.

"I hope you mean not to suggest anything indecent to the master."

"Be not concerned, Tabor; I know what I am doing," Nathanael said firmly.

"You had better. Here he comes now."

As he spoke, a dwarf emerged from the mass of people shuffling through the bazaar. The master stood apart from the other citizens of Gales, both in garb and in the commanding strides he took down to the beach. He wore a scarlet mantle hemmed with golden stripes. His pale hair and beard were straight and refined, and his once-pale skin had long been kissed by the raw sun. Stubby fingers bore many rings with jewels and gemstones to distract from the scars along his knuckles. When his beady eyes caught sight of Nathanael, the master did not extend any greeting to him but turned to address Tabor in a gravelly voice.

"Remind me, Tabor, never again to trade with Enoch," the dwarven master proclaimed. "I had to pay a ludicrous price for these chickens. Give the lad a hand fetching the last crates, and we shall set off at once." As Tabor dismissed himself to aid his son, the dwarf spun in place to look up at Nathanael. "You are late. It serves you well that Morigun's illness afforded you to take his place. Pray, do not test my patience with tardiness again. Load the last of the provisions, and we shall make for the *Wayfarer*."

"Aye, master." Nathanael said apologetically, "Master? If I might have a word with you before our departure?"

The dwarf stopped in his tracks, and intuitively, his gaze fell upon the brother and sister by his servant's side. It was abundantly clear that, just as Tabor had discerned, the master comprehended the imminent approach of an ill proposition.

"Speak quickly then," said Halruc shortly.

Nathanael nodded as he gestured to Ira and Esther. "My friends are seeking passage to the Westlands. They had arranged to sail aboard another vessel but were cheated by the master."

Halruc let out an understanding grunt under his breath as he addressed Ira. "So, Isaac is still up to his old tricks then."

"He—what?" asked Nathanael.

"Master Isaac. He and an old friend of his serving the Guard enjoy swindling those desperate enough to try and bribe their way across the sea. You heard of him offering passage at the tavern, did you not? It is the place where they like to concoct their little schemes. The bartender spreads the word through his patrons, undoubtedly earning a nice cut for himself. Exactly how much did your friend barter away, Nathanael?"

"It was not Ira's fault, but mine," admitted Nathanael. "I made the arrangements."

"Did you now?" said Halruc with a tone of amusement. "Then you are more of a dolt than I took you for."

"I will have a few words with that man upon my return," muttered Nathanael.

Esther let out a light cough as if to remind Nathanael of the purpose of their meeting with the master. With a great effort to restrain his fury at the swindlers and himself, Nathanael prepared to address Halruc with his proposition. Before he could speak, however, the dwarf raised a jewel-covered hand to silence his servant.

"So, unless I am very much mistaken, you wish for me to permit these two into my service and deliver them to shores they are forbidden to set foot upon, yes? Assuming, of course, that along our voyage to Eou Verás, they are not discovered by any galley posed for inspection."

"I am willing to vouch for their character and—"

But the dwarf raised his hand again and Nathanael's voice trailed off. The master's eyes were fixed upon Ira and Esther, their hearts pounding ever faster.

"I will not hear another word until all is laid on the table," declared Halruc. "Let us see the documents of these two."

If there had been any remaining hope for the brother and sister, it faded away as Ira pulled two sheets of parchment from his pack bearing their names and lineage. In the corner of the sheet was a section reserved for any convicted offenses. The thick black mark in this section was where Halruc's eyes flitted to before examining the documents more closely. He read and reread them several times until he turned to face Nathanael, holding their papers high for him to see.

"Is this what you believe me capable of overlooking?" he spat at Nathanael. "No citizen is barred passage to Haurth for petty crimes, but this . . . What are you doing with such ruffians as these, Nathanael?"

"Ira and Esther's pasts are of no concern to me," protested Nathanael. "In all the years of our acquaintance, they have never given me cause to doubt their loyalties, and I am prepared to stake my reputation alongside theirs. I would trust either of them with my life."

"Trust? What does your trust mean to me?" As worry began to cross the faces of the three, the master's voice softened. Yet even so, it did not lose a trace of the vitriol the dwarf was so willing to offer. "This is an imprudent proposal I would not have thought you capable of, Nathanael." After a short glare, Halruc continued, "But I know you to be an honest man. If you are willing to align yourself with these two, then I am inclined to believe in your judgment of their character."

Ira, Esther, and Nathanael all let out a deep breath of relief. But as a gracious smile grew upon Esther's gentle face, Ira's hopeful expression turned grim.

"Your words mean a great deal, Master Halruc," said Ira thankfully. "So I beg you not to think ill of me for clarifying that you have not yet agreed to have us aboard your ship."

"And so you are right," concurred the master. "For as much as Nathanael may come to the rescue of your reputations, it is not enough to alter the risk I stand to assume. Should I be caught harboring such felons as yourselves, a cell in Alaoth would take me for what remains of my life. The mariners would reduce my ship, my prize and vocation, to embers, an example to others who may be tempted to break Haurthian law. This I cannot abide. My answer is no."

In the silence that followed this denial, Ira found himself suddenly aware of his surroundings. The waters, once sapphire, now reflected the garish orange hue of the setting sun. Calls and chatter from the market sounded clearly over the rushing waves brimming the banks with foam. Halruc could not have put it more plainly, and his reservations were well founded. Ira could recall one time in Gales when illegal goods were discovered aboard another merchant ship upon a surprise inspection. For this, the magistrate revoked every contract the ship's master had ever commissioned. The crew was sent off with nothing to show for their time at sea, and the master was driven to sell his faithful vessel at a fraction of its value. In no position to make demands, the former master took what he could barter for the ship and never returned to the port.

The salty breeze wafting from the sea recalled Ira back to where he stood. The ground beneath his feet had given way, and he found his sandals sunken into the damp sands. He pondered for an instant what he might say to change the master's mind, but it was a fleeting thought.

"I cannot imagine what might drive the pair of you to sail to the land you were banished from," Halruc said to the brother and sister, "nor do I care to know. If you will excuse us, Nathanael and I must be setting off."

And with a slight inclination of his head, the master parted from their company and made for one of the two rowboats overflowing with provisions. Before the dwarf had clambered in between the barrels, jugs, and crates, however, Nathanael raised his voice.

"Could we not take them part of the way?" he inquired loudly. "The Isle of Jade is not so far off from our current course. The fleets of Haurth are hardly ever within a hundred leagues of the isles. Could they not disembark upon one of those and seek further passage from there?"

Ira's eyes widened. Finding another ship to take them the rest of the way from one of the isles might not be so difficult. It was also true that the warships of the Haurthian Navy rarely anchored at any of the desolate isles across the Bridging Sea. The master stroked his beard as he considered Nathanael, the jewels set into his many rings sparkling in the sun's vicious glare.

"You forget, Nathanael, that there remains a great risk of their being discovered at sea." Halruc reminded him. "Galleys are known for their surprise inspections."

"When was the *Wayfarer* last boarded at sea?" asked Nathanael incredulously.

"Temper your tongue, boy!" scorned Halruc. "Never address your master with such taunts again!" As Nathanael humbled himself, the dwarf went on in a business-like tone. "What price could you offer to settle an anxious master's mind?"

"We have little left to us," admitted Ira. "But we can—"

"Take your price from my wages!" interjected Nathanael.

"What?" Ira turned and gave his friend a hard shove. "Are you mad? You have Ruth and the child to consider; you are not throwing away your wages on our account."

"You lost all your savings on my account," asserted Nathanael. "So it is my charge to rectify that mistake." He looked to his master and blurted out, "Ten gold aurei from my wages. Will that satisfy you?"

Halruc let out a derisive laugh. "Ten? You insult me, Nathanael."

"Fifteen!"

Ira fought to restrain his friend from rash discourse, but it was to no avail. Such a lofty debt would mean years of labor on Nathanael's part for no profit.

"This is no small favor you ask," declared Halruc.

"Eighteen then. A more than fair price!"

The dwarf stirred with the number before countering with twenty-five gold aurei.

"Now you are the one swindling me, master. Let us settle on twenty, a generous sum for a meager risk. I warn you, I shall go no higher."

With a look at his ship anchored in the distance and a glance at the brother and sister, the master replied, "The *Wayfarer* shall anchor at the Isle of Jade to replenish our supply of food and water. It will be necessary as we shall have two extra mouths for the first leg of our voyage." Before they could rejoice, Halruc added to the brother and sister, "What becomes of you after our parting in Jade is of no concern to me. But until that time, you are—both of you— in the service of the *Wayfarer*. Now lend Tabor and the lad a hand packing the other boat."

Without waiting for a word of thanks, Halruc clambered into the nearest rowboat as a beaming Nathanael followed him. Wasting no time, Ira and Esther joined Tabor and his son in loading the last provisions into the second rowboat. Though Tabor asked no questions, he could not help but express his amazement at Nathanael's currying such favor with the master. When the last jugs of fresh water and a few sacks of potatoes had been loaded, Tabor's son and Esther seated themselves awkwardly between the crowding supplies. Ira and Tabor heaved the boat through the dense sand until it came afloat. When the icy waters had risen to their knees, the men lumbered in and took hold of the oars. In unison, they struck the sea and thrust their tiny vessel with mighty heaves to follow Nathanael and Halruc's lead. They fought against each surge of the impending waves. Over and over again, the boat was gently raised before the inevitable crash over every wavecrest. As they went, Esther and the young sailor took hold of those provisions most susceptible to tumbling out of the vessel. When the vicious billows hailing towards the banks were behind them, Ira and Tabor's strokes lightened in the steady open waters. Past a myriad of plain boats and their fishermen casting nets into flame-colored waters, the men beckoned their transport towards a tall and wide merchant ship.

The breadth of the *Wayfarer* was elevated as it bobbed between the swarm of unremarkable fishing boats. The faded paint along its ledge revealed a veteran ship's reputation. The scarlet trim met at the bow where a wooden osprey was mounted; its golden coat chipped in places. Though not as young as a virgin vessel's, the oak planks making up the hull were joined as seamlessly as the day it was constructed. Not one splintered or rotting board was to be found. A laced sail of clean scarlet was furled about the not-yet-hoisted yard. As their rowboat approached the *Wayfarer*'s port side, two rope ends were tossed over the ship's ledge and landed in the men's laps.

"Can you tie a bowline?" Tabor asked Ira.

Ira nodded and followed Tabor's lead. They tied the lines securely around barrels, jugs, sacks, and crates one by one. As soon as a knot was taught, they would tug the ropes, and the items were carefully hoisted onto the deck above. When the rowboat was empty but for its passengers, the two lines fell once more, followed by a dangling rope ladder. Tabor took his line and ran it through a small hole in the bow of the rowboat. Ira found a second hole on the boat's stern and did the same as Tabor's son began to climb. Ira tied a final bowline through the hole as Esther followed the young sailor up the ladder, gripping its rungs tightly as she went. Tabor ascended next, and then Ira, swaying with every step up the vessel's hull.

Coming aboard the *Wayfarer*, the newcomers found themselves in the heat of an organized commotion, the sort only to be found with a seasoned crew and master. No sailor on deck spared a moment's notice for the two strangers in their company. A steady patter of sandals rippled across the planks as dwarf sailors crossed in all directions, performing various tasks. All of them were garbed in scarlet tunics with their unique sashes of rigid patterns tied about their stocky waists. Ira counted seven dwarves in the scuttle, eight counting Halruc, who was overseeing all preparations from the raised quarterdeck at the ship's stern. Standing beside the master was an elf, the only one other than Halruc dressed in a mantle rather than a tunic. He wore a sash with flowing patterns and was engrossed in a pocketbook, which he flipped through without noting any of the happenings around him.

Nathanael was engaged in hauling a stone anchor from the harbor's depths. Two of the dwarves, brothers, it would seem by their identical sashes and kindred midnight manes, lifted the rowboat from the water by the lines Ira and Tabor had tethered. An auburn-haired dwarf was posted as the helmsman, gripping the two rudder oars tightly. As he propelled them forward and backward, sailors peering over the ship's ledge affirmed the motions of the rudders fixed on either side of the *Wayfarer*. Below deck in the cargo hold, someone was calling out the many goods and their quantities as one of the dwarves tacked them off on a wax-coated tablet that was the ship's manifest. When the entirety of the shipment had been accounted for, the sailors looked to their master on the quarterdeck.

"Hail the yard!" hollered Halruc.

A chorus of "Aye, master!" rang in the briny air as every sailor scurried to the mast and grabbed hold of a long rope. Esther shuffled aside as Ira joined the crew along the length of the halyard. Tabor, the tallest of the sailors, gripped the line frontmost, followed by Ira, Nathanael, Tabor's son, and the seven stout dwarves. As they heaved, many crew members finally took notice of their two new companions. Despite the curiosities on deck, no inquiries were made as the broad arms of man and dwarf slowly raised the yard. Every lug of the halyard raised the trunk wrapped in its furled sail a little higher. As their heaves grew rhythmic, a voice from the rear of the line broke into song. Before long, a choir of sailors had joined in a jovial shanty.

> *The master has called my number today*
> *The time is now; I must away*
> *The debts are many; I have not a pound*
> *For now, I am to service bound*
> *To wealth and gold, my soul is sold*
> *For now, I am to service bound*

When the timber yard was aloft and secured, the colossal scarlet cloth was released into the coastal breeze. As it gently swept across the deck, the monstrous sail caught the fullness of its breath and lunged ferociously. The sailors grasped either of the sheets to restrain the bucking sail. Sandals squeaked on the moistened deck as those remaining sailors set the braces of the mounted yard.

I kissed my bride and set out the door
A wealthy man I was not born
I shall labor and slave 'til next we touch the ground
For now, I am to service bound
To wealth and gold, my soul is sold
For now, I am to service bound

With the braces held taut, all hands joined on the sheets until they too were fastened to the ship's port and starboard ledges. With the finishing tether, the scarlet sail flooded whole and rippled no more. A soft moan accompanied the vessel's gentle lurch as its bow dipped marginally towards the water before rocking back. A thunder of boisterous cheers let out as the *Wayfarer* began to gather speed. The elf muttered something to the auburn-haired dwarf, who thrust the rudder oars opposite each other. The ship veered to port until they were pointed west towards the blazing sun basking along the horizon. One of the dwarves hustled down the ladder to the hold and returned shortly with an aged fiddle. As Nathanael made to introduce Ira and Esther to the company, they were interrupted by the instrumental strums and another canorous refrain.

When next we hail to homely shores
With riches and gems in mounds and troves
I shall spend my share, save not a pound
And then again, be service bound
To wealth and gold, my soul is sold
Forever I am to service bound

The celebration rang on as many of the crew leaned over the ship's ledge to bid farewell to the fishing boats as they passed.

Nathanael was too engulfed in the festivities to notice as Ira took his leave of him. He and Esther ventured to the stern of the ship and gazed towards the banks of the port. The garrison's polished gray masonry stood out amidst the shorter sandstone dwellings. As the excited chatter of the crew mingled with the purring sounds of waves and gales, Ira closed his eyes and breathed in the familiar tang of the sea, swimming in the memories of former days beneath sapphire sails.

CHAPTER IV

THE WAYFARER

A watery desert spanning beyond the eye served only to remind its voyagers of their irrefutable isolation. Despite the vapid surroundings, no galley or ship could ever truly count itself alone. For as far as it sprawled, the Bridging Sea concealed the life she bore beneath the cusp that separated her from the sky. A few short days into the *Wayfarer*'s journey, some of the creatures of the deep surfaced to offer the sailors their unbidden company. A throng of sirens, out of sight but not unheard, echoed their notes of temptation to the vessel from afar. The canticle was wordless and not hearty like the tunes the dwarven sailor Puck enjoyed bowing on his fiddle. The alluring voices of the maritime ladies struck in every sailor's soul the inexplicable desire to drown himself so he might hear their tender melodies loud and clear. At the urgent command of the master, all the men on deck filled their ears with strips of cloth, some rather begrudgingly, and none were permitted to remove them until Halruc was certain the nymphs' song was behind them.

The sea-dwellers were not the only creatures that greeted the *Wayfarer* as she trekked westward. Flocks of wild ospreys traversed the air, gliding wherever wafty breezes would carry them. Once in a while, the odd messenger bird would pass overhead, sailing with purpose and direction with a small leather sack bearing letters to ships, isles, or mainlands many leagues beyond. On their fourth day at sea, the merchant vessel came upon a scintillating reef in a patch of shallows where hundreds of seahawks circled above. The ospreys would take turns to swoop into a dive, outstretching their long legs and bearing a set of sharp talons. With an almighty splash, the hawks would plunge at the shoals and emerge the next moment with wriggling fish clasped in their claws. The spectacle was mesmerizing to the sailors who had grown bored with the monotony of their labors, but their enjoyment of the display was short-lived as a hefty gust caught the sail and hailed them onwards.

Indeed, the elated mood felt by all upon the ship's departure had dissipated reliably soon. Worn from their duties or lazy in their idle time, that part of the day when every sailor seemed at his cheeriest was mealtime. Esther had been tasked with preparing breakfast and supper when it came time for the day and night shifts to trade their posts. This meant ensuring that no more than the day's allotted food provisions were prepared now that two more were aboard the vessel. The ship's detour to the Isle of Jade would mean a chance to replenish their supplies. Nevertheless, Halruc insisted that Esther limit the provisions to air on the side of caution.

As Master Halruc divided the crew into night and day shifts, it was no surprise to Ira when he found himself delegated to the "nighters," as they were called, while Nathanael joined the "dayers." Ira supposed this was Halruc's way to ensure the old friends could not become distracted from their duties. It was hardly necessary, as the two crews often joined one another on deck after having a good rest in the cargo hold. All the servants of the *Wayfarer* wore identical scarlet tunics; Ira wore the sash of Érnog's ancestors tied about his waist like the other dwarves.

Weary as he was adjusting to his nocturnal labors, Ira fell most comfortably into the routine of a sailor. At each sunset, he and the other nighters would rise from their hammocks, eat a bit of supper, and then climb through the hatch to relieve the dayers. Between that time and daybreak, Ira and the other nighters would light the lanterns across the deck, take the helm in turns, adjust the yard to catch the strongest gusts, and otherwise wile away the night in each other's company. At sunrise, the dayers would emerge well-rested and ready to resume their posts, while the nighters claimed their breakfast before grabbing some shut-eye. With each meal Esther prepared, there came a small portion of cheap mead from the vineyards of Carmel. This was a common practice on every ship, an effort to prevent any malady from spreading amongst the men. Whole crews brought down by flu or fever could count themselves lucky if their numbers remained unchanged by the time they returned to the mainland, if they returned at all.

To Ira's relief, no one aboard the *Wayfarer* seemed to hold any ill will towards Esther for the mark she bore. Though her mark was the sort which denoted a criminal past, her otherwise handsome features and gentle demeanor quickly earned her favor with the rest of the crew. Many sailors of the provinces were accustomed to laboring with those holding petty crimes to their names, as those workers were reliably cheap for masters to take on. As it happened, one such sailor had already been in the service of the *Wayfarer* when the brother and sister had joined their ranks, a mute dwarf with a mat of auburn hair. His tongue had been cut out by the Provincial Guard some years ago, a punishment often dealt for something the guilty party had said to deeply offend a governing entity. As it happened, no one aboard the ship could so much as attest to the voiceless dwarf's actual name. According to Nathanael, his document of identification, kept in Halruc's cabin along with all the others, was smudged and illegible where the dwarf's name was concerned. As he could neither write nor utter a single syllable, the crew had long ago taken to calling him the mute.

Though Ira had not asked it of her, Esther elected to rest in her hammock during the day so she might join her brother on deck during his shifts. Every night, she sat on the quarterdeck steps in quiet contentment, watching them work or immersing herself in a book under the lantern light to pass the evening. Ira was relieved to find Esther nearly as pleased to be in the company of the crew as she had been in the House of Érnog. Though the addresses made to her were short and simple—a cordial nod or a genial thanks for a meal—no gesture failed to lift her spirits and broaden the smile beneath her veil. Indeed, most of the sailors appeared to enjoy the presence of a lady on the ship, though perhaps none so much as Tabor's son. It had not escaped Ira's notice that the lad's eyes routinely glinted towards Esther whenever she joined the nighters on deck with a book in her lap. One morning, as she offered them their breakfast below deck, the young sailor managed to trip over a crate a moment after he was caught beaming at Esther with a boyish grin. Ira hid his smile behind his bowl of pea soup as the lad hastened to his hammock, a little red in the face.

He was known as the lad by the whole of the ship, though this was neither a sign of immaturity nor a mockery perpetuated by his crewmates. The boy and his father shared the same name, a rare but heard-of practice across the provinces. Those families known for passing along a father's name to the eldest son were those whose ancestors had followed a particular trade for several generations. The pendant Tabor the greater wore around his neck was one passed down for centuries, father to son, sailor to sailor. Though traversing the sea was the trade of his forefathers, Ira had learned that the burly man was also the proprietor of an olive grove in the Vastlands of Héribon. It had formerly belonged to the father of Tabor's wife before his passing. And for the greater span of his youth, the lad, alongside his mother and four siblings, had tended the grove and sold its fruits and oils. This was until Tabor had managed to admit his son into Halruc's service when a vacancy had arisen a year ago. Under his father's tutelage and a watchful eye, the boy, then of four and ten, had shown himself to be a reliable member of the crew. To avoid the confusion of having two sailors of the same name, the *Wayfarer*'s new crewmate was thus dubbed the lad by his companions.

Alongside Ira, the mute, and the lad were three other nighters who moiled beside them under the star-strewn sky. Puck, the musical dwarf, and the two dwarven brothers, Ossel and Ram. All were appreciative of there being an extra crewmate to endure the long nights with, though Ram had not initially been warm to the newcomer's arrival. No doubt, his apprehensions arose from the fear of his wages being lessened with another sailor to share the voyage's commission with. Shortly after their departure from Gales, the dark-haired dwarf had gone to speak with the master in his cabin below the quarterdeck. Ira could only suppose his and Esther's presence being the reason for the private convention, for when the dwarf returned shortly after, he was far more gracious to the pair of them. It seemed Halruc had divulged enough to settle the curious minds of the crew without delving into such detail that might reveal the infamy of the *Wayfarer*'s latest additions.

Shy of a week since their departure, the sailors under the night sky were enjoying one of the idle calms their shifts regularly afforded them. With no course corrections to be made and a strong wind billowing in the sail, they could pass their spare time on deck however they pleased. Ossel was taking his turn at the helm, conversing airily with his brother. Ira and Esther watched as Puck played short notes on his fiddle beneath the mast. The mute was listening intently to the melodies while the lad lay on his back, staring into the hovering void. The young sailor was not the only one with eyes for the heavens. The elf who sailed with them, named Manoque, was peering into the twinkling stars at long intervals. Occasionally, he would lower his gaze to the pages of his trusted pocketbook and scribble with a sharpened reed dipped in ink before staring again into the abyss. Manoque had a long face, a sheen of tawny hair, sharp features, and eyes that brilliantly reflected the creamy gleam of the crescent moon. He was not a common laborer but a skilled navigator and one of the few elves born and raised in the Eastlands. While the position of the sun or moon could tell even the most novice of voyagers what direction they hailed, the guidance of the stars was paramount to traversing the Bridging Sea with utmost precision. His talents being of little use while the stars were shrouded by daylight, Manoque regularly joined the nighters on their watch to redirect the ship's course whenever necessary.

The multitude of glittering stars danced in unison as the *Wayfarer* swayed and dipped over bounding waves. The elf consulted the yellowing pages of his book once more before turning on the spot and striding towards the master's quarters. Ira and the other nighters rose to their feet as Manoque rapped on the cabin door on the port side of the quarterdeck.

"New heading, master!" the elf called in a waking voice.

An acknowledging grunt sounded from behind the door, followed by the emergence of a dreary Halruc. His pale hair and beard glowed in the lantern light as the master donned a cloak and let out a muffled yawn as he lumbered up the steps of the quarterdeck. Halruc spent most of his time on deck with the dayers while Manoque rested but insisted on being present for every alteration of their course. The navigator directed Ossel to take them a tad further north, and the dwarf obeyed as he heaved the rudder oars opposite one another. As the bow angled to starboard, the scarlet sail above began to violently shake and rattle. At once, the other nighters scampered to the port and starboard ledges of the *Wayfarer*. They planted their sandals, loosened the sheets only as much as needed, and hauled the two braces. The yard rotated by the will of the sailors' brawn as a creaking wail from the thick timber sounded overhead. With the wind bucking towards them from the east, the nighters brought the yard about and angled it northwest. The sputtering of the wind ceased as the rippling sail caught the mighty gust once more. When they had secured the braces again, the nighters tethered the sheets once more and looked aimlessly at their master.

Halruc nodded his approval and stepped sleepily back to his cabin without a word. Their conversation with the master on the banks of Gales was the only time Ira or Esther had heard Halruc offer any words beyond orders on deck. Nathanael had assured his friends that this was routine and that the dwarf's behavior was in no way altered by the brother and sister's presence aboard his ship. As Ossel allowed Ram his turn at the helm, the other nighters resumed leisurely activities. The hatch to the hold swung open, and Nathanael hoisted himself on deck. A small purse was jingling in his hand as he strode to the quarterdeck steps where Ira and Esther were seated.

"I wish it were more, but it is a start," he said, placing the sack into Esther's hand. She examined the contents to find a number of bronze and silver coins. Immediately, she outstretched her hand to return the purse.

"We have told you already," she insisted. "You owe us nothing. If not for you—"

"If not for me, you two would not have squandered so much on a sham. Nothing can amend that now, but this will help. It is not much, only the winnings from the game below deck, but you shall require much more if you are to secure passage from Jade to Haurth."

"You repaid us in full when the master took us on," said Ira determinantly. "We mean to trade some of our possessions to fund the remainder of our voyage, so your coin is nothing to us. Now take it back, Nathanael."

Nathanael raised his hands in hopes that Esther would stop trying to return the winnings. Ira knew his friend to be stubborn when set in his ways, a quality they shared. Taking the purse from Esther, Ira wandered towards the ship's ledge.

"Well, as no one here desires it . . ." He wound back his arm and aimed a throw for the dark waters.

"All right! All right!" cried Nathanael, reluctantly taking back the jingling sack as he shot his friend a look of annoyance, covering a hint of amusement.

"You shall need every bit you can scrounge for Ruth and the child," Ira informed him, "now that you are twenty gold pieces in debt to the master."

As they joined Esther on the quarterdeck steps, Puck's bowing of short and soft tunes drowned out the whistling winds of the evening. A roar of excitement from the sailors below emanated through the open hatch. The lad turned his attention from the stars to the hatch, an envious gaze in his eyes.

"Do you play?" Ira called to him.

The lad jumped at the address and quickly collected himself before replying.

"Father does not allow it," he said with a note of longing in his young voice. "He says I would fritter away my wages from boredom if I were to take to gambling."

"Your father is wise to deter you," attested Manoque as he scrawled in his pocketbook. "It is no good throwing away your earnings in a game that is mostly chance."

At this, Nathanael made an effort to hide his purse of winnings from the lad's view. The elf jotted his final notes on the weathered pages and was about to stow the book in his satchel when the lad asked, "What do you write in there?"

The elf looked from the lad to the leather-bound book in his hand.

"Would you like to see?" he asked.

With a look of embarrassment he tried to hide, the lad muttered something that sounded like "Cannot read." As common as illiteracy was in the provinces, the young sailor carried it like a shameful secret. Manoque strode over to the lad and patted him on the shoulder.

"I doubt there are many on this ship who could write their own name, let alone read. But there are plenty of skills in this life to hold value in, lad. I have sailed these waters for many years and have never met anyone as young as you capable of mastering a vessel like this."

A feeble grin grew on the lad's face, his eyes still fixed on the book in Manoque's hand. "Could I have a look at it anyway?"

The elf gave a light chuckle as he offered up the little book. Bidding them all goodnight, Manoque stepped down through the hatch as a loud groan echoed from the gamblers below. Holding it like a great treasure, the lad examined the various scribbles and shapes of the book with abstract interest. Squinting his eyes under the dim lantern light, he absorbed every detail, no matter how meaningless, on each page before turning to the next. So taken by unknowing fascination, the lad gave a start when he noticed Ira, Esther, and Nathanael all watching him attempt to make sense of Manoque's writings. Hastily, he closed the book and glanced away from them.

"Did you ever wish to learn?" asked Nathanael.

"Our house cannot afford the lessons, what with so many brothers and sisters."

"Would you like me to teach you?" asked Esther sympathetically.

The lad's gloomy expression vanished in an instant.

"Could you?" he asked eagerly.

"If you would like," she said with a smile. "Perhaps when you return, you can teach your brothers and sisters how."

"Will I be able to read that well?"

"I see no reason why not."

"I thought in the Eastlands, only great masters and scribes could read and write. I never thought someone with a—"

The lad caught himself before he finished, but he knew he had offended as Esther drew her veil close to the mark along her cheek. Again, he turned away in bitter shame at his thoughtless remark. Ira and Nathanael sat quietly, not daring to speak amidst such an uncomfortable moment. But Esther, feeling the lad's supreme regret for a momentary lapse, raised her voice with care and gentility.

"I have never tutored anyone before," she said, "but I am sure I feel up to the task. We could start with letters and make our way to forming smaller words. If you are not too tired, we ought to be able to fit in lessons after your shifts."

Thankful for her forgiveness and the willingness to teach him still, he looked wide-eyed at Esther and gave her a broad grin.

"Could we start now?" he asked energetically.

Esther laughed as he handed her Manoque's pocketbook. She opened it to one of the pages heavily scrawled with notes and began to run her finger across each letter, reading them aloud as she went. Under his breath, the lad repeated each letter to himself as Esther followed the lines. Ira thought it best to leave the teacher and her student to their studies and told Nathanael he was going to refill his waterskin.

He descended the ladder through the hatch and stepped into the crowded cargo hold. A lantern overhead swayed in perfect opposition to the *Wayfarer*'s subtle rocking. The flickering of the oil light waned as it spread to the dark innards of the bow, between towers of crates, barrels, jugs, and sacks. Hammocks were strung up in those small vacancies between the brimming stacks of exports bound for the Hallowed City. Beneath the hatch was the only bare portion of the hold. Here, the recently woken dayers were gathered around and absorbed in a game of twelve lines. Tabor contemplated his next move across from a dwarf with sandy hair named Ishcaur. Two more dwarves were observing the game: Cercur and Dromo. Cercur was the youngest dwarf aboard the ship; his beard and hair were longer than Ira's, though not quite as lengthy as those of his dwarven companions. Dromo, on the other hand, was the only one with more years than the master. Ira had spoken least with the stoic and balding dwarf, as he said hardly any more than the mute. Ira strolled by the company as Tabor examined the board littered with round chips, each topped with a bronze assarius. On his search for one of the freshwater jugs hidden amongst the supplies, he passed Manoque resting in his hammock, arms crossed over his chest. As Ira clambered towards the bow, Tabor triumphantly skipped one of his chips in a diagonal pattern over four of Ishcaur's. A cry of excitement shook the planks of the hull. Manoque's head lifted in alarm before, and with a grunt of annoyance, it fell again into a weary sleep.

"I cannot understand why you insist on trying your luck with me time and time again, Ishcaur," boasted Tabor gleefully as he collected the chips and coins he had crossed.

"I notice your mood has taken a turn for the better since Nathanael left the game with half of your purse," gloated Ishcaur. He and Cercur chortled at the remark as Tabor's smile faded from his lips. Dromo, meanwhile, held the same steely demeanor he always did through levity or upset.

"What about you, Cercur?" asked Tabor, disregarding his companion's slight. "You have not had a game all night."

"Perhaps on the return journey," said the young dwarf in a reluctant tone. "At present, I have not an assarius to my name. The Guard came to collect the other day." There was a collective grumble amongst the dayers at this remark. "Figure this: one of them was raised in our village. I have known him since he was only a lad. And now that he has joined up, he thinks he can come to my home and demand further payment from our house."

"What was the tax this time?" inquired Ishcaur.

"Who knows? He had no time to make one up before I ran him off our land." A chorus of hearty laughs met these words. "I tell you, the Guard is a parasite. They are no better than the legions were when they governed our lands, perhaps even worse."

"Let us not go that far," said Ishcaur cautiously. "I despise the Guard as much as any, but you were young when the legions patrolled our lands. You do not remember those dark days as well as those of us who suffered most under the mariners' vile rule. At least under the Guard, it is our people in uniform that we subject ourselves to."

"And what good is that?" asked Cercur. "Are we content to bend the knee to tyrants merely because they come from our homes and villages?"

"You sound like that fanatic we heard in Gales," said Tabor.

"Is any of what he said untrue? It seems the magistrates have only trained the sheep to fight on behalf of the wolves."

"And who do you regard as the wolves, Cercur?"

"Who else? What good has come to the Eastlands under empire rule? By all accounts, the High Court and the Provincial Guard are no better than Emperor Darius and his legions."

"No darker days were ever known than those of the last sovereign," mumbled Dromo. The weathered sailor's rare remarks always seemed to carry with them an ominous tone. When the dayers were recovered from the chilling commentary, Ishcaur cautiously addressed his young crewmate.

"Be careful where you utter such sentiments, Cercur. If any of the Guard were to hear you speaking like this, you would be—"

"Fined and sent on my merry way, so I might continue to pay for the Guard's feasts and fine wines," finished a jaded Cercur. "It does not change that it would have been better all-around had the empire released the Eastlands from Haurthian rule all those years ago."

"I will not deny the truth in it," interjected Tabor. "But you know as well as I that the premier and the governors will never break the union for the sake of the common man."

"When man craves liberty, the ruler tightens his grasp," grumbled Dromo.

"Quite right," agreed an uncomfortable Tabor, "and garnering loyalty by force has been the downfall of every unjust ruler through the annals of history. That was the downfall of Darius the Damned."

"Indeed, I can still recall the screams as the mariners scourged the ports on Darius' orders," lamented Ishcaur. "Many I knew were imprisoned for speaking against the empire and its mad sovereign. Others were not so lucky as to earn a cell."

"There was never a rejoicing so thunderous as that which rang at the news of the emperor's death," remarked Tabor.

"Served him right," proclaimed Ishcaur, "he and all those traitors who abetted his efforts to enslave the Eastlands."

"Were they killed as well?" asked Cercur.

"I wish. Those found guilty were banished from the Realm of Haurth. A general and admiral, I heard, and the royal children of the slain emperor."

"What of the empress consort?"

"She died some years before Emperor Darius met his doom. Rebecca was her name. Or was it Rachel? I do not recall."

"I heard," muttered Tabor, "that the prince and princess passed through Gales shortly after their banishment, whatever their names were. Of course, the traitors were promptly run out of the port. Probably crawled into a hole and starved themselves for their shame."

Trying desperately to remember what he was searching for, Ira stood frozen in the dark recess of the bow. Vivid memories long repressed flooded his mind, drowning all around him. A boy and girl in adolescence mockingly hailed by the galleymaster to the seaside street. The boy asking in the local tavern for a room. A high wail piercing the air. His sister lying on the floor with a deep gash across her cheek. A man with a square jaw standing over her with a whip. The boy grabbing a cheese knife from a table, bearing it at the man. The bleeding of their feet as they trudged down the trail to the village of Squall.

Ira's stillness in the feeble lantern light managed to draw the attention of Ishcaur.

"Looking for something, Ira?" he called to him.

All speech was lost to him. He clambered carelessly through the thicket of supplies back to the hatch and up on deck, his waterskin dry in his shaking hand.

CHAPTER V

THE HORDE

When the cusp of dawn finally dismissed the nighters from their posts, Ira elected not to join the others for breakfast. He descended through the hatch and marched straight to his hammock, yearning for the sweet release of a dreamless sleep. He swayed endlessly between heaps of provisions and goods, his eyes shut tight and his mind racing. The steady creaks of the *Wayfarer*'s hull and the crashing of the bow against the sea were not loud enough to drown out bitter memories. The sailors' callous remarks poisoned Ira's thoughts as his weary body longed for undisturbed rest. There he lay in silent agony, trying with all his might to remember how to fall asleep.

Before he was aware he was in a slumber, the deafening ringing of a bell on deck violently awoke Ira to his senses. Instinct threw him out of his hammock, and he landed with a painful grunt on a sack of grain. Ignoring the ache in his side, he and the other nighters scuttled drearily to the hatch. They scrambled up the ladder and winced as they met the shrewd light of day. As their eyes came into focus, they saw Ishcaur cease the incessant ringing of the bell hung from the mast as he beckoned the nighters to follow him. They darted behind him to the stern of the ship, where they met the rest of the crew staring over the ledge to the east. Esther and Nathanael took no notice as Ira joined them. He peered over the heads of the stout dwarves and felt a lurch in his stomach as he spotted the cause of all the commotion.

Less than half a league away was the faint outline of a sickly ship tailing the *Wayfarer*. A rusting ram of bronze was fixed to the bow of the warship, and embroidered upon a charred black lateen sail was a blurry yet horrendous golden serpent coiled upon itself. The emblem of the Pirate Horde struck crude fear into the sailors' hearts as they stared dumb and hopeless.

"What do we do, master?" Cercur called nervously from the helm.

All eyes turned upon Halruc, his own gaze fixed on the foreboding vessel. He scowled at the looming threat until he could muster the strength to tear his eyes from the sight. He stormed from the ledge, followed closely by the crowd of anxious onlookers. They followed him as he wandered about the deck in a fretful daze. No man drew breath as the master paced in stifled thought.

"Manoque," he called at last, "how far to Rover Bay?"

At once, the navigator dived into his pocketbook to consult his notes and maps. The crew closed in around him, hoping for a glance at the pages. The elf muttered frantically under his breath as he deciphered their current whereabouts and the distance to the nearest isle.

"The Bay is nearly two days north by northeast of our position," said Manoque.

Under the baking sun, a chill raised the hairs of every man on the deck.

"Could we escape under the cover of night?" suggested Puck.

"No," said Halruc with a glance towards the morning sun, "the galley will be upon us well before dusk."

"So what can we do?" implored Ishcaur.

Halruc did not answer. In the dead silence, Ira raised his voice. "What weapons have we?" he asked.

The tense stares veered from the master to the man who had been a stranger less than a week prior. From the sea of incredulous looks, a single berating laugh sounded beneath Ram's scruffy midnight beard.

"If you wish to shed your own blood, boy, that is no concern of mine," the dwarf growled derisively. "But the rest of us are not so eager to die at the hands of marauders known for staining the sea crimson."

"In case it had escaped your notice," retorted Ira, "that ship is gaining, and escape is beyond us. So, if you only care to save your own neck, I suggest you gather your strength and all the weapons we possess."

"I do not take orders from the likes of you, felon."

"You would be wise to."

"Silence!" roared Halruc. The master marched forward and gripped both sailors by the collars of their scarlet tunics. Ira was pulled down to the eye level of the two dwarves as Halruc glowered at them in turn, speaking in a hiss only they could hear.

"Do not forget your place aboard this ship, either of you! I am the master of the *Wayfarer*, and any orders to be heeded will come from my lips alone. If you wish to speak plainly, you will reserve yourselves before the rest of the crew and come to me in privacy. Neither of you is ever to speak out of turn again. Do I make myself clear?"

The crew watched uncertainly as the intense affair unfolded. The master's narrow eyes did not waver in their conviction until, at last, Ira and Ram nodded their assent.

"Right then," said the master for all to hear, "the situation is grave, and we have no room for error. If the Horde manages to give us a broadside, they shall board us by the dozens, and we will all be done for. So, distance shall be our ally."

"And what shall we do should they catch up with us?" asked Nathanael apprehensively.

The master looked up at the scarlet sail, which was brimming with the salty breath of the sea.

"When the warship is within range, we shall set its sail ablaze. They will have oars to carry them on, but their speed will be hindered, perhaps enough to afford us the advantage. Lad, grab a bucket and collect the oil from the lanterns—every drop. The rest of you, fetch the weapons from the rear of the hold. Bring up the pit, too, and start a fire. Now off with you!"

The sailors stood momentarily idle. Then, with a call of "Aye, master," a sudden frenzy broke out as the whole crew dived through the hatch one after another. There was a noisy racket in the hold as they shuffled barrels and crates around in desperate search. At last, Ossel uncovered a stack of shields, a pack of bows and quivers, and a second pack containing a dozen rusting swords. Ira found his own pack beneath his hammock and pulled from it Érnog's dagger before ascending with the others. On deck, the array of aged armaments was laid out to be distributed. Gladiuses lodged in their scabbards were tugged and yanked while a few bowstrings snapped as the burly dwarves drew them. Round shields of oak were warped and cracked in places. Ishcaur and the mute hoisted the iron pit used for cooking through the hatch and set it on deck. The lad poured some of the oil he had scavenged into the pit as Manoque struck a piece of flint. The sparks set the oil-soaked wood scraps alight as Cercur stood trapped at the helm, helplessly watching the preparations unfold.

As the sailors began wrapping arrow tips in strips of cloth, Ira turned to his sister and placed Érnog's dagger in her hand.

"Stay below deck," he ordered her. "Do not come out for any reason."

Esther opened her mouth to protest, but her brother's adamant glare stole her words. Begrudgingly, she clambered down the ladder and, with one last look at him, closed the hatch behind her. Over the stern's ledge, Ira could see the outline of the pirate galley growing ever clearer. A throng of oars on either side of the vessel could be made out, pummeling the spangling waters below. Their swift strokes thrust in accord as the warship gained on them. Even from a distance, the galley's hull looked nasty, like moss on the gray stone giants of the Eastlands. The planks appeared worn from ages of neglect, as did the unpolished ram plowing through the sapphire waves. Something else was fixed on the warship's deck near the bow, a wooden construct visibly younger than the rest of the aged ship.

"Catapult!" Cercur called over the commotion on deck.

Every head turned towards the hailing ship. Cercur was right. A newly built catapult large enough to hurl small boulders made for another weapon in the Horde's deadly arsenal. Ira approached Halruc and spoke to him in an undertone.

"That catapult will have a greater range than any of our archers."

Halruc made no reply. He was engrossed by the sight of his crew's preparations and the fear growing in their eyes with every stroke of the pirates' oars. Dromo stared cynically at the scabs of rust tainting his blade. Ishcaur's wavering draw of the bow made for a poor show of confidence in his aim. And Ram, with a look of disgust at his tattered shield, cast it aside to inspect another.

"Have you sailed aboard many galleys, prince?" Halruc asked quietly. Ira did not immediately answer, as the old form of address took him momentarily aback.

"I served as an officer aboard the admiral's galley for some years," Ira replied.

"And can your experience offer these men any reasonable hope?"

Ira aggressively pondered those naval strategies he had engrossed himself in throughout his youth. As he did, he watched the lad take up a sword lying next to the idle anchor, his breathing short and shallow. Then, in his moment of need, a tactic of a galleymaster he had once studied under dawned at the forefront of Ira's mind.

"There is one maneuver I know of. It may be our salvation, but if executed improperly, it will surely spell our demise."

The master eyed the prince skeptically, then looked to the gaining warship before muttering, "Tell me."

The crew assembled on deck in ranks like a curious militia. Puck, Dromo, Ossel, Ram, Ishcaur, and the mute stood in a line facing the *Wayfarer*'s starboard ledge. Bows were held at the ready, as the dwarves' burly arms made them ideal archers. A blazing pit was set before them, and their swords remained sheathed at their sides. Behind them, along the deck's port side, stood Ira, Nathanael, Tabor, Manoque, and the lad with gladiuses and shields at the ready. Halruc and Cercur remained at the quarterdeck, overlooking the armed assembly, with nothing to do but wait.

The Horde vessel was only a few ships' lengths astern, coming up along them on the starboard side. Once it had garnered a sufficient lead on them, the pirate galley would veer to port and pierce the merchant ship's hull with its rotting ram. In its nearness, every ominous feature of the warship was sharpened, from the sharp fang of the golden sea serpent to the figures clad in black bearing their grimy swords. Faint echoes of jeers and howls scraped across the waves and through the wind. Only by the strict edict of their master's orders did the sailors of the *Wayfarer* stand firm as the warship came level with them.

As deep blue waters adopted a lighter hue, a burst of fire erupted from the galley's bow as a flaming boulder hurtled into the searing sky. It rose gracefully, growing ever larger as it arched, hailing towards the *Wayfarer*. The crew recoiled in fright, but the master did not waver. His gaze followed the boulder's path through the sky and into the sea, where it bore a monumental splash on the starboard side. The sailors shared a collective sigh until their impending threat recalled them to their senses. Ira looked to the lad who was nearest the bow. The young sailor had sheathed his sword and held the tethered stone anchor in his arms. Halruc raised the hairy hand bearing his sword, his eyes unflinchingly set on the rudders of the Horde ship. The galley now had a short lead over the *Wayfarer*. Expectancy became the sailors as they, and most especially Cercur, awaited their master's imminent command. The white noise of their surroundings faded into nothingness until the galley's rudders spun, and Halruc hurled his arm down with a blaring warcry.

Cercur thrust the rudder oars with all his might as the lad heaved the anchor over the starboard ledge. Merchant ship and galley swerved inward, each angling its bow towards the other. It was plain to the eye that the agile warship's veers were far sharper than the merchant vessel's. As dwarven archers lit their oil-soaked arrowheads in the fiery pit, a pang of dread swept over the deck. The sailors fought every instinct to tear their eyes away from the ram posed to strike their hull. Then, with a sudden tug at the bow, the *Wayfarer*'s laggard pivot became a mighty career. Manoque nearly toppled over as the anchored ship was yanked hard to starboard. The planks creaked and cried under the vicious strain.

The two ships were nearly upon one another, but the *Wayfarer*'s arc was tighter than the Horde's. At the last second, it hurled parallel to the galley, now on its port side, narrowly avoiding the strike of its rusting ram.

It happened in a matter of seconds. There was an almighty gnashing of planks as the two hulls scraped against one another. Several unexpectant pirates lost their balance as the primed crew of the *Wayfarer* planted their sandals firmly on deck. Wasting not a moment, the dwarves let loose their flaming arrows into the heart of the midnight sail. Six punctures gleamed upon the serpent emblem as the merchant ship sped opposite the warship, snapping a mass of pirate oars as it went. At Halruc's command, the lad cut the rope and released the anchor as the dwarven archers abandoned their bows to draw their swords and shields. While the two ships were momentarily alongside one another, eight feral raiders managed to leap over the *Wayfarer*'s ledge and onto the deck. The Horde pirates varied in stature and size but bore the same dark, mangled hair, grizzly features, yellow teeth, and arid olive skin. A haunting odor of blood stained the crisp sea breeze as they unleashed their sullied blades. With another warcry, Halruc summoned the primal courage in his sailors as they hurled at the barbarians. As Ira bounded at the raiders, his sword pelted into action, the warrior within having awoken from a deep slumber.

A torrent of clattering steel resounded across the deck. Though they carried no shields, the brutish pirates proved formidable with their ferocious blows. The dwarves paired up against the brigands nearest to them, the height of their foes making it a rigorous effort to strike offensively. Puck and the mute swiped at one mangled pirate's bony legs to no avail. They were too preoccupied defending themselves as the raider's blade hammered their splintering shields. The lad was tossed aside by Tabor, saved from a monstrous pirate who had swung his gladius to sever the young sailor's head. Tabor's height and brawn were nothing to that of the giant. Yet without hesitation, he bombarded the fiend with a boorish volley from his sword, followed by a thunderous smack of the shield across the pirate's face. The brute hardly rendered the attacks. Manoque and Nathanael had partnered against a toothless brigand with a filthy mat of hair. The two gladiuses belted down upon the one while they used their shields to corner the Horde goon. Once they had pinned their foe against the ship's ledge, they clouted him again, sending the brigand into the sea with a howl and a tremendous splash.

As the lad scurried up to the quarterdeck to guard Cercur, he passed Ira in the midst of a fray with a raider that hauntingly resembled a skeleton. Despite his haggard appearance, the skeletal pirate's bludgeons were powerful, as he struck repeatedly and without wear. Ira stood his ground, shuffling his feet as the pirate's strokes grew rabid and unpolished. As the skeleton aimed a barbarous pelt at his head, Ira swept his sandals across the dampened deck and slid beneath the thrashing arm. He brought himself upright, facing the pirate's backside, and wasted no time in delivering a fatal blow into the ribs of the gaunt foe.

Retracting the crimson gladius, Ira glanced towards Halruc and Ossel, who were brawling with a marauder who wore a maniacal grin. Ossel took a harsh swipe to his sword-bearing arm. The blade dropped to the deck, but before the pirate could fell the injured dwarf, Ira's weapon came to Ossel's aid. His sudden appearance created diversion enough for Halruc to thrust the tip of his blade up and into the raider's gut. The black tunic ran red, and even as he fell limp, death did not steal the disdainful grin from the pirate's lips.

"Up with you, Ossel!" said Halruc, pulling the dwarf back to his feet. "To the quarterdeck! Go!"

Ira returned the fallen sword to Ossel's good arm as a whiz cut through the sound of blaring steel. A splinter silenced the noise as a burning arrow pierced the plank beside Ira's foot. He and Halruc turned on the spot and saw, to their dismay, the Horde galley tailing them once again. Patches of sky could be seen through the burnt holes in the lateen sail. Yet neither they nor the destruction of half the galley's oars had managed to impede the warship's speed. Horde archers stood upon the bow, sending fiery projectiles into the air. To his horror, Ira saw one of the arrows strike the *Wayfarer*'s scarlet sail, leaving a glowing gash in its wake.

"Take out those archers!" Halruc hollered to Ira over the chaos.

Ira nodded and peered between the shuffling feet of allies and foes for a stray bow and quiver. In his search, he caught a glimpse of Tabor wincing in pain as he held himself up against the starboard ledge. A smoldering arrowhead protruded from his blood-soaked leg, and the giant raider held a grimy gladius over him, ready to strike. A young sailor's yawp cried out as the sword plummeted. The blade found its target, and Ira was as surprised as Tabor to see the giant's weapon miss him entirely and sever the sheet that tethered the sail's clew to the ship's ledge.

The scarlet sail's loosened corner whipped uncontrollably in the gales. As the clew jerked in every direction, the *Wayfarer*'s speed began to falter. Ira aimed a blow at the giant, but the colossal raider thwarted his assault as he grasped him by the wrist. With his leg pierced and pouring blood, Tabor heaved his weapon with all his might at the giant. The raider dodged the feeble attack and gave Tabor a swift kick to the head, knocking the sailor unconscious. With a vile grin, the raider dropped his sword and used that gnarly hand to choke Ira and raise him by the throat. His sword-bearing hand still restrained, Ira mustered every bit of energy he possessed to punch, batter, scratch—anything to return the air to his lungs. His head was growing dizzy as his fingertips started to tingle.

Without warning, the giant winced in pain and fell to his knees. His grip slackened, and Ira dropped to the deck, gasping for breath. He could see a pool of crimson oozing from the pirate's ankle. Esther was crouched behind the giant, her arms outstretched and Érnog's dagger held aloft. Her eyes were filled with fright as the giant took up his forsaken sword and limped towards her, leaving a thick trail of blood behind him.

"No!" croaked Ira. Only then did he realize he had lost his sword. He searched desperately around him for his weapon—any weapon.

Before the brigand could reach Esther, a lean figure leapt from the quarterdeck and landed between the two. The lad thrust the tip of his sword at the giant, who caught the blade in one of his gnarled hands. The giant's fingers and palm dripped with blood as he threw the lad's weapon aside and swiped his own sword at the young sailor. The blade grazed a lock of the lad's hair as he and Esther recoiled. It was then that Nathanael burst into the fray to pelt the brute with a barrage of futile blows.

"Where are my archers?" cried Halruc as he peered towards the galley, now less than a ship's length from the *Wayfarer*.

Ira regained his breath but could find neither bow nor sword to claim. He did catch sight of Ram and Ishcaur grabbing hold of the flapping starboard sheet as yet another pirate took a swing at the pair. Ram abandoned the sheet and made to duel the brigand on his own. Ishcaur, with the help of a dazed Tabor, labored to retether the sheet and regain the *Wayfarer*'s speed. But the sheet was the least of the ship's worries as the giant set his aims upon severing the halyard. If the line bracing yard and sail was broken, there would be no escape from the pursuing warship.

Before the giant could deliver the *Wayfarer*'s fatal blow, Nathanael knocked the giant's sword away with a vicious swipe of his own. The gladius tip turned then to be driven into the pirate's chest, but not before the giant had tossed Nathanael to the deck and stomped ferociously on his weapon. The rusted blade split in two. With hardly more than a hilt, Nathanael knelt defenseless as the brigand's bloodied hands clasped him around the neck, thrusting him onto his back. Finally, in his desperate search for a weapon, Ira spotted in the pool of the giant's blood Érnog's dagger. With not a second to lose, he lunged for the knife, closed his fingers around it, and hurled it across the deck. The point of the blade lodged deep in the giant's upper arm. Unphased by the blow, the brute, still choking Nathanael, gazed at the blade with crude amusement. A shaking Nathanael caught sight of the embedded knife as well. Seizing his chance, he yanked the dagger free and thrust it up and into the giant's heart. The monstrous pirate's breath faltered as he drew his last and toppled limp onto the deck.

Ira lumbered towards his panting friend and hoisted him to his feet. As Ram finished off the last of the boarded pirates, more flaming arrows struck the scarlet sail, now riddled with searing holes. Esther, the lad, and the mute had taken up shields against the projectiles to protect Cercur, who was incapable of defending himself as he manned the helm through the chaos. The remainder of the crew was posted along the ship's stern, loosing arrows at the galley from behind mutilated shields. It was of no consequence to the pirate archers perched on their warship's bow. Their fiery barrages at the scarlet sail were crippling the merchant ship's speed. The sickly bronze ram was near enough to graze the *Wayfarer*'s hull as dozens of marauders brandished their filthy swords.

"Prepare to be boarded!" Halruc bellowed to his crew.

One look at his companions was enough to tell Ira they understood the imminence of their fate. But as a dark look of acceptance came over every other sailor, the lad's somber gaze was replaced by one of inspiration. His withering shield dropped with a clatter as the young sailor belted from Cercur's side towards the *Wayfarer*'s bow. Ira's eyes turned from the warship to the lad who grabbed a bucket and darted back to the quarterdeck. The attention of every other sailor was collected as, with a mighty lob, the bucket was cast high over the ship's stern. The glistening contents arched and cascaded gracefully on high before they drenched the deck of the Horde warship. A burning arrowhead drawn by one of the pirate archers was caught in the oily wave, and the galley's bow was instantly engulfed in a blinding inferno. Devilish orange flames rose into midnight smoke. Howls of agony crossed the waters even as the distance between ships grew. The blaze swallowed the black sail and golden serpent whole as the halyard snapped, plunging the yard through the charring deck and emitting a mighty waft of embers.

There was no great rejoicing aboard the *Wayfarer* as the wreckage diminished into a far-off light and a tall billow of smoke. In the absence of a foe to combat or an urgent duty demanding their attention, the winded sailors glanced at one another with a lost look about them. As his heavy breathing gradually eased, Halruc faced his servants, whose hair and tunics were bathed in sweat and splattered with blood. And with his former address of a master rather than a warrior, the dwarf issued a brief set of orders.

"Set the spare anchor. Mend the damage. Check for leaks. Tend to the wounded."

And without waiting for a chorus of affirmation, the master shuffled between the fatigued sailors into the privacy of his cabin.

The remainder of the day passed in uncomfortable tranquility. When the master reemerged on deck, washed and garbed in a fresh mantle, he did not call out any further orders to his crew. Nor did he drive the sailors to labor at their usual quick pace. There were plenty of minor cuts to go around after the vicious quarrel, but luckily, the arrow to Tabor's thigh was counted as the worst injury sustained. The puncture was washed with mead before Esther dressed it with a thick layer of cloth stripped from what remained of the tattered sail. In its place, Ira, Nathanael, Manoque, and Puck laced a virgin scarlet sheet upon the yard soon to carry them on. Below deck, the other dwarves had nailed fresh wooden planks over cracks along the hull's port side where the two ships had scraped against one another. Boiling tar was brushed to seal the planks, leaving a rank odor that flooded the hold. The dwarves gasped for fresh air every time they popped through the hatch with buckets of the little water the ship had taken. Those bodies of the felled pirates were carelessly heaved overboard for some maritime predator to claim while the deck was scrubbed clean of scattered crimson stains.

Violet skies reflected in the still waters as the restored *Wayfarer* prepared to set off into the night. To the crew's surprise, however, the master informed them that they would remain anchored through the night and set off again at daybreak. As the hold still reeked of hot tar, the company elected to have their supper together on deck. With the sickly remnants of the day removed, the spirits about the *Wayfarer* lightened at last, and a grand celebration ensued. Festivities of the night proved to be the perfect remedy for their collective toils, and Halruc, in a giving mood, treated the sailors with his vat of wine from the Western vineyards of Maer. The succulent nectar poured new life into the mouths of the weary as they raised their tankards in rapturous spirits.

Music and cheer rang for leagues beyond. Under the radiant moonlight and flickering lanterns, sailors took it in their turn to regale the crowd with various accounts of the conquering day. Duels were flamboyantly recounted in the company of Puck's fiddle and its whimsical bows. Even old Dromo's usual stoicism was replaced by a glad, if not joyful, demeanor for the evening. There was laughter, whooping, and applause, and each performance ended with a toast to some or to all. Everyone, even Esther, was hailed in the toasts, but none so much as the lad whose cunning had saved the day. When every last detail of the Horde's demise had been hearkened to no less than twice, a ring of dance broke out. Though he refrained due to his injured leg, Tabor watched in amusement with Ira, Esther, and Nathanael as the merry jig ensued. They laughed as the lad stepped into the gaiety with cheeks rosy from the wine. Dromo observed with a short crease of a grin beneath his aged beard, and though he was repeatedly invited to join the circle of dance, Halruc's uncommon generosity found its end as he refused his sailors the privilege of such a spectacle. Voices rang as bodies spun to the lively tune birthed from Puck's fiddle.

Wey, hey went the wayward bard
One bright and sunny morn

He was fiddling here and fiddling there
Across the plains of corn

Then the people of the plains did say
"Be off, bard, on your way."
So, dancing with a fiddle in hand
He traipsed about all day

Wey, hey went the wayward bard
One breezy afternoon
He was fiddling here and fiddling there
Across the Cliffs of Huen

Then the people of the cliffs did say
"Be off, bard, on your way."
So, dancing with a fiddle in hand
He traipsed about all day

While his merry companions skipped and sang with gusto to every creature of the deep, the mute broke from the ranks of the dance to offer a stubby hand to none other than Esther. A bewildered look came over her as the lady found herself entering the jigging circle hand in hand with the dwarf to many cheers and acclaims. Before long, the mute was relieved by Manoque, then Ishcaur, Cercur, Ossel, and Ram. Esther beamed as she passed from partner to partner, her raven locks whirling and gleaming in the luminous night.

Wey, hey went the wayward bard,
One dark and chilly eve
He was fiddling here and fiddling there

Across the Bridging Sea

Then the creatures of the sea did say
"Be off, bard, on your way."
But the bard did stay, and with the fossegrim play
Into the sunny morn

Wey, hey went the wayward bard
As he drowned so far from shore
He was fiddling loud for the watery crowd
As the kraken ate him whole

As the lad took Esther's hand in the dance, even rosier in the cheeks than before, Halruc offered Ira a full tankard of wine before taking a seat beside him.

"They have not a clue who they owe their lives to," the master muttered to him. Ira knew not how to respond as he watched the festivities unfold before him. "You are risking far more than encounters with the Horde by taking this journey," continued Halruc. "So, why would the children of Emperor Darius dare to venture back to a land that cast them out?"

As Esther twirled about with her young partner, Ira considered how much he cared to divulge to the master. On another night, he might have leaned towards reservation on so personal a matter. But something about the near sharing of a watery doom inclined Ira to answer Halruc with some degree of truth.

"My sister's mark, branded in cruelty and vitriol, has barred her from starting a new life ever since we set foot in the Eastlands. Had I . . . It is my fault she bears the outward shame that ought to have been mine. There is but one place in the known lands where she might know peace in her lifetime. It is a garden that resides in the Westlands. The mariners are forbidden to enter the sacred grounds. There, Esther will be free to leave the past behind as we live out our lives in quiet solace. There is nothing I would not do for her. There is no risk I would not take."

As the music carried on over the calls of soaring ospreys and the gentle brushing of waves, Ira labored with all his might to memorize Esther's beaming face as she jigged without tire, her patterned veil forgotten upon her shoulders.

CHAPTER VI

THE MIDNIGHT GATHERING

Twinkling stars swam circles around the moon and over Eou Verás. While lanterns were doused throughout the city streets, those flames blazing within the Temple of Érosai were fed with oil and kindling by the priests. The pits flared at the feet of the pale statues, bathing the courtyard in a soft, fiery hue. The gentle glow and the priests' low hymns passed between the pillars, barely reaching the two villas situated beside the temple. From the smaller dwelling, there emerged a figure in a plain tunic. His faint shadow gave him away in the dark surroundings as it followed him along the path to the larger villa. As the figure approached with a batch of woolen blankets in his arms, the sentry posted at the door stepped aside to permit him entry.

His bare feet made no sound as he stepped lightly through the stone corridor. Passing the stairs descending to the kitchen and the sitting room, where the embers burned feebly in the fireplace, the figure came upon the room that he sought. The door crept open with the tiniest of creaks, and he slipped silently into the bedchamber. Majestic furniture filled the space. Ornate ceramics and hung tapestries depicting legends of old basked under the moonglow. Atop one of the bedside tables was a porcelain water pitcher and a royal gladius with a dark gem rooted in the hilt. The thick blankets were laid on the floor. A thin hand reached for the idle sword until a soft grunt from under the sheets caused the looming figure to reconsider. He retracted his arm and instead pulled from the folded blankets a glistening kitchen knife. The young heart raced as the blade was raised over one of the two slumbering figures, the one with the long mane of mahogany hair. His hands twitched as a slow, deep breath was drawn, followed by a short gasp of horror. The wide eyes gleamed as the elf awoke with a start to face the assassin.

The knife plummeted as Lysias heaved his body towards the bedside table. The steely point bore into the elf's right shoulder and was instantly withdrawn, with a streak of crimson upon it. Lysias' desperate fingers made to clasp for his gladius, but they found instead the handle of the decorative pitcher. Provoked by desperation and searing pain, the premier heaved the pitcher with his good arm and smashed it upon the intruder's head before the kitchen knife could strike again. Water and porcelain shards sprayed the room as the shrouded figure keeled over, and his meager blade clattered to the floor. Lysias sprang to his feet, seizing the jewel-encrusted gladius as the assassin looked up in fury and fright. Blood coursing down his forehead, the man crawled backwards away from the point of the sword until he was pinned against one of the hanging tapestries. The night sky shone into the bedchamber, illuminating the young and familiar face of the temple servant.

Lysias stood alert and armed in his night garb, when a horrid thought swept over him. His eyes darted to the other side of the bed and then to a corner of the room, where his lady stood rigid and pale. Filia's golden hair waved gently in the breeze as her pale eyes shifted between the servant, her husband, and his shoulder. Lysias glanced down at the stream of blood pouring down to his fingertips but had not a mind to care. His primal concerns were reserved for the young assassin under his blade. Filia strained her voice to shout for the sentries, who shortly came bustling into the bedchamber. Wasting no time with pointless questions, the elven soldiers seized the servant gruffly by the arms as the master of the Temple Guard rushed to the premier's side.

"Take him away!" barked the master sentry. The order was obliged, as the grimacing young man was hauled out of the room without so much as a struggle. "I will fetch one of the servants to tend to your wound, premier."

"No!" bellowed Lysias. "The servants are not to leave their quarters under any circumstances!"

At once, the master sentry gave an apologetic bow and fell silent as Filia peeled herself from the corner to collect a water basin from one of the tables. She brought it to the bedside and beckoned her husband to sit beside her. Lysias noticed that the arm bearing his gladius was still aloft despite the threat's removal. With an effort, he lowered the blade to his side and seated himself as the lady stripped and wadded cloth from their sheets to wash his shoulder. Even as the oozing of blood ceased and the wound was firmly bandaged, Lysias did not slacken his grip upon the sword still in hand. The master sentry stood idle and did not utter another word until Filia had finished her mending.

"The sentries will escort the prisoner to the cavern tonight," the elf assured his premier, "and I shall personally stand watch outside your chambers until morning."

"Belay that order, gairose," replied Lysias grimly. "Send one of your men to collect the governors. Deliver them to the temple at once. I shall meet them there, as will the prisoner."

After a brief look of apprehension, the master sentry gave an obedient bow and called the order to one of the armored elves in the corridor. Not bothering to don his scabbard, the premier remained attached to his sword as he and the lady were led out of the villa and onto the moistened grounds. The pack of sentries paraded the couple up the winding path into the garden set between the Temple of Érosai and the base of the crescent range that stretched to the sea. In the heart of the garden was a baldachin composed of four marble pillars supporting a ringlike canopy. The glistening shrine was dressed in barren wisteria vines winding about. Shrubs and buds not yet in bloom held as little color in the sanctuary as the peaks rising from the yard's edge in patches of green and gray. The escort strode through the neatly trimmed grass and past those round stones, which sealed the entries to the mountainside tombs.

A parade of sandals clapped across the marble courtyard. Temple priests with thuribles of incense gazed in shock and concern at the sight of the premier's blood-spattered tunic. A number of chairs were fetched by the sentries. As Lysias and Filia awaited the arrival of the governors, they sat with the eyes of guards and statues beaming down upon them. Firelight danced upon the towering figures of emperors and empresses past, their pale throne cold and empty. Filia lifted her gaze to the heavens high above the roofless temple while Lysias studied the faces of the ancient sovereigns. In the elf's quiet meditation, the last of the stony busts between the pillars called out to him. Despite the blazing pit beneath him, the emperor's features were shrouded in shadow and darkness.

"Do you know his name?" Lysias asked the lady softly.

"Jesse," replied Filia calmly, her eyes still fixed upon constellations on high. "He came here from the provinces last spring."

Scurrying footsteps rattled across the ornate floor as the six governors hastened through the archway to the premier's side.

They, too, were dressed in sleeping tunics under their traveling cloaks. Lysias did not stand to greet them but acknowledged them with a short inclination of his head.

"By the Light!" exclaimed Doracaen at the sight of the premier's bandaged shoulder and crimson-stained garb. At once, the governors sprang into a barrage of anxious queries.

"Say it is not so. One of the servants? It is unheard of!"

"Do we know his motivations?"

"Where is the assassin now?"

"Did he act alone?"

"Rumor will reach the city by the morning; what shall we tell them, premier?"

The relentless torrent made Lysias' head throb violently. Lifting his right hand to touch his temple, the forgotten wound on his shoulder caused him to wince at the gesture. Pain and fury mucked together as the gladius in his other hand slipped from his sweaty palm and fell with a clang. The echo wavered throughout the courtyard as the silenced governors stared in alarmed embarrassment at their behavior. Taking their seats in the circle, the four men and the two dwarves made no further utterance while they awaited the premier's invitation to speak. Once the elf had recovered from his lapse, he addressed the troubled members of the High Court.

"Allow me first to say that I am grateful to each of you for answering my summons. I know you all have questions concerning what has unfolded this night, and the same can be said for myself and my lady. The prisoner will be brought forward soon, and you have my leave to interrogate him to your heart's content. However, I am resolved to answer but one question here and now, the question that will inevitably bear answers to all others. Why?"

"Indeed," concurred Anthazar, "what does a servant stand to gain from the murder of the premier and Lady Filia?"

"I do not believe Jesse's intentions ever involved bringing harm upon me," said Filia.

"An assault in the royal bedchamber is an assault on my love and my life," Lysias said firmly to her.

"Well, let us waste no more time in the absence of he who stands to enlighten us," said Valcor.

"My thoughts exactly," replied Lysias. "Gairose! Bring forth the prisoner."

The master sentry bowed and scuttled to the temple's rear, through the garden, and out of sight. Governors and sentries alike waited soundlessly in chilling anticipation. Moleu sat with one of his thick legs shaking of its own volition. Périlles wrung his hands together as he stared vacantly into the distance. The agonizing quietude was broken by the rippling of iron upon stone. The governors leapt to their feet as the young man was dragged in chains across the courtyard. The servant Jesse did not attempt to stride on his own, more out of spite it appeared than due to his ankles being bound so close together. The sentries surrounding the High Court spun to face outward, their sheathed swords at the ready as the defenseless captive was hauled nearer. Jesse was forced to kneel as he was placed before the leaders of the empire. He might have been praying were it not for the scowl, which lacked any trace of penitence.

Lysias reached for the floor and closed his fingers around the hilt of the fallen sword. Suspenseful breaths formed gentle mists from the governors' lips as the premier glowered upon the young assassin. Jesse fought against his trepidations as he glared at the elf standing over him. The premier did not so much as blink before the young servant, his gladius held in ominous dormancy. The longer he clung to inaction, the more Lysias reveled in that fear he struck into Jesse's ever-rushing heart.

"Enough of this!" shouted Anthazar with impatience. "You made an attempt on the premier's life. This court demands to know why!"

When the young man's gaze parted from the elf's, he shot a nasty look at the governor and spat upon Anthazar's feet. The sentries unleashed their swords, but the premier was swifter. The tip of the royal blade rested perfectly on Jesse's throat. Rage swelled in the servant's eyes, his lips laboring to restrain the words of loathing he yearned to bellow to all the Hallowed City below. When Jesse finally did speak, it was with a low voice and unwavering conviction.

"Why? Why did I take the necessary action to protect my people and my homeland? Even in the face of the truth, the High Court is blinded by vanity. The Eastlands have already lived under the empire's tyrannical rule once in my lifetime. I shall not stand by and watch it happen again."

"Tyrannical?" sneered a bewildered Périlles. "Need I remind you, boy, that the leaders of the court serve all lands of the Haurthian Empire? To compare this governance to that of Emperor Darius' betrayal of the Eastlands is a mockery of all we have built these last twelve years. The Legions of Haurth were removed for the establishment of the Provincial Guard. The premier resigned his rightful title of emperor so we of the new provinces could serve the interests of our people. All this was to ensure peace across the Bridging Sea. If this be tyranny in your eyes, then may I never be so blind as you."

"So says the lap dog feeding from the premier's table scraps."

"Dogs, are we?" bellowed Périlles as the dwarf, Doracaen, restrained the man so much taller than himself.

"You would return the mariners to their bloody regime in the provinces!" roared Jesse. "I heard it from your very lips. This census will be the undoing of any peace left in the empire."

"On that account," Héribon interjected calmly, "no decision has been made as to whether the mariners will head the census in the provinces. Nor will any such ordinance pass until there remains no other course to amity."

"What you would call amity, others would deem subjugation. Tell me, governors, when did you last voyage to the lands you preside over? Power and the luxuries that accompany it have kept you a thousand leagues from the struggles of your people. We are pillaged, starved, and sickened by the thorns of your failures. Magistrates and the Guard serve only to take what little we scrounge for ourselves. The tyranny of the throne was traded for that of lackey governors beckoned by their elven master."

"Curb your tongue, assassin!" snapped Périlles.

"The trust of my people has been betrayed for the last time! We demand our release from the Haurthian Empire and its corrupted rulers!"

The declaration soared through the courtyard and bounded off the pillars, resounding like a malicious choir. With the point of his gladius still upon Jesse's throat, Lysias used the flat side of the blade to raise the servant's chin and meet his gaze.

"'We?'" asked Lysias sternly. "You mean to say you know of other brigands aligned with your sentiments of mutiny?"

"It is no short list of those who have suffered under the High Court's reign," Jesse remarked callously. "We had plenty of allies in the provinces before I came to serve here, and I have since been assured that our numbers grow by the day."

Moleu muffled a gasp with a plump hand as Périlles pointed frantically at the kneeling prisoner.

"This is exactly what we have been warned against!" cried Périlles. "This is sedition of the highest order! The ruffians are spreading the weeds of treason across our lands! They may already have the numbers to lead a revolt against the empire!"

"Have you heard nothing?" snarled Jesse. "My people's only desire is liberation. War is a tool of the oppressor."

"You will reserve yourself to speak when spoken to!" hissed Périlles.

"The assault came from a temple servant, yes?" Moleu muttered to the governors. "What of the others? Could they have a part in this mutiny as well?"

"The other servants knew nothing of my plan," said Jesse quietly.

"What had you hoped to achieve from the premier's murder?" inquired Filia.

"The safeguarding of my homeland. We servants are invisible to the court as it handles the affairs of the empire. But I have served in this temple, and I have witnessed the premier poisoning the minds of the governors against those they claim to care for. Do not blame yourselves, governors; leeches live to suckle for themselves without the concern of others. No, I hold you responsible, premier. You temporarily resigned the position of emperor rather than abdicating forever your right to rule as sovereign. Others may have thought you noble for such a surrender of power, but not me. I see now that you have found a more secretive way to conquer behind your portrait of righteousness. By the governors' leave, your legions will occupy the provinces and allow you to tighten your grasp over those who would abandon this dictatorial empire. With your death, I might have freed the East from your dominion. But by my stroke of the blade or another's, this treachery will end in your death."

Calls of ospreys filled the crisp night air. The audience of Jesse's vile address was at a loss for words. Doracaen stroked his long beard in a fit of stress as Filia closed her eyes ruefully. Anthazar took a seat and covered his face with his hands. Finally lowering his sword from the prisoner's chin, Lysias gave the young man a disdainful look as he pondered the servant's mutinous vendetta.

"Tonight," the premier declared forcefully, "you will see the inside of a cell. If there be mercy in this world, you will live to be an old man in such surroundings. At this hour, I will make no such promise."

As the elf turned away, the sentries hoisted the prisoner by the arms and hauled him towards the grand archway facing the dark and the valley and sea beyond. Some of the governors muttered to themselves, while others gaped in the face of the night's bitter revelations.

"Can it be true?" asked Héribon solemnly. "Do our people oppose us as much as Jesse has led us to believe?"

"If one traveler is led astray, others are sure to follow in his wake," said Valcor ominously.

"It will do us no good to dwell on uncertainties now," said Anthazar. "We will find no more answers tonight. Let us return to our homes and gather what sleep we can. Further discussion can wait until the morning."

There was a general murmur of agreement as the governors rose from their chairs. Before they could take a step, the premier's rigid voice halted them.

"This meeting has not yet been adjourned, governors."

The temple sentries stood a little taller in their places. Filia looked at her husband concernedly as the men and dwarves traded curious glances.

"Premier," said Doracaen sympathetically, "you have been through a great ordeal tonight. Allow your body to rest and heal, and we may reconvene in the—"

But a steely glare from the elf was enough to silence the dwarf. Rejoining the circle, the governors forced their postures upright and contorted their tired faces to appear more alert. The premier did not take his seat but glided to the middle of the gathering and lifted his eyes to the guiding light of the stars and the moon.

"When the Haurthian Empire was birthed a thousand years ago, the first sovereign, Emperor Daethros, ordered this temple to be erected as a monument to the one who had shown him the way to the salvation of a wartorn realm. It was Érosai, the Light, who first foretold Daethros the humble soldier of the union which would bring forth a peace to last for all ages to come. And it was Érosai who was honored as this temple was built without roof or cover and christened in his name. The first sovereign wished for those who entered this sacred place to look up and discern all the glory of the Light. Likewise, as we seven are gathered on this most dreary of nights, we are called to recognize the vile deeds of the Dark." As he spoke, the governors lifted their eyes to the vast abyss. Filia's gaze, however, did not part from her husband. "There can be no further denial of the civil threat that faces the Haurthian Empire. This union has stood for more than a millennium, and I, for one, will not surrender its fate to the wicked will of the Dark."

"What are you saying, premier?" asked Valcor guardedly.

"I am voicing my clear and unwavering support of Governor Périlles' proposal to deploy the Legions of Haurth to preside over the census." Wide-eyed horror struck many of the governors' faces. Filia started to rise from her chair but was halted by the hand of the premier. He did not meet her gaze but allowed his eyes to pass over those seated in hesitant contemplation. "The mariners," continued Lysias, "will apprehend those with a criminal record to suggest a possible association with Jesse's seditionist movement. The census will provide Western soldiers ample opportunity to conduct a thorough search for these traitors. As the bulk of these offenders will be found in the bustling ports, which can only serve to conceal their presence and numbers, I see no reason at present to dispatch the mariners into the remote parts of the provinces. I do believe, however, that the census ought to include those islands scattered across the Bridging Sea. They are known to serve as havens for many unflattering individuals. Not to mention, the militias that govern those desolate isles are hardly to be considered trustworthy."

With pride, Périlles rose and addressed the court in a booming voice.

"I stand in full support of this measure. Rooting out separatists from law-abiding citizens will enable the provinces to flourish once again. Aye."

The governor remained standing as he glanced eagerly around at his companions.

"Drastic actions taken in the wake of dark happenings rarely stand the test of time and duty," said Anthazar cautiously.

"At your behest," retorted Périlles, "we seven delayed taking action against a known threat. And for this, one of our own was nearly slain! Your unceasing denial of this impending threat, Anthazar, will be this court's undoing!"

"I have never denied the gravity of the forces that oppose us," stated Anthazar flatly, "but it was the mere contemplation of dispatching the legions that prompted Jesse to take such drastic measures. Fanning the flames of unrest will not mend the tears of the empire. Nay, I will not give my support to such an ordinance."

Anthazar turned to the other governors for support, but none met his gaze. Moleu's leg shook rampantly still, and his thick olive cheeks flushed crimson.

"They have given us no choice in the matter," the portly governor said nervously. "If we do not act now, our restraint will be taken as weakness."

"Restraint can also serve as mercy," pleaded Anthazar.

"You may voice your tone of mercy when it is your bedchamber invaded in the night," said Lysias harshly.

At this, Anthazar fell silent like a chastened schoolboy. The court waited silently as Moleu took a deep breath to utter, "Aye."

He rose unsteadily from his seat and stood alongside Périlles and Lysias. The three looked down upon the remaining governors, searching for the last necessary vote. Héribon appeared even thinner in the firelight, his aging eyes darting between the two dwarves on either side of him. Valcor's snowy beard shook as his teeth chattered in the cool night air. Doracaen's fingers were clenched as the orange flames reflected upon his white knuckles.

"We had agreed to postpone any involvement of the legions until after the Guard had carried out the census," muttered Doracaen.

Périlles opened his mouth to speak, but Lysias approached the dwarf and gently laid the hand of his injured arm upon the governor's shoulder, his gladius still clutched at his side.

"And it would have been so," the premier said ruefully, "but we cannot afford to wait any longer. We must act now."

With a deep breath, the governor rose to his feet and nodded his approval. Périlles and Moleu sighed with relief as Lysias patted Doracaen's shoulder and turned to face the last two governors. The elf made a point to avoid Anthazar's gaze as he addressed Héribon and Valcor.

"The eyes of rulers past look upon us now," he said with a glance at the starry void overhead. "The ordinance has passed, but I should still wish to proceed in union with the court."

The man and dwarf looked at one another with unease before Héribon rose slowly to his feet.

"If this is the course we are bound to, let us follow it together. Aye, I am with you."

There was a murmur of approval from the standing company. Anthazar looked up from his feet to meet Valcor's remorseful gaze.

"May I request that the Provincial Guard assist the Legions of Haurth in carrying out the census?" the dwarf asked the court. "Their efforts will be received far better if local regimes aid the mariners."

The premier and the other governors spoke amongst themselves before nodding their assent. With great effort, the dwarf rose and joined the others, who welcomed his presence. A silent and final invitation was extended to the lone governor. Anthazar looked to the lady seated across from him and recognized the disquiet in her pale face.

"A union against one's better judgment is no union, but a falsehood," stated Anthazar vehemently. "I will ask no man here to change his vote, and so I pray you grant me the same favor."

Chilling gusts from the mountain range swept through the temple pillars and whispered the peaks' mumbling tune. The premier called for a tablet and stylus, and the master sentry sent one of his cohort for the requests. As the shadow of dawn traipsed along the watery horizon, the ordinance was taken down in the premier's own hand and sealed with six marks. Anthazar fought to muster an appropriate address for his companions. But before he could find the words he wished to express, the premier was striding with his lady and their escort back along the path leading to the royal villa.

CHAPTER VII

FABLES OF THE WEST

Through a rainless storm of gray sea and sky, the *Wayfarer* ferried amidst rabid waves thrashing from all directions. Deafening squalls howled in a sickly chorus. With each crash of the vessel's bow against ocean swells, misty waters splashed upon the deck. The nighters tilted opposite the dips and bobs of the ship, their soaked feet and squishy sandals planted around a dim light swinging from the mast. Worn, wet, and dreary, the sailors held their pale hands close to the lantern's warmth and shuddered in unison as yet another icy spray drenched them to their core. Puck's eyes were glossy and fixated upon the meager flame. Ossel pressed a hand to the sodden dressing wrapped around the healing lash on his arm. One of Ram's outstretched hands reached too close to the fire, and he recoiled as the iron case burned his fingertips. While Ira's and the dwarves' thick beards dripped chilling salt waters, the lad's bare chin had grown clammy in the elements. The olive color in his face was lost, and his teeth chattered violently under a pair of blue lips.

Numbed to their environment, none of the sailors paid mind as yet another blunt wave pounded the *Wayfarer*. That was, until the lad's feet gave way, causing him to slip and fall upon the moistened deck. The nighters howled as their companion started to slide towards the ledge and the raging torrent. Ira lunged and caught the lad by the collar of his tunic before he could gain enough momentum to be hurled overboard. With the dwarves grasping his free arm, Ira yanked the young sailor back onto his feet. The unexpected grapple with death shocked the lad into paranoid awareness as he panted and clung to the mast for support.

It had been another bitter night for the crew. The conditions remained too severe to attempt tacking the sail against oncoming winds. Wearing ship was the only alternative amidst such rabid waters. This maneuver involved the helmsman veering the ship in broad circular patterns so as to harness the wind as their ally. Each time the *Wayfarer* rounded, the other nighters would loosen the sheets and braces, allowing the formidable gusts to swing the yard to an angle best suited to carry them onward. Tedious as it was, wearing ship was far safer than tacking, which required immense force on the part of the crew to haul the yard manually against the bucking gales. If executed improperly, tacking could cause a vessel to lose all momentum and fall at the mercy of the pummeling waves. Nary a sailor had ever returned to land after a tacking had gone awry in a brutish storm.

Upon the quarterdeck stood Manoque, Halruc, and the mute. The master was keeping a keen eye on the deck as the mute manned the helm with his hairy hands frozen to the rudder oars. Manoque squinted into the perpetual cloud cover for any sign of a constellation, but it was a fruitless effort. The elf had been unable to peer through the thicket since they had entered the storm the night before last. Neither the sun nor the moon had been sighted since then, yet the navigator had not the leisure to abandon his search. A significant dilemma for the nighters and dayers wearing ship so often was in Manoque's charge of charting the *Wayfarer's* present course. Without so much as a guiding light to consult, it was nearly impossible to determine their precise heading or whereabouts.

The murky morning sky had only just cast off the nighttime's black abyss, which, to the nighters, had lingered for a chilling eternity. Contrary to his usual routine, Halruc had not left the crew's side once through the dreadful night. The lines under the dwarf's eyes had darkened beneath his pale brows as he searched the rippling horizon for any landmark in the gray desert. Another icy gust mingled with the elf's frustration brought Manoque to the point of shutting his pocketbook with a loud clap of the pages.

"I have not a clue where we are!" fumed the elf loudly enough for the sailors to hear. Meeting their desperate glances, Manoque collected himself and spoke to the master in a low tone. "Best as I can tell, our destination is that way." He pointed a shuddering finger over the starboard ledge into the dull void. As the eyes of the nighters followed its direction, a luminous bolt of lightning struck distantly at the exact point Manoque had gestured to. A choir of thunder rumbled as the mute's white knuckles tightened upon the rudder oars. "Must we make for the Isle of Jade? This storm will set us behind schedule as it is."

With a short glance at the banished prince, Halruc affirmed the importance of anchoring in Jade before continuing to Eou Verás.

"How far back will it set us if evade the heart of the storm?" the master asked through his soggy beard.

"By the time we clear this cover, it could mean days," replied Manoque.

The master contemplated, shifting his gaze between the most direct course to Jade and the weary sailors huddled around the flickering lantern. As another streak of lightning was born from the cloudy thicket, Halruc shook his head.

"We will stay our heading and correct course once the worst is behind us." At these words, the dripping nighters let out heavy sighs of relief. "The crew is drained as it is, and I have no wish to meet the kraken this day."

At these words, the lad's eyes darted at the master, a frightful expression etched upon his face. Halruc called for Ossel to summon the dayers to their posts. The dwarf let out a wavering "Aye, master!" and lumbered away from the lantern's scanty warmth to open the hatch. He called into the hold over the roaring wind and stepped aside as the rest of the crew clambered on deck to assume their duties. Each rested sailor jerked as they were greeted by the frigid gales and morning mists. The dayer dwarves' long, dry hair and beards whipped in the winds bellowing at them. Tabor took his time hoisting himself through the hatch, limping on his good leg once he had clambered on deck. The wrap on his leg showed a spot of crimson where the Horde arrow had struck him. Despite the injury, Tabor walked with a greater stride each day and did not allow the wound to hinder his duties in the slightest. Nathanael was last out of the hatch. He fought against the wind up the slippery steps to the quarterdeck. Upon his relief from the helm, the mute dwarf struggled to pry his icy fingers from the rudder oars. With great tenderness, the nighters lowered their aching bodies through the hatch, down the ladder, and into the hold.

The air in the belly of the *Wayfarer* was like a breath of fire upon the sailors' clammy skin. A hearty aroma from a simmering pot filled their dripping nostrils, awakening the beaten nighters to how very hungry they were. Before they could sit down to their breakfast, however, Esther offered each of them rags to dry themselves and fresh tunics to replace the sodden ones latched to their bodies. In the privacy between towers of cargo, the nighters undressed and dried themselves as Manoque descended the ladder and shut the hatch behind him. The noisy wails became far off, muffled by the creaking planks and the swells thumping against the hull. The sailors and the navigator sopped up as much frigid saltwater as they could with their rags. The dwarves repeatedly wrung their manes and beards, dripping endless streams from the thick tangles. Despite his best efforts, Ira could not manage to rid himself of the icy feeling that lingered beneath his own damp beard.

When they emerged in warm tunics, the sailors seated themselves upon crates around the pot that Esther was stirring. Her veil lay draped across her shoulders as it had remained in the week since the Horde ship's raid. The shadow of her scar could hardly be made out in the dim lantern light as she offered the weary crew bowls of pork stew and slices of dense bread. The nighters offered their thanks as they drank in the nourishing breakfast with immense pleasure. Their shivers and shakes eased as the warmth of the broth coursed into every ache throughout their bodies. Puck let out a sigh of delight as he smacked his lips. Holding his bowl in one hand, the mute exercised the movement of his fingers, still locked in an unnatural grip from his time at the helm. The lad drank so quickly that he began to sputter and had to stop to catch his breath. As Manoque gave the youngster a hard slap on the back, Ram and Ossel slurped their stew while they stared at the hanging lanterns swaying against the *Wayfarer*'s steady rocking.

They sat in quiet contentment until the sounds of creaks and billows were broken by the lad who had finally caught his breath.

"What did the master mean?" he asked uncertainly. At a loss for what he was speaking in reference to, the huddle offered him a curious look. "About the kraken," he continued. "The master said he did not wish to meet the beast. But he was not being serious, was he?"

Pairs of eyes wandered toward one another as if considering the best answer to give their young companion. After some time, Ram spoke with a casual air about him.

"There is no point in dwelling on it, lad," the dwarf said as he set down his bowl to wring his midnight mane once more. "The creature is an omen as old as sailing itself, but there is hardly any truth to it. Countless ships have been lost in storms more violent than this. The mysterious nature of the sea and the beasts that linger below her surface long ago inclined sailors towards a fantasy of their own making. Far-fetched rumors flooded the ports and taverns of a monstrous squid that never leaves survivors and that no man has ever set eyes on. Awfully convenient, if you ask me. Yet the rumor served its purpose, giving the loved ones of lost sailors a place to lay the blame for their grief. It is a far greater comfort than admitting to the ill fate that even the most veteran sailors might encounter on their voyages."

The lad stared unassuredly at the dwarf as Puck lowered the bowl from his lips to chime in.

"I would not be so quick to dismiss the kraken as a figment, Ram. There are plenty of sea-dwellers widely known that prey upon trekkers of the Bridging Sea. How many fools have ventured too close to a fossegrim in their travels? You have witnessed the lures the sirens cast with their tantalizing hymns. Is it so unthinkable that there may be some truth in the legend of the kraken?"

"What is a fossegrim?" asked the lad curiously.

"A water man who lurks in the rocky shallows," said Ram with a mock-worried tone, "waiting to shipwreck sailors by enthralling their minds with his deadly fiddle. Sirens and fossegrimen . . . It would seem by your account, Puck, that music and song are the greatest dangers we face at sea. Why not thrill us with an exhibition? Go, fetch your instrument. See if you can bewitch me into dancing a jig."

Ossel chuckled as Puck returned annoyedly to his breakfast, but the brothers' chortles were cut short as they caught the mute's grim glare from across the simmering pot.

"Oh, come now, mute," jested Ram. "Surely, you do not also give credit to these fantasies."

Without hesitation, the speechless sailor gave a resolute nod. Caught between affirmers and naysayers, the lad appeared to regret raising the topic of maritime beasts at all. For this reason, Ira gave himself leave to enter the discourse.

"It is unwise to make light of such things, Ram," he said solemnly. "Provoking the sea has been the demise of sailors more seasoned than any on this ship. The Bridging Sea commands respect from her voyagers, as does the *Wayfarer*, and that respect is duly earned." Ira then turned to address the young sailor. "The master only spoke of the kraken out of caution, lad. Tales say that the great squid prefers to inhabit the most restless of waters, like those thrashing in the eye of a storm. Given how widespread this cover is, I see no reason to fear our encountering the beast in our travels."

With an understanding nod, the lad lowered his gaze and returned his attention to the remainder of his stew. He downed it with a final slurp, wiped his mouth, and turned to Esther.

"I am ready for our next lesson," he said in a far more eager voice.

"You have had a long night," said Esther concernedly. "Why not continue our lessons once you have had a rest?"

"No!" exclaimed the lad, forcing himself upright. "I am not at all tired, really!"

After some additional coaxing, Esther assented to the lad's pleas. Since their first reading session, the young sailor had learned to recognize several letters as well as sound out some smaller words. He was not the only one who had taken an interest in improving his literacy either. Nathanael had joined in his spare time whenever the lady and the lad elected to study on deck. Ossel, Puck, and the mute had also taken to watching the pages and listening intently when Esther spelled or sounded out words from the book Torzara had gifted her. Sure enough, as Esther seated herself on the crate beside the lad's, the dwarves' attentions were instantly gathered as she opened *Fables of the West*. She began reading slowly from "The Ode to the Parocen Troves," allowing the lad to sound out those words he recognized as her finger traced the pages. By the time they had finished the poem, even Ram had lent an ear to listen to the treasures uncovered deep within the Western mines.

"Well," said Esther when they finished the sonnet, "what would you like to read about next?"

The lad considered the question before asking, "Are there any stories about great battles? Warriors of old and triumphant tales?"

"Certainly. There are a number of poems with verses dedicated to heroic figures of eras long passed. Likewise, this book also contains those laments of the vile and wicked who tainted the history of the Westlands."

"No doubt, Mágna will have a chapter to himself," interjected Ossel, as all but the lad let out a solemn sigh.

"Who?" asked the young sailor.

"My word, lad!" exclaimed Puck. "Mágna the Snakeheart is only the most notorious pirate who ever plagued these very waters."

"The dwarf who birthed the horde of ruffians that assaulted this vessel not a week ago," said Manoque. "His time was generations ago, yet as you have witnessed, the Pirate Emperor's dark legacy lives on in his stead."

"I did not know the pirates had an emperor," remarked the fascinated lad.

"Not a real one, mind you," said Ira. "Not by any true meaning of the word. Mágna was known most widely as the Snakeheart. But the title of Pirate Emperor was the one the dwarf bestowed upon himself after an age of terrorizing the Bridging Sea and any who dared to cross it."

"I believe there is a page or two about his rise and fall in here," said Esther as she perused the pages of her book.

She stopped as she came upon an elegy entitled "The Sons of Veroise." As she offered it to the young sailor, he asked, "Would you read it?"

With a gentle smile, Esther began to read aloud. All ears in the hold turned to listen as her soft voice recited the verses of old.

In ages past, when black sails roamed
And realms were ruled apart
A Horde of brutes traversed the sea
Striking fear into sailing hearts
'Twas Mágna the malevolent
Who wrought great havoc afar
Upon the Augur, *Dominion in hand*
He pillaged souls for the Dark

THOMAS USLE

A brood of beasts, the pirate commanded
From brigands to creatures of deep
For Mágna bartered with the vile sea snake,
To feast on vessels it reaped
The woes of the East had trumpeted
Across blue skies to the West
Empress Veroise pledged to save the realms
And to sea, the emperor was sent

When two fleets met, a clash ensued
'Tween soldiers and pirates of dread
But Mágna hailed a victor's crown
Stole from the emperor's head
When tragedy reached the temple's ears
The sons of Veroise set sail
United beside the Eastern men
The Horde would not prevail

In the mighty fray, the snake did join
As Mágna hailed for its aid
But the cunning beast turned foe to all
Thrashing ships to watery graves
'Twas one Eastern warrior that felled the beast
To save the union's last
But the sons of Veroise had met their fates
By the mountainous serpent's wrath

The line of the empress ended that day
As she forfeited crown and right
So the one who felled the beast might reign
O'er the lands he would unite

When Esther had finished the elegy, the sailors hanging on her every word were consumed by the haunting tale as a look of understanding crossed the lad's face.

"So Mágna killed the emperor and took the crown for himself," he said solemnly. "That is why he awarded himself the title?"

"Yes," Esther replied quietly, "the elven sovereign, Empress Veroise, deployed her husband, the emperor consort, to end Mágna's deadly rule. But the Haurthian fleet was overwhelmed. In those days, the Horde had multitudes of warships, far more than the dwindling numbers that straggle on today. After besting the fleet and the emperor consort, the Snakeheart forced upon the royal elf the ultimate act of cruelty. Mágna commanded him to take his own life, and in the wake of his grand defeat, the emperor consort did the pirate's bidding." No breath was drawn in the hold as Esther recounted the harrowing legend. "And in a final act of disdain, Mágna raised his dark sword, Dominion, and severed the elf's head. He ordered the fleet's survivors to deliver the sickly trophy to their empress, keeping the crown for his own."

"Dominion?" said the lad. "Like in the poem?"

"A fitting name, too," said Manoque. "*Invocar*, the sword is called in the Western tongue. The souls stolen by that gladius are too many to count. Folks in the provinces still say the Snakeheart held the power to command the will of the sea itself. If you ask me, Mágna carried with him a vicious curse, bringing all he ever touched to ruin."

"You do not mean that, Manoque," Ram said loftily. "Tell the lad tales if you would like, but do not go about filling his head with ideas of curses and enchantments looming over all of life's atrocities."

"I tell you," said Manoque, "the *Augur*, the sword Dominion, the trail of bodies. To say all in Mágna's wake was cursed is hardly a farce, Ram, not to mention those other haunting enchantments we know to be real. Mystics, creatures of the deep—"

"Are nothing but horrid deeds and beings," interrupted the dwarf. "You would have the lad believe that every tragedy is brought about by dark forces beyond our understanding."

"I would have him understand the world as it is," muttered Manoque.

The mute offered Manoque a hearty nod of approval. Before Ram could retort, his brother inserted himself into the discussion.

"You have to admit, Ram," said Ossel, "that if ever a curse existed, it would surely have been Mágna who carried it."

Ram did not reply as he and Manoque each returned to their bowls of stew, which had nearly gone cold.

"So, after the emperor consort was murdered," the lad said to Esther, "the empress sent her sons to avenge him?"

"No," said Esther, "quite the contrary. When the head of the sovereign's husband was brought to the temple in Eou Verás, Empress Veroise forbade the princes to pursue vengeance against Mágna. Veroise did not wish to see any of her sons perish at the hands of the Horde, as their father had. You must understand, however, that this was the first time a royal had been slain by enemy forces in the empire's history. It is true that the emperor consort was not of royal blood. His name is not even remembered by most, even for the sake of his tragic end."

"Nevertheless," added Ira, "the princes were determined to end the Horde's terrible reign once and for all. They disobeyed their empress, and the six elven princes set off with a fleet of galleys to hunt down Mágna and his vicious band. The princes called upon the free men of the Eastlands to join in their fight so they might secure the safety of both mainlands. And so, a rally of warships sailed from Eastern shores and joined their new allies. After months of scavenging the Bridging Sea, the united forces met the pirate fleet south of the Savage Peaks, and a great battle ensued."

"But none of the princes returned?" asked the lad in a hollow voice.

"Not one," uttered Ira. "They and many others were slain that day by the monstrous sea snake. *Éalbenthen*, as it is called in the Westlands. A hundred ships and thousands of men, elves, dwarves, and pirates met their doom by the towering serpent's fury. The once-trusted ally of the Horde betrayed Mágna and unleashed its wrath upon all. Every sword turned upon the éalbenthen, but the snake was too powerful. That is until one warrior, a man of the free Eastlands, delivered the fatal blow to the scourge of the Bridging Sea and saved the last survivors. The remaining pirate warships fled to the Mortal Spires to take refuge. The battle was won, but victory came at a heavy cost.

"When the last maritime forces of the new alliance returned to Eou Verás, the empress fell to her knees in mourning for the ancestral line that was to end with her. For this reason, she ceded the crown to the man who had vanquished the sea snake and saved what was left of the allied fleet. And as the Second Line of Sovereigns began, the Eastlands were formally joined to the Haurthian Empire, creating a union that would last for ages to come. In tribute to the memory of the lost princes, the six realms, which would one day be governed as the provinces we know today, were each given the namesake of one of the fallen sons of Veroise. This was Emperor Lysias' parting gift to the elf widow as she departed from the Hallowed City to live the remainder of her life as one of the people."

"But," said the lad with a puzzled expression, "the elven line could not have ended. What about the premier? Is he not descended from Empress Veroise? Did he not claim his birthright and usurp the crown from Darius the Damned?"

Ira could not repress the instinct to glance towards his sister as she lowered her gaze to hide a tear. Fortunately, the other nighters' attentions were fixed on Ira, and so none took notice of Esther's lapse.

"It is true," said Ira with an effort to keep his voice passive. "Premier Lysias is a descendant of the last elven empress. No doubt, he was named for the one who assumed the sovereignty after his ancestor abdicated her right to rule. Veroise left the Hallowed City and settled in some remote part of the Realm of Haurth. It would seem she lived in anonymity for many years before she remarried and, despite her age, bore another child. The First Line of Sovereigns was restored."

"Then why did she not return and reclaim the sovereignty?" asked the lad.

"She could not. Had Veroise elected to temporarily resign her title, she might have assumed the throne again. But once an individual has abdicated their position, it cannot be reclaimed."

"But her descendants could, and one of them did. So why did none before the premier come forward?"

Ira gave a light chuckle as he faced the inquisitive young sailor. "You ask many thoughtful questions, lad. In reference to this query, I expect your guess is as good as mine. Others have asked why none before Premier Lysias revealed themselves as heir to the First Line of Sovereigns. Perhaps Veroise kept the secret for her own, and it was only discovered after her passing. But if I were to venture a guess, I would say that it was far more likely that Veroise and her descendants knew the truth and elected to live as commoners in the Westlands. Power and riches hold great sway over the masses, but true hearts often yearn for those treasures most often taken for granted. I suggest that the former empress and her renewed line were most happy leading the sort of simple life that the sovereignty could never have afforded them."

The lad pondered these words long and hard. Perhaps he was struggling to comprehend how anyone could willingly deny themselves all the gold, gems, and glory the empire had to offer.

"How did the premier come to defeat Emperor Darius?" asked the young sailor.

This query, Ira had not the heart to answer. Nor did he wish to subject Esther to the recollection of those memories that had plagued their minds for twelve years.

"Another time, perhaps," he said to the lad. "We seem to have strayed from the elegy we were listening to."

A tad disappointed but nevertheless interested in any topic of legend, the lad posed another question.

"You never said what happened to Mágna. Did the éalbenthen kill him, too?"

"That remains a mystery," Puck chimed in. "No survivors of the battle could say whether his warship, the *Augur*, was sunk or if it was amongst those taking refuge in the northern range. All that is known is that neither the Snakeheart nor his infamous vessel were ever sighted on sea or land again."

"Indeed," said Ira, "there are few today who lived through the age of the dwarf pirate's bloody reign, and I doubt whether any personally bore witness to the carnage Mágna wrought."

"But you are mistaken, Ira," interjected Ram. "The Snakeheart vanished no less than half a millennium ago. Who would be alive today to give a personal account of his reign?"

"There are those who are said to have dwelled in the northern glens of Haurth since before the time of Mágna," said Manoque without looking up from his bowl. "It is a sacred place where life began in the Westlands, born by the Light and the Dark. Legend says those who dwell in Vistérae live on in blissful immortality."

"Yes, yes," said a jaded Ram. "I have heard of the fables of the garden, Manoque. By the way, there seem to be some gray flecks in your fine locks. Why not venture there yourself for a taste of eternity?"

"I see no appeal in an endless life," the elf muttered with a note of annoyance.

"Well, I say it is a farce," proclaimed Ram, "much like the dreaded kraken to which you are all eager to lend your fear. Can anyone attest to these immortal inhabitants? Does anyone here know of one who has seen the sacred glen with their own eyes?"

"I have seen the garden," said Esther, "and I have met those you speak of."

All eyes in the hold fell disbelievingly upon the lady. Puck's mouth gaped as he spilled some stew on his fresh tunic.

"What is it like?" asked an awestruck lad, his eyes brimming with wonder and intrigue. Esther did not immediately reply. A reminiscent smile crept upon her face as she appeared lost in her own marvelous trance.

"There is no other place I shall ever know as its equal," she said softly. "It is where yearning souls go to take refuge from the pangs of life. Blades upon emerald hills spread wild across the mounts to the west. Blustery cliffs of sable stone overlook the black sands washed by the tide. A river born from a stream spreads wide into a waterfall, encasing a secluded cove. Waters have never held so much life or taste as those that flow freely through the garden. And the air . . . I had never breathed before the day I found myself wandering about that winding glen. If you could only savor the breeze that traipses through your hair and upon your lips, you would long to see the place in your most fanciful dreams."

As the winds outside called and waves pounded against the hull, the nighters sat in their private imaginings of such a paradise as that described to them. No one, not even Ram, questioned how Esther could have a personal account of the northern haven. His sister's words were enough to recall the senses and memories of Vistérae to the forefront of Ira's mind. Hearing another speak of its majesty in such vivid detail somehow made the place all the more real. It assured him that it was indeed a memory and not merely a persuasive mirage.

"Well," said Puck as he rose and stretched his arms, "I believe I shall turn in. Thank you for the meal, Esther, and for the stories."

Ossel also dismissed himself, followed shortly by Ram. The mute also rose, offered the lady a kindly smile, and shuffled with the others through the towering stacks to their respective hammocks. As Manoque parted from the huddle around the pot, the lad whispered to Esther, "What did Manoque mean when he said life was 'born by the Light and the Dark?'"

"That is a far more ancient tale," she replied, "not one you would likely find written on pages. It is older than the written word and has been passed down orally for generations. What is based in truth versus myth, I could not say."

As the fascinated lad leaned in closer, Ira smiled and excused himself for the night, bidding the lad not to stave off rest too long. When his tired body was slung in his hammock, Ira closed his eyes and listened as Esther delved into the story they had first heard as children.

"Well," she began, "it is said that in the great beginning, there were two. The Light and the Dark. *Érosai* and *Caurenthen*, as they are named in the Western tongue. And in their might and majesty, the pair of deities formed the world itself. The void was divided into day and night, sky and sea, all of creation in balance with one another. And between the air and the waters, Érosai and Caurenthen created the earth. All the lands were as one at their birth, with the great northern peaks serving as the isthmus between the emerald West and the golden East. And yet, in all the life they formed apart, the two deities found their creations lacking. And so it was that with two hands, the race of elves was shaped from the wild fields of wheat as tenders of the land. Likewise, dwarves were sculpted from the forest trees as crafters to shape the world around them. The young beings met and settled in the garden where the dawn first greeted them, and they called it *Vistérae*, birth in their native language."

"Peace prospered for many years in the green garden, and Érosai was glad. But in the imbalance, Caurenthen grew spiteful. And so it was that with one hand, he bore a chasm in the earth that stretched all the way to the coast. From the depths came sickly creatures born of the Dark, thrashing in the waters below the cliffs. As the maritime beasts set out to the wide sea before them, a throng of feral beings crawled from the chasm and flooded into the garden. They were primitive creatures, a ghastly imitation of the garden's inhabitants. Hunched on all fours and hairless, with leathery green skin coating their jagged features. The band of ferals scampered across the glen, slaughtering the innocents with their gnarled fists and pointed teeth. The elven farmers and dwarven craftsmen possessed no tools of war to defend themselves, and many were slain that day. When the mayhem Caurenthen's jealousy had wrought was discovered, Érosai was outraged. The wrath of the Light came swiftly upon the ferals, sinking the land that connected the peaks from east to west. The remaining savages were banished to the isolation of the northern range. Soon after their narrow survival, many of the elves and dwarves migrated south to seek refuge in other parts. Those whose trust in the Light remained steadfast elected to stay in the garden, and their fidelity was rewarded with Érosai's blessing of eternal life."

Over the steady creaks of the *Wayfarer*, Ira thought he could hear from his hammock the faintest sigh of amazement uttered from the lad's lips. He wondered if the other nighters had already fallen asleep or if they, too, were lying awake listening to Esther's tale of the great beginning.

"What of man?" asked the lad. "Was he not also given life in the garden?"

"No, he was not. In the wake of Caurenthen's betrayal, Érosai looked to the untarnished shores of the East to start anew. With one hand, he washed humanity from the sands. It was a pure creation, all that could give splendor to the Light. But in a desire to maintain the balance, Érosai made an offering to Caurenthen and allowed him to place amidst the new life a part of his being. And so, in the knot of a tree, a piece of the Dark was left to be undisturbed by those of humanity who wished to live in harmony. With this act, the creators were content to allow the race of man to endure in their absence."

"Ages passed, and life in the East flourished. Peace and communion were heralded, and all was as it ought to be. Then, one day, a man who had given way to jealousy was wandering through the forest and heard a soft voice calling to him. The voice, no more than a whisper, a hiss, came from a magnificent tree, and the man followed its calling. There, he found embedded in the bark the power that had lain dormant for so many ages. Temptation became him as the man ripped from the knot the last gift of the Dark. With this power in hand, the man went to the brother he envied so and slayed him where he stood. This first act of malicious will shattered the peace throughout the Eastlands, and all of humanity knew of the man's sin. As punishment, he was cast adrift in a small boat hailing towards the Savage Peaks, and the race of men was left to pick up the pieces of the lost amity."

"Neither land would ever know true peace now. The balance would never prosper in this mortal plane. With one final gift to offer, Érosai was given leave by Caurenthen to cast into the night sky a luminous star to shine above all others. Both ends of the world saw its brilliance, and the people in the West heard the star's calling. And so it was that a ship of elves and dwarves followed *Arisa Lae*, the Star of the Sea, into waters never before crossed. They voyaged many leagues beyond their homeland until, at last, they came to harbor on Eastern shores. And as the people of the two lands met under the light that had bridged their worlds, Arisa Lae faded into the darkness, never to be seen again."

Beyond the stacks of cargo and provisions, Ira thought he heard a stirring near the place where Ram's hammock was hung.

CHAPTER VIII

THE GALLEY

Thin streaks of light passed through gaps in the deck's planks and into the dim cargo hold. One of these beams passed over Ira's lids, rousing him to his waking senses. Rested but still stiff from the night's labors, Ira shifted gently in his hammock to set his bare feet upon the cool floorboards. He laced his sandals, refilled his waterskin, and lumbered between the stacks of cargo towards the hatch. All of the other hammocks were vacant except for the lad's. He was slumbering soundly on his back, one of his arms hanging loose over the sack, the other resting over *Fables of the West* on his chest.

When Ira emerged on deck, he was greeted by blue skies, a warm sun, and a tender breeze in the early afternoon. If these pleasant conditions held, it would be an ideal night for sailing when the nighters assumed their posts. The *Wayfarer* was trekking north now, no doubt to correct for the time they had sailed blindly through the shrouding storm. Over the starboard ledge, the host of bleary gray clouds from which they had hailed lingered in the distance. Faint cracks of lightning illuminated those dark patches still billowing in the east.

Upon the quarterdeck, Halruc and Manoque consulted the elf's map while Ishcaur manned the helm. Esther was seated in her usual spot upon the steps of the quarterdeck. On one side of her was Nathanael, whittling away at a small block of wood in his hand. It appeared to be the vague figure of some four-legged creature. Ira suspected that when finished, the carved beast might serve as a toy for his impending son or daughter. On Esther's other side, Tabor was replacing the dressing on his punctured leg. He lobbed the old, bloodied wrap over the ship's ledge and trickled some water over the wound before tying it with a clean strip of cloth. Dromo and Cercur were spending their leisure time around the mast with Ossel, Ram, Puck, and the mute. The dwarves were engrossed in excited discussions of the Circus of Lark and the chariots they favored to win the tournament. Old Dromo did not offer much to the conversation, but the mute seemed to have found his own way to engage with his companions. At the mention of each racer and his horses, the dwarf's head would either nod with zeal or shake with doubt.

Talk of the famed charioteer, Haron the Brute, was interrupted by the changing winds noted as the scarlet sail began to ripple and waver overhead. Without so much as a word from their master, the dayers leapt to their feet and took to resetting the sail in a harmonious rhythm. Ira weaved between the hustling sailors as he made his way to the steps to sit beside Esther.

"I hope the lad did not keep you up too late," he said as they watched the crew prepare to swing the yard about.

"It was nearly midday by the time I could persuade him to get some sleep," chuckled Esther.

"He ought not to have kept you from your rest."

"I do not mind, truly. He is quite bright and certainly persistent. We are less than a week from Jade, and I intend to teach him all I can in that time." As they watched the yard swing and catch the southern breeze, Ira heard Esther say under her breath, "I ought to have offered lessons to the children back in Squall. I know they would have enjoyed it as much as the lad." But as she made this remark to herself, her hand reached up to touch the long mark along her olive cheek.

At that moment, a young voice carried across the ship to the quarterdeck.

"Master!" called Cercur.

The dwarf was gripping the starboard sheet with one hand and pointing over the ship's bow with the other. Halruc and Manoque looked up from the charts to follow the direction of Cercur's finger. The other dayers had ceased their work of tethering the braces to gaze while the nighters scattered about the deck to search for some landmark in the distance. Ira rose from the steps to get a better view, but not before the master's booming voice answered the question before any sailor could pose it.

"It is a Haurthian galley," said Halruc. He did not raise his voice, yet the grim nature of his words carried across the deck with ease. A throbbing in Ira's chest grew rapid at the master's words. Ira abandoned Esther and hustled to join Ossel, Ram, and the mute along the bow. Any hope he had of the master's being mistaken was swept away by the far-off yet clearly discernable silver star embroidered upon a sapphire sail. The galley carrying a cohort of Western soldiers was positioned along the *Wayfarer*'s current course, poised to detain anyone forbidden to cross the Bridging Sea.

"I shall not stand for this idleness!" Halruc barked at the dayers. "Tend to your posts and tether the braces!"

The distracted dayers set to work again, but with a notable loss of liveliness in their steps. Splinters of dampened wood ground themselves under Ira's nails as he clenched the ship's ledge. The dwarves next to him were no longer staring at the Haurthian warship but at the man and woman they knew to be voyaging under less-than-legitimate circumstances. Tearing himself from the bow, Ira strode violently across the deck, ignoring the darting eyes around him as he went. He dared only to glance at his dearest friend as he passed, but the brief glimpse of Nathanael's anxious expression only made Ira's insides turn more violently. Esther was on her feet, clutching her hands together in a feeble attempt to cease their trembling. Halruc dismissed himself from Manoque's company and came to Esther's side as Ira joined them.

"Why have we not altered our course?" Ira whispered to the master.

"They will have already caught sight of us by now," answered Halruc solemnly. "If we veer unnaturally from our heading, it will be taken as a sign that we mean to avoid inspection."

"We can hide below deck," muttered Esther, "in the keel. They will not find us there."

"That is the first place they will search for stowaways should they come aboard," said Halruc. "And we do not know for a fact that they will. This is a simple merchant ship. Galleys of the Haurthian Navy tend to reserve boardings for the port inspectors."

"And should this galleymaster elect to come aboard the *Wayfarer*?" asked Ira in an undertone. "Can we not at least hide our documents?"

"This is no crew of a hundred rowers, prince, where documents are miscounted and lost. I assure you, the mariners will not be so careless as to mistake a crew of fourteen for a crew of twelve."

"Then what are we to do?"

Halruc did not speak as he took in the sight of the ever-nearing galley to the north. Even beneath his thick, pale beard, there was no mistaking the grimace, which was even graver than that last seen on the day of the Horde's pursuit.

"We will hide nothing from the galleymaster. Do not raise your voice while your master speaks!" hissed Halruc as he quelled Ira before he could utter a word of protest. "I have passed many inspections in my time, and I have known of those foolhardy enough to attempt concealment from the mariners. The cost . . ." The dwarf's voice trailed as he fell into fretful thought before regaining his composure. "If we are boarded, the both of you will stand alongside the rest of the crew in plain sight, though perhaps not so innocently plain. Indeed, I would be remiss not to advise the lady to don that veil of hers again." As he spoke, Esther raised the scarlet cloth from her shoulders and draped it over her head. "While we remain at sea," continued Halruc, "the mariner's prime concern is for what we bring into the Westlands, and our manifest is as commonplace as any other vessel's. Interest in who enters the Realm of Haurth is routinely left in the charge of the ports. But if fate is not on our side today, we will all abide by the galleymaster's orders without question or reservation."

And without waiting for a reply from either brother or sister, Halruc parted from their company and rejoined Manoque upon the quarterdeck.

The master addressed the rest of the crew with similar orders on how they were to proceed should their ship be subject to inspection. When all had been said, the dayers did not attempt to busy themselves. Instead, they joined the nighters along the bow to captively watch as the galley grew nearer. The forbearance about the *Wayfarer* was similar to that preceding their recent encounter with the Horde. Only this time, the crew felt no burning anticipation for their own sake. Glances shifted between the approaching warship and their new companions. Amidst the pirate galley's pursuit, Ira had been relieved to have tasks, preparations, and plans to occupy his anxious mind. No such distraction would serve him now. All that was left to them was to wait and hope. As the galley's mighty hull and glistening ram bore through the sea, the outlines of armored figures grew clearer against the broad sapphire sail. Upon the bow, one of the mariners raised a golden pennant on a wooden post. The signal waved side to side, high enough for the merchant vessel to discern. Somewhere in the back of Ira's racing mind, he could hear Halruc's distant calls to furl the sail and make ready to anchor.

While the dayers took to loosening the sheets and hauling in the sail, the mute passed them by and descended into the hold. Moments later, the auburn-haired dwarf clambered back on deck, followed shortly by the lad. The young sailor was examining the strange scene through sleepy eyes, Esther's book still in hand. The sight of the Haurthian galley awoke him to the grave nature of his summons, yet he dared not ask any questions. When the clews of the sail were furled, Cercur cast the stone anchor over the ship's ledge. The crew watched in abject awe as the galley, propelled by three banks of oars, came along the merchant ship's port side.

Even amongst the finest warships he had known in his naval service, Ira could not recall ever beholding a warship so colossal as this one. The broad sail was hoisted swiftly by the mariners shuffling about the deck. The faint bellows of officers calling orders stretched the distance between the ships. The hortator's rhythmic beats from the lower deck boomed loudly as with a final thump of hammer against drum, the band of rowers came to rest. In unparalleled unity, the oars were raised and retracted into the galley. Anchored but a ship's length from the *Wayfarer*, a regal rowboat and a boarding party of a dozen Western soldiers were deployed into the open waters.

Unconsciously, the sailors backed into a huddle along the starboard side of the deck as Halruc remained stationary at the mast. Esther grasped Ira's hand viciously as the hooks of a step ladder latched upon the *Wayfarer*'s port side ledge. One after another, elven mariners ascended the ladder and stood opposite the pack of sailors in a rigid line. Sunlight bounded off their round shields and glimmering helmets, with long sheens of hair tied back uniformly. Tunics beneath iron chestplates held more blue in their dye than the sea itself. After the mariners were collected on the deck, a dwarven officer rose from the step ladder, followed by the master of the mighty warship.

To the surprise of many of the *Wayfarer*'s company, the galleymaster was neither an elf nor a dwarf but a man. It was not unheard of, though so few men resided in the Westlands, and even fewer rose to such an esteemed rank as gailaum in the Haurthian Navy. He was bare-faced, and his long mane of gray hair resembled that of his elven brethren. But the olive skin and hardened features common to the race of man could not be hidden beneath his regal helmet. His station and that of the dwarven officer beside him were apparent by their bronze armor and short capes. The dwarf's cape was of plain blue, and the man's silver cape bore fine sapphire embroidery. The galleymaster also had attached to his belt the traditional tassels to signify his rank and stature amongst the maritime forces. As the man's garb gave his position away, Halruc's fine mantle also denoted him as the one in charge, so the galleymaster approached him first.

"You are the proprietor of this vessel, are you not?" inquired the man.

"I am, sir. Master Halruc of the *Wayfarer*, hailing from the Port of Gales, at the service of the Haurthian Navy."

Halruc bowed courteously to the galleymaster, who respectfully inclined his head to the dwarf.

"I am Gailaum Zaccai of the galley *Requiarda*." The man called Zaccai broke his gaze from Halruc so that he might pace about the deck. Ira could feel his body tense up as the man's eyes drifted over the huddle of sailors. The galleymaster did not appear the least bit interested in the crew. He was too preoccupied with the scars the *Wayfarer* had sustained from the encounter with the Horde warship. "I hope we find you and your vessel well," said Zaccai, examining a scorched plank at his feet. "Has your ship been long in need of repairs, Master Halruc?"

"No indeed, gailaum," said Halruc calmly, ignoring the indignant nature of the remark. "Upon our departure from Gales, the *Wayfarer* was as pristine as the day she was christened. The damage you see before you is the aftermath of a raid perpetrated by the Pirate Horde. It was my fortune to escape with my life and those of all in my service. Though I think it fair to say that our vessel surely felt the cost of the attack."

"This was the Horde's doing?" asked the dwarven officer in a mixture of shock and admiration.

"I would attribute more than fortune to you and your loyal crew," said the galleymaster. "Very few have evaded the grasp of those brigands so long as to recount the tale. Pray tell, where did their warship encounter you?"

"We must have been some fifty leagues south of Rover Bay."

"I see. Our sources have indicated the pirates favor the northern waters this time of year. I shall pass along this information so our fleets might intercept any other Horde vessels before they happen upon innocent travelers." Halruc nodded his thanks to the galleymaster, who continued his observation of the deck. "Would you have one of your men fetch your ship's manifest?"

Halruc called for the lad to retrieve the wax tablet from his cabin. The young sailor knew the tablet well, though he was not yet skilled enough to decipher its contents. The lad glanced nervously at the statuesque mariners as he passed them by on his way to Halruc's cabin beneath the quarterdeck. The soft sounds of rummaging could be heard across the still and silent deck. Finally, he emerged with the tablet listing the exported goods from the provinces, their quantities, and their final destinations. He handed the manifest to Halruc, who in turn offered it to Zaccai. The galleymaster's eyes passed over it briefly before it was turned over to his fellow officer. The dwarf beckoned half of his squad to search the ship. Without hesitation, the elves dropped through the hatch and began a noisy examination of the hold and its contents. The clatter of crates and barrels being pried open and tossed about filled the afternoon air, cut only by the calls of their contents from within the hold. While the dwarven officer noted those exports confirmed on the manifest, the galleymaster addressed Halruc in an unnaturally casual tone.

"Your manifest indicates that this shipment is bound for Eou Verás. Yet as we came upon you, your vessel was hailing north rather than west to the mainland. Has your navigator been struggling in his duties?"

Ira could see in the corner of his eye Manoque grinding his teeth at this remark. The galleymaster was baiting the crew with his slight at the elf. Not even the most deficient navigator could so mistake a ship's heading. Zaccai knew perfectly well that the *Wayfarer* was not sailing directly to Eou Verás. But to confess now to their harboring first in the Isle of Jade would only serve to arouse further suspicions. Halruc was cornered between false ineptitude and willfully veering from his commissioned destination.

"My navigator has performed his duties most adequately," said Halruc after a moment's contemplation. "Indeed, you are correct, gailaum. My vessel is currently sailing north to the Isle of Jade for repairs. She has weathered much along this journey and, as you can see, is in dire need of a proper fix. My crew has done all in their power to maintain her, but we all have our limits."

"North to Jade?" the galleymaster repeated in a tone ripe with both intrigue and suspicion. "That is a long way from your intended course. The Hallowed City is much nearer, and I assure you, the city's shipwrights are the finest in all the empire."

"Were it not for the storm we only just emerged from," said Halruc, "our course to Jade would have been a more direct one. Of course, I hold no blame against my navigator for the delay. And with no disrespect towards the great shipwrights of the Westlands," he added with a strong note of cordiality, "a master entrusts very few to the welfare of his ship. The dwarf who headed the construction of the *Wayfarer* resides in Jade, and none but he has mended her since she came into my charge. I hope you will forgive an old master's eccentricities when it comes to his most prized possession."

It was an elaborate dance the two masters shared as they stepped around the truth hidden in their words. Ira hastened to hide his amazement at Halruc's quick thinking with so brilliant a work of fiction. It was, however, abundantly clear that Zaccai's skepticism regarding their alternate course was not entirely swayed. Before the man could question Halruc further, he was recalled by the dwarven officer's report of the manifest being perfectly in order.

"I shall also require the documents of your servants, Master Halruc, as well as your own," said the galleymaster.

As Halruc stoically beckoned the lad again to his cabin, Ira found himself incapable of drawing air. He felt the urge to shake throughout his body, but all feeling was lost to him except for that deafening pounding in his chest. There was no escape; this was the end he had brought his only living kin to. Seconds passed like an eternity as he, Esther, and Nathanael stood pallid behind the dwarven sailors, awaiting the impending doom. When the lad finally returned, he offered a small stack of parchment to his master. After a flicker of hesitation only the crew seemed to note, Halruc handed over the documents to Zaccai. Ira raised his eyes to the beautiful sky, wondering if he would ever again enjoy its splendor from the Isle of Ruin.

"Master Halruc, none of these documents bear the mark of the census," the man noted bemusedly. "Why have your servants not reported to their magistrates?"

The sailors looked at one another, searching for any who might know what the galleymaster might be referring to. Ira looked in disbelief and saw that Zaccai had not examined all the documents but only the topmost ones in the stack.

"I beg your leave, gailaum," began Halruc, "but I cannot claim to know what you are speaking in reference to."

"Really? Are you unaware of the ordinance passed by the High Court, mandating every citizen of the empire to report to their magistrate's office for a census?"

"By the Light, we had heard nothing of a census when we departed from Gales nearly three weeks ago. Had I been aware of such an ordinance, I should not have permitted any of my crew to sail without first abiding by the High Court's decree. I give you my word, gailaum, that each of my men will report to their magistrate upon our return from Eou Verás."

"You misunderstand," said Zaccai pointedly. "No ship is permitted entry to the Realm of Haurth unless all aboard bear documentation in accordance with Haurthian law. I am afraid that I must ask your vessel to return to the provinces at once."

Robbed of those riches awaiting them in the Hallowed City, the crew of the *Wayfarer* appeared on the verge of lashing out. Amidst the huddle of bitter sailors, a young voice cried, "But we have come so far! You cannot—"

His father's hand clasping his shoulder and a grave look from the master silenced the lad's outburst. But his deeply affronted expression was nevertheless shared by his companions. Halruc took a moment to collect himself before speaking in the most reasonable tone he could muster.

"Gailaum Zaccai, my servants and I have labored for hundreds of leagues, and as you can see, our ship has already had its share of tribulations. To turn back now would come at drastic expense to myself and my crew, not to mention how this failure to fulfill my commission on schedule will tarnish my reputation with vendors far and wide. I implore you to allow us to complete our voyage. As soon as our shipment is delivered, we will return to Gales with haste."

"I cannot allow it, Master Halruc. Your commission will have to wait until all in your service are in compliance with the High Court's ordinance."

Miserable groans sounded from the weary sailors as Zaccai lowered his gaze to the documents he shuffled in his hand. Then, with a terrible lurch in his stomach, Ira saw the man's eyes turn from a lazy glance into a widened stare. Esther's hand slipped from his own as she pulled her veil so close that it pressed taut against her cheek. The rest of the crew was too preoccupied with their own dismay to notice the sudden alteration in the galleymaster's demeanor. Ira could not see Halruc's face, but the dwarf's hands clenched so hard behind his back that the pale scars along his knuckles could be made out. When the man looked up from the parchment, he did not acknowledge Halruc's presence in the slightest. He only had eyes for Esther.

"Arrest this woman!" boomed the galleymaster.

Even the officer and the mariners jumped at their master's sudden outburst. Shimmering swords were drawn as the sailors tightened their huddle around Esther. Manoque and Tabor positioned themselves on either side of her while Ira and Nathanael covered her from the front. They were plainly visible above the heads of the dwarves and the lad. As the galleymaster's eyes fluttered between the two young men protecting Esther, a gleam of comprehension dawned beneath his helmet.

"Am I left to guess which of you is the disgraced prince and son of Emperor Darius?" the man said derisively.

Nothing could have prepared the crew for these words or for the answer given as Ira raised his voice.

"I am he."

The mariners, bearing their gladiuses, murmured disbelievingly to one another. The huddle around Esther slackened as the sailors gaped at the brother and sister they had come to know and respect. Puck ridiculed the proclamation loudly, declaring the precedent unfounded and impossible. A scornful glare was carved beneath Ram's dark brow as he and Ossel traded meaningful looks. Manoque abandoned Esther's side as Tabor pulled his son away from the disgraced royals. The lad's amazed expression was not his usual, filled with awe and wonder. It was tinged with the pang of a most intimate betrayal. Only one remained steadfast at the prince and princess' sides. As the galleymaster strode across the deck towards the banished pariahs,

Nathanael dared to block his path. In doing so, he was instantly met by the raised points of several Western gladiuses. Though he did not waver in his convictions, the voice of his dearest friend brought Nathanael back to his senses.

"Do not be rash," Ira whispered sternly at him. "Think of Ruth and the child; they need you. You cannot—"

But before Ira could finish, Zaccai had gripped him by the hem of his tunic and tossed him forcefully to the mariners.

"Shackles!" bellowed the galleymaster.

Ira made no struggle as the mariners threw him on his knees and fastened the cold irons around his wrists. He wanted desperately to tell Nathanael not to mourn for whatever fate awaited him and Esther, and especially not to hold any blame upon himself. He could have told him such well before the mariners boarded the ship; why had he not? But Ira could say nothing aloud in their present company. Any admission of Nathanael's role in getting the prince and princess this close to the Westlands would surely land him in shackles himself. Ira tried desperately to express his message with a look but became distracted at the sight of his sister being chained.

"There is no need—"

"I will decide what there is a need for, Prince Ira!" barked Zaccai. "You and the princess are already in violation of your exile! It is a privilege that I allow you to draw breath after the treachery you and your kin have committed!" The galleymaster turned to Halruc with a look of utter disgust. "You, Master Halruc, will accompany us aboard the galley *Requiarda*."

Halruc made no protest but asked in an almost indifferent tone, "Am I also under arrest, Gailaum Zaccai?" The man did not answer him but gestured the dwarf towards the step ladder still hung upon the ship's ledge. "What is to become of my crew?" the master asked casually, as though all that had taken place was not of the slightest concern to him.

"The torlaum and the mariners will stay aboard your ship until I have uncovered their innocence or complacency in this grievous crime." said the galleymaster.

At that moment, Ram rushed forward and pleadingly addressed the man.

"We knew nothing of who these two were!" the dwarf hollered indignantly. "By the Light, I swear—"

"That is enough, Ram!" growled Halruc.

Zaccai did not appear disturbed by this outburst but eyed the sailor curiously before beckoning the master again towards the step ladder. Halruc obeyed without another word as Ira was lifted from his knees and shoved across the deck beside Esther. Ira chanced one last look at the crew and immediately wished he had refrained.

Halruc descended the ladder into the rowboat first, followed by Zaccai, then Ira, Esther, and the pair of mariners accompanying them. The prince and princess took longer to climb down, what with their hands so tightly bound. When all were seated in the boat, the mariners began rowing. Within no time at all, their meager transport was bobbing beside the pristine hull of the regal warship. A step ladder was already mounted for them upon the galley's ledge. Esther went first this time, with Ira following closely behind. Their chains jingled against the steps as they steadily heaved themselves up towards the deck. As Ira ascended alongside the galley, his first inclination was to admire the craftsmanship that had born her. There was not a crack or gap all along the polished cedar planks. His youth had been filled with dreams of commanding such a vessel, battling hordes of pirates, and conducting expeditions into uncharted waters. But as Ira landed on an all-too-familiar deck flooded with blue-clad soldiers, the dreams of that intrepid boy faded into dreadful reality.

The galley *Requiarda* was far wider than the *Wayfarer* and more than twice as long. The deck was flat, with the helmsman and his rudder oars level with the rest of the ship rather than raised on a quarterdeck like most merchant vessels. A gap in the center of the deck stretched the ship's length, affording a narrow view into the lower levels, where at least a hundred resting rowers sat gulping from their waterskins. Down below, behind the hortator and his drum, were the officers' quarters and a small cabin brimming with armaments. Every mariner, be he elf, dwarf, or man, carried a glittering gladius by his side at all times. Spears, bows, and shields hung in the lower deck, ready to be taken up at a moment's notice.

Zaccai was the last to emerge on deck and at once led the party of Ira, Esther, and Halruc through the sea of stares. They passed the helmsman and reached the stern of the galley, where an arched canopy was propped over an ornate desk and chair. It seemed the galleymaster was to question the three infractors together rather than separately. At first glance, the study's canopy appeared to be a simple cloth of the same hue as every other sapphire stitch aboard the warship. As Ira looked more closely, however, he noted several delicate weavings upon the fabric, culminating in a grand tapestry. Before he could make out the patterns and shapes, the galleymaster cleared his throat loudly. He was not seated behind the desk as Ira had expected but standing erect at Halruc's side, eyeing the desk intently. The meaning of this was lost to Ira until his eyes adjusted to the study's darkness enough to discern another figure already seated before them.

Behind the desk, preoccupied with the composition of a lengthy letter, was an elven officer. His helmet sat on one corner of the desk, and his sheen of mahogany hair was tied back behind a pearly cape. Ira recognized the cape immediately, as well as the tassels hung upon the elf's polished belt. The admiral looked to be roughly the same age as himself, making him quite possibly the youngest appointed to his station in the history of the Haurthian Navy. Zaccai cleared his throat once more to announce their presence, and the admiral lifted his gaze shortly. He scrawled his last words on the parchment before him, set down the reed, and offered his full attention to the galleymaster.

"Praelaum," began Zaccai, "it is my unfortunate duty to report the uncovering of numerous violations aboard this merchant vessel. Firstly, the ship's proprietor, Master Halruc, and every one of his servants have neglected to report to their magistrates' offices for the census. Secondly, the—"

But the galleymaster was cut off by the admiral before he could continue.

"Thank you, Gailaum Zaccai," the elf said sedately, "but I should prefer you to relate these violations to me one at a time. This way, I might hear each report in full and address every charge before continuing onto the others." Less than enthused yet understanding this to be an order rather than a mere suggestion, Zaccai inclined his head cordially. Then, turning to the dwarf, the admiral went on. "You understand, Master Halruc, that failure to comply with a mandated census is a most serious offense against Haurthian law. What justification can you offer for your crew's collective failure to abide by the empire's ordinance?"

Zaccai opened his mouth to speak, but the elf beckoned him to remain silent.

"As I have already informed the gailaum," began Halruc, "when my vessel departed from Gales almost three weeks ago, there had been no proclamation of a census anywhere in the provinces. We were none of us aware of being in any violation of empire law; otherwise, my ship should never have set out."

The admiral nodded kindly to the dwarf as he considered this.

"Under normal circumstances, this would seem a perfectly reasonable explanation." With this, the elf glanced momentarily at Ira and Esther, their wrists bound in chains. "However, it would seem there is more to the story than a premature departure from the provinces. I presume, gailaum, this man and woman have a role to play in the other allegations you have to bring forward."

"Indeed, praelaum," said Zaccai bitterly as he crossed the study to stand beside the seated admiral to face the accused. "What this dwarf neglected to mention is that two in his service are the banished children of the malevolent Emperor Darius. They and Master Halruc have been in violation of Haurthian law since the moment they set sail."

At this, Esther stared helplessly at the planks under her feet. Zaccai handed over the prisoners' documents for the admiral to examine. Outside the study, the sea breeze brushed against the canopy, rattling the tapestry noisily as it blew. After combing the papers extensively, the elf's inquisitive gaze shifted to Ira, then to Esther, and then between the two several more times. This reaction, it seemed, was less than the galleymaster had expected and hoped for, and so Zaccai again raised his authoritative voice.

"Had we not intercepted this vessel, praelaum, the prince and princess would have harbored in Eou Verás despite their banishment from the Realm of Haurth. No doubt, the disgraced children of the last emperor know full well that they cannot pass undetected by the port inspectors. There can be no rational reason for their voyaging this far without a plan to avoid detainment, and I suspect I have uncovered that plan. Halruc confessed that his ship, when we met it, was sailing to Jade to obtain repairs he could readily receive in the Hallowed City. So costly a divergence from his commissioned course must hold some greater reason and intent. I suggest that the prince and princess bribed the dwarf to take them as far as Jade so they might acquire further transport to some remote part of the Westlands from there."

It was then that Halruc finally traded his steady candor for a tone of sheer indignation.

"I have held my tongue up until now," he said in his gravelly voice, "but I will not stand for the slander of my reputation! The *Wayfarer* has never seen a bribe under my command, nor shall she ever!"

"Furthermore," Zaccai continued over the dwarf, "the mere presence of the prince and princess aboard a vessel crossing the Bridging Sea is a clear infraction of empire law. As per the ordinance barring the passage of any citizen with a criminal record—"

"I know perfectly well what is dictated in the laws of our empire, Gailaum Zaccai," said the admiral patiently. "You are speaking in reference to that ordinance that was enacted to apprehend Horde raiders and any suspected to be affiliated with the ruffians' band. As I recall, that law led to the capture of many pirates who had commandeered trade vessels so as to lure passing ships into unknowing traps. Tell me, gailaum, have you any reason to suspect Prince Ira or Princess Esther to be in any way associated with the Pirate Horde?"

"I . . . I do not," said Zaccai sourly. "But, praelaum, it still holds true that the prisoners had every intention of willfully harboring in the Realm of Haurth against the terms of their banishment. I need hardly add that Master Halruc is directly responsible for enabling this felony. Neither master nor servant has condemned this accusation as false, and I firmly propose we detain this dwarf immediately so we might escort all three to Alaoth at once."

Ira was not preoccupied with thoughts of how the galleymaster had pieced together the near entirety of the arrangement Nathanael had struck with Halruc. He had no thoughts for what might become of Halruc when he inevitably faced trial for abetting their scheme. He was not even concerned about what might be running through Esther's mind at the moment of their imminent ruin. His sole focus was on the admiral, silently contemplating the magnitude of their crimes.

"It occurs to me," said the elf after a long while, "that the prisoners have not yet been offered a say against any of the charges laid before them. Prince Ira, Princess Esther, I invite you now to speak freely."

Having been drowned in a sea of others' voices for so long, Ira knew not where to begin. He tried to summon some answer—any answer to serve as their aid—but not before Esther raised her voice.

"There was no bribe," she said simply. "Halruc's employment of us was entirely legitimate. My brother and I were each promised a fair share of the commission upon our return to Gales."

"I see," said the admiral, and with a note of curiosity, he continued. "And why do you suppose Master Halruc allowed two such infamous figures entry into his service?"

"That, I believe, only my master could answer for."

All eyes turned toward Halruc. The dwarf gave careful consideration to his words before voicing them aloud.

"Who Ira and Esther were before they came to serve aboard my ship is of no interest to me. When I first met them, I was assured of their trustworthiness, and I have not since been disappointed. They have each earned my respect to a degree seldom found anywhere across the Bridging Sea."

"Be that as it may," muttered Zaccai, "it does not change the gravity of the charges you and your—"

"For how many voyages have Ira and Esther been in your service, Master Halruc?"

Something in the admiral's inflection seemed to prompt a particular answer to this query. Ira could not comprehend. This was, of course, to be their only voyage in Halruc's service. Had there been others . . . And then it dawned on him. With a final desperate hope, Ira answered for his master.

"Esther and I came to serve aboard the *Wayfarer* some years ago," he said firmly. "In that time, we have labored for him along a number of voyages."

Zaccai was utterly dumbstruck by the gall of such an admission. "Is this true?" he demanded of Halruc. "You have employed and harbored these felons for the span of several years?"

After a moment's consideration, Halruc hesitantly replied, "Aye, this is true."

"And did any of these commissions take your ship to the ports of the Westlands?" asked the admiral.

"Aye, a few," answered an unsure Halruc, "as well as a number to the northern provinces."

"Well," said the galleymaster, "I shall be sure to include this in my report to the arbiter. A trial may not be necessary with a witnessed admission of guilt."

"On the account of there not being a trial, we are agreed, Gailaum Zaccai," said the admiral, "though it would seem we differ on our reasonings. This new information strikes me as an affirmation of innocence rather than a proclamation of guilt. Had the prince and princess even once stepped foot on Western soil, they would have rightly been apprehended by port inspectors and tried for violating their banishment. Master Halruc, as well, would have been arrested as an accessory to their crime. As neither has occurred in all of their voyages, it would seem the brother and sister have never disembarked from their vessel while anchored in lands they were forbidden to enter. Am I correct in this assumption?" With adamant certainty in their answers, all three of the accused nodded their heads. "Well then," continued the admiral, "it would seem Ira and Esther have indeed adhered to the terms of their exile from Haurth. Albeit," the elf raised a hand to quell an outburst from the galleymaster, "rather loosely. But at this time, I find no reason to prosecute this master or his faithful servants. Laumin, unshackle this man and woman at once."

Ira fought to restrain his urge to rejoice as the mariner behind him unlocked the chains around his and Esther's wrists. They smiled at one another, but as he looked at his master, Ira saw that Halruc remained as impassive as when he had been on the verge of a criminal trial. Zaccai, meanwhile, was in a state of infuriated shock. Before he could whisper a word of protest into the admiral's ear, the elf raised his voice again.

"I would like to add that it would be most unwise for the prince and princess to remain in your service after this voyage, Master Halruc. While I have not found sufficient cause to prosecute, it is a delicate line of the law that you tread on in your employment of them. Upon your return to Gales, I expect Ira and Esther to seek their fortunes elsewhere, far from the shores of Haurth. Do I have your word?"

"Praelaum, I wish to question the other sailors in this dwarf's service," said the galleymaster adamantly, "so we might confirm whether or not—"

"I have given my verdict, Zaccai," proclaimed the admiral. "Let the matter rest."

The galleymaster silently fumed behind the admiral's chair as Halruc dared to speak once more to the elf.

"You are most fair, praelaum," he said graciously, "but if I may ask one final indulgence of you. Would you permit me to send one of your messenger birds to my vendors in the Hallowed City? I wish to convey to them the circumstances of my failure to deliver on schedule."

"Of course. If it be your wish, I should be glad to authenticate each letter with my signature and seal. Gailaum, would you see that Master Halruc is given parchment and reed? And have an osprey fetched from below deck. In the meantime, I would like to have a private word with Ira and Esther as they wait for their master."

Begrudgingly, Zaccai accompanied Halruc and the two mariners out of the tent, flatly refusing to glance at either Ira or Esther as he went. Alone in the study, the elf arose from his seat and stood tall behind his desk.

"Praelaum," began Esther, "we cannot thank you enough for—"

But the admiral quieted her with a respectful raise of his hand and a gentle "please." Then, peering over Ira's shoulder to observe if there were any outside the study within earshot, the elf spoke in an undertone.

"Regardless of your release, I hope the both of you are fully aware of the danger you placed yourselves in by voyaging this close to the Westlands. Under another's judgment, the consequences may have been dire. I ask for no gratitude or debt for my verdict, only that you adhere to my warning. For your sake, I beg you to never again sail upon these waters."

Perhaps it was the admiral's sincerity that prompted Ira to speak with a degree of candor he had not felt warranted until this moment.

"Why have you redeemed us, praelaum?" he asked. "We who are so reviled in the eyes of the empire."

"Retribution should not be eagerly sought. Blood for the sake of blood serves only to corrupt the soul. Furthermore, I do not believe the sins of a father ought to be cast upon his children. I judged what stood before me, and I found no guilt."

As he said this, the admiral met Esther's eyes without so much as a flinch towards the long mark beneath her veil.

When Halruc had composed the last of his letters, the admiral authenticated each and placed them into a leather pouch fastened to a seahawk's tawny back. The mariners watched suspiciously as Ira and Esther freely crossed the galley's deck at the admiral's side while the officers muttered to one another in disbelieving tones. It seemed Zaccai had already shared the details of the former prisoners' identities, if not also the circumstances of their release. The galleymaster signaled across the way to the dwarven officer still aboard the *Wayfarer* that he and his mariners were to return to the galley *Requiarda*. Before their parting, Halruc and the admiral exchanged a few quiet words, which ended in a mutual bow. As Esther made to follow Halruc down the step ladder, the admiral offered his hand to help her over the ship's ledge. With a final gracious look at the elf, Ira descended the steps, followed by the mariners who would return them to their vessel.

The sailors' surprise at their master's return was nothing compared to their shock at the release of the prince and princess. With a sour reluctance, the officer and his mariners returned to their rowboat, each with a harsh scowl etched under their helmets. When the crew was once again alone, there was no discussion and no questioning of any kind. Bewilderment was the expression of some, and for others, incredulity. As he and Esther stood apart from their onlookers, Ira thought it had been infinitely easier to stare down the glowering galleymaster than to face the disdain of his fellow crewmates. But as the murmuring sailors returned to their posts or leisures, the deepest cut was felt by Esther as the lad came forward to return *Fables of the West* before silently trudging away.

Under the dusk, rays of moonlight cascaded over the watery plain's surface, reflecting a mesmerizing gleam upon the polished planks of the galley *Requiarda*. The main deck was nearly deserted, but for the pair of elven mariners standing watch upon the bow and two dwarven soldiers posted outside the admiral's study. One of the dwarves struggled to remain alert as he listened to the soft brushing of waves against the hull and the shuffling of parchment behind him. Another noise, that of creaking steps ascending from the lower deck, renewed the drowsy mariner's vigilance at once. Two figures emerged on deck, their armor basking in the radiant night light. As the young elven officer strode towards the bow, Zaccai stepped into the admiral's lantern-lit study.

"All rowers are settled in for the night, praelaum, as are those mariners not due on watch tonight."

"Very good, gailaum. That will be all for the evening. You are relieved."

The elf resumed shuffling several marked letters over a comprehensive map of the Bridging Sea until he found the one he sought. He examined the report in one hand while tracing a vessel's course upon the map with the other. As he marked with a reed the current whereabouts of the galley noted in the letter, the admiral's attention was diverted by Zaccai's frozen figure. The graying man was preoccupied with the sapphire tapestry draped over their heads. The delicate weavings of a noted Western artisan portrayed several primitive ships with sails of red, blue, or black surrounding a monstrous snake of sea green. In the Realm of Haurth, monumental triumphs and tragedies of old were often memorialized in some form of the arts.

"May I offer you a drink, Zaccai?" asked the admiral.

With a short but cordial "No, I thank you, sir," Zaccai returned his gaze to the ornate tapestry. The elf watched the man briefly before setting down the reed and the letter. He rose and fetched from the table in the corner a small jug emanating a floral scent. The admiral poured the scarlet nectar into two tankards and offered one to Zaccai, who quietly accepted it. The man drank heavily from it before lowering it from his lips to watch the drink of the Western vineyards sway in his mug. The elf also took a sip before placing his own tankard on the desk, away from the parchment and the map.

"Zaccai, should you wish to address your praelaum verily, I would have you do so in the privacy of such a moment as this."

The galleymaster considered the proposal momentarily before speaking to his admiral in a tone ripe with concern.

"Very well, praelaum. If I am allowed to speak with a certain degree of liberty, I must confess that I cannot quell my reservations concerning our release of the prince and princess."

The admiral considered his companion before asking, "Would these reservations be considered objections were you speaking to another?" The hesitant galleymaster made no answer to the inquiry, and so the admiral continued. "What are your ambitions, Zaccai?"

"I beg your pardon, sir?"

"Your ambitions. Your aims as gailaum of the galley *Requiarda* and as a servant to the Realm of Haurth?"

"What does any soldier yearn for, praelaum? To have his name and conquests immortalized in stone, painted upon walls, and stitched into tapestries. To hail grand victories and to give all glory to the empire."

"Valiant pursuits," remarked the admiral, "no less than I would expect of a faithful servant such as yourself. Personally, it is of little concern to me whether I am revered or forgotten in the annals of history. It is not my endeavor to be remembered as anything but a loyal servant to the empire who met the challenges of his day with honor and dignity. Duty to others ought to always precede the glory of self. The latter shall follow in due course if it is well merited."

"Naturally," agreed Zaccai, "but Praelaum Ambrose, we are commissioned to defend the integrity of our empire across the sea and lands. Setting free two banished traitors, while deemed just in your eyes, might be considered differently by others. Would it not have been more favorable to allow the arbiter or the High Court their say on the matter?"

"It was considered," said Ambrose thoughtfully, "but I stand by my verdict. The law is written, Zaccai, and we are merely its humble deliverers. Furthermore, in my years of service, I have found that mercy tends to yield fruit where others have declared the soil barren. The prince and princess will return to the provinces, never again to cross these waters, and so the matter is ended. Peace, Zaccai, will endure so long as conviction and clemency are justly dealt."

The call of an osprey sounded over the canopy as the admiral and the galleymaster stood in silent reflection. After taking another sip from his tankard, Zaccai said, "I believe I shall turn in now. Good night, praelaum."

"Good night, gailaum. You have served your empire well today. Rest so you might serve her again tomorrow."

With a bow, the man turned and set off across the deck and down the steps to his quarters. As Ambrose made to return to his charts and reports, the young elven officer requested entry into the study. He was bidden to enter and offered the admiral a scroll and a short letter only just arrived by messenger bird. Ambrose dismissed the officer and opened the letter first. A chilling draft wafted across the stern of the galley as the disquieted elf dropped the letter in hand to unfurl the scroll and read a copy of a new ordinance bearing six marks of the High Court.

CHAPTER IX

THE CAVERN OF SOULS

Hardly a whisper had passed from the Temple of Érosai into the streets of Eou Verás since the night so widely discussed. News of the failed attempt on the premier's life had first met a baker in the city early the following morning. One of the temple servants sent on an errand had been quick to share what little he knew of the night's happenings. By midday, the vague yet captivating story had reached the ears of all throughout the Hallowed City. Rumor overcame truth in the ensuing gossip, and those elves and dwarves who reserved themselves to only what was known as fact had more questions than answers for their chattering neighbors. What was observed and reiterated countless times over was that no civilian had since set eyes on the premier, Lady Filia, or any of the governors. Moreover, temple sentries were now charged with fulfilling those errands in the city formerly designated to the servants.

Once repetitious discussion and speculation had grown dry and tasteless, talk of the assault in the premier's bedchamber began to subside. To an outsider of the Hallowed City, it might have appeared as though the population had returned to a relative state of normalcy. One notable difference, however, was the civilians' ceaseless attempts to glimpse something or someone of consequence within the temple grounds. The courtyard appeared perpetually vacant from the crowded plaza, with not even a temple priest in sight. Nevertheless, the sentries posted about the grounds and the plaza had the frequent task of ushering citizens along their way should they linger in their daily passages.

One night, a week after the city was first flooded with rumors, a tight swarm of five tall figures emerged under cover of darkness from the temple's towering archway. Trotting down the steps and into the plaza, the sentries led the way, with the premier in a dark traveling cloak at their center. Through the icy morn, the escort marched along one of the many paved streets. Their journey would not be brief, but a chariot would surely have awoken many slumbering citizens and drawn undesired attention. As they came to the outskirts of town, the dwellings thinned until the road split into two paths of trodden earth, both leading towards the northern range. The wider of the two led on a gentle incline towards the pass set between two towering peaks. The premier and his guards passed up this road to follow a narrow trail winding eastward along the mountainside.

Sandals trod through the tall grasses that concealed the shallow path. Boring mountain gales rattled those sprouting greens engulfing the elves' bare legs. The higher the party trekked, the more their bodies leaned into the swelling gusts billowing over and around the protruding boulders scattered along the range. As the city behind them grew distant, the night sky began to fringe along the sea to the east. When the colors of the day had nearly surfaced over the watery edge, the company came upon its destination. Built into the green and gray mountain at the end of the path was a chiseled stone wall with a mighty door. One of the sentries stepped forward and pounded his fist thrice upon the thick slab of granite. Awaiting an admittance, the escort stood with the lofty breeze against them as the soft chirps of the warblers greeted them. The sentry made ready to pound again when the granite door opened with a shrill scraping noise. A uniformed dwarf faced the five, a burning lantern held aloft to shine on the faces of the new arrivals.

"Yes?" the dwarf muttered in a low and tired voice.

"The premier and his escort," announced the sentry, "requesting entry to the cavern."

The dwarf stifled a yawn as he stepped aside. The arrivals crossed the threshold into a lantern-lit corridor burrowing into the heart of the mountain. As the dwarf heaved the massive door shut behind them, the feel of the peaks' breath was instantly lost, replaced by dank air dripping upon the elves' skin.

"This way," said the dwarf, leading the company down the flickering corridor. The guard's escort was hardly necessary, as there were no alternate passageways along the way to turn into. As they marched, they passed nearly a dozen other dwarves seated on benches underneath hanging lanterns. Bows were propped against the carven walls, and one of the guards was snoring loudly as they passed. As the premier's face came to be recognized in the lantern light, the other guards bolted to their feet and stood with unflinching attentiveness. Still slumbering soundly, the last guard was awoken as he received a swift kick from one of his companions, though the escort paid it little mind. The further they delved into the mountain's core, the more laborious the elves' breathing grew. Their kind was not so acclimated to this sort of encroaching environment as the race that had carved these passageways during the Battle of the Blooming Vale.

When they finally reached the corridor's end, the escort stood in a wide circular den with a large desk and several branching pathways. The office, while dim, was notably brighter than the rest of the cavern. From behind the desk stood yet another dwarf.

The warden bowed low as Lysias stepped forward from his place between the sentries.

"Premier," said the warden with a second courteous bow, "my guards and I stand humbled and honored to serve you. You are here to see the prisoner, Jesse, are you not?"

"Do not presume to be privy to what business the premier holds upon his visits, warden," stated the premier with a peeved glance. Before the warden could voice a thousand apologies for his forwardness, the elf went on. "But as it happens, your presumptions would be correct. Which cell does the prisoner reside in?"

"Number twenty-six," answered the warden eagerly, "allow me to escort you personally."

"Thank you."

As the company followed the warden through and along one of the passages hailing from his office, Lysias strode with the hand of his injured arm resting upon his sheathed gladius. Since the night of the attack, the sword etched in gold had hardly left his side for even a moment. The dark jewel encrusted in the hilt did not reflect the lantern blazes as they marched down a narrow stairwell. Occasionally, a small hole in the walls would feed spurts of fresh gales into the passageways, only to be lost to the flood of dense, torrid air filling the mountain. The corridor turned, and they came upon a guard posted outside the door marked twenty-six. Ordering him aside, the warden inserted a rusted key into the lock, turned it, and hurled the iron door open.

A grotesque smell seeped out of the aged cell. Even the warden could not repress the faintest of retches as he stood aside. Two of the sentries went first, and the premier bid the other two to wait for them in the passageway. Lysias stepped into the moldy cell and, to his surprise, found an old lantern burning on the damp stone floor. Prisoners were hardly ever afforded the luxury of light in the Cavern of Souls. No cell within the mountain had ever seen a drop of sunlight. In the faint firelight, Lysias made out the figure of a young man propped against the wall opposite the door, with the two sentries standing on either side of him.

Jesse's face had grown thin, his hair ragged. The servant's hands appeared boney enough that, had he the strength, he might slip them through the shackles binding him to the cell wall. A plate with a slice of rotting bread lay untouched beside a tin tankard of water. The prisoner glanced lazily at his new visitor and immediately lost interest at the sight of the premier. Distracted first by the ghastly sight of the young man, Lysias had not taken notice of another figure lurking in the corner of the cell. The stranger's dark cloak shrouded his body, even by the light of the lantern at his feet. Only a fine braid of ashen hair reflected his presence as Anthazar turned to face the visitor with mild shock.

"Premier," the governor said with a short bow, his voice incapable of hiding his surprise at the newcomer. Lysias neither bowed nor spoke, but his hand rested upon the hilt of his sword, clutching it tightly at the sight of the man. The elf stood paralyzed in the doorway, his eyes shifting between governor and prisoner. "Well," Anthazar said hastily, "it appears you have another visitor, and I believe I have outstayed my welcome."

The governor refastened his cloak and strode towards the doorway. As he made to leave, he found his way blocked by the premier, still fixed in the threshold. The elf's eyes flickered as he read those parts of the man illuminated by the lonely flame. Shadows painting one side of the governor's stoic face lent him a weary appearance. Anthazar stood uncomfortably still before the one in his way until the premier leaned close to whisper in his ear.

"Did I not instruct you and the rest of the court to remain in hiding until you received my summons?"

"So you did, premier," replied the governor nervously. "I beg your forgiveness for my lapse. We are all restless with questions unanswered, you most of all, I imagine. Perhaps we may convene at my villa after your session with the prisoner. There is some knowledge I wish to share with you and the court. Now, if you will excuse me, I will be off. I do not much care for these mountain ways."

This much was apparent. Anthazar's breathing was deepening and quickening the longer he stood before the premier. Feeling those same effects that were festering in the man, Lysias stepped aside.

"I will not be long," the premier noted. "Wait a while longer, and the sentries may see us both back to the city."

Though visibly uneager to remain in the cavern any longer than necessary, Anthazar nodded his assent. He joined the sentries in the passage as the warden shut the door with an echoing clang. Lysias stared at the prisoner, taking in the fullness of those haunting effects that had plagued his features in only one short week. Despite his being deprived of any company in that time, it was abundantly clear that Jesse's only yearning in this moment was to return to his solitude.

"Up," commanded the premier.

The young man did not so much as blink as he stared emptily into the corner of the cramped cell. A swift kick from one of the sentries caused the young man to recoil in pain before he begrudgingly rose to his feet, staggering a bit as he stood. Jesse's face contorted to appear firm in the face of his adversary, but there was no mistaking the toll the cavern had already taken on him.

"You are not eating," remarked the premier, nodding to the plate of untouched bread. Jesse made no reply but glared disdainfully at the elf before him. "Arrogance in the face of defeat is a most childish ploy. I had hoped these walls might offer you some time for reflection, yet I find no evidence of it. That said, it seems the mountain has at least managed to tame that wicked tongue of yours."

Jesse drew a long, hoarse breath before opening his cracked lips. "Defeat?" The dry and feeble voice stole what little youth still lingered in the man's withering body. "You would have me believe that I have been thwarted—that all of this was for none. The Premier of Haurth would have me rot in a cell or hang by the rope so the cause of liberation might die with me. But I am not alone in this cell, nor am I alone out there. You know the truth in what I told you that night in the temple. You would not be here if you believed it to be a lie."

"There was never any doubt in your motives or your radical convictions," said the premier. "I can only presume the same sentiment extends to the rabble you have aligned yourself with in the provinces. But no matter; with your assistance, I am sure we can quell the efforts of any other brigand who might seek to bring the Haurthian Empire to ruin."

Jesse let out a single sardonic bellow that, in a healthier body, might have resembled a laugh.

"Is this the bargain you expect me to snatch up? That I should live as an informant and a puppet to serve the whims of the High Court? The fires of rebellion have been set ablaze, thanks to me. My name will forever be heralded by the people who have longed for freedom from your empire for generations."

"Pride does not become you, boy," said the premier. "Because of your actions, two dozen vessels carrying the finest soldiers of

Haurth are sailing for the ports as we speak. They will snuff out those traitors you have aligned—"

"My actions?" barked Jesse. "You and your governors were the ones who sought to invade and occupy the Eastlands, to enslave those who spoke against your tyranny. I—"

"Your actions were precisely what deemed it necessary to deploy the legions. The Provincial Guard has failed to root out the sickness plaguing the Eastlands, so it falls to the uniforms of Haurth to reinstate peace once more. Should your accomplices attempt to hide, the mariners will track them down. Should they raise arms against us, I shall purge the fortress armory of its every weapon to quell their attacks. When all is done, my mariners will have restored the union to its former glory. You and your accomplices have only yourselves to blame for what is to come. Do you still believe you will be championed as a martyr for the tribulations you have brought upon your homeland?"

The iron links rattled violently as Jesse's hands shot for the premier's throat. His lunge was abruptly halted by the chain's end tethering him to the wall and a blunt jab to the gut from one of the sentries' sword hilts. Jesse curled over onto his knees, sputtering and gasping for air.

"The occupation has been set into motion. There is nothing you can do to prevent it now. The legions will comb the lands in search of your accomplices, starting with those named in the letters we recovered from your quarters in the villa. Your kin in the Province of Anthazar will also be taken into custody and questioned for good measure. Make no mistake; I take no pleasure in performing these duties. I have no wish to see the ports needlessly ransacked. The innocent should not suffer to protect the guilty from their due justice. However, occupations can be ruthless dealings, even for the guiltless. I offer you this one chance to do right by the people you claim to care for. In exchange for your kin being spared a cell beside your own, you will offer up the names and whereabouts of every seditionist ally you have ever come across, as well as any citizen who has ever championed or aided your cause in the slightest. Upon their apprehension, they too will offer up the names of those they have plotted alongside. Once this treachery has been thoroughly purged from the lands, I shall recall the legions at once and reinstitute the governance of the Provincial Guard. Those who have remained loyal to the empire will be free to begin a new chapter of peace in the Eastlands. But until that time, my mariners will scour the lands for those who would see this empire brought to ashes."

The prisoner, still panting violently, mustered the strength to raise his head so he might glare at the elf standing above him.

"By the Light," hissed Jesse, "I shall rot in this cell for all eternity before I betray my brothers to their deaths."

With a disappointed sigh, Lysias tapped a finger upon the gladius sheathed at his side. "What business did Governor Anthazar wish to discuss with you?" asked the elf.

As Jesse looked up at the premier, a twisted smile grew upon his cracked and bleeding lips. "Surely, you would not trust the word of a man who nearly stole your life."

The tapping of the elf's finger ceased at once as a choleric grimace spread across his pale face.

"A galley will soon arrive to escort you to Alaoth. You will spend what remains of your miserable life there in a cell such as this. I shall return once more to see you off before your departure. If you do not surrender your allies by then, the innocents who suffer will suffer on your behalf."

The premier nodded to the sentries who marched from Jesse's side to the cell door and pounded on it. Taking the aged lantern with him, Lysias stepped through the threshold into the narrow passage as the warden locked the door behind him. The dense air no longer tasted of aged mold, though Lysias felt it clinging to his skin still.

"If you will follow me, premier," said the warden genially, "I shall see you back at once. The governor is awaiting you in my office as we speak."

Lysias hardly noticed the steps he took as he followed the warden and the sentries back the way they came. They entered the wide circular den and found Anthazar alone in deep thought.

"Very good," the governor said at the sight of his party. "Thank you for your time, warden. We shall be on our way now."

"If I may encroach upon the warden's hospitality a while longer," said the premier to the dwarf, "I should like a moment to speak with the governor. Warden, might we use your office for a private word?"

The dwarf eagerly obliged them as he and the sentries shuffled into the long corridor to ensure none of the other guards disturbed the members of the court. When they two were alone, the premier's demeanor towards the governor at once turned cold and cynical.

"You have willfully disobeyed me by coming here tonight, Anthazar," spat the elf.

"Premier—" began the governor.

"Under the shroud of night and against my explicit commands . . ."

"That is not—"

"What other secrets have you kept from the court? For how long have you been convening with the assassin? Answer me!"

Anthazar took a deep breath before uttering, "Every night since the attack."

A boiling rage seared in the elf's chest. He turned from the governor, unwilling to face the one who had defied him so, who had communed secretly and repeatedly with his assailant.

"And when," snarled the premier, "did you intend to inform the court of your conventions with the traitor?"

"The moment I had collected that knowledge that we have sought for a week now," stated Anthazar firmly. "Despite my best efforts, Jesse has hardly yielded anything more than what we learned that first night."

"But you have collected some knowledge of consequence?"

"I believe so. He did not divulge much, but I can confidently say that Jesse was not exaggerating when he spoke of the numbers his movement is garnering. He boasted of there being some hundreds at least aligned with the seditionists somewhere in Anthazar. And his correspondents across the other provinces would suggest there being some thousands conspiring across the Eastlands."

The elf's grasp upon his sword grew tighter with the governor's every word.

"And did the prisoner offer up where these conspirators may be found? Certainly, for a movement as large as this, there must have been gatherings of some kind."

"Jesse would not say. I have not yet earned that degree of his trust, though I believe I am making progress."

"There are other means of procuring the whereabouts of these traitors," the premier uttered in a hostile tone.

"I imagine," said the governor hastily, ignoring the elf's dark implication, "that crowds of such magnitude could not assemble in remote areas without drawing attention to themselves. It seems we were correct in assuming the ports would serve as their cover and haven."

"And yet," said the premier softly, "that does not dismiss the possibility of fellow conspirators residing beyond the ports."

"No. No, I suppose not."

The two stood in mute contemplation, listening to the soft whistles of the breeze blowing through the burrowing air holes of the mountain.

"So, this is the force that stands against us," said the premier. "I do not hide the fact that I am thoroughly vexed by your approach to retrieving this information. However, I am appeased in one respect. That your sessions with the prisoner have brought you some peace of mind regarding the occupation. Now, the court may proceed with the census in unity."

But the countenance of the ashen-haired man was anything but peaceful.

"Premier, you do not mean to say that you still consider the legions' occupation a prudent course of action?"

"Unreservedly," stated the elf.

"How can this be, knowing now the numbers that grow in our opposition? This is not some rogue band of agitators to be dealt with swiftly. These are thousands of dispirited men who require only the smallest of sparks to ignite a revolt that would divide our empire forever! If we are not careful—"

"If the mariners do not act now," interjected the premier, "and snuff out these seditionists, their numbers will grow still. Once they have amassed an army greater than our own, they will revolt to oppress the Westlands with vile tyranny."

"They wish for no such thing; Jesse has already attested to that. These men yearn for liberation so they might establish their own rule. They have no aims to dictate the governance of Haurth."

"And you would trust the words of a traitor to the empire? One who would gladly see your governance overthrown?"

"It is not too late for an appeasement," pleaded the governor. "Call for ambassadors from the Eastlands to join us in the Hallowed City. Let us hear out Jesse's allies, and we may yet avoid bloodshed."

"No ambassador will ever again enter the Temple of Érosai," said the premier darkly, "not at the invitation of a ruler they despise. Nor shall I meet these brigands on their shores. Bloodshed has already come to our doorstep, Anthazar, or have you forgotten that it was that prisoner who first drew swords against this empire?"

"The act of one misguided soul. Are thousands to pay the price for Jesse's transgressions?"

"You do not think that if afforded the opportunity, his companions would slay every member of the High Court? Or do the lives of the premier and his lady weigh so light compared to that of an assassin?"

"I . . . I . . . ," stammered the governor. "I will make no excuses for Jesse's actions, and I will gladly see him pay for his attempt on your life and Lady Filia's. But the governors and I were appointed by you to serve the interests of our homelands. The moment the legions begin scouting the provinces for those who question the empire, it will be seen as the first sign of a civil war. I beg you, premier, postpone the ordinance until we have had an audience with the seditionist leaders."

His knuckles white upon the hilt of the gladius, the premier took a calming breath before replying. "Any opportunity for peace is behind us."

The elf extended his other hand to place upon the governor's shoulder consolingly, but Anthazar recoiled in a fit of rage.

"This is madness!" the man shouted, his voice echoing in the dome above. "Are you so prepared to fracture the last sliver of trust our people hold in us? Open your eyes, Lysias!"

Instantaneous regret came over the governor as a throbbing pain grew in his chest, the elf's steely glower bearing down upon him.

"You take too much liberty, Malachi." hissed the premier. "Coming here in secret, fraternizing with a murderous traitor, openly defying the commands of your premier. Consider your loyalties when next you unleash that wild tongue of yours."

Anthazar's remorse for his own unflattering outburst was chased away by the elf's callous remark. With cold tenacity, he uttered, "I serve at the behest of the premier, but I do not answer to the ruler of the Westlands. My loyalties will always align with those of the citizens of Anthazar. As bleak as the future may look for our empire, this governor shall never draw swords against his own people."

And turning from the elf, he strode down the flickering corridor and through the distant doorway leading to the winding mountain trail.

CHAPTER X

THE LAST EMPEROR

The sailors aboard the *Wayfarer* no longer savored the taste of salt in the air. Its tang on their lips served as a ceaseless reminder of their coming so close to a prosperous commission, only to be cast off with nothing to show for their labors. To make matters worse, the master had proclaimed that their voyage was to be further prolonged. The *Wayfarer* was not to return immediately to Gales. They were first to make for the Forager's Cove to restock their supply of fresh water and provisions before carrying on to the Port of Mason. It was Halruc's belief that several of their goods might garner a moderate price in the northern provinces. While the crew privately dreaded the extension of their journey, the master's gambit to abate destitution was not met with any expressed opposition.

By all accounts, the sailors had begrudgingly accepted that they would receive no compensation when, at last, they harbored in Gales. The goods long stowed in the hold would be fortunate to scrounge prices half what Halruc had paid for them. If all the cargo was offloaded in Mason, it might only be enough to offer the master the chance to secure another commission that might save the *Wayfarer*. After all the toils they had endured to come so far and lose so much, the jaded sailors were content to offer their labors further. For the master to profit enough so they might remain in his service was enough for them, at least for the time being.

The routines aboard the merchant vessel carried on as usual, except for the new habit of sailors falling silent in the company of the outed children of Darius the Damned. Ira continued his duties alongside the other nighters, though the dwarves and the lad largely carried on as though he were not present. Likewise, the dayers, save Nathanael, quietly ignored his presence, even in the confinement of a lone ship traversing the wide sea. Since their departure from the Haurthian galley, Nathanael had been repeatedly questioned as to whether he had known his friends' true identities, but he flatly refused to answer any of the queries for the accusatory tones they held towards Ira and Esther. To make matters worse, an allegation first voiced by Ram seemed to have festered into an unspoken belief amongst some of the crew. The dwarf had accused Ira and Esther's presence aboard the *Wayfarer* of being the driving factor behind their being forbidden from anchoring in the Hallowed City. Halruc immediately dismissed the falsity and swore that the next to utter a word against one of his servants would be cast into the sea by the master himself. No one, not even Ram, dared provoke the dwarf in his incensed state, but the hushed rumors persisted nonetheless.

Ira grew indifferent to his being shunned by the sailors. What behavior he could not stand for was their likened treatment of Esther. The lost favor of those she had come to regard so highly had profoundly struck her heart. Even the lad who had grown so fond of the lady had ceased approaching her for reading lessons and, in fact, had ceased approaching her at all. In this, however, Ira suspected he had seen Tabor's hand more at play than the sole conviction of his son to avoid the marked princess. Unable to escape the shame aboard so small a vessel, Esther reserved herself to the dark corners of the hold and refused to join any on deck. She still cooked meals for the crew, which openly detested her, but left them to serve themselves at the changing of the shifts. Esther spoke to no one, not Nathanael as a friend, nor to her brother, who felt her pain as his own. Nathanael endeavored to try harder to retrieve her from her lonely state, but Ira knew his sister's heart and mind intimately enough to understand her desperate desire for solitude.

"It is my fault," he said one night to Nathanael, who had offered his company as Ira manned the helm. This post was presently most favorable to the prince, affording him isolation during his shifts from all but Manoque. Thankfully, the elf routinely reserved his attention for the stars and his charts. Even so, it was difficult to converse with Nathanael, with a recurring sense of having one constantly listening in.

"No more yours than mine," murmured Nathanael as he eyed the elf beside them. "Or have you forgotten my part in getting you so close to the gallows?"

"That is not what I meant," said Ira solemnly. "I am not speaking of mine and Esther's being here tonight, not exactly. All that has happened—every agony since we stepped foot in Gales those twelve years ago—might have been forgone. Had I challenged my father and his treachery, had I only . . ." But Ira trailed off as he caught several eyes watching him from across the deck. Ram and Ossel eyed him curiously as they spoke quietly to one another. Upon meeting Ira's gaze, the mute and the lad turned quickly to look at Puck, who swiftly returned to bowing his fiddle. "Well," continued Ira, "there is no hope for her now. I am the reason my sister was driven from her homeland. I am the reason she was branded with the mark that stole her only chance of starting over in the provinces. And now, I have broken my promise to her, too weak to deliver her to the only place she could ever have found peace."

"How many times must I tell you?" scolded Nathanael. "Your father's sins were his own. Let them fade with his memory, but do not take them upon yourself."

"And why should I not?" whispered Ira. "Why should the sins of a guilty father not also be the penance of an equally guilty son?"

"You know as well as I that your guilt pales to that of Emperor Darius."

"But Esther's soul is guiltless, whole, and pure. Yet she bears the shame that I allowed to befall her. For that, my guilt measures equal to that of my father."

The rest of the night passed in silence between the pair, and morning came as a sweet but fleeting release from Ira's aching mind as he fell exhaustedly into his hammock. When he later awoke to the blistering light bursting from the open hatch, he turned away from it to rest longer. Before he could drift into sleep again, his dormant attentions were drawn by a faint discussion coming from on deck.

". . . said and done to secure their freedom. It would have been all the better for us had the galleymaster taken them away to rot in a cell."

It was Ram's voice, which was met with a mumbling chorus of agreement.

"My concern," said Ossel, following his brother's declaration, "is how Halruc could have kept such a thing from us, his loyal servants. We have a right to know who we sail beside and break bread with."

"Now, wait just a moment," chimed in Ishcaur. "I understand your sentiments as well as any other, Ossel. But none here have the right to demand anything but what we are owed for our service. The affairs of others aboard this ship are between themselves and the master alone."

"How can you say that, Ishcaur?" added Puck. "We have all heard your laments about Darius the Damned's rule too many times to count. Now you are content to live in the company of his treacherous offspring?"

"Indeed," said Ram, "what good has come aboard this ship since the felons' arrival? Pirate raids and barred passage. So many misfortunes were never wrought upon a single voyage before."

"Cursed is the ship that carries dark omens," muttered old Dromo in his low, monotonous tone.

"Oh, give it a rest, Dromo," griped Ossel. "We have had quite enough of your haunting proverbs."

"But can you honestly say that there is no truth in what he says?" asked Ram pointedly.

"What I do not understand is how a prince and princess could have passed unnoticed in the first place." The lad's voice was unmistakable to Ira's ears as he listened from the hammock.

"We all knew they were bartering passage for some reason or another," replied the lad's father, "what with the lady's mark and Halruc's assurance that they would not receive a share of the commission. I must admit, though, I never imagined it to be anything so sinister as—"

"So sinister as what, Tabor?" His friend's presence in such a conversation caught Ira momentarily off guard until he discerned that Nathanael must have only just entered the huddle of gossip.

"This," said Ram melodramatically, "from the one who befriended such traitors as the cursed children of the last emperor. You knew perfectly well who they were, boy. Do you deny it?"

"I deny nothing," stated Nathanael firmly. "I have known them for many years now and count myself lucky to consider them as dear to me as my own kin."

"You surprise me, Nathanael," said a disappointed Ishcaur. "I never would have thought it possible."

"What brought the banished children to admit themselves to you anyway?" inquired Tabor.

Nathanael did not at once reply. From his hammock in the hold, Ira felt a waft of shame come over him for the answer to Tabor's query.

"I was never supposed to know their secret," answered Nathanael solemnly. "When I first came to know Ira nearly a decade ago, it was on a hunt with my brothers in the hills beyond our village. He told us he and his sister had grown up in the Port of Lark before settling in Squall. I thought nothing peculiar of this, and my brothers and I soon came to regard Ira in high esteem for his generosity and kindness. Some years later, Ira and his master, Érnog, came to stay with me and my kin as they passed through Kevah on their way to Gales. While they were staying with us, Érnog mentioned something in passing that caught my attention. As we discussed the great chariot races in the north, the tanner said that Ira had never been to Lark but had long yearned to visit so he might witness the great circus. Something about this remark stirred in the back of my mind until I recalled one of the first things Ira had ever told me during our acquaintance. It hardly seemed possible that my friend would lie about such a thing. That is, unless it was meant to cover for an unflattering truth. I tried to no avail to forget what I had heard. But my mind raced for some time after with dark speculations of what might motivate a trusted friend to conceal his past in a lie."

"The next time Ira joined us for a hunt, I seized my chance and confronted him while my brothers were away. I divulged what Érnog had let slip and connected it to his lie about being raised in Lark. I accosted him rather harshly that night. All I knew and believed of my old friend was in question. And to my great astonishment, Ira confessed the entirety of his tainted history to me, leaving no stone unturned. He told me all concerning his upbringing in Haurth, his father, the emperor, the tale of his banishment, and his marked sister, whom I had not yet come to know. It almost seemed a relief for him to confide the long-hidden truth in someone beyond his home in Squall. And in all he confessed to me, not once did Ira offer any plea in defense of his reputation. When my brothers returned and we settled in for the night, I lay in the wild barley, looking up at the stars and contemplating the banished prince's story. And when a new day was upon us, I scolded myself for every curse I had ever uttered against the children of Emperor Darius."

The profound silence following Nathanael's words ached Ira even more than the recollection of all he had told his friend that night. From his hammock in the hold, it was impossible to discern how the sailors on deck were receiving this tale. After some time, Puck's voice carried through the hatch to Ira's ears.

"Setting aside your attachment to an old friend," he said, "you mean to say that the testimony of the prince was enough for you to pardon both he and his sister?"

"If that be the case," interjected Ossel, "then why not share what he told you that night? If his story is enough to redeem them in our eyes, then let us hear it for ourselves!"

"If you wish to know the truth," replied Nathanael coldly, "then you are free to ask for it from the source. But I will not betray my brother's trust to appease a loathing mob."

"Say what you will to protect them, Nathanael," barked Ram viciously, "but the remnants of the House of Darius are paying for their treachery. Your 'brother' deserved far more than what came to him. At least the princess bears her guilt upon her face, and it serves her right. If I—"

Before Nathanael could summon a fierce enough punishment for the dwarf's cruelty, the huddle's attention was diverted as Ira thundered through the hatch. The effect was instantaneous. Struck dumb, the dayers and nighters seated around the mast watched the prince pass them, taking a fuming Nathanael along with him. Ram, out of spite more than anything else, held his tongue as he glowered at the pair making their way towards the quarterdeck. Cercur was posted as helmsman beside Manoque, though their attentions were hardly upon the sea. Before Ira could take a seat on the steps, the elf addressed him.

"The master wishes to speak to you in his cabin."

Ira looked to Nathanael, who appeared just as confused by the invitation as he was. Nevertheless, he acknowledged Manoque for the message and set off to the side of the raised quarterdeck. He meant to glare at Ram as he glimpsed the gossiping crowd but was distracted as his eyes fell first upon the lad. While the dwarves and his father were all watching the prince with unflinching intrigue, the young sailor averted Ira's gaze and stared into his lap to hide a contrite expression. Recalled to his errand by the short door on the quarterdeck's port side, Ira rapped against the wood and waited. When a gruff voice from inside answered, he ducked his head and stepped into the tight room.

Ira did not stand up straight so as to avoid knocking his head against the shortened roof. Halruc was seated behind his desk, engrossed in a ledger heavily laden with notes and scrawls, with a stubby, bejeweled finger pressed against his temple. He held the ledger in the sunlight pouring through the porthole overlooking the ship's stern. Behind the master's chair was a short sleeping rack situated beside a number of multicolored mantles hung on various pegs. There was also pinned against the wall a humble portrait of a dwarven sailor. The prince thought the sailor depicted in ink bore the faint resemblance of a young Halruc. Ira stood awkwardly hunched over, awaiting his master's invitation to speak. The dwarf glanced at him shortly before returning to those margins of his ledger, which denoted the sorted debts of the *Wayfarer*.

"You wished to speak with me, master?" Ira said casually. Halruc made no response but turned to the next page of columns and notes. This detached sort of manner was not entirely unwarranted. The master and his criminal servant had not shared any intimate conversation since the day they stood before the vindictive galleymaster and the merciful admiral. As he had not the faculty to speak candidly then, Ira felt compelled to address those happenings aboard the galley *Requiarda*. "It is long overdue, master," he said, "but I feel compelled to apologize for—"

But Halruc's voice cut across his own, though the dwarf's eyes did not flicker from the pages of the ledger.

"Your apologies are neither sought nor accepted," the master said stoically. "The promise of wealth blinded me enough to permit two felons into my service. This vessel has been my life all these years, and I nearly squandered her in greed. Keep your apologies, prince; they do me no good."

"Be that as it may, it was on our behalf that you were compelled to lie to the—"

"If I lied aboard that ship, it was not for your sake, nor the princess'. Playing the part of a noble master who would employ an infamous but good man was the only ploy at my disposal. What might have become of you and the lady was the least of my concerns." Any preconceived notions of gratitude towards Halruc quickly faded from Ira's mind. "I did not summon you here to recall what has already transpired. By Manoque's estimations, the *Wayfarer* shall reach the Forager's Cove by sundown today. When we harbor, the crew will scavenge the island for parties willing to purchase any of our shipments. I do not imagine we will offload much without a prearranged buyer, but we shall attempt it all the same. For the duration of our stay in the Cove, you and your sister are to remain aboard the ship."

Ira comprehended the master's meaning in this order at once.

"You wish to avoid any chance of our being discovered in the Cove."

"Precisely. The galleys of Haurth do not frequent the island, but I have seen local regiments govern with ruthless manners. So, we shall err on the side of caution and keep the both of you out of sight. Do I make myself clear?"

"Master, I am afraid I must disappoint you on this account. I have not yet given up hopes of taking my sister to the Westlands." For the first time, Halruc gazed up from the ledger in his hand. His disapproval was unmistakably felt by Ira, who went on before the master could berate his desperate plan. "Nathanael bartered our way here at great personal expense, and Esther and I shall never make it this far again should we return to the provinces. I mean to find a ship in the Cove bound for Haurth to secure passage aboard. We have little coin, of course, but the isles are known more for trading than for sale. Esther and I shall depart from your company once we reach the Cove, and there we shall remain until I can bargain our way to Vistérae."

The dwarf scoffed as he closed the ledger with a snap and set it on his desk. Halruc turned his chair to face Ira directly, folded his hands in his lap, and looked at the man like a father ready to scold a child.

"A wiser man would take what luck came his way and run with it. You escaped the justice of the empire with your life and your freedom, against all odds. And now, you wish to tempt fate further, hoping to achieve a different outcome. You would be a fool to risk so much for some garden."

"The garden is the only place my sister will ever be free," said Ira sharply. "I will not have her live to be an old woman knowing only scorn and ridicule from those around her."

The only sounds in the tiny cabin were wafts of cool sea air passing through the porthole. Master and servant stared at one another, each determinant in his way.

"Very well," Halruc said, picking up his ledger again. "I shall not attempt to hinder your vain quest. I only hope you will reconsider trekking this dangerous path. If not for yourself, then for the lady, else she pay a price graver than that of a mere mark." He dismissed his servant with a wave and cast his eyes upon another page of narrow margins. As Ira opened the cabin door and stepped out, the master's voice caught him. "The *Wayfarer* shall remain in the Cove for a day or so while we tend to business. Should your plans alter before then, you will both have a place aboard this ship."

With a nod of thanks to the master, Ira closed the door behind him. He glanced towards the dayers applying themselves to the braces while Ram remained in huddled speech with the other nighters collected around the mast. Wishing for isolation in some place other than the cramped hold, Ira strode to the stern of the ship so he might watch the sunset. As he rounded the corner of the quarterdeck, he found that another had claimed the spot before him. Esther sat upright, leaning against the planks constructing the master's cabin and supporting the raised quarterdeck, her scarlet-patterned veil whipping in the breeze like an untethered clew. With a feeling that he was intruding upon her privacy, Ira turned to leave.

"You hold too much against yourself, brother," her gentle voice called to him. As he looked at her with mild confusion, she nodded towards the porthole above her head feeding cool air into Halruc's cabin. "For all these years, you have carried a guilt with you that was unjustly placed. If I could have one thing in this life, I would see you forgive yourself and forget the past."

At Esther's invitation, her brother sat beside her. Together, they gazed over the *Wayfarer*'s ledge at the sky, which was bleeding pink and orange hues across thin layers of cloud. Ira wanted to speak plainly, but the prospect of the master hearing his words through the porthole made him reconsider, as did the backs of Cercur and Manoque's figures upon the quarterdeck. Leaning around the corner to check they were otherwise alone, Ira spoke in a soft voice meant only for the ears of one.

"The day I forgive myself is the day I make amends for my soul. And it will not be long now. We will both start our lives anew when we reach the garden, far from loathing glares and beyond the reach of the mariners. I will fulfill my promise to you, sister."

"Not every want and wish is afforded in this life, but is that so bad?" she asked. "It is like you told the lad that night. True contentment can be found in a simple life. Our home in Squall was indeed simple, yet never lacking in love. If that cottage along the banks was the last luxury I was afforded in this life, I should strive to be grateful for all that was mine."

"But for all the love Érnog and Torzara could give, they would not have you spend your days in a land that shamed you. They would have you live freely, even at the cost of losing you. I have not forfeited hope of reaching the garden. I will take you there."

"And if you cannot?" asked Esther in a hollow voice. "What should become of us if we cannot reach Haurth? What if the ship leaves us in the Cove and we cannot even return to the provinces? Are we to be stranded yet again from any life we have ever known?"

Her voice cracked, and a tear ran down her cheek beneath her billowing veil. Ira knew not what to say and so took her hand in his own and held it firmly.

"Perhaps," he said after a long while, "we can search for passage to Haurth only as long as the *Wayfarer* remains in the Cove. If nothing comes of our search, we may return with them to Gales and make our way back to Squall."

Esther blinked away another tear as she nodded in agreement. They sat together and watched the sky bloom with wide lavender shades. As the world around them bathed in color, Nathanael rounded the corner and asked to sit with them. He leaned against the quarterdeck on Ira's right and joined them in the tranquility of the scene. A short while passed before he broke the silence.

"Would you have ever told me?" he asked his friend. "Had I never suspected anything? Would you have confided the truth in me?"

Ira considered the question and, moreover, what answer his friend might hope to hear. After some thoughtful contemplation, Ira replied, "No, I doubt I would have told you or any other the truth. There were times when I wished even Érnog and Torzara had not been privy to our tarnished legacy. For each person who knew the truth, the past was all the harder to escape. Though people of Squall never knew who Esther and I truly were, her mark was enough to shun all of the House of Érnog from their good graces."

"But whenever I ventured to Kevah for bison skins, I was but a common tanner's apprentice and a friend. Villagers would inquire after my sister's well-being, and I could speak of Esther with a brother's pride. After some time of knowing you and your kin, I knew that I could confide the truth, or at least some degree of it, in you without being ousted in shame. Yet I elected to live in falsehood. Make no mistake, a part of me was relieved when you aired the discrepancies of my past to me. After confessing to you, I even considered sharing all with your brothers as well. But in the grand scheme of things, I would have been content to remain completely isolated from the life I had led before. To live and die as no more than a tanner's apprentice and a good man would have been a liberation to my soul."

Unsure of what to think, Nathanael swam stoically in his friend's answer. He made to speak when another joined the company of three in the small space between the quarterdeck and the ship's ledge. The young sailor traded glances with Nathanael, Ira, and, most of all, Esther. He opened and closed his mouth several times but seemed incapable of uttering a single word. Lost for where to begin, the lad stood uncomfortably as he lowered his gaze and uttered, "I have behaved poorly."

Brief as it was, his remorse could not have been more sincere. Were it any other, Ira might have found it challenging to forgive so quickly.

"Will you sit with us?" asked Esther.

As the lad took his usual place at her side, the faint crease of a smile grew upon her lips. The four sat together to watch the sky, which had sprouted braids of magenta and scarlet along the sea's edge. Marveling in the brilliant hues, Ira yearned for this peaceful scene to linger on, undisturbed by life and tragedy. But as surely as the dark would soon shroud the light, Ira knew he would soon face the inevitable question from the lad more inquisitive than any he had ever known.

"Will you tell me your story?" the young sailor finally asked after a long, quiet stretch. "I have heard enough, quite enough, from those who know little of the truth. Nathanael knows your tale in full, and he remains faithful to you. I should like to know it too, if you are willing."

As Ira considered the lad, he glanced at the porthole above them. The privacy of the hold would be preferable to the looming feeling of the master's hearing every word of the prince's tale. Yet Ira felt that weighed against the other sailors' intentions for the truth, Halruc's would come second only to the lad's.

"What would you like to know?" asked Ira.

The lad considered for a moment, apparently trying to narrow his inquest to something more specific than Ira's life story. Finally, he answered, "The emperor, your father. Aside from his failed ploy to dominate the Eastlands, little is told of him. What was it that led him to ruin?"

Ira looked at his sister. "Shall I recount the tale, or would you prefer to?" he asked her.

"Let it be from your lips," Esther replied quietly. "I have not the heart for it."

"Very well then." And with a deep sigh, the prince began. "When our father ascended the throne after our grandmother's passing, there was already unrest in parts of the empire. It came from East and West alike, but these instances were few and far between. The crown was never without its opposition, even before the Eastlands were joined to the Haurthian Empire. I was a boy when Prince Darius assumed his role as the empire's sovereign. Perhaps youth clouded my perception at the time, but the new emperor appeared to be just in his rule. Like those before him, he repeatedly sent for emissaries from each of the Eastern Realms, which were not yet established as the provinces. Men and dwarves, respected lords and leaders of their homelands, served as members of the Emperor's Court, bringing the hardships of their people before the sovereign to handle as he saw fit."

"The court also included the general of the legions, the admiral of the naval fleets, and the sovereign's firstborn who would one day take his father's place. The emperor would summon the members of the court to convene in the Temple of Érosai every few months, and I was determined to learn all I could from his ways. Poor harvests, seasons of malady, and raids were amongst the concerns chiefly raised during our conventions. But even then, scattered talks of releasing the Eastlands from the empire were brought forward by the six emissaries. Such had been the case even before Emperor Darius sat upon the throne, or so I was then assured by the admiral."

"Why had citizens wished to break from the empire for so long?" asked the lad.

"From what the emissaries related, it was a matter of subjecting themselves to a governance so far removed from themselves." At the puzzled expression on the lad's face, Ira expanded the point. "What it means is that the people in the Eastlands had no desire to answer to a sovereign who felt none of their sufferings. Almost every emperor and empress who ruled since the Haurthian Empire was founded had known periods of abundance, health, and safety. The price for such prosperity was allegiance to the empire and the legions of mariners stationed across the lands as stewards and enforcers of the law. Many citizens were content, even glad to pay such a price while luxury reigned. But in seasons of strife, the sacrifice of independence tasted most bitter to those who felt it at its deepest. There will always be those who believe they would be better off serving as their own masters."

"And do you agree now, looking back on it all?" asked the lad.

"I believe the strength of rule relies entirely upon the strength of the constitution held by the ruler," answered Ira thoughtfully. "And to my infamous father's credit, his response to those calling for the Eastlands' release from the empire was, for a time, admirable. Throughout my youth, Emperor Darius repeatedly sent the six emissaries to convene with those wishing to break from the empire so they might better understand their reasons and aims. Their findings were then related to the emperor, either by correspondence or in the court's periodic conventions. Plans to establish an Eastern policing body to replace the mariners were formulated. Several taxes that were crippling homes and families were struck down. I even heard my father once voice his consideration of forfeiting further attempts to salvage the union and instead grant the Eastern Realms their long-sought freedom."

"What?" exclaimed the lad incredulously. "No, it cannot be true; how could it be? Emperor Darius, free the Eastlands? It is not possible."

"Were my memory any weaker, I might not believe my own words," said Ira. "But it is true."

"So what happened? What could have altered the emperor so?"

"This," said Ira solemnly, "is where we delve into the unknown. Neither Esther nor I can truly account for the change that came over our father preceding his imminent demise. When I reached the ripe age of five and ten, Admiral Litanius of the Haurthian Navy proposed to the emperor that I take up the commission of an officer aboard his warship, the galley *Obysarr*. Under his tutelage and that of the vessel's newly appointed galleymaster, I would learn to command a singular warship as well as an entire fleet. The prospect was endearing to me. The admiral's galley had only just returned from a quest to uncover the den of the Pirate Horde's fleet. Though their quest had been fruitless, I wished for nothing more than to join the ranks of the officers so I might learn from the greatest soldiers of the empire."

"My father concurred that I was of the appropriate age to take up such a commission, and I was appointed to my first naval post. At the same time, Esther, who was not yet two and ten years of age, was to journey to the northern garden to study under the wisest priests and sages of the Westlands. Like princesses before her, she was to become a scholar and ambassador for the crown and of the people. Our commissions were as much for our benefit as for our father's. Esther was to be a peacemaker, and I a peacekeeper. And so, we set off on our separate journeys. As members of the Emperor's Court, the admiral and I were to be recalled to Eou Verás whenever we received our sovereign's summons. But I had no idea it would be so long until I next set eyes upon my young sister."

The soft creak of a plank from the helm momentarily distracted Ira from his immersion into vivid memory.

"What was it like as an officer?" the lad asked eagerly. "Did you duel many pirates? How many warships did you sink?"

Esther, despite herself, could not repress a smile at the lad's awe.

"Need I remind you, lad," chuckled Nathanael, "that you have also encountered a Horde galley and lived to tell about it?"

Under his breath, the young sailor muttered something that sounded like "Not the same." Ira knew all too well that in the mind of an idealistic boy, a narrow escape from a pursuing vessel could not compare to the vision of a coordinated breach, boarding, and assault inflicted by a crew of soldiers clad in shimmering armor.

"Yes, lad, we discovered and sank a few Horde vessels in my time—only a few, mind you. However, the bulk of my adolescence was spent aboard that galley, learning the ways of the ship and the sea. We traversed the Bridging Sea countless times, and some of my happiest memories can be traced to those simple days upon the briny waters. As an officer, I trained under the guidance of the galleymaster in the art of swordsmanship, naval tactics, and commanding the mariners at their posts. In addition, the admiral consulted me on matters of the fleets while having regular correspondence with the general of the Haurthian Army. Praelaum and praedaur were charged with safeguarding the sea and lands across the empire, and I was fortunate enough to study under both. Throughout my years of service, I earned the mariners' respect, not merely for my title of birth but as an officer and a leader."

"As my emperor had promised, I was repeatedly recalled to the Hallowed City to join his court, as were the admiral, general, and Eastern emissaries. These gatherings occurred every few months for the span of four years after I joined the cohort of the galley *Obysarr*. And with each return to the Temple of Érosai, I watched my caring father and noble sovereign change in word and manner. At first, I thought little of his alteration, attributing it to the time we were apart or an odd fit of stress in his duties. But over those four years, every word of unease in the Eastern Realms seemed to spark a dark countenance in Emperor Darius."

"Any notions he once held of satiating those who questioned his rule were cast asunder. Needless taxes were levied in the Eastlands as a punishment for infidelity to the crown. Before long, the emperor was demanding that the emissaries reveal the names of the traitors he had once asked them to commune with. Even more mariners were stationed in the East, apprehending any who dared to speak against their sovereign. Pretty soon, the paranoid emperor became convinced of the six realms' intentions to amass an army and enslave the empire under their own rule. And this mad notion became the crutch of every cruel action he took against the innocents. It is a miracle that such rabid actions did not irrevocably fracture relations between East and West."

"But, but why . . . I mean, how come . . ."

"Why did I not oppose my father in any of this?" Ira finished. "Why did none of the Emperor's Court defy his notorious means of quelling opposition?" He looked to Esther, wishing with all his being to give any answer but the truth. "We did oppose him. Throughout the sovereign's growing madness, we objected, even pleaded with him to renounce the measures he took against those he had vowed to serve. But the emperor's word is law. And even in his worst fits of insanity, I saw my father assume an unnatural state of calm when he found it necessary. Even when I knew his ploys to be radical and wrong, the sovereign's words were always enough to convince a part of me to believe him when he spoke of their uniting the empire once more. A father's reassurances and a pat on the shoulder were all it took to sway my youthful gullibility. Yet even as I sounded my assent with the emperor and his mad ways, my former opposition lingered in the back of my mind, trapped behind a cloud of blind allegiance."

"I was not the only one to fall under the influence of my father's sly tongue and persuasive ways. I watched as the other members of the court set aside their own reservations to be in accordance with the emperor. But the consensus of the court never seemed to last long. There were many nights following our conventions in which I lay awake, resentful of my own weak will. It was like waking from a strange dream, only to recognize it as a nightmare of your own making. But even beyond the court's conventions, I could not summon the strength to oppose my father, the mighty sovereign. I wrote many times to Esther, still dwelling in the north, and we both pleaded with our father through our letters when away from the temple. I dare say the other members of the court did the same. But Emperor Darius was determined, convinced that vile force and sheer will would reunite the Haurthian Empire. The cost of such an end was of little consequence to him."

"Then, at one of the court's last meetings ever to be had, the emissaries entered the Temple of Érosai armed with gladiuses at their sides. Their people had been impoverished, arrested, and even slain by the mariners sworn to protect them. The treachery in the Eastlands would no longer be stood for. The six proclaimed their collective resignation from the Emperor's Court and demanded Emperor Darius release their lands from Haurthian rule. My father just stood there, a pale reflection of the noble sovereign he once was. He took his time examining the defectors and their weapons, his fingers dancing upon the hilt of his own. At last, my father agreed to discuss the terms of releasing the Eastlands, but he would only speak with the emissaries. Not even the Temple Guard was permitted to stay. And against our better judgment, the remaining members of the court abided by the emperor's command."

"The admiral, general, and I stood idle with the sentries in the garden behind the temple, all of us unsure of what to do with ourselves. We awaited a summons which never came as day faded into night. I was on the verge of falling asleep against one of the trees when . . ." Ira shuddered as the tragic remembrance returned to the forefront of his mind. ". . . when a piercing howl echoed from within the temple. We sprang to our feet and rushed into a scene that locked every man in a horrid trance. The six emissaries of the Eastern Realms lay in a pool of crimson upon the marble courtyard, bloodstained swords locked in their death grips. Emperor Darius was transfixed over the massacre, his own gladius without a spot of blood upon it."

The lad, usually so inquisitive, was at a loss for words. He and Esther sat close to one another as the chill of the ocean breeze swept across the ship. As Nathanael stared at the setting sun, Ira could feel the weight of the breaths his friend drew.

"I would give anything to know the truth of what was said and done that night," Ira said after a long and solemn reflection. "My father insisted that the emissaries had gone mad at his refusal to release their lands. He claimed that the men had threatened to kill themselves and frame the emperor for their deaths. As martyrs, they would ignite an uprising that would only be quelled by the Eastlands' release or civil war. It was a ludicrous story, yet there stood the emperor with not a drop of blood from the tip of his regal blade to its jewel-encrusted hilt. I saw, yet I did not believe. And all of us who bore witness to the ghastly sight knew that the agitated citizens of the Eastlands would not believe it either.

"By the next morning, news of the emissaries' suspicious deaths had already flooded into the Hallowed City, and rumors of the emperor's ludicrous tale coursed alongside it. War seemed inevitable, yet there was still one course by which the fractured empire might be saved from itself. My consideration of taking so drastic a measure had plagued my mind for some time. And in the wake of the emissaries' deaths and an all but imminent civil conflict, there seemed no alternative. You see, lad, centuries ago, a law was written concerning a sovereign's right to rule. It was decreed by an empress of old that any descendant of the royal bloodline could challenge the reigning sovereign for their birthright to the throne. "*Méne caiar*," the contest of right. The law was predicated on the belief that if a sovereign was defeated in ritual combat by one of royal lineage, then it was the will of Érosai that his challenger should ascend as ruler. Here was the answer to the tyranny of Emperor Darius. Only I could end the madness. The sovereignty was to be mine someday, but there was nothing stopping me from ending my father's rule prematurely. Nothing, that is, except my own reservations."

"I could have ended the war before it even began; I could have granted the Eastern Realms their freedom and restored peace across the Bridging Sea. I knew there was no other way, and still, I allowed my selfish considerations to sway me towards inaction. Was I to be known to all as the emperor who murdered his own father to claim power? Could such an act, even for the sake of others, damage my soul irretrievably? In doing so, would I eventually give into madness only to become just like Darius the Damned? Could my sister ever forgive her brother for committing—for even considering—so heinous an act? For all my reservations, not one was held for my father's sake. The good man and leader I had once admired was lost to me. I could have taken his life with ease, and the only remorse to follow would be for how his death would define my legacy. I was not prepared to do what was necessary, though I was the only one who could challenge the emperor. Or so I believed."

"The day after the emissaries' collective demise, the admiral, general, and I were summoned to the Temple of Érosai for the court's last convention. As we were joined by my father, already swimming in battle preparations, another figure clad in sapphire and bronze strode into the courtyard. It was the galleymaster of the galley *Obysarr*, the one who had guided my officer's training for the last four years. An elf named Lysias."

"What?" exclaimed the lad. "You were trained by Premier Lysias all those years?"

"Back then, he was only Gailaum Lysias. You can imagine my surprise to learn that my mentor was the long-lost descendant of the First Line of Sovereigns. Yet, as the temple priests combed through the elf's scrolls and documented lineage, there could be no denial of this miraculous revelation's validity. And as the priests affirmed the galleymaster to be a true descendant of Empress Veroise and her royal ancestors, Lysias wasted no time in invoking the right of méne caiar against the reigning sovereign. Forgoing all ceremony and tradition entailed with the ancient ritual, my father unleashed his sword and thrashed at the elf like a feral beast. Before I knew what to make of the scene, Lysias had run my father through with the tip of his blade. His eyes rolled upwards, the sword fell from his ashen hand, and he collapsed in the very spot where the emissaries had gone cold."

"The right to rule was restored to the line of elves with which it had begun. Lysias was set to ascend as the first elven emperor in more than five hundred years. That was, until he announced his resignation of the sovereignty. Instead, Lysias reserved himself to preside as premier over the Realm of Haurth alone. Not long after, the elf handpicked six leaders of the Eastlands to govern their respective realms. The Guard of the newly established provinces enlisted Eastern men to steward their lands while the legions were recalled to their duties in the West and the Bridging Sea. All of this, along with the demise of the dreaded Emperor Darius, was enough to forgo civil war and secure tranquility throughout the lands. Even now, I must admit to my admiration for how my former gailaum salvaged the Haurthian Empire from utter ruin.

"What happened to you after . . . after?" asked the lad.

"I was arrested for treason, along with the admiral and the general. We were held in the Cavern of Souls to await trial as accessories to Emperor Darius' tyranny. Days, possibly weeks, passed as I lay chained in that mountain. All the time, I longed to speak to my sister, to know that she at least was all right. When it came time for me to face Haurthian judgment for my crimes, I was brought before an audience of the arbiter and the new premier. But I was not alone in my trial. Standing in the temple courtyard beside me, shackled and weeping, was Esther."

"I cannot remember my words from that day, but they would be of no consequence now. Nothing I said could convince the justice of the empire of my sister's innocence. The daughter of a mad tyrant, even one beyond the emperor's conspiratorial counsel, was believed to be as guilty as the son who had betrayed his empire. And Lysias . . . Lysias was already of the belief that I enabled, even encouraged, my father's treachery. I hold no blame against him for it; my inaction gave him every reason to believe the worst of me. I only wish I could have swayed his mind and the arbiter's for the sake of my sister. Esther and I stood together as we were convicted and banished from our homeland. We were stripped of the patterned colors worn by the royal family. My unshorn hair was cut, a sign of disgrace in Western culture. We were outcasts, traitors, pariahs to the whole of the empire."

"But Lysias won the sovereignty by means of méne caiar. Could you not have reclaimed it the same way?" observed the lad.

"It is true," admitted Ira quietly. "I could have challenged Lysias. But I could never have bested the one who taught me all I knew in the ways of the sword. And had I lost, Esther would have been left alone in a world that despised her, all for my desperation to cling to something already gone. No, I could never have challenged Lysias. I had no desire to kill him. We had come to know each other well in the years we served beside one another. He even had a mariner son about my age, though I never met him. Lysias was a good man, and I knew he would serve the empire better than a disgraced prince ever could. It was because of him that Esther and I did not face a graver sentence. I saw his intimate conferences with the arbiter spare us from a life in Alaoth, possibly even from the gallows. And after our trial, the premier ensured that Esther and I were permitted to remain in Eou Verás for our father's funeral. The last emperor was laid beside his ancestors in a mountain tomb, his regal sword set upon his chest by the premier himself. It was more than our father deserved, and for that, Lysias will always have my thanks."

"What became of the other members of the Emperor's Court?" asked the lad.

"I do not know for sure; their trials followed our own. I later heard rumors that the admiral and general had been stripped of their ranks and reduced to beggars. At the time, I had not a care for them as my sister and I boarded a Haurthian galley bound for the Eastlands, never to return to our home. The prince and princess set foot in Gales as infamous criminals, and our arrival was mockingly heralded by the galleymaster who delivered us. The banished children of Emperor Darius could not escape the jeers and scorn that day. I attempted to find us lodging for the night, but the word of the pariahs in the port spread like wildfire. As my back was turned, a vindictive man furious at the House of Darius came forward with a whip in hand, and he . . ." Ira broke off as he glanced towards his sister. She did not return his gaze. The breeze coursed through her scarlet veil as she lifted a hand to feel the long mark upon her cheek. "I should have seen it. But I could only muster the selfish strength to pull her out of there in time to save my own outward reputation. I had failed twice, first as a prince and again as a brother. And now, my sister will forever bear the mark of a violent felon, a mark branded in vitriol."

A morose expression festered upon the young lad's face as he looked upon a tearful Esther. "I did not . . . ," he said in a penitent voice. "I . . . I should not have . . ."

"I understand," whispered Esther, taking the lad's hand. She looked then to her ashamed brother and said, "I would not have you bear a mark alongside mine for anything in this world."

"I know," replied Ira, "but your selfless nature does not exempt the guilt that is rightfully mine. Inaction and cowardice are the sins I will carry with me until the day I die. I only thank the Light for sending one with the strength to do for the empire what I could not."

Somewhere in the dusking sky, the cry of an osprey could be heard. Ira searched for the seahawk overhead as the lad sat with the prince's tale in great solemnity.

"You must miss your former life terribly," said the lad. Though the remark was not specific in its address, Ira knew it was not he the young sailor was speaking to.

"At times, it is all I can think of," replied Esther. "And in others, I count myself amongst the luckiest of souls. The love of friends and relations weighs greater than all else through life's trials and tribulations. It is a wonderful thing we all have to cherish."

"I hope . . . I hope you will someday consider me a friend."

Esther offered the lad a tender smile as Nathanael rose from his place against the quarterdeck and stretched his arms to the fading sky.

"Well, I have been absent long enough from my duties," he said, "though I doubt I have been missed. You two," he added to Ira and the lad, "had better prepare for the change of shifts."

Esther remarked that she was going to fetch a drink and prepare supper. As Ira made to get up, the sound of rustling feet sounded around the corner. He glanced over the quarterdeck and saw nighters and dayers scuttling away towards random parts of the deck. Ira did not know whether he was more cross at the eavesdroppers or relieved to have no more secrets aboard the *Wayfarer*. He, Esther, Nathanael, and the lad emerged from the stern of the ship to meet a crew averting their gazes from the prince and princess. What feelings served as the driving forces behind these aversions remained unclear until, at last, one dwarf stepped forward and silently faced the brother and sister. The mute only stared at them, trading glances with Ira and Esther in turn. Underneath his matted auburn beard and brows was an expression of understanding that words could never have conveyed as he extended his hand to offer a dripping waterskin to Esther. Esther offered her own silent thanks to the mute as she graciously accepted a draft.

From the helm, there came a sharp whistle, jolting every observing sailor from the present scene.

"Land ho!" called Cercur from the rudder oars. A wave of scarlet tunics swept to the bow for a better view. On the eastern horizon were several glimmering specks flittering in a sea of pale darkness. The Cove's many burning lanterns were huddled like a fallen constellation. The master's cabin door flung open as Halruc marched across the deck to join the spectators. As he passed him by, the dwarf offered a slight inclination of his head towards Ira and Esther as he called for Cercur to take them into the harbor.

213

CHAPTER XI

THE FORAGER'S COVE

In the illumination of the blazing swarm of lanterns, the island grew vaguely more perceptible as the *Wayfarer* made its approach through the dark waters. Boulders and earth were gnashed together, forming gentle mounds brimming with shadows of lush tropical trees against the evening sky. Dark outlines of anchored boats and vessels bobbed lazily along the Cove's outer banks. Standing guard on either side of the harbor entry were the stone busts of two singing sirens. At one time, the water nymphs' carvings may have been called handsome, but the wavy sheens of hair and slender figures had been drastically weathered by age and element. Their once shapely faces were coarse and jagged, and one of the nymph's long arms had snapped and crumbled at the base of its scaly tail.

The *Wayfarer* drifted into the Cove, where it met a small village set just beyond the shoreline. One sand-sprinkled road followed level around the crescent harbor, while others rose along the hills. Dwellings in the quaint community had been erected from slate and sediment resembling that of the shallows beneath the merchant ship. Along the winding streets packed with homes and shops were ragged tents littered with goods awaiting sale. To the best of his recollection, Ira could find no significant change to the Forager's Cove, with the exception of the sandstone tower rising as high as the hilltop cypresses.

The Haurthian Navy had little reason to travel to inconsequential islands such as this other than to resupply fresh water and provisions. When Mágna the Snakeheart and his dark sword, Dominion, came to plague the Bridging Sea, cohorts of trained mariners were stationed upon the remote islands to protect their citizens. But as pirate raids grew scarce, the ransacking of ports and their riches grew common. The mariners were thereafter returned to their original posts of guarding the waters and the two mainlands. In the absence of any local and legitimate governance, colonized islands across the known world created their own establishments in their nominal communities. Some flourished for generations; others crumbled in less than a fortnight. What veteran voyagers of the East and West did know was to always be wary of harboring in these isolated societies. One could never be certain whether they might arrive to find civilized order, vile tyranny, or rabid anarchy. It, therefore, came as no surprise when Halruc gave the order for the *Wayfarer*'s meager armory to be dispersed amongst the sailors.

"A needless precaution, I dare say," the master assured them as Cercur emerged on deck with the bundle of rusty gladiuses and scabbards. "Nevertheless, I expect all of you to remain in pairs as you comb the streets. Manoque and I will fetch the necessary provisions to take us as far as Mason. The rest of you will scrounge the Cove for buyers of our shipments. Return with the highest bids you can barter out of these islanders, but no trade is to be considered official until I have had the final say. Cercur and the mute will remain on watch aboard the *Wayfarer*."

A chorus of "Aye, master" sounded as the rowboat was removed from storage and set into the coral-strewn harbor. The crew crammed together in the small vessel and hailed towards the bank. Ira could see Esther staring towards the *Wayfarer* and the mute dwarf, watching them from the bow.

"We will have time to bid our farewells if we do secure passage to the West," Ira muttered to her. "For now, Halruc's knowledge is enough."

The rowboat beached upon dry sands only a few paces from the road spanning the shoreline. As the packed crew hobbled out of their vessel, a man clad in a ragged white tunic and an antique iron chestplate approached them from the village. His face was all cheer and cordiality, but his hand rested at the ready upon his sheathed weapon.

"The Chief of the Levies bids you welcome, travelers," the man said loftily. Something in the airiness of his words reminded Ira sickly of the magistrate back in Gales. "I have been sent forth to greet you as well as to collect on the toll."

"Toll?" exclaimed Puck cynically.

"For anchoring in the harbor," the man informed them.

"And who are you to demand payment from us?" asked Halruc cynically.

"I am a Levy of the Cove," the man said assertively. "My men and I are charged with maintaining the welfare and protection of our humble island. Of course, you are more than welcome to forgo the harbor toll and take your vessel to the outer banks. I would warn you, though, that it is a long and rocky path to the village from anywhere but the harbor." The sailors were ripe with annoyance. Even Halruc made no effort to hide his displeasure from the levy. "Just a meager toll," the man assured the master.

"How much for the night?" asked Halruc.

"Ten denarii."

Ram huffed as he stared about the vacant harbor. Halruc countered the levy with four denarii, which was stoutly refused as the man claimed he could accept no less than eight.

"Very well then," said a passive Halruc, "we shall heed your advice and anchor elsewhere."

Before any of the irritated crew could clamber back into the rowboat, the levy called out to the master with the ask of five. Halruc consented and paid the man as his sailors paired up to comb the island for trade deals. The natural couplings of Ram and Ossel, as well as Tabor and the lad, split off first to venture into the village, followed by Dromo and Ishcaur, and then Nathanael and Puck. Halruc offered no words to the final pair left on the beach but did shoot the prince and princess a wary glance as he and Manoque set off down one of the winding roads.

"Where is the tavern?" Ira asked the levy.

"Huh? Oh, down that road, by the watchtower," the man replied distractedly, adding Halruc's silver to his jingling purse as he strode away.

Ira might have guessed as much. Most of the shops and tents along the roads had been vacated for the night, but moving shadows could be narrowly glimpsed within the larger establishment across from the sandstone tower. There was the place they might inquire about any ships headed west for Haurth. They strode along the street, past grungy strangers and curious onlookers. As they went, Ira discretely passed Érnog's dagger into Esther's hand. She hid the blade in the folds of her dress as Ira's eyes darted towards every passerby, his hand resting on his aged sword. They glimpsed Tabor in one of the tents along the dirt path, speaking to a local vendor. As his father discussed business, the lad was occupied sniffing the contents of one of the jars for sale.

They passed them by as, from around the tent, there came a high, shriveled voice from a pile of dirtied rags.

"Come closer, child," the voice called. "Let me see your face."

Ira and Esther were hardly near enough to catch the eerie summons as the lad peered around the edge of the tent to see where the sound had come from. Upon second glance, Ira saw that the heap of rags was, in fact, a person—a woman, it seemed—by the pitch of the voice. She was wrapped in layers of frayed cloth and seated against the nearest shop wall. The beggar hardly moved as the lad came closer. Were it not for the pocket in her layers exposing a patch of olive skin and a pair of pale eyes, the heap would not be discernible as a living being.

"Closer, yes, closer, child. I wish to tell you something."

Tabor was too consumed in negotiations with the vendor to notice the voice or his son's disappearance from the tent. From the ragged layers emerged a lank, bony hand reaching to take the lad's. The gesture brought instant clarity to Ira as he sprang from Esther's side towards the young sailor. Yanked backwards by the collar of his tunic, the lad stumbled to the ground as the pauper woman's outstretched hand grazed one of Ira's fingers. Tabor charged from the tent at the sound of the strange commotion as the lad was being helped to his feet by Esther. Grabbing his son by the arm, Tabor snatched him away from the lady with an instinctive glare. The burly man's spiteful expression towards the princess slowly faded as he saw a hurt Esther lower her gaze. The tensions were interrupted by a high, haggard voice that made Ira and Tabor draw their weapons and point them at the rags.

"Fire . . . death . . . raining on high," uttered the beggar woman. "Shrouding all . . . consuming all . . . fire . . . death . . . fire . . ."

The vendor whom Tabor had been in conference with limped on his walking stick out of the tent. At the sight of the rags beneath Ira's blade, the man hollered in fury.

"Back! Back you!" he bellowed. To Ira's astonishment, the vendor began prodding away not the beggar woman but himself. As Ira recoiled in pain, the limping man turned his walking stick upon the pauper. "I told you never to return here! Off! Off with you, witch!"

The man jabbed his stick again, but only at the air around the heaps of aged cloth. Even as he barked more threats at the beggar woman, the vendor gradually retreated, horrorstruck and pale in the face. All the while, the same sullen words called from the heap. "Death . . . fire . . . death . . ." The lump of rags slowly stretched upright and shuffled away up the road. The high, uttering voice turned to shrill, haunting cries the further she lumbered along. When the beggar was far removed from the scene, the vendor turned his rage upon the lad.

"Mad child! Do you wish to curse us all? You may think it a joke, boy, but mystics are no laughing matter on this island!"

The lad stood dumbstruck and bewildered as to the reason for the vendor's lashing out at him. Still fuming, the limping man bid Tabor a swift and discourteous good evening before trudging back to his tent.

"What was that about?" asked the lad.

"Islanders can be a bit funny about their ways," said Tabor, "especially when it comes to mystics."

"People with an unusual enchantment upon them," Esther said in response to the lad's curious face.

The lad appeared on the verge of asking more about mystics when Ira cut him off.

"We ought not spend the whole night speaking with one another," he said to Tabor. "Let us be about the master's tasks. We will see you back on the ship."

As Ira and Esther started up the road again, Tabor called out to them.

"Thank you," he said with an apologetic glance at Esther. "Thank you both."

The appreciation for their protection of his son was acknowledged with a gentle smile and nod from both brother and sister. They strolled along their way towards the shimmering lights and lively chatter pouring out of the tavern. Ira fought to keep his aims clear as they approached the establishment, but the beggar's screeching words would not cease their sickly echoing inside his head.

As they came upon the stony tavern, Esther pulled her veil a little closer, and the both of them felt for the blades they carried. With a deep breath, they passed through the entry and underneath the doorway's carving of a snake coiled about an anchor. The place was brimming with patrons, all seated upon aged sacks around many low tables. Simple cushions were commonplace in such public establishments, as the luxury of chairs was hardly to be expected anywhere beyond the Westlands. Nathanael and Puck were discernible amongst the crowd, what with Puck being the only dwarf amongst the many islander men. The sailors were conversing with a man at their table with sun-kissed skin and unkempt hair. Ira peered through the sea of heads until he spotted the bartender pouring drinks behind a stone counter.

"Stay close," he muttered to Esther under his breath. They made their way around the tables toward the other end of the room. A few chattering heads turned to observe the strangers as they went, while others remained engulfed in their merry diversions.

When they reached their companions' table, Ira begged their pardon for the intrusion and asked if Esther could join them while he spoke to the bartender. The islander at the table, who was introduced as a local whaler, obliged the request and beckoned Esther to sit with them. With a reassuring glance from Nathanael, Ira parted from them and made his way back through the crowd of patrons. He found a place along the stone counter next to a pale man with a thick coat and long gray hair whose tankard was being refilled.

"And for you?" the bartender said to the new arrival.

"I see a few sailors in tonight," Ira commented casually. "Where are they all headed?"

"All over, I suppose," said the man in a bored sort of voice.

"Any of them heading west?"

The man shrugged. Apparently peeved by Ira's senseless questioning, the man turned away to occupy his time elsewhere.

"Where can I find a vessel bound for Haurth?" Ira asked in a low, blunt voice.

Perhaps for the sake of getting the man to either buy a drink or leave him alone, the bartender considered the inquiry.

"The levies might have heard something. Nothing happens in the Cove without their say-so. I would ask them, or better yet, try their chief."

This information, while advantageous in the bartender's eyes, was anything but to Ira. Halruc had warned him against crossing paths with anyone of authority who might not take kindly to the discovery of him and Esther.

"Thank you for your help," said Ira, "but I think I shall—"

"Beg your pardon, chief. Do you know of any ships headed westward?"

To Ira's horror, the bartender was addressing none other than the long-haired man beside him. As the chief rounded on the inquiring traveler, Ira's impulse to look away was halted by an unexpected realization. The chief was not, in fact, a man but an elf. Beneath a disheveled mat of gray hair, his pale complexion, bare chin, and pointed ears made him perfectly discernible from the scruffy men about the tavern. Then, a second, more startling revelation came upon Ira as he recognized the elf's face through the eyes of his youth—through the eyes of an officer training under his admiral.

"Litanius?"

Ira could not help himself. The sight of his former mentor stole all other thoughts from his mind. Once the esteemed Praelaum of the Haurthian Navy and a member of the Emperor's Court, the elf had shriveled into a feeble reflection of his former self. Ira gaped as the chief examined him through a drunken daze.

"As I have told you before, David," the elf sputtered to the bartender, "I am only to be disturbed if someone wishes to buy this public servant another round."

Downing the last of his drink, the chief slammed his tankard on the counter, sending drops of wine flying.

"Litanius, it is me, Ira."

"Ira . . . Ira . . ." The elf repeated the name to himself, straining to find its meaning somewhere in the recess of his memory. "I once knew a lad by that name. A good soldier, a good man. You are not him; he died a long time ago."

"No, Litanius, I did not—"

"He and that sister of his, now what was her name?"

"Esther and I are alive. We were—"

"They are dead, I say!" he bellowed out of nowhere. Hardly anyone in the tavern paid mind to the chief's sudden outburst.

"The prince and officer I once knew died long ago. So, tell me, who is the man before me who ventures to my island? A whaler? A tradesman? A pirate, perhaps?"

"I was a tanner's apprentice in Anthazar before I came here."

"Well, now, that is a fine practice. Not one I would have chosen for a man of your talent, but beggars we were made. You seem to have done all right for yourself."

"It seems I am not the only one, chief," replied Ira as he took in the discolored iron chestplate beneath the elf's heavy cloak and the formerly white tunic stained with streaks of spilled wine.

"Chief? Come now, Ira, we shall have none of that formality here," said Litanius in drunken cheer. "Certainly, this post is far from commanding the empire's fleets, but the refreshments are sublime. Bartender! Pour my dear old companion a drink. Let us toast this merry reunion!"

The bartender refilled the chief's tankard and offered Ira his own. They drank together, and Ira stifled a cough at the bitter taste of vinegar. Beside him, the elf downed his tankard once more and slammed it again upon the counter.

"Litanius," began Ira, "I am in need of your assistance. Esther and I have come here seeking passage to—"

"Is she here too?" interjected Litanius. "Where is she? Let her have a drink with us as well!"

"Later, perhaps. Do you know of—"

"What is your hurry, young Ira? Relax. Sit a while. Your troubles and errands will await you in the morning." The chief gave a drowsy look about the room before leaning in close to whisper with his sour breath. "Listen, Ira; no one is sorrier than I for . . . well, it was cruel, the whole ordeal." Ira did not reply but took another sip of the vulgar wine. "Had I acted sooner, I might have saved Darius from his dark fate and the two of us from the aftermath."

"It was in my power to end the emperor's terrible reign, not yours," said Ira consolingly. "I am sorry banishment has brought you to this present state."

"Banishment?" replied Litanius. "I was never banished from Haurth. I came to the Cove of my own volition some years ago."

"Well," said Ira in surprise, "thank goodness for that. I suppose the arbiter stripped you of the admiralty, then. Is that when you came to govern here?"

Litanius took a long draft from his tankard before replying. "No, I remained praelaum until I retired a year after your father's rule was ended." Opening his cloak, the elf revealed a set of tassels identical to those the admiral of the galley *Requiarda* had worn upon his belt.

"What of the general?" asked Ira. "Did he remain at his post?"

"No, no, he was banished shortly after your trial."

"Help me to understand then," said Ira darkly, "why the general, my sister, and I were fortunate to escape with our lives while you retained your freedom and station for the same crimes we were found guilty of." As the elf averted his old companion's gaze, Ira's voice turned bitter and accusatory. "Explain yourself."

"We were all of us condemned men," said Litanius hollowly, "accessories to a warmongering emperor. I would have been sentenced alongside the rest of you had it not been for . . . well, it was all I could do to secure my own liberation."

"Had it not been for what?" grunted Ira.

"He told me your conviction was imminent. He said the arbiter would not grant me a pardon if I came to your defense."

"Who? Who told you this?" demanded Ira. When the elf did not meet his gaze, Ira's indignation swelled as he uttered, "Lysias?"

"I tried to persuade him to appeal on your behalf, but he said you were a lost cause."

"And you were not?" muttered Ira.

"I was. I was to be reduced to a lowly pauper like the rest of you unless . . . unless I testified against you and the others. Unless I swore that you all encouraged the emperor and his mad plans and that I had done all in my power to sway the court from pursuing war against the Eastlands."

"Encouraged my father?" scoffed Ira. "How could you perjure us so? And what reason could Lysias have for wishing the rest of us to be condemned?"

"There had to be scapegoats for the empire's treachery, pariahs to take the fall and wash away the sins preceding Lysias' regime. He considered the banishment of the empire's traitors to be the only means of securing the fealty of the agitated Eastlands. I gave my aid to the premier's cause, and in exchange, I was pardoned from any association with the last emperor's vile deeds."

A livid heat coursed under Ira's skin as he took back every word he had ever uttered in defense of the galleymaster who taught him and the premier who rose to power.

"Curse the elf and curse you!" spat Ira.

"I took no pleasure in your condemnation," hissed Litanius, "but can you honestly say that if offered the same chance, you would not have grasped at freedom as well?"

"And what of my sister?" muttered Ira. "She had no part in any of the court's affairs. Did you even lift a finger for her sake, or does her life count for so little in your regard?"

"Ira," said the elf, his voice edging towards aggravation, "the daughter of a mad tyrant, no matter her innocence, would never be acquitted by trial nor in the eyes of the people. I risked my only chance at redemption pleading for your defense at all. You should be so grateful for what I—"

Before his sword had left its scabbard, Ira felt a jolt from behind his foot, and his back hit the floor with a sharp thud. His head spun as he stared up at the thatched tavern roof. The chief stood above him in drunken vigilance, the point of his blade resting under Ira's chin. The tavern's patrons turned their attentions towards the pair in eager hopes of an ensuing brawl. Esther was gaping at the sight of who it was standing over her brother. Nathanael made to unleash his sword, but Ira caught sight of him in time to wave off his approach.

"Age has not yet stolen my prowess, boy," said Litanius sternly as he recoiled his aged gladius to offer a hand. Ira did not accept it and instead pulled himself to his feet as the islanders groaned and resumed their discourse.

"So after all these years," Ira said as he massaged his back, "this is what has become of you. A tax collector posing as a protector."

"I resent that," said Litanius casually. "My levies and I have fended off many a raid since we established order in the Cove. Such services do not come without their price. It is true; the Horde has not dared to besiege my island for some time now, but I cannot help it if business is good."

The elf gave a sly grin as he patted the inner pocket of his cloak, melodically rattling his purse.

"If you never lost the admiralty or your reputation, then why did you come to the Forager's Cove in the first place?"

"Who said I never lost my post?" retorted the elf. "The arbiter acquitted me of all charges as they related to your father's treacheries, but the respect a praelaum commands about his fleets is not so easily restored. A year after you were banished, the premier appointed an esteemed galleymaster to succeed me as admiral. At the time, Lysias was struggling to garner the allegiance of the new governors. I imagine his resigning me from the post was mainly a ploy to earn the respect of the Eastern leaders. They never quite forgot the position I held during Darius the Damned's reign. I had already been exiled from all decent society in Haurth. And when my title as praelaum was cast away, my reputation amongst the Western people was scorched beyond repair."

"Imagine my pity," said Ira sardonically.

"I do not claim my misfortunes were undeserved," added Litanius. "My efforts to evade them only delayed their arrival. Rather than wallow in seclusion for the rest of my days, I sought to regain any shred of my former dignity. Mastering a vessel of some trade seemed the appropriate path for one with as many years behind the helm as I. A whaling ship took me on for a short spell until a shortage of provisions brought us here. When I arrived, the levies were no more than a ragged militia. Here was my chance, at last, to renew my purpose as a leader. I forfeited the prospect of mastering a vessel so I might master this island. The Cove, this insignificant rock, has become my grand vocation. I shall never rise above this station, and someday, another stronger than I shall covet all I have built here. This is to be my atonement."

A boisterous cheer from one of the tables rang across the tavern as the man and the elf stood quietly at the counter. Ira only drank from his tankard, so he might have some reason not to speak. The sour taste that coated his tongue distracted his mind enough to recall Ira's reason for coming to the tavern.

"I did not come here to rekindle memories of old. I am seeking a vessel sailing for Haurth. Do you know of any in the Cove?"

"What concern is it of yours?"

Under his breath, Ira replied, "Esther and I are bound for Vistérae."

Litanius gave a deep sigh. "Hoping to live out the rest of your days in the place that mariners are forbidden to enter?" he said with a note of annoyance. "Willing to risk a death sentence should you be caught and face the arbiter again? You said you had a life in the provinces, yes? Return to it and bother me no longer."

"There is no life in the provinces for her," said Ira. He nodded towards the table where Esther sat between Nathanael and Puck. The shadow of her mark ran along her cheek under the flittering lanterns. Litanius glimpsed her briefly before returning his gaze to the contents of his tankard. "Will you help us?" asked Ira.

"I am sorry for her misfortunes," said Litanius ruefully. "But if any knew that I aided the children of Darius the Damned, I could . . ." But the elf's words trailed as he looked upon the man and recognized the boy he had once known. After another long gulp, the elf wiped his mouth and muttered, "Let me ask around."

Ira inclined his head toward the elf but had no present wish to remain in his company. "Esther and I can be found aboard the *Wayfarer*, should you—"

At that moment, the chattering room fell unnaturally quiet. Ira and Litanius looked for the source of the disturbance and found two figures standing in the entryway, both clad in sapphire and silver. From behind the mariners came an elven officer in blue and bronze, surveying the crowded tables before raising his voice to address the hushed patrons.

"By decree of the High Court," announced the officer, "a census of every island, province, and realm of the empire is to be conducted by the Legions of Haurth. All islanders and travelers will offer up their documents for inspection."

Ira's eyes darted to Esther, then to Nathanael, and back to Litanius as two more mariners entered from the road.

"They cannot discover you," hissed Litanius. "We shall go through the back to the watchtower; you can hide from the mariners there. Go, fetch your sister."

Ira took the tankard from Litanius' hand as well as his own while the soldiers began examining the many patrons' documents. Crossing to the far side of the tavern, Ira set the half-empty tankards before Nathanael and Puck as he took Esther's arm and helped her to her feet. They strolled innocently towards Litanius, standing at the back door. Halfway there, a man across the room was seized by one of the Haurthian soldiers. Esther's arm shook as she clung to her brother. The officer across the way looked over the detained man's document with stern animosity.

"Theft and failure to comply with tax laws," the officer read aloud. "Not much, but he may know of others we seek. Take him to the galley."

Ira and Esther fought against the impulse to sprint to the back door. They were a few paces away when . . .

"You there!"

They froze as one of the mariners started marching between the tables to the brother and sister. Ira made ready to reach for his sword as Esther clutched the dagger at her side. As the soldier drew nearer, Nathanael snatched Puck's tankard of wine and spilled it upon himself. Rising to his feet, Nathanael bellowed, "You drunken oaf!" and shoved the dwarf onto the floor. The disruption caught the attention of all in the tavern. After a moment's confusion and a glance from Ira, Puck comprehended the scheme and thumped Nathanael hard in the gut. The staged brawl drew the tavern patrons into an onlooking huddle as the mariners attempted to break up the fight. Ira and Esther did not wait to see the outcome as they followed Litanius' lead through the back door into a tight room brimming with barrels and jugs.

"What about them?" Esther asked desperately.

"I imagine they will be all right," said Litanius, leading the way, "so long as neither has any criminal record."

Another door hidden between two stacks of barrels led them outside into an alley between the tavern and the next shop over. They strode along the narrow passage until they came to its end at the roadside. The watchtower was just across the way. Litanius' arm halted their strides as he gestured for them to remain quiet and peered around the tavern's corner.

"There are more of them in the streets," said the elf. "I count half a dozen headed this way."

"Do we go back?" asked Ira. "Hide in the storage room?"

"No, the mariners inside will check there soon enough. Ira, give me your sword." The request deeply affronted Ira, whose grasp on the hilt only tightened. But the urgency in Litanius' eyes stole all reason from him as he begrudgingly handed over his scabbard and sword. The elf added Ira's gladius to his belt, opposite his own. "All right," he said, hiding the blades beneath his heavy cloak, "follow my lead."

Litanius positioned himself behind Ira and Esther and began to walk with his hands grasping the hems of their garments. The three ambled across the road towards the sandstone watchtower, not daring to turn their heads in the slightest.

"Halt!"

They were trapped in the middle of the road. As another elven officer and his squad of mariners approached, Ira glimpsed behind them many scattered mariners leading men writhing in shackles towards the shore. A rowboat on the sands was pointed towards a Haurthian galley anchored beside the *Wayfarer*. Echoing wails pleading for help cried over the dwellings from other roads in the village.

"Not to worry, torlaum, I have these two," Litanius said officially to the approaching officer. "There are others attempting to flee inspection down the road. I suggest you send your soldiers to apprehend them before they get too far."

"Halt!" the officer repeated as Litanius took another step towards the tower, still gripping Ira and Esther forcefully. "The census is being conducted by the legions. You"—he glanced disdainfully at Litanius' stained tunic and rusted chestplate— "have no authority here."

"I am Chief of the Levies, the guardians and governing body of the Forager's Cove. One of your officers in the tavern bid me to escort these two brigands to the watchtower."

"That will not be necessary," said the officer, who beckoned two mariners holding iron shackles forward.

"Is this how a former praelaum is to be treated for his years of service?" demanded Litanius with an air of indignation. Relinquishing his hand from Esther's hem, he threw aside his cloak to reveal the admiral's tassels hung upon his belt. Even in their faded state, the fine cords could not be mistaken for counterfeit. The officer stared in disbelief as he cast an inquisitive gaze upon the elf.

"And what corpse did you rob those off of? Unless . . ." The elven officer gave the chief a cynical laugh. "Can it be the disgraced admiral? I say, Litanius, you have indeed fallen from your station."

"Be that as it may," said Litanius through gritted teeth, "I still serve the empire and the High Court."

"Not in this matter. Now, hand over the prisoners."

The fingers of the mariners behind their leader danced upon the hilts of their sheathed swords. With great reluctance, the chief released his grip upon the brother and sister's garments and resignedly raised his hands. Two Western soldiers stepped forward, chains rattling sickly in their hands. The shackles had nearly closed around Ira's wrists when . . .

Without warning, a loud hiss of steel cut the air as the tips of Litanius' dual swords were thrust into the soldiers' iron chestplates. The attack was registered instantaneously, as with a fiery rage, the officer and his remaining soldiers unleashed their weapons and hurled at the chief. Litanius cast his cloak aside to toss Ira his blade just in time for him to deflect a lash aimed at the elf's head. Esther darted for cover towards the tavern as the distant scattering of blue uniforms along the shore abandoned the apprehended prisoners and hustled towards the fray. An outnumbered Ira and Litanius deflected the elves' coordinated attacks from all directions. Their own blows had little effect, as the glimmering shields opposing them refused to miss a single strike aimed at their hosts. Afforded not a moment's rest, the prince and the admiral were backed against their whims until they found themselves cornered against the base of the watchtower.

There was a sharp whistle from above. A streaking arrow plummeted into the elven officer's glistening helmet, striking him dead in an instant. The soldiers' attacks ceased momentarily as cruel instinct told them to search for the arrow's sender. It was long enough to afford Ira and Litanius their chance. Catching the remaining mariners off guard, the two barreled around the three and pinned them against the watchtower. Ira struck one soldier in the side as a second arrow whistled into the collar of another. While Litanius engaged the last of the squad, Ira turned to face the wave of Haurthian soldiers thundering their way. He took up a felled mariner's shield and braced himself. As the sea of sapphire neared, a band of crudely uniformed levies emerged from the shadows to meet them. At the same time, a throng of enraged islanders brandishing swords flooded out of the tavern to join the Cove's protectors. Clarion warcries trumpeted all around as the street plunged into battle.

Having defeated the last mariner cornered against the tower, Litanius joined Ira, and the two flung into the conflict together. Amidst the gaggle of fighters, Ira could discern Tabor, taller than even the elven soldiers. He bore his gladius down upon the mariners who clung to their shields for protection. Ira thought he had glimpsed Nathanael somewhere in the chaos, and he was sure he had seen the shortened figure of a dwarf in the scrimmage as well. Harsh groans and painful cries followed pings and swipes of steel. Thick beads of sweat flung from impelling limbs as the cold evening air turned dense and heated. From atop the tower, the levy archer, who had rescued Ira and Litanius from certain death, continued sending howling arrows into the mayhem, each tip finding its mark. As a swiping blade created a lengthy lash in Ira's tunic, narrowly avoiding his chest, another's gladius ran the mariner through the back and out of his stomach. As the body fell, a dwarf with pale hair was revealed, his bloodied sword grasped in a hand decked with gemstone rings.

"We heard the commotion!" panted Halruc as he and Ira paired against another blue uniform. "We have not the numbers to fend off this many!"

In the swarm, Ira recognized more familiar faces. Not far from him and the master, Ishcaur suffered a deep gash to his sword-wielding arm. His gladius fell to the ground as he ducked to avoid a strike to his head. Before another fatal thrash could be delivered, the dwarf barreled a ferocious fist into the elf's kneecap with his good arm. A thunderous crack of bone was followed by a roar of agony as the mariner keeled over. Manoque, Dromo, and Ossel were huddled with a couple of levies as they dueled several sapphire-clad soldiers beside one of the shops. Ira was about to rush to their aid when, in the corner of his eye, he spotted the lad fending off a brutal mariner all on his own. The young warrior fumbled backwards onto the dirt road as his weapon was pelted out of his hand by a vicious blow of the soldier's gladius. The fearful lad made to scurry away from the looming mariner's reach until another figure came between them. The savior was not armed with a sword but with the blade of Érnog shaking in her palm.

Ira wanted to hurl himself at the soldier, to take his life brutally and without hesitation. But the way to Esther was blocked by another in blue and silver. Ira made every attempt to fell the mariner, but the elf continued to skirt each of his vicious attacks. He could only watch helplessly as a crimson-stained sword was held high to strike the lady bearing only a dagger in her defense. Ira roared over the commotion as the blade plummeted. Then, out of nowhere, the sword's path was disrupted as it suddenly spun in the air away from its intended target. The mariner's helmet was also sent hurling away by the force of the mute's tackle. Wasting no time, the dwarf, drenched from his swim to join the battle, pounded his knuckles into the soldier's temple, knocking him out cold.

A weary Ira labored to fend off the evasive mariner's blows. The shock of an arrow whizzing so close to his head was followed by immediate relief as it struck the mariner before him dead. As Ira made to rush to Esther's side, he tripped and fell over a body hidden in the throng of fighters. His sweaty face was coated in dirt as he stared into the vacant face of the slain islander beside him. He dazedly looked around him and, for the first time, took in sight of the many bodies strewn about the road. Mariners and men alike were sprawled about, their brothers stepping over and around them to continue the senseless brawl in their stead. Ira could not tell which side now had greater numbers, but he could see through the legs of those still fighting two rowboats hailing from the anchored galley. The small crafts were brimming with dwarven mariners armed with bows and quivers.

"Up with you, prince!" shouted a bloodied Litanius, pulling Ira to his feet. "We are not out of the fray yet! More are on the way!"

"Esther," muttered Ira, "I have to get to—"

"Look out!" cried someone from the throng.

Heads reeled as a ball of light hurling from the harbor blinded the fighters to their surroundings. The fiery projectile struck the archer's tower with an explosive crack, sending chunks of sandstone showering over the battle. Duels were abandoned as rubble sprayed across the road and darkness shrouded the street.

CHAPTER XII

THE TRENCH

The world was spinning in an empty void. A splitting pain in his head greeted Ira as he came to his senses. He labored to open his lids, but a stabbing light from above stopped him as his head spun more violently. Ira tried to focus on any part of his body that was not throbbing or numb. He was lying on his back; he was almost certain of it. Rousing his fingers to life, they swam beside him through coarse sand warm to the touch. He opened and closed them several times before noting an incessant ringing in his deafened ears. The shrill monotone noise, once realized, was impossible to ignore and chafed Ira more than even the blinding light. Desperate for any discerning sense to return to him, he pried his lids open as scolding daylight struck his dry eyes.

The sun was high above as Ira painstakingly sat up on the bank. The effort of this simple task caused him to vomit on the sand beside him, but the reflex served to relieve some of his aching. He gazed bleakly towards the harbor, trying to remember how he had come to be on the beach. A vague memory of clashing swords lingered in the back of his mind. Whether it was a memory of old or a new one, he could not recall. As he touched a hand to his spinning head, Ira felt a wad of cloth plastered above his ear. The tender spot felt as though it had been struck by some blunt object. Blood and sand were muddled together on his fingertips as

Ira recoiled his hand from his midnight hair. Though his hearing was still impaired, a muffled moan managed to cut through the ceaseless ringing.

On his left was an elderly man lying beside him on the shore. One of his legs was wrapped in thick bandages, and his foot was pointed in an unnatural direction. The man made no coherent words. He only moaned and muttered to the sky and the seahawks swarming overhead. Glancing up from the broken soul by his side, Ira saw that he had been laid in one of three lines on the beach. Women and children were shuffling between the injured with strips of cloth and dripping waterskins. Some of the wounded were upright, like Ira, while others lay still on crimson sands. The man to Ira's right had lost all color from his face. The body drew no breath as a hand rested peacefully upon the deep hollow in his chest.

A shadow crept over the dead man as a woman knelt beside Ira to offer him fresh water.

"What happened?" he said, but he could hardly discern his own words through his clouded ears. The woman's reply was equally muffled, but Ira thought he could make out something about a galley, a catapult, the tower, and his head. He was about to accept a draft from her when the gentle face beneath a plain veil summoned a terrific realization to his spinning mind. The woman dropped the waterskin as Ira sprang to his feet and nearly collapsed from dizziness. Staggering between the lines of bodies, he searched from one face to another in a fit of panic, praying not to find the familiar face of a young lady. The shore was littered mostly with the bodies of men, but at each feminine figure he came upon, Ira halted to examine the victim's blurry features before setting off again in a waking horror. Some of the women and children tending to the injured tried to calm Ira from his frenzy, but to no avail. The lines of wounded and dead were coming to an end as Ira began to wonder whether she might have taken refuge in the village or aboard the *Wayfarer*. He was ready to forfeit his search on the beach when he spotted a hazy figure kneeling on the sand, a patterned scarlet cloth clutched over her midriff.

A stabbing chill coursed through Ira as he rushed to the woman using her veil as a healing swathe. Only when he was by her side did Esther's dismal face come into focus. A tear fell from her cheek onto the wadded veil pressed, not over herself as it had first appeared, but over a head lying in her lap. If the wound to the short figure's head were not so deep, it might have remained hidden beneath his long auburn hair and beard. Esther's eyes did not flinch from the mute's as her brother kneeled beside her. The ailing dwarf's labored breaths were quickening every second as she dabbed gently upon the gash oozing into his thick mane. Words were absent as the gasps grew fainter under the sound of gentle waves ebbing and flowing upon the banks. The sailor's eyes drifted from the lady's face up to the bright sky and flickered their last upon the new day.

"He pushed us aside, the lad and me, when the tower . . ." Her voice was barely a whisper, as though she dared not disturb the dwarf resting still in her lap. "I cannot even mourn him by his name."

Ira would have given anything to have the ringing return to hinder his hearing again. The brokenness in Esther's voice was more unbearable than any pain searing in his body.

"Is the lad all right?" he asked.

"Yes, he and the others are fine. They are digging the grave just down the way. You should go to them; they will want to know that you are awake."

"In a bit," said Ira, watching her with a brother's concern.

"Go to them," she insisted, "there are others who require my aid."

"It can wait."

Esther looked up and gave him a hollow smile. "I will come and find you later." Carefully lifting the mute's head from her lap, she rested it gently upon the sands before rising to her feet. Ira watched as she strode into the harbor until her feet were submerged. There, she washed her veil of the dwarf's blood with each low surge of the crashing waves. On another day, the Cove might have been a beautiful place, with its pale blue waters and coral reef dazzling beneath its surface. As he took in his surroundings, Ira spotted a tall mound of freshly dug earth beyond the shore and away from the village. He was about to head over when he received a tap on the shoulder. Standing over him was Nathanael.

"Grab his legs, will you?" he said quietly, nodding to the lifeless dwarf.

Ira obliged him. Together, they hoisted the mute's body and carried him along the water's edge. Several footprints were etched in the sand leading to the grave site, hailing to and from the beach and the village roads. A broken pillar of sandstone remained upright where once the watchtower stood guard over the Cove. Its collapse had been severely felt by the neighboring shops, and the once-busy tavern was reduced to rubble and ruins. From the shoreline, Ira could make out a few stray limbs protruding from the heaps of debris veiling the road. As he and Nathanael neared the dug-earth mound, they were passed by Tabor and the lad on a return journey to the village for another victim. Their numb gazes lingered as father and son recognized the dwarf in their companions' arms. The detached lad said nothing but trudged on behind Tabor to fetch the next body.

When he and Nathanael reached the edge of the mound, Ira peered into a wide trench to see the dwarves of the *Wayfarer* hard at work. Their arms and legs were blanketed in layers of earth as their spades heaved the ground beneath them. Even the master had joined in the excavation. Consequently, Halruc's finely woven mantle was sullied beyond repair, though he showed no sign of care. They dug with fierce strikes of their spades as though the labor might tire them enough to drive away all terrible thoughts. No dwarf, not Dromo in his aged state, nor Ishcaur with the deep lash upon his arm, broke a sweat as they bore into the thick dirt edging the sandy beach. The soil offered little challenge to those who were naturally built for moving and shaping mountains of stone. Ira hoped the dwarves would not cease their work long enough to notice the one he and Nathanael carried. But as they laid the mute gently beside the other cold bodies, the sound of burrowing spades fell silent. Neither of them wishing to stand idle in the rueful moment, the two men parted from the sailors' company to fetch another victim.

Over and over, Ira and Nathanael trod from the trench to the shore and village in a monotonous cycle of morbidity. No conversation was shared as they repeatedly passed Tabor, the lad, and those men who had not lost their lives in the evening's conflict. Amongst the islanders at work were other men not native to the Cove. With no crew of Western soldiers to receive orders from, the hired rowers of the Haurthian galley had offered themselves to aid in the village's recovery. The levies, it seemed, had begrudgingly accepted the rowers' help, though they did not refrain from showing their resentment towards the men for their association with the defeated mariners.

The sight of the Cove militia brought to mind someone Ira had not seen since the tower's debris had knocked him out cold. He kept his eyes peeled for the elf's pale face as he and Nathanael combed the rubble-paved road for the dead. As they excavated their third victim from a pile of sandstone, Ira caught a glimpse of Litanius through the colossal wreckage of the tavern. With the help of Manoque, the chief had removed a chunk of the wall to reveal the vacant face of the departed bartender. After all the former admiral had revealed to him the previous night, Ira could not tell whether he felt relief or resentment at the sight of his once-trusted ally. Litanius had risked much to protect his sister and himself from the mariners last night; there was no point denying it. But was it enough to excuse the admiral's false condemnation of them—the condemnation that had set in motion every misfortune of the last twelve years? No, this, in Ira's mind, could never be fully pardoned. The carnage of the Cove mingled with private fury as Ira yearned for the chance to unleash his wrath upon the elf, not only for Litanius' betrayal but for the one who had convicted the prince and princess in the name of appeasing the masses rather than delivering true justice. But as his rage swelled amidst the mournful surroundings, Ira was recalled to his better senses and cursed himself for presently dwelling on his own bygone misfortunes.

By the time the trench grave was thoroughly excavated, some seventy islanders and levies had been lined up to share their final resting place. When it seemed the last of the fallen had been collected, Ira noticed a cluster of men peering at something near the crumbled watchtower. He managed to shuffle to the huddle's center, where he found the attraction to be a pile of bloodied rags covering a frail body. The mystic, reduced to a beggar woman, lay sprawled on the ground, a crimson stain upon her exposed head.

She was not aged as her shrill voice had suggested her to be. She even appeared kind and gentle, with her lids closed over her pale eyes. No man dared approach the body, as the intensity of their stares suggested the same haunting thought. The crowd's tension was shattered with a collective gasp as Ira threw caution aside and hoisted the beggar into his arms by his lonesome. As one of her limp hands brushed against his own, Ira felt a cruel relief as death prevented the woman from calling out another eerie message to plague his days to come.

The huddle parted wider than necessary as he carried the mystic down the road towards the trench. The women and children were gathered there already, as well as the wounded who had the strength to join them. Ira was not met with any objections as he climbed into the trench and set the beggar woman on the soft earth. With the help of Nathanael, Tabor, and Manoque, they respectfully laid the cold bodies in their communal grave. Tears of the onlookers were shed for strangers and loved ones alike. As he held in his arms a boy no older than his own, Tabor could not restrain a shudder as he placed the body beside that of an elderly woman also caught in the crossfire. When the last body, that of an auburn-haired sailor, was settled in the trench, Halruc tore a clean strip off his tarnished mantle and laid it respectfully over the mute's eyes. Muffled cries and parting words came from islanders gathered around. Ira held Esther's hand as they and the crew of the *Wayfarer* stared at one who remained as silent in death as he was in life. The dwarf's innermost thoughts would follow him in anonymity to his eternal slumber. Knowing no other way to properly honor him, the sailors shared a quiet eulogy for their nameless companion.

When all others had left the site, the dwarves took up their spades again, and by dusk, the mound had been returned to the trench. The islanders and galley rowers settled that night around bonfires along the shore, none of them eager to be isolated in their mourning. Across the harbor, the bodies of the mariners had been indifferently piled into a great heap. The soldiers of Haurth were paid no mind that night as a mellow anthem was bowed by Puck to the souls of the departed. The fiddle's notes ambled across the harbor and echoed back like a siren's mesmerizing voice cherished by a lonely voyager.

Around their fire, the sailors of the *Wayfarer* cared not enough to ask their master what plans the new day would have in store for them. Tomorrow's troubles could wait, and yesterday's seemed foreign and distant, the worries of someone else untouched by life's harrowing tribulations. They watched the Haurthian galley sway gently in the harbor with no crew to command her. A rowboat filled with the Cove's levies was hailing from the warship back to shore. Perhaps their chief had tasked them with looting the vessel for any valuables it might carry. Ira could not bring himself to care what Litanius and his militia might be up to. He sat on the dry sands between his sister and the lad as the company watched their fire diminish into glowing embers.

"Esther said there was an enchantment upon that beggar woman," the lad said softly to Ira so only he could hear. "That is why none but you would carry her body, is it not?"

"Some would call it enchantment; others would deem it a curse," Ira replied in the same low voice. "Mystics bear the gift of foresight, the ability to see what has not yet come to fruition. They have existed for ages, and long ago, they were heralded by emperors and empresses for offering their prophecy by means of a single touch."

"What could be so bad about that?"

"Because, lad, when foresight offers bad tidings, frantic hearts scurry to blame the messenger. Consider, for a moment, how you would react if you were warned of something terrible and inevitable yet to come. What would you do?"

"I . . . I would do anything to prevent it."

"Of course you would, as would I and anyone else, for that matter. You can imagine the terror it wrought whenever witches and druids offered vague and haunting premonitions. Soon enough, people began speculating that the mystics were not, in fact, predicting calamities like famine and pestilence but creating them at will. Though there was no means to give proof to the idea, the prospect of curses being set upon rulers and their lands deeply frightened the empire. For this, the seers were ousted from society by the sovereign of the age. Despite their newfound infamy, it was rare to ever hear of a mystic being murdered in cold blood. Those already mad with fright feared most a curse being laid upon them by a dead spirit. To this day, mystics and their kind have either faded into rarity or else hidden their true nature from the world around them."

Before the lad could question the topic further, Ira received a tap on the shoulder and turned to see the tall figure of Litanius standing over him.

"A word, Ira?"

Halruc shot the chief and his servant an inquiring glance as they stepped out of earshot of the company.

"I sent a few of my levies to search aboard the galley," Litanius said in a hush. "They returned to me with this letter from the gailaum's study."

The elf offered him an unsealed scroll. Ira took it and read the Western scrawls in the dim firelight.

To the galleymaster of the galley **Benúra**, *April the twelfth, the year one thousand and seventy-six of the Haurthian Empire.*

By decree of the High Court, the empire census, formerly to be carried out by local governing forces, will now be conducted by the Legions of Haurth in the ports of every realm, island, and province under empire jurisdiction. The galley **Benúra** *will sail immediately for the Forager's Cove and collect all pertinent information of every household and individual.*

Furthermore, the mariners of the galley **Benúra** *are to procure any information that may relate to the seditionist movement arising in the Eastern provinces. Any individual found to be affiliated with or suspected of having knowledge pertaining to the seditionist movement is to be apprehended and considered dangerous. Individuals with a harsh criminal record are to be considered suspect.*

Once your mariners have completed the census of the Forager's Cove, the galley **Benúra** *will sail for Fortress Mariner to deliver the apprehended. Upon your arrival, your prisoners will join others being held interim at the fortress before they are escorted to Alaoth for trial.*

We will expect your arrival no later than April the twenty-third.

Cordially, General Concleor of the Haurthian Army

Ira had to reread the letter several times to ensure he grasped its whole meaning.

"The general expects the galley's arrival in less than a week," he remarked. "When it does not show . . ."

"He will send reinforcements to investigate what has become of it and its crew," said Litanius with an ominous glance at the pile of mariner bodies across the harbor.

Ira gazed at the many islanders comforting one another around their bonfires. "These people will be arrested the moment reinforcements arrive. What is Lysias' aim in all of this? It is the same violent path that led my father to ruin. What could have driven the High Court to such measures?"

"We can dwell on that later," said Litanius. "For now, we must concern ourselves with sending the women and children at least to safety."

"The letter claims the legions are reserving their efforts for the ports. If the events of last night are any indication of the census' conduct, others will have been reduced to warzones. We must send the families to those remote parts of the provinces; there, they will be safe from harm."

"Not for long, I expect," remarked Litanius. "When the general learns of what transpired last night, the legions will scour the mainland for the responsible party."

"We have no other course of action. The best we can hope for is to evade Western forces long enough to go into hiding."

"Yes," agreed Litanius, "but when they do find us, we must be prepared." The elf glanced towards the huddles around the bonfires and said, "I must inform the people to make ready to evacuate the Cove."

"I must speak with my crew as well," said Ira. "With this information, voyaging to Mason is entirely out of the question. Halruc will not be pleased."

The two went their separate ways: Litanius to the islanders and rowers and Ira back to his crew. There, he conveyed in full the contents of the letter shown to him by the chief and how it related to the *Wayfarer*'s plans.

"Am I to understand," Halruc said gruffly after Ira had finished, "that we are to expect this same sort of mayhem on the mainland as well?"

"We can no longer assume the ports are safe," said Ira. "The galleymaster's letter indicates the legions have already begun to arrest in significant numbers. They are prepared to detain anyone they deem suspect of aligning with the seditionists. Such a purge of the ports will not be short-lived."

"What have we to fear then?" boomed Ram. "No one here claims any allegiance to that treasonous lot. I say we continue to Mason and scrounge what we can for this cargo."

"No one on this island had connections with the seditionists either, Ram," said Nathanael coldly. "Look around and tell us that the ports will be in better shape than the Cove."

"Do not claim any authority in the matter, Nathanael," spat Ram. "You only wish to protect your friends from empire forces."

Esther lowered her gaze as Ira locked eyes with the dwarf. They glared at one another through the wisping fire that separated them. Before Nathanael could retort, Tabor interjected.

"It is the master who commands where we go from here. So both of you, quit your squabbling!"

This last part was particularly directed at Ram, whose jaw clenched reproachfully under his midnight beard. As his sailors looked to him for direction in the madness, Halruc wrung his stubby hands as he stared into the dying flames.

"To risk arrest or face destitution, are these the only paths before me, prince?" he inquired thoughtfully.

"If my master knows of a more favorable course, I will gladly follow it."

Halruc's reluctance to sound a decision prompted some of his servants to quietly discuss their thoughts and opinions with their neighbors around the fire. As Manoque eyed him with a questioning gaze, the master declared, "I should like to speak with this chief myself. If there is a plan for the islanders' refuge from the Cove and the ports, I should like to be privy to it."

Without another word, Halruc rose from the sand and strutted towards the fire that Litanius and several other men were gathered around. Intrigue made all but Ira, Esther, and Nathanael follow the master along the shoreline to join the huddle.

"So, it is back to Squall for us then?" said Esther passively.

With a glance from Nathanael, Ira stated, "I think we must. There is no safer place for us now, and I would hate to think of what might happen to Érnog and Torzara if the mariners should stray from the ports. The people of Squall might spread all sorts of rumors about the House of Érnog. And you," he said, turning to Nathanael, "you must return to Ruth and your kin. Kevah is only a day's trek from Gales."

"I know," Nathanael replied emptily.

"They will be all right," Esther assured him.

"I know."

From down the shore, antagonizing voices erupted in the somber night. The three turned to find the outbreak coming from the distant fire, where their crew stood facing Litanius and the crowd of men. Ira, Esther, and Nathanael rushed to the scene in time to catch the chief's last words.

". . . without your help. But if we are successful . . ." Litanius trailed off as the three joined the bickering huddle.

"What is—" began Ira, but Cercur cut him off.

"Ira, what is all this about?"

"Did you expect us to offer ourselves for your mad conquest?" barked Ram.

Ira's stunned expression was answered by Litanius' interjection. "This plan was entirely my own; Ira knows nothing of it."

"Will someone please explain what is going on here?" said Nathanael loudly.

"This delusional elf wants to lay siege to Fortress Mariner," said an incredulous Ossel.

Ira had no words. He gaped at Litanius' gall for proposing such a radical idea. Not even the Horde had been so rash as to maraud the island fortress since the days of the Snakeheart.

"We have the chance to deal a crippling blow to the Legions of Haurth before they can further devastate our lands." Litanius proclaimed assertively. "To rush into hiding now is to only delay the inevitable. Sooner or later, the mariners will come for us. When they do, we will require strength in numbers and weapons if we are to stand a chance against them. Both can be acquired within the fortress. A vast armory is kept within its walls, along with hundreds of citizens wrongfully taken prisoner who would gladly take up arms alongside us. But these men, friends, relations, our brothers will shortly be delivered to the Isle of Ruin. Once there, they will not likely return. If we do not act now, it is only a matter of time before we join those buried in the trench."

There was a murmur of agreement from the islander men and rowers around the fire, but the crew of the *Wayfarer* did not appear the least bit swayed by the chief's gallant speech.

"It cannot be done," scoffed Manoque. "Noble intentions are not enough to trump radical plans. How are we, a band of commoners, to defeat cohorts of trained soldiers and seize their stronghold? Why should anyone believe it possible?"

"Because I know the fortress and its every stone," answered Litanius. He looked to Ira as he said, "I know it from my days as admiral of the empire's navy. I know her safeguards and those ways around them." With the tip of his gladius, the chief began to trace the outline of the fortress in the coarse sand. "The siege will take place on two fronts. The first team will consist of myself and those rowers who came here aboard the galley *Benúra*." He gestured to the cluster of men standing behind him. "They have agreed to sail the warship to Fortress Mariner and anchor her at the southern docks. Once there, I will lead an intimate squad clad in mariner garb into the fortress. I shall pose as the galleymaster, who currently resides in the heap of dead mariners across the way."

"While we enter from the south, a second team made up of my levies and the islanders," he gestured to the men across from him, "will approach in rowboats from the north. Under cover of darkness, they will pass unseen and beach upon the fortress perimeter. By then, the imposter mariners and I will have neutralized the sentries posted in the turrets along the northern wall. When the wall is secure, we will send down climbing ropes for the beaching team below to ascend and join us. With so many breachers, we cannot expect to remain in secrecy for long, but we cannot demand the fortress' surrender without a proper show of force. So, when we are inevitably discovered, the rowers hidden aboard the galley *Benúra* will breach the southern gate, and we will surround the mariners from all angles. By then, my squad of imposters and I will have made our way into the keep, where we will compel the general to issue an immediate surrender of the fortress."

When the chief had finished his elaborate plan, Ira's mouth was not the only one gaping.

"Are we expected to risk our lives on this mad conquest rather than return to protect our homes and kin?" asked Ishcaur. Ira could see Tabor through the crowded huddle, pulling the lad closer at these words.

"Every man here is willing to send his kin to safety while we take the fortress," retorted one of the men around the fire.

"Where are the women and children being sent?" asked Ira.

"To the forest of Gideon," said Litanius. "It is not as far from the Port of Bramble as I would wish, but the thicket should afford them adequate cover from the legions until we rejoin them."

"A few swords and a couple of prisoners are not enough to rival thousands of trained Haurthian soldiers," stated Puck.

"Not forever, no," admitted Litanius, "but should we garner a force strong enough to challenge the legions, it may be possible to drive them from our lands for good."

"Even if it is possible," said Nathanael, "if we could amass such a force and purge the armory of every sword and shield, there is one issue you seem to have overlooked. The success of your siege depends entirely upon you and your squad of imposters passing unnoticed. Your warriors do not look the part. The race of men is seldom found in the ranks of the mariners, and so many in one place will undoubtedly give away the scheme."

"True," said Litanius, "though I look the part and know the mariners' ways, I cannot accomplish this feat alone should I be discovered. This plan is sound, but I require the aid of others to ensure its success."

"And we have told you already," said Ram harshly, "none of our company will have any part in this radical ploy."

Ira observed the grim expressions of the dwarves and Manoque as he finally comprehended their meaning. They were all descended from Western lineage, and Litanius intended for them to don the mariners' garb.

"It is not that we do not pity those taken prisoner . . . ," began Puck.

"Suppose the sentries discover us; are we to be sentenced or slain as well?" asked Cercur desperately.

"You ask a great deal of those whom you do not know, chief," said Halruc coldly.

"In the face of righteousness, a great deal is always demanded of those who claim it," said Litanius.

"And I make no claim to it," the master replied gruffly.

"Of course not," barked one of the rowers. "We all know the first allegiance of dwarves is to their trade and treasures. To those plagued by greed and self-interest, the welfare of others is merely that."

"I tell you," pleaded Litanius, ignoring the rower's harsh outburst, "this plan is our only chance. With Ira leading the beaching team, and I—"

"I will have no part in this," said Ira simply. Now Litanius was the one gaping as the grim gazes of his crew turned upon Ira. He could feel the weight of the lad's utter dejection from across the flames. Before the chief could counter his remark, Ira felt himself being yanked by the arm away from the fire. When they were out of earshot, Esther faced him with a look of unbridled indignation.

"How can you abandon these men in their time of need?" she said in a low, stern voice. At once, Ira was taken aback by this sudden alteration in his sister's demeanor.

"I have a duty to uphold," he whispered to her. "I swore to Érnog and Torzara that I would never leave your side, and so I shall not. There are plenty of men already committed to following Litanius."

"But he needs Halruc and the others," said Esther. "If you do not join him, they most certainly will not. As for me, I will be quite safe with the other women and children in Gideon."

"Not if you are discovered," Ira said with a glance at her cheek. To this point, Esther knew she could not dispute.

"Then I shall come with you to the fortress."

"Absolutely not!"

"I will be just as safe hidden aboard a ship with you as I would be on land with the other refugees," she retorted. Now, it was Ira who reluctantly had to agree with her. When next she spoke, it was with her usual tone of thoughtfulness and gentility. "Our duty to others must always be placed above our own self-interests. You know it as well as I, brother, and you could not stand to leave these men to such a dangerous undertaking any more than you could stand to leave me without a protector. I shall not make you choose between the two, and so I will accompany you to the fortress. I will be quite safe aboard the *Wayfarer*."

"Assuming the crew will follow me into the fray," Ira replied uncertainly.

"They will."

He could tell there was no dissuading her. With a heavy sigh and a reassuring smile, he and Esther returned to the huddle around the fire.

"Forgive me, gentlemen," Ira said loud enough for all to hear. "Please do not consider my initial reservations any reflection upon the validity of the chief's plan. Litanius is a great leader and renowned strategist, and I trust him in this matter. I was, at first, preoccupied with my own selfish intentions. But this ordeal is greater than any one man, and to save even one life from tyranny carries with it the weight of the world." He looked at the lad and smiled as he said, "I should be proud to join your ranks to defend our lands. That is, if my companions will join me."

Though he addressed the company of the *Wayfarer* as he spoke, his eyes were fixed upon the master. Before Halruc could answer the call, Ram's boisterous voice and sardonic tone rang through the night air.

"The words of a mad emperor's son do not carry any sway with me, Prince Ira."

All eyes around the fire flickered towards the outed pariah as shock, rather than angst, crossed their faces. Nathanael was ready to come to the prince's defense when Ira's hand told him to back down.

"I make no denial of my past life," Ira said to the crowd, "nor do I absolve myself from any blame you may hold against me. It was my failure to end a mad sovereign's reign that brought great suffering to your lands. None of this can now be changed. But perhaps, be it the will of the Light, this cause may be my atonement. I offer myself to you, not as a prince but as a man, for courage and conviction shall always triumph over title and rank. I ask no favor of any here except that which I should merit through word and deed. If I am beyond your forgiveness, so be it. But I shall strive until my dying breath to earn your trust."

There were no outcries of remonstrance while the men around the fire traded glances and hushed whispers. Likewise, the company of the *Wayfarer* exchanged a mixture of thoughtful expressions until their master summoned the dwarves and Manoque for a private council. As Ira, Esther, and Nathanael watched their companions converse in undertones away from the fire, Tabor and the lad crossed over to humbly address the prince and princess.

"I have misjudged you, children of Darius," Tabor said firmly. He looked prepared to go on in detail, but Ira wasted no time awaiting further repentance.

"Let us leave bad things in the past, Tabor."

The burly man grinned graciously at the prince. "It would appear my son is becoming a better man than I each day," he said as he patted the lad on the shoulder.

"The true mark of a dutiful father and a fine son," said Esther with a loving smile.

Ira chuckled as the lad's cheeks flushed in the firelight. He almost took no notice of the nudge Nathanael gave him as Halruc and their companions dispersed from their intimate huddle to rejoin the crowd. Ossel could be seen muttering something to his brother, who appeared not the least bit pleased. The chief stood tall as the master approached him to say, "What are our next steps?"

As Litanius began to detail the preparations necessary for evacuating the women and children, Nathanael whispered to Ira, "Needless to say, I am following you."

It need not have been said. There was no more use dissuading him than Esther. Yet even as he offered his thanks for the fidelity of a dear friend, Ira ached for the sacrifice Nathanael was enduring on his behalf.

"I will see you by Ruth's side before long," Ira said to him. "I swear it."

"And I shall eagerly await that day," said Nathanael, "but if she could speak to me now, this is where my Ruth would have me, standing by my brother in his time of need. And she is not alone; my kin will look after her until my return."

But Ira could not help but notice a familiar vacant stare in his friend. It was the same expression he had first seen that day as they rode across the golden barrows beyond the village of Kevah.

256

CHAPTER XIII

THE DEPARTURE

Glimmering drops of dew caressed the blades of grass and trickled upon bushes and buds in the temple garden. The emerald life did not hold its usual brilliance with the morning fog swimming about. Shadows were lost as sunlight refused to break through the vast gray thicket. In the center of the garden stood the baldachin, erected of pure white marble, akin to the statues in the courtyard. Though the season was upon them, the wisteria vines winding along the stone canopy remained as bare in the spring as in the winter.

Kneeling at the base of the shrine was Lady Filia. Despite the absence of daylight, her golden sheen reflected bright as ever beneath her sapphire veil. As the elf matron sung in quiet prayer, a soft pair of footsteps and a long royal robe brushed the wet grass with a faint rustle. The premier removed the scabbard and sword from his side and set them upright against a slender tree before approaching his bride.

"I cannot recall the last time I saw shrubs and vines so lifeless," said Filia as her husband knelt at her side.

"Their time to bloom will come," said Lysias, "when the conditions are ripe. And when they do, their colors will shine out brighter than ever before."

"I am not so certain," she said as her fingers danced upon the stem of a closed white lily. Lysias gazed at the gray wisps careening about the temple pillars and the garden's barren flora.

"The ship is to depart for Alaoth today?" she asked.

"It is," replied Lysias.

"Perhaps the arbiter will show him mercy. There may yet be remission in Jesse's heart."

"Stains of the soul are not so easily washed out, Filia."

"No, yet it is the charge of those standing in the light to show the lost their way. Absolution is a long and arduous path, but it begins with the humbling of one's soul. Is any man truly beyond that?"

Lysias made no reply as he watched the mist coat the hilt of his gladius and cloud the dark gem embedded in it.

"In vain, I have tried to reason with Jesse, but he is stubborn—fixed in his ways. He and his accomplices threaten to destroy all that the court and I have built. Had they approached peacefully, I would not have considered their aims to be sedition. But hostile defiance cannot be disregarded, lest it burn like a wildfire."

"To love what is good, one must recognize that which would have goodness corrupted," whispered the lady. "Jesse's actions were his own, kindled by the impulse to protect his home. Do not lose sight of those intentions that led you to reveal yourself all those years ago. Érosai will guide the way for those who have ears for listening."

Lysias looked into her pale eyes and took her hands in his own. "*Emanium ide*, with you as my guide, I shall never wander astray."

Though her lips curled into a smile, disquiet lingered behind the lady's loving gaze. As Lysias searched for the words to ease her heart, another set of footsteps came marching upon the garden grounds.

"Premier," said the master sentry with a bow, "the governors await your presence."

With a parting glance at his bride, the premier rose to his feet, took up his sword from beside the tree, and strode towards the temple pillars. The courtyard, like the garden, was flooded with billows of hazy fog. The hanging clouds shrouded any view of the Hallowed City beyond the gaps between the pillars and statues. As Lysias strode across the marble floor towards the mahogany table, soft echoes of troubled voices met his ears.

". . . at such a time as this?"

"It is long overdue; I make no denial of it. That is why it can wait no longer."

"And for what? To bargain and make pacts with traitors who call for your demise? Be sensible, Anthazar . . ."

"It has been decided; I shall not be dissuaded from my errand."

"And what errand would that be, governor?"

The premier's grip reflexively tightened upon his sword as he paraded into the courtyard, where five governors were seated around the table. Standing above them was Anthazar, drawing deep breaths as the elf emerged from the haze. The mists shrouded the blue and silver sentries posted about the courtyard's edges. Those colossal statues of sovereigns past were mere shadows in the heaps of gray, the blazes at their feet outlining the towering figures. As he joined the rest of the court, the premier did not take his seat but stood opposite the ashen-haired man across the table.

"I beg your pardon, governors," said Lysias casually. "I seem to have interrupted you. Pray, what were you discussing?"

When the standing governor did not reply, Doracaen raised his voice. "Governor Anthazar was just sharing some news of his as it pertains to the affairs of the High Court."

"Dear me, it must be urgent if its annunciation could not wait for the presence of the premier," Lysias remarked coldly.

Even through the dim hues of the fog, what little color lived in the governors' faces vanished as they looked anxiously towards the man opposite the elf.

"Forgive me, premier. I meant you no disrespect," said Anthazar apologetically. "In fact, I am glad all are now present so I might share the details of my voyage with the court."

"Your voyage?"

"Yes, indeed. It occurs to me that I have been too long removed from my homeland, and most especially from the hardships of those I serve. For that reason, I have arranged passage to the Province of Anthazar aboard the galley, which will first deliver the prisoner Jesse to the Isle of Ruin. Upon my arrival in Gales, I intend to fulfill my vow as governor and address the strifes of my province and people. Consequently, this means I shall be taking a temporary leave of absence from the court's regular assemblies. Though it is not my wish to be parted from you all, I hold no reservations about leaving the welfare of the empire in such trusted hands as those of the governors and the premier."

Those wanton thoughts and feelings held towards the governor in the Cavern of Souls were renewed as Lysias discerned the true purpose of the governor's conquest.

"No doubt, Anthazar, one of your errands in the Eastlands will be to seek counsel with the leaders of the seditionist movement," remarked Héribon.

"Should any remain amidst the ongoing census, yes, I shall seek them out," admitted Anthazar firmly. "Though I expect there will be many awaiting trial in Alaoth by the time our galley has escorted Jesse to the prison isle."

"And you mean to interrogate the accused yourself when you reach Alaoth?" said Périlles callously.

"I am sure the arbiter will be grateful for any knowledge I can acquire of the seditionist movement and its followers. Needless to say, I shall have regular correspondence with the court and relate all of my findings as they are uncovered."

"I am afraid not, Anthazar, for you shall not be leaving Eou Verás at this time," said Lysias harshly. The eyes around the table flickered in unison towards the elf. "The mariners are charged with implementing the census, and the arbiter with trying those traitors apprehended. Your charge remains here with your constituents. You shall not abandon the court in its time of need."

"And for how long are we, the rulers of East and West, to proceed in ignorance of our opposition?" asked Anthazar pleadingly. "We have already received reports of the unrest the census has wrought in the ports, and there is no sign of its dissipating anytime soon. These 'traitors' you call them, for all their dissenting beliefs, are nevertheless citizens of the empire. They are not our enemies! Must thousands flood the cells of Alaoth before we raise a finger to mend the divide ourselves? For how long must we attempt to achieve amity by means of force? This is not—"

"That is quite enough, governor!" spat the premier. "Your belligerent protests have grown wearisome. This court does not entertain notions of peace with those who raise arms against the leaders who serve them. Making wartime concessions with such brigands is a fool's errand."

"Premier, while I recognize the truth in much of what you say," remarked the dwarven governor, Valcor, "the lands of East and West are not at war."

"Premier," Moleu said peaceably, "while we, the court, remain in this period of uncertainty, where is the harm in the governor's search for answers? By all accounts, it would seem the court stands to benefit from any information we may—"

But the portly governor lost his voice as Lysias' palm struck the mahogany table in a fury that shook its occupants.

"Have I not made myself clear?" barked the elf. "The governor stays, and that is the end of it!"

The sentries in the far corners of the temple glanced cautiously through the mist towards the table. No governor dared to speak until the premier had regained some of his former composure.

"Respectfully, premier," said Anthazar firmly, "such an exercise of verdict is not in your power to make. In the absence of a reigning sovereign, the rulers of the respective realms and provinces are free to come and go as they please. As such, the arrangements for my voyage have already been made. Once this meeting is adjourned, I shall head to the cavern to fetch Jesse before we depart for Alaoth." Examining the premier's bitter expression, the governor adopted a kinder demeanor and said, "I would not take such action if I did not believe it necessary for the welfare of the empire."

The two chairs on either side of the table stood vacant, forgotten by their occupants. Between them, the governors' eyes fluttered between the elf's fingers clenched about his sheathed gladius and the man who would dare defy the one who appointed him to his station.

"If you are determined," said Lysias with a reluctant finality in his voice, "then I shall not be the one to stand in your way.

Governor Anthazar, I give you leave to part now for your journey."

At this, the ashen-haired man bowed low in gratitude to the elf. As his cloak was fetched by one of the sentries, the governor bid his farewells to the rest of the court. While the others offered their companion well wishes and safe travels, Périlles merely inclined his head as Anthazar came to his side. Just as the governor was prepared to depart from the temple, Lysias circled the table to address the man in a low voice.

"My outburst just now was most unseemly, Malachi. I beg your forgiveness."

"It is already forgotten," replied the governor. As he turned to leave, Lysias caught him with his words.

"Will you allow me to see you and the prisoner safely to the harbor?"

"Of course," Anthazar replied politely, "I would be glad of the company."

"Very well, then," said Lysias. He turned to the table and announced, "I shall not be long. If you would please remain on the temple grounds until my return, we shall resume our session shortly."

The men and dwarves muttered their assent as the elf's cloak was summoned. Surrounded by the sentries and their master, Lysias and Anthazar strode through the grand archway, down the steps, and into the city draped in a gray veil. Wagons, carts, elves, and dwarves were parted by an invisible force as the royal escort approached the edge of the Hallowed City. Up the narrow path they went, following along the north side of the crescent range bathed in murky fog. No conversation was had as the premier and the governor made their way to the cavern entry, greeted the eager warden, and followed the dwarf down the winding corridors to the cell marked twenty-six.

"If you have no objections, premier," Anthazar said outside the cell door, "there are a few matters I wish to discuss with Jesse before our departure. Would you care to join me?"

"Thank you, I would," replied Lysias graciously. "As it happens, I have some parting words for the prisoner that I would like you to hear as well."

"As you wish. Let us address him together then."

As the warden turned the key and unleashed the cell's rancid air, the sentries who made to enter were halted by the premier's hand.

"The governor and I shall have a private convention with the prisoner."

"Premier," began the master sentry reservedly, "I think it unwise to—"

"He is frail and unarmed," remarked the elf as he showed beneath his cloak the hand still resting upon his regal blade. "Should we require your presence, you shall be summoned with haste."

With this, Anthazar took up the warden's lantern and carried it into the shallow den as the iron door closed behind Lysias. The flame fell upon a body curled in the corner and reflected upon the grimy chains binding the withering man. Jesse was more bone than flesh, his cheeks and eyes sunken under his tangled hair. Anthazar set the lantern down and made to approach the figure but was deterred as he caught the premier's uncertain gaze.

"Why do you continue to refuse food and drink, Jesse?" the governor asked with a sideways glance at the untouched mug and plate in the opposite corner. Jesse did not look at the man speaking but only stared with unmistakable contempt at the elf.

"You will stand when your governor addresses you, prisoner," commanded Lysias. Only when the young man broke his glare to look upon the ashen-haired man did he heed the order. Drawing thick, raspy breaths, Jesse sluggishly raised himself from the cold stone floor, using the wall for support as he did.

"I hope this reluctant demeanor will not be our companion as we sail to Alaoth," said the governor.

A hint of surprise crossed the prisoner's vacant face as his dry lips opened to croak a single word.

"We?"

"Yes, we. It has been arranged that I shall personally accompany you to the prison isle. Perhaps the time at sea will allow us the chance to better understand one another."

"You should count yourself fortunate, prisoner, to have found so steadfast an ally in Governor Anthazar," said Lysias. "It was his decision alone to join you on your final voyage."

Another croak filled the cramped, grubby cell.

"Why?"

"There will be plenty of time for that discussion later," said Anthazar. "But the premier has come to address you, so I shall take up the conversation no longer."

Making a bleary effort to stand tall before him, Jesse glowered upon the premier as a drop of blood trickled from his cracked lips, his shackled hands twitching and rattling their chains. As Anthazar removed himself to the opposite corner of the cell, Lysias studied in silence the servant's haggard face.

"Am I to take this spiteful conduct to mean that you still refuse to offer up your accomplices and their whereabouts?" asked the premier. Whether done in sheer contempt or for the exhaustion of his fragile voice, Jesse made no reply as he turned his head away. "In that case," continued Lysias, "it would seem my journey here was in vain." Then, without warning, a long-fingered hand sprang from beneath the cloak and locked its fingers upon the prisoner's jaw. A bewildered Anthazar took a step closer as Lysias forcibly pivoted the weakened man's head to face him. Jesse made no retaliation but kept his eyes averted from the elf's gaze. As his other hand tightened upon the dark sword beneath his cloak, Lysias refused to speak again until, at last, Jesse's eyes flickered to meet his own. "When you reflect upon your days as a younger man from a cell very much like this, remember that it was I who held dominion over you and your lands." The prisoner's deep, hoarse breaths grew short and rapid as the premier gently released his hand from the man's jaw. Jesse remained stoic and motionless, the lantern light flickering in his sunken eyes. Turning to Anthazar, the premier said with a tired voice, "With your permission, governor, I shall leave you here and charge the sentries with seeing you to the harbor."

"I understand," replied Anthazar as he gave the elf a timid bow. "Be well, Lysias."

"And you, governor. May your journey see only clear skies and steady waters."

And with a parting glance at his companion, Lysias rapped on the cell door. It swung ajar and closed again behind him as the elf bid two of the sentries to remain on guard until the governor was ready to depart.

When the premier and his escort returned to the Temple of Érosai, the governors were not awaiting him in the courtyard. The morning haze had dissipated at last, and the polished eyes of the First and Second Lines of Sovereigns followed Lysias as he strode through the temple, the elf neglecting their gazes as he went. He came to the garden situated behind the great throne, and there he found governors, as well as his bride, immersed in their preoccupations. Lady Filia was feeding the shrubs fresh water from a ceramic jug depicting the historic contest of the brothers Arieh and Zev. Héribon sat on a bench, wringing his frail wrists. Valcor paced beside the stone baldachin as Périlles whispered to the stout Doracaen, stroking his beard. Moleu was alone by the flowerbed, running his pudgy fingers through his dark hair. The premier's arrival need not have been announced, as the eyes of the garden found him at the temple's edge.

"Thank you for your patience, governors," said Lysias. "Shall we resume our meeting with old business first?"

"Premier," said Périlles cordially, "allow me to convey our sincerest apologies regarding Governor Anthazar's earlier remarks. When he first told us of his plan, we tried dearly to dissuade him from taking reckless action. Personally, I have never—"

"What Périlles means to say," interjected Doracaen, "is that we know the governor stepped out of line in forming his plans without first seeking the counsel of the court. We who are loyal to the empire shall not betray the trust you have bestowed upon us."

A hollow smile crept upon Lysias' face as he looked upon his faithful companions. "I take heart knowing such dedicated leaders stand by my side. No man could dream of being more fortunate than I."

He smiled at the lady as he and the governors strolled towards the temple to resume their session. Before the grass had left their sandals, a temple sentry came bounding from the courtyard, panting for breath.

"What is the meaning of this?" demanded the master sentry.

The arrival looked to his master and then to the members of the court before gasping, "Governor Anthazar . . . is dead."

A crash from behind them made Lysias twist in place as he saw Filia standing over the shattered pieces of the water jug. The governors did not flinch. They were all of them frozen in shared mortification.

"What?" uttered Valcor, aghast.

"By the Light," whispered Moleu, "say it is not so. How could it be?"

"We remained . . . by the cell . . . as you ordered, premier . . . while the governor . . . and the prisoner spoke in private," panted the sentry as he collected what breath he could. "After some time, we could no longer hear voices. I called to the governor but received no reply. We rushed into the cell and . . . and found the prisoner leering over the governor's body on the floor, his shackled hands clutching his throat, cursing under his breath." An icy chill was sent through the company in the garden. "The other sentry ran the prisoner through with his blade, but it was too late. The warden is preparing the body to be brought to the temple as we speak."

Even the beating sun could not warm the aching hearts in the garden. Valcor, the eldest of them, nearly collapsed from shock. Moleu managed to catch the dwarf midfall as Héribon raised his scrawny hands and covered his face in agony. Périlles scowled and hissed, "The barbarian!" under his breath.

"But this cannot be," murmured Doracaen. "After all Malachi said and did in Jesse's defense, in defense of his . . . It simply cannot be. Lysias, you were there with him; what did he . . ."

But the premier could not hear the dwarf as he staggered wearily past the sentries towards the temple courtyard, his back to the mourners in the green garden.

CHAPTER XIV

THE SIEGE

No idle hands were to be found as all in the Cove scurried about their respective duties. The village appeared in even greater shambles than the morning following the mariners' strike. Working around the unshifted rubble and collapsed dwellings, men and women scoured for any items of worth prior to their imminent evacuation. Stashes of gold and silver were removed from every home, but the rations, fresh water, and fabrics collected held their own value to the soon-to-be refugees. An exodus of so many to the mainland could not be trivialized. The women and children would need all they could gather to survive in the forest of Gideon until the men returned from plundering Fortress Mariner. Provisions would be hard enough to come by when the companies were reunited, what with their inability to seek trade in the presently occupied ports.

Over a hundred men of the Cove had pledged themselves to join in the chief's gambit to overtake the island fortress and release the imprisoned men of the provinces since the bonfire the night prior. Adding to that number the rowers formerly in the service of the galley *Benúra*, Litanius found himself commanding a cohort of more than two hundred warriors. Those men too severely wounded to aid in the siege would accompany the women and children to the mainland as they recovered. According to his charts and the fair conditions ahead of them, Manoque estimated no more than a four-day voyage from the Cove to the fortress. As the galley *Benúra* was expected by the general of the Haurthian Army no later than the twenty-third of the month, that afforded only two days for siege and evacuation preparations to be made. Though the women and children would likely be safe to remain in the Cove longer, postponing their departure was not an idea long entertained. The prospect of another unexpected warship arriving to detain their families was entirely unacceptable to the islander men. As a consequence, all vessels fleeing the Cove would set off at the end of the second day, affording no time to waste.

While many of the older boys were to sail with the women and children for their protection, Tabor was adamant that his son accompany him and the rest of the men to the fortress. To this, the lad could raise no objections. The same, however, could not be said when his father declared outright that his son would have no part whatsoever in the siege.

"Absolutely not!"

"But you will need all the help you can—"

"I will not have it! What would your mother say if I allowed such a thing?"

"I can fight; I have fought!"

"You will obey my orders, or you may sail to the mainland with the other adolescents!"

Insulted yet unwilling to be parted from his father and his companions, the lad fell silent and stared defeatedly at the sand between his toes. Ira could see from afar the disquiet Tabor felt for reprimanding his son's noble wishes to stand by his side. As a peace offering, the burly man removed the ancestral pendant of their house from his neck and placed it about his son's. Tabor whispered something to the lad before returning to his commission of gathering weapons from across the village.

Litanius had delegated various preparations to the men as they pertained to the impending siege. His levies gave accounts of all supplies and weaponry stowed aboard the galley *Benúra*. Several men were charged with stripping the iron chestplates, helmets, gauntlets, and greaves from the dead mariners piled up across the harbor. Those pieces of armor that remained in fair condition were set aside, while the damaged ones were passed along to the dwarves of the *Wayfarer*, busy at work with the local smith. Though the trade was not theirs by upbringing, the brawny laborers adapted swiftly to their duties as they mended the dents and lashes they themselves had wrought.

Ira had been eager to accept any task that might allow him to avert unwanted attention since his outing as the banished son of Emperor Darius. Litanius, however, had plans quite to the contrary. In the two days before they were to set off, Ira was appointed to train the men of the siege party in the ways of proper combat. Their victory against the soldiers of the Westlands had been, in the chief's own words, a sheer fluke. The surprise uprising of the village, the mariners' lesser numbers, and their scattered forces had been enough to turn the tides in the islanders' favor once. The same could not be said for the venture ahead of them. And so, taking them in shifts of a dozen at a time, Ira endeavored to pass along those invaluable lessons he himself had learned under the tutelage of the elven galleymaster he had once admired.

Following their teacher through mimicry and repetition, those unrefined techniques the men had long clung to were gradually replaced with those that had served the legions for a thousand years. Ira did not permit his students to practice with gladiuses for fear of causing unnecessary injury. In place of actual blades, the men used wooden posts broken into short lengths to wield alongside the recovered mariners' shields. The men did not make light of their training, and no snide remarks were made towards the prince as he watched the dueling pairs and corrected their stances, strikes, and deflections. Even Ram reserved his tongue as he and the *Wayfarer*'s crew had their lesson along the beach. As laborers were few and the work was plentiful, the lad was not permitted to join in the practice of swordsmanship. He would have no need for it on this next leg of their journey. Nevertheless, his and Esther's task of filling fresh water jugs could hold no comparison as the young sailor enviously watched his cronies learn the finer techniques of the gladius. As he trudged up the street on another trip to the well, Ira and Nathanael shared a look of pity for the lad. This was ill-timed, however, as Nathanael's momentary distraction allowed for Ishcaur's wooden weapon to jab him hard in the side.

When the dusk of the second day fell across the Cove, it was time for the men and their kin to bid farewell to one another. It would be less than a fortnight before they would meet again in the forest of Gideon. But everyone along the beach understood that even the most fortunate outcome at the fortress would not afford every house a happy reunion. When the final partings were concluded, the throng of heads on the shore crammed into rowboats and hailed to their respective vessels. The rowers returned to the galley *Benúra* and took with them as many of the islander men as could fit while the *Wayfarer* accepted the rest. The merchant ship's deck and hold were brimming with a flock of new voyagers in addition to her original crew save one. As the scarlet sail carried them once more, the sailors and their master gathered along the ledge to watch the Cove's communal grave pass them by. They and the galley hailed through the harbor entry guarded by the two stone sirens, followed by those ships loaded with the innocent and the wounded. The new faces aboard the *Wayfarer* traded places with the sailors along the ledge to watch their kin veer to follow their own plotted course for the mainland.

Shallow reefs bursting with vibrant colors were left behind as the *Wayfarer* and the galley *Benúra* bore side by side through crisp blue waters. As much as they were relieved to be gone from the Forager's Cove and its dreadful memories, the cramped conditions did the voyagers no favors along their northern trek. The perk of having extra hands on deck to assist the dayers and nighters was hardly worth losing so much space in the hold when rest was needed. Dozens of new hammocks flooded the dank belly of the *Wayfarer*, even after Halruc divided the islanders evenly between the two shifts. The galley *Benúra*, while not exactly comfortable, was well equipped to handle its capacity. Ira had seen her breed of warship sling hammocks for a hundred rowers and a crew of fifty Western soldiers within her vast hull. The Haurthian officers, meanwhile, were granted the amenity of a shared quarters along the ship's stern as well as a personal cabin for the galleymaster. As Ira caught sight of the former admiral commanding the great warship across the raging swells, he allowed himself the private diversion of reminiscing about simple and glorious days at sea.

The looming nature of their journey seemed to rob any sense of liveliness aboard either vessel. No melodies strummed from Puck's fiddle. Esther and the lad had lost interest in continuing their former reading lessons. Even though the atmosphere was ripe for one of Dromo's sparse yet foreboding proverbs, the aged dwarf refrained from sharing those inner thoughts already stirring about every man's mind. Hardly a word was spoken, except for those commands called and answered on deck, until the morning of the fourth day. Upon the pale sky's expanse, a looming shadow of a broad mountain range appeared to the north of the two vessels.

"Keep a lookout now," Halruc called to the dayers as well as those passing the time on deck. "We do not want to be spotted in the daytime."

The dwarven sailors and the lad peered over the ship's bow to search for a landmark, as did many of the islander men. The same practice was occurring across the way aboard the galley *Benúra*. All eyes squinted towards the horizon that divided the Bridging Sea from the eerie Savage Peaks. Ira stayed back with Esther and Nathanael on the quarterdeck steps while Tabor manned the helm beside Halruc and Manoque. Morning turned to midday, and still, the fortress remained unsighted. As the winds changed and rippled the sail, Ishcaur, Dromo, and Cercur were recalled by their master to help tack the ship. Once the oncoming gales were harnessed again, the dayer dwarves elected not to rejoin Ossel, Ram, and the lad in their ongoing search for the island stronghold.

It was well into the afternoon when, at last, a cry of discovery sounded from the galley. One of the last men fixed upon the warship's bow was pointing ahead towards the shadowy alps. Heeding Litanius' and Halruc's commands, the crews furled the sapphire and scarlet sails before casting their anchors into the depths. The decks of both ships were suddenly as cramped as the *Wayfarer*'s hold as several men emerged from the hatch at the announcement of their arrival. Ira, Esther, and Nathanael joined the company on the quarterdeck for a view unobstructed by the many heads swarming about.

"There it is," called out Manoque, "beneath that pass."

This observation hardly narrowed their search. The range stretched east to west as far as the eye could see, a twirling cloud cover dripping from atop the peaks, and there were many mountain passes along the way. After some time peering along the horizon, Ira finally spotted a small coral-colored speck, the old yet familiar sight the admiral and the prince knew well from a former life.

A whistle from the galley cut through the sharp breeze as Litanius began bellowing orders to the idle men on his ship. Now that they were upon the fortress, the company had final preparations to make as they divided into their respective parties. The galley's hired rowers set boats in the water below for the islander men who would be joining the rest of Ira's beaching team already aboard the *Wayfarer*. Meanwhile, Halruc, Ram, Ossel, Ishcaur, Dromo, Cercur, and Manoque prepared to cross the short distance between ships to join Litanius and clad themselves in Haurthian uniforms.

"In my absence," declared Halruc, "young Tabor will be acting master of the *Wayfarer*." At these words, the lad's eyes widened in disbelief. "You will not be alone, of course. The lady will remain aboard, too, as will a couple of the elder men to aid your escape should things go awry. Should we be overtaken or the *Wayfarer* discovered, you are to make for the mainland at once. Understood?"

"Aye, master," said the lad with an air of authority.

Halruc stared at the young sailor, not much taller than himself, and the dwarf's lips curled into an uncommon smile under the pale beard. "Then we shall see you soon, Master Tabor," and he offered the lad a parting bow.

The crew bid their temporal farewells to one another as Manoque descended the rope ladder, followed by each of the dwarves in turn. They rowed towards the galley as the islanders' boats came alongside the *Wayfarer*'s hull. When the whole of the beaching party was settled aboard the merchant ship, they hauled the rowboats up on deck. Hoisting the tiny crafts proved more difficult than usual as each landed with a noisy clatter of iron and steel. Weapons and shields were dispersed from the boats, as were various pieces of Haurthian armor, which the men donned over their common tunics. When the strange militia stood armed and ready in their polished gear, the shimmering helmets turned towards the newly appointed master to receive orders. Grinning broadly as he gazed upon his new command, the lad called out for the anchor to be lifted and the sail unfurled. They caught the wind once and departed from the galley's side.

The *Wayfarer* was to circle the fortress and approach from the north come nightfall while keeping enough distance so no sentries could spot their scarlet sail. Orders bellowed by the lad were heeded swiftly by the armored men and, most especially, by those who knew him best. It was nearing sunset when the vessel settled in those waters north of the fortified rock. With time to spare before they continued under darkness, the armored islanders were given no alternative but to set anchor and brew in what was yet to come. Time slowed to an agonizing pace as the dire task ahead of them became all the more real and imminent. Many islanders seated themselves along the *Wayfarer*'s ledge, examining their shimmering weapons or apprehensively watching the sun fall to the west.

"Well," said Nathanael as he seated himself between Ira and Esther, "I dare say this journey has been more than any of us bargained for."

Ira and Esther could not help themselves as they chuckled along with their friend.

"I think you mean more than you bargained for, Nathanael," corrected Ira. "Or have you forgotten that you are out twenty gold aurei on our account?"

"A price I would happily pay again to have you stay in the provinces."

"It seems that will be the case when all of this is over," remarked Esther.

"I know it is not how you would have it," said Nathanael consolingly, "but rest assured, you will both have a place in our home whenever you pass through Kevah. And Esther, you must promise to come and see Ruth when she has had the baby. Nothing would delight her more."

"A promise I shall be happy to keep," she replied with a grin.

It was only then that Ira noticed the lad standing by his lonesome under the mast, clutching what appeared to be one of the wooden posts used for combat training back on the Cove. Surrounded by men wielding pristine blades forged by the most renowned Western artisans, the lad held his meager weapon aloft as though it were a cherished prize. He leapt forward and swung wildly at a foe only he could see. This display continued until the men laughing around him recalled the abashed lad from his imaginings. But as he turned to stride away from the onlookers, the young warrior found himself face-to-face with the prince, clad in shimmering armor. Ira unsheathed his blade to examine its miraculous gleam before offering it and his shield to the lad in exchange for the splintered post. Esther and Nathanael grinned, and the crowd fell silent as they observed the private lesson. While he struggled with the weighty iron shield upon his arm, the lad's footwork was impeccable, and he emulated every motion of the sword as smoothly as his teacher did with the post. The two continued until dusk fell and the stars began to flicker on high. The hour was at last upon them.

Lanterns aboard the *Wayfarer*'s deck were not set alight this evening. Blending into the engulfing darkness, the scarlet sail crept gently towards the distant fortress made visible by its blazes atop the towering curtain walls. When they were within half a league of the stronghold, the *Wayfarer* was brought to anchor for its final rest of the night. Eight boats were lowered into the wavering night waters as warriors by the dozen boarded each of the vessels in turn. Tabor the greater and the lesser stood apart from the rest of the crew as the father pressed his hand firmly upon the ancestral pendant resting upon his son's chest. At the sight of this familial display, Nathanael made his excuses and left Ira and Esther to their own parting. The brother and sister gazed with affection and understanding that did not require the company of grand speech.

"Watch over them," said Esther softly.

"I will see you soon," replied Ira. Behind them, Tabor was clambering into one of the beaching vessels below. Now, the boats only awaited Ira and Nathanael's company. They looked upon Esther, the lad, and the few aged men who would remain aboard to sail the *Wayfarer* to refuge if this was to be the warriors' last night. "Remember Halruc's orders," Ira said to the lad, "and take care of my sister until I return."

The lad gave a firm nod and bid them good luck as the two men descended into the bow of the final rowboat. Ira raised himself high enough for the rest of the fleet to discern him in the darkness. He gave the signal, and the soft pattering of oars against the sea sounded as the convoy lunged ahead.

A steadier voyage in the open waters could not have been asked for. No torrential waves threatened to swallow the boats and drag their occupants into the briny depths. Yet despite the amiable conditions, the distance of half a league to shore threatened to wear the rowers to the brink of exhaustion. The men were soon taking it in turns to assume the oars, lightening some of the burden felt across the hailing fleet. Ira found himself confronted with the uncomfortable choice of either facing the menacing destination ahead or else watching the somber faces beneath the warriors' helmets. As they trekked onward, a low voice from Tabor's boat hummed gently to the party. The speech was difficult to make out over the convoy's rowing until the old familiar words of a lonely ballad reached the somber warriors' ears.

In pale north waters dwells a wide mortal range
And a haunting more ancient than time
The shadowy veil shrouds the peaks from the day
As its rovers pay with their lives

If virgin mounts held rich veins of ore
And troves of gleaming gems so divine
Son, heed an old man's words and leave treasure to rest
As the brave or foolish bid their goodbyes

The air about the fleet was changed as the voice sang its last. The expressions Ira glimpsed across the moonlit faces were neither courageous nor fearful. The look the men shared was rather one of acceptance and understanding—the understanding of their lives' simultaneous importance and insignificance for that which was larger than themselves. And so they hailed onward, rowing nearer to the citadel and their brothers held within.

With each stroke of the oars, the colossal curtain wall composed of mortar and coral sandstone rose higher from its foundation upon the minuscule isle. It could hardly be called an isle at all were it not for the fortress that birthed the desolate rock's sole purpose. Along the north wall's peak were blazing lanterns stretching between those turrets, which climbed higher still. Within each turret was a long shadow of a posted sentry monitoring the watery perimeter. As the fleet approached the shallows, Ira signaled to the rowing warriors to soften their strokes. Beyond the fortress walls to the south, the dark figure of a warship was hailing towards the southern docks to harbor. The men in the boats could only hope that Litanius and his imposter mariners would not be discovered before admitting them entry to the stronghold.

The fleet was mere paces from the dry sands when a soft rustle beneath the boats told the warriors that they had landed. With the greatest care to avoid making noisy splashes, a hundred iron-clad warriors stealthily disembarked and surged upon the shore. The boats were gently lifted and hidden behind a nearby boulder so as not to give away their presence. The swarm of men hustled lightly towards the towering wall, careful not to rattle the iron greaves upon their shins. As they came upon the base of the fortress perimeter, the warriors plastered themselves against the wall in one long line. No one dared draw too deep a breath for fear of being sighted in the narrow blind spot. In the hush, Ira and Nathanael each turned an ear towards the turret above them and cautiously listened. No call of alarm sounded from the sentry posted above. All that was left to them was the excruciating wait.

As their backs remained fixed to the coral wall, the washing waves were the only sounds louder than the warriors' pounding hearts. Every so often, Ira would lean dangerously forward to glance down the line, ensuring no man strayed too far from their cover. Down the way, the islanders were doing their own part in keeping each other in line as well as calm through the idle agony. Ira saw a warrior with a snowy beard easing the rapid pants of a young man barely beyond his adolescence. As the prince fought to steady the ruthless beating in his own chest, he closed his eyes and allowed the waves to guide the breaths he drew.

He was standing upon smooth black sands brushing between his toes. His back was pressed against a dark cliff strewn with vibrant and untamed grasses. Gales swept through the garden above, whistling with the robins, who gave their voices to the harmonic tune. The wild waters to the east held the promise of adventure for the young boy robed in the patterns of royalty.

A nudge from the man beside him awoke Ira from his distant recollection. Nathanael gestured upwards as the end of a long rope landed before them. Immediately, Ira took hold of it as two more lines plummeted to admit the warriors. He planted his feet against the curtain wall and, with great heaves, hoisted himself up the rope. Those behind him followed his lead as three chains of climbers silently ascended. Through the shadows and up the coral sandstone, they rose as the men below shuffled tight against the wall to the line nearest them. Almost halfway to the top, Ira caught a short glimpse of an observing figure within the turret above him. He hastily crouched down, cursed himself for nearly giving them away, and continued hailing upwards, his knees bent low. Behind him, the rest of the men mimicked his stance. Though this kept them close to the wall and out of sight, the climbers' squatted legs soon began to burn as much as their exhausted arms. At long last, when the top was within his reach, Ira grasped the stony ledge and peered along the wallwalk. The northern wall was indeed vacant as he hoisted his weary body between the burning fire pits, landing gingerly atop the fortress perimeter.

Ira could see into the ward below. A dozen mariners were marching across the grass towards the tower keep, situated along the western wall. Wasting no time in the open, Ira rushed into the turret beside him before the sentry posted above could spot him. He entered a circular den and, to his horror, was immediately met by an elven galleymaster in bronze armor and a silver cape. Ira reached instinctively for his sword when the elf caught his arm and muttered, "Easy now, prince."

Relieved to find the company of a friend rather than a foe, Ira joined Litanius' hiding place beneath the stone steps rounding up to the turret's lookout. Halruc was with him, garbed in the same bronze armor with a sapphire officer's cape. Nathanael hopped the ledge and joined them shortly in the turret, followed by Tabor and a steady flow of warriors emerging from the three tethered lines.

"A few of our imposters are standing guard on the ground level," whispered Litanius. "This area should remain clear, at least for a while."

"And the sentry above?" asked Ira with a glance up the turret steps.

"Dromo," answered Halruc. "Cercur and Ishcaur will have taken the next turrets over by now."

The already cramped space continued to shrink as more ascending warriors took refuge in the den.

"We have to move now," commanded Ira. "The others can follow behind us, but this many in one place cannot evade discovery for long."

Litanius agreed, and following the prince's lead, the ever-growing pack made their way down the turret's rounding steps. Swords were drawn and shields were raised as the swarm of siegers crept towards the ground level. At the base of the stairwell, Ira could see four pairs of sandals standing guard.

"Ours," whispered Litanius.

The elf took another step when Ossel's booming voice called out, "Good evening, torlaum!" The warning words of the disguised intruder echoed along the adjoining corridors as the hidden warriors pressed backwards into the shadows. Litanius managed to remove himself from sight as the legs of an officer marched past. The officer muttered a short greeting to the imposters standing guard and proceeded along the next corridor. When the pattering of footsteps had disappeared, Ossel muttered up the stairs, "The coast is clear."

The full figures of Manoque, Puck, Ossel, and Ram in their blue and silver garb came into view as the warrior reinforcements filed down the steps and onto the ground level. Ira could not recall the last time Ram had been so happy to be in the prince's company.

"All right," said Litanius in a hurried voice, "the imposters and I will make for the keep, find the general, and force his surrender of the fortress. You," he said to Ira, "take the men and free the prisoners. The only chamber large enough to hold them is the one below the eastern corridor. You know the way. Stay hidden for as long as possible, and we may yet—"

But the elf was interrupted by an alarming bellow coming from the ward. There was a sound of snapping rope, followed by horror-stricken cries and several hard thumps upon the sand beyond the fortress walls. Moments later, a monstrous horn thundered from the keep, calling all Western soldiers to arms.

"You cannot be seen with us!" Ira hissed at the ones in Haurthian uniforms. "Make for the keep; we will find the prisoners!"

The elves and dwarves obeyed without question. They barreled in the direction the officer had gone down the northern corridor as Ira led Nathanael, Tabor, and the other warriors the opposite way. Flames illuminating the narrow passage rushed overhead, the men's hearts pounding more ferociously than ever. Their straight path turned sharply at the northeast turret. As they rounded the corner, they came upon a host of mariners marching their way, weapons at the ready. The soldiers of Haurth broke into an almighty charge at the sight of the intruders. The dwarven mariners leading the way raised their bows and sent a shrieking barrage at the cluster of men. Warrior shields deflected the projectiles as the archers fell behind their elven companions, making ready to strike with their glistening swords.

Rallying cries erupted as the forces met with a resounding clash in the narrow corridor. Gladiuses and shields pounded one another in the confined mayhem. It took no time for Ira to realize that the close-quarters melee was affording the mariners a crucial advantage. Though their enemies were less than a score, only five or six pairs could duel at once in the enclosed space, forcing others to wait helplessly behind their allies for a turn in the fray. In such an environment as this, skill with a blade would vastly outweigh the quantity of warriors wielding them, and Ira could tell his men lacked the former. The outnumbered mariners were finding those weak points in the men's strikes and defenses and exploiting them to their deaths. Limp bodies stained with crimson were piling around their feet, only to be replaced by other equally novice fighters. This strategy could only end in their massacre.

"Shields!" Ira cried over the deafening conflict. At his command, the men threw their round shields together, creating an iron wall between themselves and the Western soldiers. As the mariners attempted to thrust through the gaps in their defense, Ira bellowed, "Up!" In one swift motion, the warriors drove their shields forward before sending them high towards the ceiling. The mariners' sword-wielding arms were unwittingly caught in the maneuver and cast upwards, exposing their bodies. Before the soldiers could recover and shield themselves, blades from beneath the iron wall pierced the frontline, felling six blue uniforms at once.

Ira and the warriors seized their chance and charged into the sliver of space where the felled mariners lay. The momentum proved their ally as Haurthian troops were compelled to retreat down the corridor from their assailants. A victorious cheer sounded as the men gave chase. As they rushed after their foes down the eastern corridor, Ira's mind was not set on pursuit. His eyes darted along the way, searching for the path that would lead them down to the prisoners' chamber. He could feel it getting closer when . . .

A fresh wave of sapphire and silver troops arrived from the southeast corner. The frontline admitted those retreating mariners before raising their shields into the same formation Ira had taught his men. From the pockets between these shields protruded sharpened spears aimed at skewering the warriors from afar.

"Fall back!" Ira roared to the men. His words were echoed by the others on the frontline, pushing and shoving, vying to flee from the storming spears. The stampede rumbled behind them as Ira sprinted behind his men around the northeast corner and past the turret they had first descended from. The warriors hurtled down the northern corridor until they came upon a grand archway opening onto the grassy ward. Desperate for any escape from the mariners' wrath, the men rushed into the open without hesitation. Ira could hear a commotion ensuing outside as, at last, he escaped the confined passageway. He raised his weapon, expecting to enter a battle already underway. But the ward was empty. Still, the colliding of blades, bashing of shields, and piercing cries filled the night air around them.

"Up there!" cried one of the men.

The warriors spun on the spot to stare above them. Dozens of the men who had ascended into the fortress were fending off Western soldiers along the wallwalk. The last ones up the lines had never made it to the corridor with the others. They had been discovered and trapped by the mariners, who now swarmed upon them from either end. Dwarven archers posted in the turrets about the fortress were sending whistling arrows at warriors both along the wallwalk and huddled in the ward. Ira and his men took refuge from the flurries, their shields rattling with deflected arrow tips. As he took cover, he noticed some of the projectiles were not hailing towards the siegers. A few of the archers in the northern turrets were firing at the mariners beneath them. Only then did Ira remember the imposters who had first stood guard as they ascended the curtain wall. From their respective turrets, Dromo, Cercur, and Ishcaur could be glimpsed sending streaking arrows to the aid of those warriors trapped along the wallwalk.

Flooding from the archway beneath the battle came those Haurthian troops bearing shields and spears at the men in the ward. Ira could not hear himself think over the commotion above and the bashing noises coming from the southern gate. Before he could call any redeeming command to his men, they were surrounded. Still deflecting enemy arrows, Ira glanced up at the keep behind, desperately wondering what could be delaying Litanius and the others. He held his crimson gladius aloft as he bumped shoulders with the man beside him. It was Nathanael. In the vicious scurry, Ira had quite forgotten to look for his friend. As they hid behind their shields, he searched their huddle and found the burly figure of Tabor still standing tall with the vigor to fight on. A renewed sense of dread followed Ira's fleeting sense of relief. As the swords and shields of the trapped men wavered, an elven officer beyond the circle of spears raised a hand and halted the turret archer's volleys. In the grim silence, the torlaum's Western voice called loudly to his soldiers.

"Ilthúania faenis!"

Ira raised his shield a little higher. The unnerved warriors around him began to back into one another, bracing for their collective demise. The only noise they could discern now was that of the continued bashing coming from the southern gate that led to the docks.

With a mighty crash, the wooden gate burst open to admit a throng of rowers bearing blades and shields on high. The reinforcements of the galley *Benúra* had finally broken through. They belted into the ward, brandishing their steel at the forces encroaching upon their allies. In vain, the elven officer shouted more orders to his troops. Rogue spears followed their own accord, either turning to face the onslaught or else being forfeited in favor of a gladius. Amidst the mariners' disarray, Ira and his men broke free from the circle and thrashed into battle once more. Archers above resumed their efforts as troves of vengeful rowers rushed towards the northern archway to aid their allies along the wallwalk. In the ward, swords met their marks, shields missed theirs, and before long, the Haurthian soldiers found themselves trapped in the place they had formerly held their foes.

Then, cutting across all the chaos, the same booming horn that first announced the fortress intruders was blown again from the tower high above. Every weapon in the citadel froze at its clarion call. As the panting warriors stood dormant and skeptical of the conflict's sudden intermission, Ira and the mariners looked on high. From the tower keep, a gruff voice carried across the tranquil stronghold, addressing the mariners in their native tongue.

"*Tir inojé vorsius fíja!*"

"What?" asked a breathless Tabor. "What does it mean? Ira, what—"

But his and the other warriors' question was answered as every sapphire-clad soldier laid down their armaments and knelt in surrender.

It was as though a sudden wave of exhaustion passed over every allied warrior. Ira had not, until that moment, been aware of how incredibly worn his limbs were. Dromo, Cercur, and Ishcaur did not lower their bows as, along the wallwalk, the rowers led the new captives to join their mariner brethren in the ward. Even from the grass below, the bodies of dozens of felled islanders could be seen strewn about the wallwalk, streaks of blood coursing down the coral sandstone. The sight of three severed lines still latched upon the ledge served as a dreadful reminder of those who had not managed to scale the wall before their presence was discovered. If it would not have been a poor repayment for their allies' sacrifices, there might have been victorious cheers at the feat of conquering the legendary mariner stronghold. But as the warriors collected their surrendered foes, their faces reminded Ira eerily of the happenings on the Cove. Remembering the speechless sailor and all the others lying cold in the trench, Ira's mind strayed to another group of innocents he had forgotten in the midst of all the chaos.

"Nathanael," he called wearily, "go and release the fortress prisoners. Follow the eastern corridor, and you will find an adjoining path leading to a chamber below. Once they have been removed from their captivity, the mariners will take their place."

"Where are you going?" asked Nathanael as Ira trudged across the ward towards the tower keep.

"I have business with the general."

289

CHAPTER XV

THE MAP

As Nathanael and a few warriors made for the chamber to release the mainland prisoners, Ira pushed open the tower keep's grand oak doors facing the ward. He entered to find a rounding stairwell littered with the bodies of felled mariners. Still regaining his strength from the siege, he took the steps at a recovering pace as he ascended. And with each crimson-stained body he passed, Ira glanced upon the cold faces, praying they would all be strangers to him. By the time he had reached the second landing and the trail of bodies' end, he was relieved not to have found any allies in disguise amongst their fallen ranks. Upon the third landing, a breathless Ira came before another set of wide oak doors. He pounded his fist upon the wood, and they swung open as a disheveled Manoque admitted him to the war room.

Ira was far too spent to recall any changes that might have been done to the interior of the tower's grand haven. The floor and ceiling were the same coral sandstone as the rest of the fortress. Cabinets containing thousands of scrolls stretched across every wall but that which overlooked the grassy ward below. Ira could see Ram kneeling over his brother, who was seated against one of the cabinets. A broken arrow lay beside Ossel, and a bloody wrap was being cinched around his hairy calf. Litanius, Halruc, and Puck were gathered around a polished sandstone table with round stones scattered across it. There was one in their company whom Ira did not recognize, though there could hardly be any doubt as to who he was. The dwarven general was wider around the waist than any other in the war room. His hair and beard were neatly combed, and he wore the same blue tunic as the imposter mariners, only without any armor, cape, or tassels to denote his station. The general's thick hands were bound before him, and Litanius' sword lay idle on the stone table, pointed at the captive.

"Will he be all right?" Ira called to Ram as he and Manoque crossed the room.

"He may limp for a while," answered the dwarf, "but he will recover."

"I saw the bodies along the stairwell," Ira remarked as he joined the company around the table. "What gave you away?

"A galleymaster who recognized me from my days as admiral," said Litanius. "They caught us fleeing the horn's call to arms. It took us a while to break through their forces." In a lower tone, so the general could not hear him, the elf asked, "How are the men?"

"Shaken," admitted Ira, "at least thirty dead along the wallwalk. As for the ones who did not make it into the fortress . . . I know not how many fell to their deaths."

"Is everyone else all right?" asked a timid Puck. From the dwarf's inflection, Ira could tell he was really inquiring as to whether any more of their crew had been struck down.

"The others are fine. I sent Nathanael to fetch the prisoners from the chamber so we can lock away the mariners." At this, the dwarf general let out a derisive snort. "Once the armory has been emptied," continued Ira, "we shall be ready to make for the mainland."

"I would not be so certain," murmured Halruc, "or perhaps you would care to explain this."

The master gestured to the table they were gathered around. At first glance, there seemed to be nothing of great significance concerning the polished surface or its scattered stone pieces. But as Manoque held a lantern closer to the slab, shadows of intricate etchings became plain to the weary eye. A map of the Bridging Sea and all its lands and isles was intricately carved into the sandstone. As Ira looked closer, he observed the carved likeness of a mighty galley upon those round pieces denoting the positions of the Haurthian Navy's many vessels. Hardly more than a dozen of these markers were situated in a blockade formation off the shores of the Westlands. The stone representing the galley *Benúra* sat by its lonesome in the Forager's Cove. But what drew Ira's attention most was the armada of warships stretching from north to south, all of them hailing towards the Eastlands. The galleys were not only making for the ports where some vessels had already harbored. The fleets were preparing to flood the length of the provincial coasts like a tumultuous wave of spears and swords. Some vessels had many leagues to go before reaching the Eastern banks, but Ira's heart sank as he spotted one warship but a day's voyage from the forest of Gideon and the refugees of the Cove.

"'A few galleys in the ports alone,'" said a disdainful Halruc. "Those were your very words, were they not, chief? Every weapon in the armory and all the rescued prisoners are not enough to combat an invasion of this scale."

"There must be a hundred ships hailing for the provinces," said Manoque defeatedly, "legions of mariners. How many—"

"Several thousand, at least," uttered Litanius. Turning on the captive general, he hissed, "What is the meaning of this?"

The dwarf let out another sardonic snort. "Come now, Litanius. Even in your diminished state, you cannot be all that daft." The silence around the stone map seemed to encourage the general's sense of authority in spite of his present situation. "The Provincial Guard has failed in its charge to replace the mariners almost since the moment of its conception. Heresy against the empire runs rampant in the streets. Criminals are either marked or sold to the circus rather than imprisoned. Granted, the Guard does excel in its stewardship of the tax ledgers. That may be sufficient in times of peace, but those days are behind us. When order must be restored, that commission shall always fall to the Legions of Haurth."

"To what end?" asked Ira incredulously. "Is holding the provinces ransom worth the capture of a few dissenting citizens?"

"A few?" chortled the general. "After tonight's happenings, that lie will no longer be indulged in. You and your seditionist allies shall soon pay for your—"

A violent crash shook the war room as the oak doors burst open. The general collapsed to the floor as every sword around the table was drawn. Nathanael, Tabor, Dromo, Cercur, and Ishcaur scurried towards their company with frantic stares.

"What is it?" demanded Litanius. "Is it the mariners? Have they—"

"They are not here!" panted Ishcaur. "The prisoners have gone!"

"What?" bellowed Ram, rising from his wounded brother's side.

"No, no," said Manoque disbelievingly, "no, they must be here!"

"Comb the fortress," ordered Ira. "Have the men check the western corridor and the—"

"We have searched every corridor and chamber throughout the fortress," stated Nathanael, "and there is no sign of them."

Litanius pulled the stout general up by the collar of his tunic and shook him vigorously.

"Where are they, Concleor?" the elf spat.

"Who?" asked the dwarf coyly.

A swift thump to the gut brought the general to his knees, coughing and gasping for air as the tip of Litanius' blade came to rest between the bound general's eyes.

"Now, shall we try this again?" Litanius asked sternly. "You wrote a letter to the gailaum of the galley *Benúra*. We know the men you had arrested in the provinces were being held here. What have you done with them?"

The general continued to sputter as he regained enough composure to speak.

"Is this the whole reason for your grand intrusion tonight? You meant to free that rabble and plunge the empire into further chaos? I am afraid, gentlemen, that your efforts were in vain. The prisoners you so violently sought tonight were removed from the fortress days ago."

"Where have you sent them?" pestered Ira.

"They are presently being delivered to Alaoth to be tried and sentenced accordingly for their crimes of treason."

The sailors around the table groaned a miserable groan as Ram's fist bashed the table.

"You," the dwarf barked with a finger pointed in the direction of Ira and Litanius, "it was your assurances that brought us here in the first place! You led us here for nothing!"

"The contents of the gailaum's letter could not have been plainer," retorted Litanius sourly. "The prisoners were not to be sent to Alaoth until the galley *Benúra*'s arrival. But perhaps the general would care to enlighten us on the reason for this surprise alteration."

As he spoke, the elf's gladius rested so close to the general's face that the dwarf's heaving breaths started to fog the blade.

"It would seem your information is dated, old friend," the general said callously. "The delay of the prisoners' transport to Alaoth was indeed the plan while the census was still to be carried out by those galleys and mariners that could be spared by the admiral. But thanks to that mad ruffian of your defectors' cult, the High Court amended their plans for the census, and the fleets of Haurth were set at my disposal. At once, I dispatched orders to every galleymaster under my command to sail for the provinces and to deliver their apprehended to the Isle of Ruin directly."

"No such letter ever reached the galley *Benúra*," said Litanius.

"Indeed, I suppose my orders were received by a corpse somewhere in the Forager's Cove, were they not?"

Neither the chief nor any of the *Wayfarer*'s crew answered the general's morbid query.

"What are the governors and the premier thinking?" pondered Cercur. "Provoking tensions between East and West? They would do better to grant the provinces release from the empire than to go to war with them."

"And allow your barbaric leaders to amass an army to destroy the Westlands?" hissed the general. "Never."

"Then you are as mad as Emperor Darius!" exclaimed Halruc.

Ira averted his gaze as the weight of many eyes around the table fell upon him.

"It was your treasonous lot that sparked the fires of conflict," muttered the general coldly, "just as it was Darius the Damned who nearly brought the empire to its knees. Or have you forgotten that it was he who was found standing over the six murdered emissaries who dared to oppose him? Even a clean blade and a tale of a suicidal pact could not absolve that wicked sovereign." Litanius shifted uncomfortably beside Ira as they shared the grim recollection of that fateful night. "Mark my words, you shall not be absolved for your crimes either. The Governor of Anthazar and the mariners you have slain will not go unavenged. You shall be less than embers clinging to life once the legions have answered your treachery."

"The governor?" said Tabor. "What role has the governor in any of this?"

"The role of a martyr, ever since one of your seditionist allies murdered him in cold blood. Governor Anthazar, strangled to death by the same brigand who, weeks ago, attempted to assassinate the premier in his bedchamber." The astonished faces of the crowd around him made the general let out a derisive laugh. "Can it be? Is your militia so disorganized that you are unaware of your own vicious ploys?"

"No man here had a hand in the governor's death," said Puck.

"And what of the deaths your siege has wrought tonight? These are affronts of the highest order. It will not be tolerated. We will have no treaties, no amnesties, no negotiations with you and your band of mutineers. We will have war until the day the empire is finally saved from treason and its deliverers. Whether by the sword or the gallows, you shall all meet your end."

A stillness came over the room as the general fell silent. The whispering winds swept into the keep, shaking the lantern flames that bathed the war room. Ira shared a pensive look with Litanius, who sheathed his sword and dragged the general to a corner.

"One move, Concleor," muttered the elf, "and it shall be your last."

The dwarf shot him a spiteful glare as he straightened himself up against the far wall.

"Will this wretched night never end?" murmured Dromo as he rubbed his weary eyes.

Litanius returned to their company as every head leaned over the stone map to confer in hushed tones.

"What do we do now?" asked Cercur.

"We stick to the plan," asserted Ossel, standing gingerly on his bandaged leg as he leaned against the table for support. "We make for the mainland, go into hiding with our kin, arm the people against the invasion."

"That was before we knew the breadth of the forces awaiting us," whispered Manoque with a despondent look at the galley stones hailing to the Eastern shores.

"Manoque is right," said Ira. "We have neither the means to evade the legions nor the forces to combat so many."

"Well then," said Ram, "the path forward seems perfectly clear."

"And what path would that be?"

"Submission. The only way we survive this whole ordeal is to pledge ourselves to the mariners' governance and encourage others to do the same."

The dwarf's companions gaped at him, utterly stupefied.

"By the Light, Ram!" fretted Ossel.

"Would you rather be hung for sedition? Need I remind you that I was against this plan from the start? I warned all of you what this would lead to. You, brother, are the only reason I came here tonight, and look what our efforts have wrought."

"So after all that has happened," growled Nathanael, "after all the innocents who have suffered by the mariners' wrath, you would have us offer ourselves ripe for the slaughter, and for what? That we might secure mercy under the thumb of tyranny?"

"Those who oppose the powers that be might count it as tyranny," retorted Ram. "But the loyal will be protected, even rewarded for their fealty. If you are too prideful to accept what cannot be changed, then you shall be amongst the first to reap the punishment of treason." Ram stared about the table at his scathing companions before bellowing, "Some liberties are not worth dying for!"

The reproachful air in the war room was broken as Tabor muttered, "You sicken me."

Ram looked as though he would love nothing more than to leap across the stone table and pummel the enormous man with his stubby fists.

"The way I see it," Litanius stated loudly in an effort to break the tensions, "we are at an impasse. Neither the mainland nor the islands can now be considered safe for us."

"Why not take refuge here, in the fortress?" proposed Ishcaur.

"It would be unwise to remain longer than necessary," remarked Ira. "We do not know if the general managed to send word to the fleets when our siege first began. If he did, there is little time until the galleys begin scouring the waters for us."

"So, we cannot flee, nor can we stay. Where does that leave us?" implored Manoque.

"It leaves us with that course of action that would end all conflict," said Litanius quietly. "We must free the provinces from the empire's rule."

Ram scoffed as Puck said, "The general made it quite clear that the High Court would not engage in negotiations. And now that one of the governors has been murdered, I am afraid I must agree with his sentiments."

"It is true; the High Court will never free the Eastlands after all that has unfolded. But there is one that stands to claim authority over all the lands and even over the High Court. The sovereign of the empire holds the power to recall the legions and release the provinces from Haurthian rule. All this is indeed possible if he can defeat the premier and reclaim his right to the throne."

Under his breath, Nathanael uttered the Western words, "Méne caiar."

No man situated around the stone table appeared more dumbstruck at the proposal than Ira. He tried to garner the words to protest but lost them as the faces around him swam with varying expressions. Halruc looked as though he was considering the price of a trade. Nathanael was positively marveling. Others shifted from dismissiveness to curiosity to enlightenment, as Litanius offered Ira a look not of encouragement but of finality.

"I am no one's savior," Ira stated firmly, unable to bear the silence any longer. "What you ask of me is . . . The empire will never accept a disgraced prince as its sovereign."

"If it is the will of Érosai . . . ," began Litanius.

"The will of the Light cannot overcome the mortal obstacles of men. To challenge the premier for the throne, the challengers must meet face-to-face. While Lysias remains safely guarded in Eou Verás, the right to ascend as emperor remains his."

"Then you must meet him where he dwells," said Tabor with fervor. "These men took the fortress against all odds; what is to stop them from marching on the Hallowed City as you challenge the premier to a contest of right?"

Ira laughed mirthlessly. "Besting the forces of one desolate island does not make this militia an army. Brave as they have proven themselves, these men cannot claim the most fortified city in the history of the known world."

"The city is not so fortified now," remarked Nathanael with a glance at the map, "not with so many of the fleet removed to the provinces. If we can present with forces strong enough to break through the city's defenses—"

"It would take hundreds, nay, thousands," protested Ira, "and we have not the allies!"

"Then we shall send word to the mainland!" proclaimed Nathanael. "We shall call for others to join us! Those men not yet taken by the legions, they will fight by our side to free their lands. I know they will!"

It was aggravating enough for Ira to refute the appeals of the others, but to add Nathanael's to the bunch . . .

"And if by some miracle this band of warriors overwhelms the city's protectors and claims Eou Verás," said Ira, "if I should meet the premier only to die by his blade, what will you do then? Will you slay the members of the High Court where they stand? Will you make them martyrs for the legions who will hunt you to the ends of the sea? Is the fate of every man here to be tethered to my own?"

The sailors around the table glanced at one another in search of an answer less formidable than the question posed to them.

"The fate of every man, woman, and child of the lands is already latched to your own, Ira," said Litanius solemnly. "But one fell strike of the blade, and you can rescue them from ruin."

"The people will not stand behind the son of a mad emperor on his quest for power," said Ira bitterly, "even if that power was taken to serve their interests."

"I believe on that account, every man must decide for himself where his trust shall lie," said Halruc stoically.

From behind the huddle, a gruff voice rang throughout the room.

"So, this is the wretched son of the last emperor? I will give you this much credit, Prince Ira; you are right to refuse them. Listen to their badgering pleas. They would not follow you had they any alternative. You, son of Darius, are but a means to their ends."

"Silence!" hissed Nathanael.

"Once you have granted them their freedom and the Eastlands are left to their own, will their trust in you remain? No, they will rise against you. These allies of yours will only see you rise as sovereign because they will never be called upon to answer to you."

"That is enough!" spat Nathanael.

"They will betray you to your last breath. If you doubt my words, look to the Governor of Anthazar and his dark fate. He fought against the mariners' occupation, bartered for their removal, and even entertained allowing the provinces to break from the empire. All of this only to wind up dead at the hands of the brigand he sought to aid. Your fate will be no different."

Nathanael was about to burst when Litanius interjected.

"You never mentioned the governor had advocated for the seditionists," proclaimed the elf. "What reason could a man have for murdering one who aided his cause?

"How am I to understand the mind of a senseless ruffian?" asked the general sharply. "I had word from the warden himself that Governor Anthazar had counsel several times with the one who nearly assassinated the premier. As it happens, Premier Lysias seems to have a knack for narrowly avoiding death. He left the assassin and the governor while both were still amongst the living. Shortly after that, the prisoner went mad and strangled the governor to death." Those around the table traded curious looks with one another, searching for the one who might be able to comprehend such a peculiar unfolding of events. Then the general turned toward Ira and said, "It is not you that they wish to follow, only the title you stand to gain. To them, you will always be an outcast, a pariah. No such man will ever sit upon the throne; the governors will not have it. They and the premier shall hold dominion over this empire and snuff out any who would threaten her."

"That remains to be seen," proclaimed Litanius. "Whatever you say, no power can stand in the way of . . ." But the elf trailed off as his still-moving lips lost the words they carried. The crew of the *Wayfarer* watched curiously as the chief's gaze wandered away from the general to some barren part of the room. There was a strange way in which the lights flitted in the elf's distant eyes. Ira thought to pull him aside to inquire after his state when he noticed the cusp of the day brimming the horizon through the keep's lookout.

"We have squandered enough time already," said Ira, returning the war room to its senses. "We must make haste and leave the fortress before we are discovered."

There was a murmur of agreement from around the stone map.

"But where are we to go?" inquired Manoque.

Ira considered the question for a moment. "We can take refuge amidst the Mortal Spires, just south of the Savage Peaks." This plan was met with many an apprehensive gaze. Veteran sailors knew perfectly well why those waters surrounding the shadowy mountains were never passed through. The deathly spikes threatening to sink a wandering vessel were the least of their worries. The fear blooming in the eyes of the company belonged to the creatures of land and sea that haunted the feral range. "Galleys do not wander through those parts," Ira assured his companions. "We shall not be discovered. For now, that is enough."

"And from there, will we make for the Hallowed City?" asked Puck pressingly. "Will you challenge the premier for the sake of our lands?"

Having no wish to give answer to this particular query, Ira remarked "There are the men in the ward to consider. They know nothing of what we now face, and many may rightfully wish to return to the mainland to safeguard their homes and kin." Ira glanced at Nathanael as he said, "I will ask no man to forfeit those duties which come first to him."

"Indeed," said Tabor, "protecting one's own from tyranny must take priority. And with that purpose as my guide, I shall follow you to the Hallowed City, prince, to the very steps of the temple if I must."

This pledge of solidarity took Ira quite aback, even more so as others around the table began to offer their assent to Tabor's proclamation. As Halruc inclined his head towards the prince, all eyes around the table fell upon the spiteful dwarf with the midnight hair.

"If this is the path we are mutually bound to," muttered Ram as he traded an apprehensive glance with his brother, "then I shall not be a willful hindrance. But understand, son of Darius, that if I follow you, it is out of necessity and not loyalty."

Ira looked to Nathanael, who shrugged at the dwarf's less-than-half-hearted concession.

"I do not make light of any commitment offered in this room," said Ira appreciatively, "but we cannot accomplish this feat without the aid of others."

"Well then," said Ossel, "let us see what the men below have to say."

"Wait!" blurted Manoque.

The elf hustled to one of the mahogany tables set about the room and returned to the stone map with an iron stylus and a sheet of parchment. With great precision, he sketched a copy of the lands and islands, including tick marks where the Haurthian warships were presently located.

"And what are we to do with him?" asked Ishcaur, pointing a stubby thumb at the general in the corner.

"He can join the mariners in the chamber below," growled Halruc.

"No!"

The abruptness of the chief's voice startled the company. Litanius, noting the wild expressions around the table, took a calming breath before he spoke again. "We should lock him in the cell aboard the galley *Benúra*. We may wish to interrogate him further. Besides, the general of the legions could make for a mighty bargaining tool."

It was a sound thought and one that might have garnered more immediate support were it not for the strange tone in the chief's voice. The rest of the war room glanced cautiously towards the one who knew the elf best.

"All right," concurred a hesitant Ira. "Tabor, take the general to the galley and—"

But even as he spoke, Litanius had already hoisted the bound dwarf to his feet and led him out of the war room to the rounding stairwell.

"Finished," said Manoque, folding the crude but accurate map of the Haurthian fleets and stuffing it inside his shimmering chestplate. "When we return to the *Wayfarer*, I can draft several more to send across the Eastlands. The citizens must be warned of where the legions are heading."

"We will require a flock of ospreys then," said Halruc. "Ishcaur, Cercur, find the fortress mews and fetch the messenger birds to the galley, no less than a dozen. We shall reconvene with the men below and deliver the news. If they will follow us to Eou Verás, all the better. If not"—Halruc glanced towards the galley markers scattered about the sandstone map— "let us speak to the men."

"The mews are in the southwest corner of the fortress," Ira called to Ishcaur and Cercur as they set off ahead of the others.

Ram wrapped an arm around his brother as Ossel limped on his impaled calf down the tower stairwell. The rest of the crew followed slowly behind them, each of them brewing in thoughts of the uncertain journey ahead. Ira's mind was conflicted, divided between two persons he had considered forever lost. Was the prince turned apprentice to be reborn again as the emperor who would save the provinces from tyranny? Would the death of one warmongering premier be enough to restore the legacy and honor of his kin? For the first time since their separation, Ira's thoughts settled on his sister, the outcast. The garden would have offered her quiet dignity for as long as she lived. But were her honor restored . . .

Ira swam in his ponderings of family and duty all the way down to the grassy ward. The place was empty, but for the lifeless bodies strewn across the grounds and along the wallwalk.

"They will be at the docks," remarked Halruc, approaching the southern archway.

It was only then that Ira noted the dispirited man beside him. Nathanael's face was as doleful as the heavy way he sauntered, and Ira felt shame for so desperately considering the consequences of his own kin without a thought of his dearest friend's.

"We will join you in a bit," Ira called to Halruc. "Nathanael and I are going to search the corridors for any stragglers before we depart."

The master gave his consent, and as they came to the grand archway, the two men turned left into the southern corridor while the others continued straight ahead towards the docks. Their sandals clapped upon the coral sandstone floor, rippling off the walls and down the lantern-lit pathway.

"The men might elect to return to their homes," Ira said casually as they strode. "For the sake of their families, who could blame them?"

"They will certainly wish to return," remarked Nathanael, "but they will join you, Ira, all the way to the Hallowed City, as will I. There is no point arguing to the contrary. In the grand scheme of things, I may be little more than a pebble chucked against a swelling wave. But you stand to command the tides and the sea itself."

"But Ruth . . . the child . . ."

"I shall do all in my power to return to them," he said somberly. "But if my sacrifice brings you one step closer to rescuing them and others from harm, I will gladly follow you to my dying breath."

Ira knew not how to respond, but the silence as they trod through the corridor seemed answer enough for Nathanael. As they neared the corner that turned onto the eastern corridor, a pair of hushed voices could be made out over their footsteps. The speech might have been missed if not for the reverberating echoes of the stone enclosures.

"You are sure?" breathed a frantic voice. "You are absolutely positive?" It was Litanius.

"What has come over you?" said the wary general.

"And a rough midnight gem. Those were your words, were they not?"

"Good gracious, yes, yes, I am quite sure of it! Now let go of me, I say!"

Ira rounded the corner to find the squat general pinned against the wall, his short legs dangling in the air. Litanius' hands were clenched into the dwarf's tunic as he held him aloft like a predator toying with his prey.

"Litanius!" Ira and Nathanael leapt forward and yanked the elf's grip loose. The general collapsed to his knees, gasping for air, as Ira threw the chief against the wall. "What has come over you?"

The elf appeared pallid in the frail light of the corridor. His whole body was trembling, his lips incapable of forming words. The wavering eyes darted rapidly between Nathanael, the general, and Ira. The dwarf, with his hands still bound, made to rise to his feet. He glanced subtly in the direction of the chamber where his soldiers were being held. It was enough to provoke Nathanael into unleashing his blade and pressing it against the place where the dwarf's thick neck hid beneath a heavy mound of beard.

"I must speak with you," Litanius muttered anxiously to Ira.

"I am listening," replied Ira impatiently.

"No," hissed the elf, eyeing the other two, "not them."

"Whatever you have to say to me, you can say to Natha—"

"No!"

His sharp voice traipsed through the corridor and off into the distance. Ira examined the nervous figure critically, trying with all his might to discern what could have possibly been the onset of this radical behavior.

"All right," said Ira quietly. He looked to Nathanael and whispered, "Take the general to the galley; we will be along shortly."

Nathanael, though hardly eager to leave his friend with the unhinged elf, nodded his assent and led the dwarf down the way they had come by the point of his sword.

"Now," began Ira, "would you care to—"

But Litanius hushed him before he could utter another word. His jittering body turned unnervingly still as he turned a pointed ear to listen for the receding footsteps of Nathanael and the general. When only the crackling sounds of the lanterns above remained, Litanius spoke with unbecoming intensity.

"Ira, you must face Lysias; you must ascend as emperor! Too much is at stake if you do not!"

"I have already told you," Ira said exasperatedly, "the empire will never have me as its sovereign, and I have no wish to convince the people otherwise. Besides, if the men in the provinces will not join us—"

"But you must!"

"You are behaving like a madman, Litanius; what has gotten into you?"

Still pinned against the wall by Ira's hand, Litanius glanced towards both ends of the corridor to ensure they were, in fact, alone.

"There is a dark curse lurking in the Westlands," the elf murmured in a low voice, "a power unlike any other known to this world. If you do not claim the throne, many more will suffer under its terrible enchantment."

Ira peered questioningly into the elf's eyes. There was not a trace of jest to be found in their gaze.

"A curse?" said Ira skeptically.

"A sword," whispered Litanius.

Ira scoffed as he released the hand that pinned the elf against the wall. "A hundred galleys pillaging the provinces, and your concern is over one sword?"

"Do not trivialize what I speak of, boy!" hissed the elf. "That was once my mistake, and I have paid dearly for it. This is not some common steel of a poorly smith. It is a relic, an ancient gladius laden with a dark enchantment. The sword that has led countless souls to their demise now rests in the hands of the Premier of Haurth. If you do not end Lysias' cancerous rule, he will enslave the empire and slaughter anyone who stands in his way."

This was too much for Ira to absorb. A cursed gladius? The power to enslave an empire?

"Why should I believe a word of what you say?"

"Because," Litanius said darkly, "before Lysias carried the sword Dominion, it was wielded by your father, the emperor."

CHAPTER XVI

THE ADMIRAL'S LAMENT

"Dominion?" Ira said incredulously. "Invocar, the blade of the Snakeheart? My father wielded—"

"The Pirate Emperor's infamous weapon," Litanius finished morbidly, "yes."

The elf and the man's gazes did not flinch from one another until Ira broke the silence with a strange chuckle.

"It cannot be. Even if my father had come to possess a weapon with so devious a history, that does not make it cursed. Besides, you know as well as I that Invocar vanished with Mágna centuries ago. They were last seen together aboard the *Augur*, and that warship was never sighted again after the fall of the Sons of Veroise."

"So many were led to believe, but they would be wrong," said Litanius. "The *Augur* did indeed vanish through the ages until I discovered her remains." The elf paused as though awaiting an objection from the man, but Ira merely stared at him, lost in perplexed thought. "The voyage before you came to serve on my vessel, I was commissioned by Emperor Darius to scout for the long-rumored lair of the Pirate Horde. No praelaum before me had discovered a trace of the raiders' hideaway, and so I directed the galley *Obysarr* to sail where others would not dare. We crept through the Mortal Spires and searched along the shallows of the

Savage Peaks in search of the pirates' ancient refuge. It was all we could do not to collide with the multitude of rocky spikes and send ourselves to the depths, not to mention the maritime creatures and feral beasts we evaded along the way. Then, after months of fruitless expedition, I found her. The ruins of a once-mighty galley were beached on the gravel shore where the tide had abandoned her. The sail had been reduced to wilting strands, and its planks were marred from ages of decay. Yet the vessel's carven name was as clear as ever. It was the *Augur*."

"I could not believe my eyes. Exhilaration swelled in my officers and me as we came ashore to investigate the wreckage. But our eager anticipation was swiftly tempered. We ventured into the belly of the ship and found ourselves standing in a sickly boneyard. As we examined the remains, it was abundantly clear that the pirate crew had not gone to rest peacefully. No creature with a soul could have ravaged their bodies so. It was impossible to tell how many had been butchered, with bones ripped, broken, and scattered throughout the rotting crypt. And beneath all the haunting remains, mounds of archaic gold and gems shone out in their undying brilliance. Were they all the riches the world had to offer, nothing could have tempted me to claim a single coin for my own. That same foreboding expression I wore was shared by my officers, who dreaded every instant spent in that warship."

"I was prepared to recall my men back to the galley *Obysarr* when one of our company called our attention to a particular relic amongst the ruins. Lodged in a set of mangled ribs was a gladius unlike any I had seen before. It was coated in dust and grime, yet the sword gleamed still from its sharpened blade to the midnight gem in its golden hilt. There was no mistaking it for the weapon of some common pirate. This was the sword that had terrorized the sea and lands for an age—the gladius of the Snakeheart."

"So," said Ira warily, "you recovered Dominion and brought it back to Haurth to present to the emperor. It is a chilling tale, I give you that, but hardly enough to suggest a looming enchantment set upon the *Augur*'s precious horde."

"You never held your father's sword, did you?" said Litanius. "No, of course you never. It is not a sensation you would soon forget. I can still recall the moment I released Invocar from that ancient wreck. My fingers curled about its hilt, and an almighty wave coursed through every part of me. That gladius was made an extension of my very being, and I drank its strength with unbridled splendor."

"Strength?"

"Not of the body, mind you, but of the will. Reservations and inhibitions held no sway over me; nothing was beyond my grasp. I remained mere flesh and bone, but my spirit was free, unhindered by the material world. I . . . ." Litanius' starry-eyed gaze turned suddenly cold as he recalled himself to the fortress corridor where he and Ira presently stood. "It was as glorious as it was disturbing to be in the presence of that which was all at once so great and terrible."

"But we could not leave it for another to find. Moreover, I was curious to know more about the sword's unique properties. I thought perhaps the Western smiths or the temple priests might uncover the blade's ancient secrets. So, I wrapped the relic in an old cloth taken from the pirate warship, and Dominion sailed with us back to our homeland. In a private convention with the emperor, I presented him with the trophy of our voyage. By the gleam in his eyes as he took up the blade, I saw the reflection of that strange power that had washed through me. Emperor Darius concurred that the weapon must be studied and so commanded me to say nothing of the *Augur*'s or Dominion's discovery. I held some reservations in this order, but nevertheless, I pledged my silence to the matter and passed the command along to my crew."

"You could have told me," insisted Ira, "I would have kept the secret."

"I know it, but the liberty was not mine. At any rate, I thought there was little reason to share our findings with you until we better understood the recovered relic."

"So, the smiths and priests did uncover the secrets of Dominion?"

"If so, I was never privy to the knowledge gained," said Litanius. "Months of inner speculation passed at sea, and still I received no word from the emperor regarding the sword. Finally, a letter arrived recalling the admiral and the prince to rejoin the Emperor's Court. Surely, I thought, a report of the relic's uncovered mysteries would await me upon our return. You can imagine, then, my astonishment at entering the Temple of Érosai to find Invocar sheathed at the emperor's side. At once, your father took me aside and informed me that the greatest smiths and sages in the land had found no sorcery within the blade. I contested the matter most severely, but the emperor would hear nothing of my protests. Furthermore, Darius insisted that everything surrounding the finding of the *Augur* was to go on as a secret—that news of the infamous warship's reappearance would unsettle the lands it long ago preyed upon. Despite my deepest objections, I consented to keep the whole mystery of the pirate vessel to myself and never again raised the subject of the dark gladius to my sovereign."

"But that settles it then," remarked Ira. "If the masters of crafts and spirits could find no enchantment in Dominion—"

"Your father lied, Ira. There was and remains a curse upon Invocar, and he allowed himself to be consumed by it."

"So you have told me repeatedly," Ira said with harsh annoyance. "Yet you offer only paranoid speculation to support your mystic claim. Why should I believe this sword is all you claim it to be?"

"Because," said Litanius silently, "we have both of us fallen under its spell before. That wicked gladius bears the power to corrupt the thoughts and deeds of others. The power of will itself. To strengthen the convictions of the host. To conquer the foe into submission. Enthralling minds and possessing bodies—this is the weapon we stand against should we embark to Eou Verás to free the provinces. This is what you will come to face when you and Lysias are fatefully reunited."

Alone in the flickering corridor, the prince and the admiral stirred in the unnatural chill that wafted over them.

"You mean to say," uttered Ira, "that I—that we—have been unknowingly altered by such an enchantment before?"

Litanius did not meet the man's gaze as he spoke. "In all our conventions with the emperor along his descent to madness, did you never find yourself speaking or acting in a manner that felt foreign to you? As though another was taking you along a path against your will and better judgment?"

Lost for words in his scattered mind, Ira fought to organize his thoughts over the pounding heat in his head. To recollect thoughts of a younger self, absent of present wisdom, was to recall oneself as painfully callow for having ever been so blind. Ira's memories of the court and its members' inability to sway the emperor from madness had long been tainted by what was reaped thereafter. But as he considered the horrid prospect of there being truth in the elf's words, it came as nothing short of a relief when Litanius spoke again and disrupted his racing mind.

"I was not aware of the influence being cast over me for a long time after I delivered Dominion to its new host. It was in others that I first noted a series of unnatural shifts in speech and character. The Eastern emissaries, for instance, had always yearned for a peaceful resolution to the unrest in their lands. You will recall the day Emperor Darius first abandoned prospects of amity with the seditionists and ordered more legions to the East. How restless were the emissaries when the emperor first proclaimed it?"

"They offered my father several warnings that day," muttered Ira, "and warned him again many times after."

"And yet, that evening, the opposed emissaries consented to follow their sovereign's decree. Even after the mariners' hardened governance was proven a mistake, each of the court's conventions began with the emissaries' opposition and ended with assent. I could not account for how such a change came over those loyal men of the Eastern Realms. Our gatherings were so few and far between; I considered the possibility that I did not know the emissaries as well as I had presumed and attributed the same reasoning to the general's peculiar shifts in character. But you, Ira . . . I sailed beside you for months at a time and had come to know you as an officer, a prince, and a friend. And through the court's many sessions, it was that temporal change I beheld in you that frightened me the most. As your father delved deeper into paranoia around that which he could not control, I watched as your protests turned to assent in a manner most contrary to the man I admired so."

"As our conventions with the emperor turned from thoughtful discourse to dogmatic endorsements, I began to watch more closely the one whose verdicts were never long questioned. Only then did my own alterations become apparent to me. Those objections I so meticulously expressed to my sovereign would inexplicably fade into a sort of waking dream, present yet a struggle to recollect. No more than a reassuring touch from the emperor, perhaps a few words, and my reservations were replaced with affirmations a part of me knew to be nonsensical. The day would pass in a mind not my own before my better senses would return as I questioned how I could have behaved in such a manner. Was I going mad? Had my constitution weakened to the point of blind servitude to he who was trekking the path to the empire's fracture?"

Every word rang incessantly in Ira's mind as clouded memories of old sharpened with painful comprehension.

"I was convinced my ineptitude was to blame," whispered the elf. "That was until the emissaries broke free from Dominion's sway long enough to challenge their emperor. Until they declared their fervent resolve to break their realms from Haurthian rule. Until . . . until your father was found standing above their bleeding corpses with an unsullied gladius." A look was enough to tell Litanius that Ira now felt the whole meaning of that grim spectacle and the ludicrous tale of six Eastern leaders murdering one another in a fit of insanity. "The emissaries may have died by one another's blades, but it was Invocar who commanded their deeds."

Anguish at a father's harrowing deceptions was now muddled with rage at the breadth of such a betrayal. Ira wanted to lash out— to break something in a physical manifestation of the wrath boiling within. The stony surroundings of the corridor deprived him of that pleasure, and so he turned upon the one who had reserved the dark secret to himself for so long.

"Four years I sailed beside you in ignorance," spat Ira, "while you silently reeled in the truth I deserved to know, that all of us deserved to know! I reserved myself from invoking the contest of right only by the influence of my father, the influence which you observed!"

"I knew no truth in my dark speculations until that fateful night!" retorted Litanius. "After the dreadful truth was confirmed, I was determined to share all with you. But by then, it was too late. Rumors of the emissaries' bizarre demise had already flooded into Eou Verás. And before I could prompt you to challenge your father for the right to rule, the heir of the First Line of Sovereigns had come forward to covet the throne. And now, he has coveted that curse that leads the empire to war and ruin as it nearly did twelve years ago!"

Amongst the many uncovered truths of his father's heinous deeds, Ira had entirely forgotten the one whose revelation had wholly altered the course of his life and that of his beloved sister.

"Both Lysias and I came to service aboard the galley *Obysarr* after the *Augur*'s hushed discovery," said Ira. "He challenged my father out of duty to protect the empire from a civil war; he knew nothing of Invocar's presence or power. How could he . . ." Ira's trail of spoken thoughts faltered as a look of shame plagued the admiral's pale face. "Because you told him. When we were locked in the cavern awaiting trial, you told Lysias all you had meant to confide in me."

"I was not prepared to see another ruler fall to the temptation of that blade's enchantment," said Litanius defensively. "When Lysias came to my cell, the instrument of Emperor Darius' demise accompanied him. The new premier admitted to his own suspicions of the blade's mystic properties, and so I divulged to him all that I have told you here and now. When the whole sickly truth was laid out, the gailaum who had served his praelaum faithfully for four years served me once more. As the general and the children of Darius were condemned to lives of infamy, I was shown mercy and reinstated to my post commanding the fleets. Furthermore, Lysias heeded my pleas and forfeited Invocar's power as he placed the dark blade in the tomb of its fallen host. There, it would remain in anonymity for the ages, never to be disturbed again." Then, with a look of dismay, Litanius uttered, "Or so it should have been."

"But can you be certain Dominion has returned?" inquired Ira. "Perhaps Lysias did not—"

"I assure you, the premier carries the Snakeheart's blade as we speak. From the moment Concleor informed us of the governor's strange demise at the hands of a seditionist ally, I knew what must have been the cause. When you and your friend happened upon me interrogating the general, he was confirming my worst suspicions. Concleor described in vivid detail that sword, which he has seen at the premier's side for years now."

"We must tell the men," stated Ira. "If the governors have sent the legions under Invocar's influence, the people must know of—"

At that moment, Litanius' hands shot forward and thrust Ira against the cold wall.

"No one can know of Dominion!" the elf hissed fervently. "Not your friend, not your sister, none of them!"

"But this will expose Lysias and break the empire's trust in him!" muttered Ira, fighting to free himself from the wall.

"It will do far worse than that! A revelation of this magnitude would shatter our civilization beyond repair! If people, against all odds, did believe such a curse as Dominion's was carried by their trusted leaders, more than the High Court would feel the chaos wrought. Disorder and mayhem would run rampant throughout the empire, insatiable and unending. There would be nothing to salvage once Lysias' rule was ended."

When the elf had finished, he suddenly became aware that he was still pinning Ira against the wall and at once released him.

"I have not said I will challenge Lysias," Ira remarked quietly.

"No, but you must, Ira." It was not a demand but more of a simple truth in the way Litanius said it. "You must, if only to ensure Invocar never corrupts the sea or lands again."

"But surely, in the hands of one with noble intent and constitution, Dominion would command peace and unity. Could not the instrument of division also be wielded to mend the fractures of an empire?"

"Have you failed to comprehend the meaning of all of this?" asked Litanius incredulously. "The power to guide the will of others is simultaneously burdened by the fear of what lies beyond our mortal capacities. I do believe your father first leaned on Invocar in hopes similar to your own. But he clung to that power as those unnatural persuasions he himself had pervaded cracked and turned others upon him. Once you invoke méne caiar and kill Lysias, Dominion must never again be allowed to pervert another soul, even for the good of others. Bury it. Drown it in the sea. I care not how you dispose of the sword. But that power and the knowledge of it must die with us."

Drowned by the overwhelming revelations of the night, from those in the fortress keep to those in the vacant corridor where they stood, Ira's mind drew himself back to his first and most crucial duty as a brother.

"If I follow the path set before me, it is not for myself that I do so."

"No emperor is called to serve his own whims, Ira, but to live and die as a servant to his people. The power to rescue the empire rests with you alone. Will you abandon the calling set before you or abandon yourself in its acceptance?"

As Ira made to answer, a noise not their own startled the admiral and the prince. A pair of sandals echoed towards them as Nathanael rounded the corner.

"We informed the men of our plan," he said with a grin. "And they are with us, all of them. We can send for others to join us once we have set off, but they will follow us to Eou Verás. That is, if Ira will challenge the premier."

"All of them?" asked Ira incredulously.

"Every one," said a beaming Nathanael.

"Well then," said Litanius, "let us not keep them waiting, prince."

Together, they strolled through the long pathways leading towards the docks. As they went, Ira caught the elf mouthing the words "Tell no one." The prospect of withholding the secret of Dominion weighed as heavy as the voyage now cast upon him. Would such a dark revelation truly sink the lands into perpetual mayhem, as Litanius had prophesied? Might its unveiling instead serve to cast away that shadow looming over the empire? Before Ira could consider the matter further, he was standing in the grand archway, looking down upon the docks. The galley *Benúra* and another anchored warship drifted in the shallows, ready to make sail. The *Wayfarer* would be awaiting their return in the waters to the north. A throng of warrior men, as well as an elf and a few dwarven sailors, looked upon the banished prince with bated breath.

With a final glance at Nathanael, Ira mustered his strength and called out to the docks, "We make for the Hallowed City!"

ABOUT THE AUTHOR

Born and raised in Sierra Madre, California, THOMAS USLE currently resides in the greater Chicago area where he serves as an employee of Students for Life of America. A reader by hobby and an author by passion, Mr. Usle enjoys those simple pleasures of life, chief among them the company of good friends and family relations.